# The Ottoman Cage

# *The Ottoman Cage*

## BARBARA NADEL

*All the characters and events portrayed in this work are fictitious.*

THE OTTOMAN CAGE

A Felony & Mayhem mystery

PRINTING HISTORY
First UK edition (as *A Chemical Prison*) (Headline): 2000
First U.S. edition (Thomas Dunne/St. Martin's Minotaur): 2005
Felony & Mayhem edition: 2008

ISBN-13: 978-1-933397-84-9
ISBN-10: 1-933397-84-5

Published by arrangement with Thomas Dunne/St. Martin's Minotaur,
an imprint of St. Martin's Press

Manufactured in the United States of America

To Jan, in Remembrance of Times Past

The icon above says you're holding a copy of a book in the Felony & Mayhem "Foreign" category. These books may be offered in translation or may originally have been written in English, but always they will feature an intricately observed, richly atmospheric setting in a part of the world that is neither England nor the U.S.A. If you enjoy this book, you may well like other "Foreign" titles from Felony & Mayhem Press, including:

*The Rainaldi Quartet,* by Paul Adam
*Soviet Sources,* by Robert Cullen
*Cover Story,* by Robert Cullen
*Love in Amsterdam,* by Nicolas Freeling
*Because of the Cats,* by Nicolas Freeling
*Gun Before Butter,* by Nicolas Freeling
*Death of a Dissident,* by Stuart Kaminsky
*Black Knight in Red Square,* by Stuart Kaminsky
*Season of the Monsoon,* by Paul Mann
*The Ganja Coast,* by Paul Mann
*Yellowthread Street,* by William Marshall
*Belshazzar's Daughter,* by Barbara Nadel

For more about these books, and other Felony & Mayhem titles, or to place an order, please visit our website at

www.FelonyAndMayhem.com

or contact us at

Felony and Mayhem Press
156 Waverly Place
New York, NY 10014

# The Ottoman Cage

# 1

THE OLD WOMAN looked sadly up at the open door and sighed. 'Of course there was a time, Officer, when this was a usual thing. Not'—she added rather sourly—'that you would remember.'

There wasn't a lot that Sergeant Farsakoğlu could add to that besides agreeing with the woman.

'What with the tourists and now all these wretched infidels from across the Black Sea. When I was a young girl Turkey was for the Turks and one could leave one's door open without worrying that you'd be robbed or murdered in your bed, but now...'

'Yes, right, Mrs, er...'

'Yalçin.' She smiled. 'My husband owns the grocer's shop opposite.'

Both Sergeant Farsakoğlu and her rather small, swarthy companion looked across the road at a tiny basement-level shop, the mean doorway of which was currently blocked by several large cases of Coca-Cola bottles.

'So,' the sergeant continued, turning back to the

woman who was still smiling very proudly in the direction of her property, 'do you happen to know who owns the house, Mrs Yalçin?'

'An Armenian lives there. Lives alone. I don't know his name though. Very polite and private he is, dresses very well. Next door might know his name, you could always try there.'

'Yes, I may well do that.'

The house the two police officers and the elderly woman were talking about was one of those wooden nineteenth-century affairs that had, in recent years, become so popular with foreign tourists. Many of them, in response to this popularity, had been converted into what had become known as 'Ottoman Mansion Hotels', presumably so that foreigners could boast about having slept where the old aristocracy used to lay their heads. The fact that some of these houses had originally been built for quite ordinary citizens was not spoken of within foreign hearing. This particular building, and the one next door to it, which had already been converted into a hotel, was however rather special in that it had actually been built on to one of the side walls of the Topkapı Museum. Offering as it did both wooden quaintness and proximity to such exotic joys as the royal treasury and the imperial harem, it was rather strange that the owner had continued to maintain the house as a private residence. As Sergeant Farsakoğlu's companion, the redoubtable Constable Cohen, had been heard to mutter, 'If I had this place I'd turn it into a hotel, retire to Bodrum, lie on the beach and do what I do best.' And that was indeed the scale of income that such a place could attract, if put a little crudely.

'And how long, to your knowledge, has the door been open like this, Mrs Yalçin?'

The old woman paused for a moment before replying. 'Well, I noticed it first thing this morning, at about seven o'clock.'

Sergeant Farsakoğlu looked at her watch. 'It's now six and so—'

'Eleven hours,' put in her colleague, 'assuming that it was opened at that time. Which it may or may not have been.'

'We'll go in and have a look,' said his superior, 'just to make sure.' Then, looking up at the lowering storm-blown clouds above, she added, 'It's not the sort of day to have your doors wide open.'

The old woman smiled and, her duty as a citizen done, turned back and walked towards her shop.

The house, although wide and tall, comprising three storeys plus basement, was curiously dark. But then when your back wall is an ancient, windowless palace fortification, light can and does enter only via the casements that look out on to the street. This, together with the iron greyness of the darkening October sky outside, lent the rooms that the officers walked through a sombre and, by virtue of the shallowness of the property, extremely claustrophobic feeling. Indeed two armchairs and a settee completely filled the living area on the ground floor; it was almost impossible to manoeuvre around them.

As Sergeant Farsakoğlu led the way out of the living room and into the kitchen, Cohen murmured, 'I'd go out of my mind living in a place like this!'

On the face of it, the kitchen was really very well off with regard to equipment. There was a stove, large refrigerator, numerous cupboards and work surfaces upon one of which was even a very modern-looking blender. For some reason that Cohen assumed was to do with his superior being a woman, Sergeant Farsakoğlu started looking through the cupboards and inside the fridge. Not that he paid her movements very much attention, transfixed as he was by the 'Girls in Swimwear' calendar for 1982 that hung over the sink.

'Empty.'

Cohen barely registered what had been said. 'Eh?'

'The cupboards and the refrigerator are all empty.'

He turned to look at her. She was very attractive for a policewoman: tall and willowy and, when she chose to let it down across her shoulders, possessed of the most fantastic mane of chestnut-brown hair. Cohen replied whilst wrestling with a terrible desire to imagine her naked: 'So?'

'Well, normally,' she said, 'people who live in a house have some food around with which to feed themselves.'

He shrugged. 'Maybe. Although if this man lives alone he could go out to eat.'

Sergeant Farsakoğlu looked doubtful. 'What, all the time? Even just for a glass of tea?'

'Mmm. I see what you mean, but...'

'But what?'

He smiled. 'Men can be a little bit lazy, I suppose, when they're on their own. Single men have, well, you know, other things on their minds.'

She gave him a look that informed Cohen more eloquently than words that now was perhaps the time to stop talking about what single men might or might not get up to, and start being a little serious about the job in hand.

Looking slightly puzzled, Sergeant Farsakoğlu moved out of the kitchen and mounted the stairs. As he ascended behind her, Cohen childishly grinned at the prospect of entering various bedchambers with his lovely superior.

The first floor was taken up by two identical and, as far as those little individual touches that characterise people's 'own' rooms were concerned, featureless bedrooms. They had beds, covered with matching yellow counterpanes, one chair each plus chests of drawers which Sergeant Farsakoğlu soon established were as empty as the kitchen cupboards had been.

'It's almost as if the occupant has recently moved out,' Sergeant Farsakoğlu observed as she pulled one of the counterpanes aside to reveal a plain, uncovered mattress.

'People do do runners sometimes,' Cohen observed, 'particularly when they're behind with the rent.'

'I don't think that's a possibility. Mrs Yalçin said that the Armenian who lives here wore nice clothes and was very polite, which doesn't sound to me like the sort of person who would default on rent.'

Cohen shot her a rueful smile. 'Anybody can default on rent, Sergeant, believe me.'

She smiled. 'The fruits of your considerable life experience, Constable?'

'Yes, well...' Cohen cleared his throat in that obvious way people do when they want to change a subject. 'Perhaps someone's just been in here and stolen all of Mr Armenian's personal stuff then, eh, Sergeant?'

'Perhaps.'

She moved back towards the stairs once again. 'Come on,' she said, 'let's take a look up there. If we don't find anything, we'll do the basement before we leave.'

'OK.'

Unlike the rest of the house, the entrance to the second storey was not accessed via a hall area; as the officers ascended, they found it obscured from their view by a door placed right at the top of the stairs. It was, so Sergeant Farsakoğlu mused, almost as if this part of the house were separate from the rest of the building—like a self-contained apartment for a tenant or sub-lettee. In the context of an ordinary, working-class Istanbul dwelling such an arrangement was not unusual. Here, however, in this great, wide house clinging to the edge of the mighty Topkapı Palace, it seemed, for some reason she couldn't logically fathom, odd. And in keeping with the sergeant's weird feelings about it, the door, unlike that which may have belonged to a totally separate tenant, moved aside easily under the light pressure from her boot.

At first, and quite reasonably in a room in which the blinds were drawn, neither of the officers could see anything beyond their own shadows falling across the edge of the dark brown carpet beneath their feet. Cohen moved rather closer to Farsakoğlu than he knew she would like but then moments of tension like this gave him all sorts of excuses. He cleared his throat before whispering, 'If he's asleep in here and we wake him up...'

'Hello?' Farsakoğlu said in a loud, authoritative voice as she simultaneously switched on the large chandelier that hung over the equally large bed. Cohen was for a moment quite lost in admiration for her forcefulness until he saw the figure facing away from them on the top of the bed-clothes.

'Sir?' she said, again with some forcefulness, enough at least to rouse a sleeping person.

Not of course that this person did rouse from his sleep. And as the smell from the soiling of his trousers finally reached their nostrils the two officers knew that he wasn't going to react to any of their entreaties—ever.

Çetin Ikmen was not a patient man. He could have hung around for the waiter to come and give him another drink of his choice but quite frankly he really couldn't be bothered. So, grabbing hold of what he hoped was the brandy decanter, he poured a nice healthy draught into his glass and then drank with obvious pleasure. Had he not been at the home of his very best friend, Arto Sarkissian, he would have acted with more propriety—or at least that was what he told himself as he hurled a massive gulp down his throat. It felt good too, the warm, comforting taste of alcohol. The drink and the cigarette he was holding in his other hand also had the advantage of giving him something to do, which he needed very badly for, as well as feeling hideously uncomfortable in the unaccustomed dinner jacket he was wearing, he also felt very out of place amongst Arto's other guests.

Çetin and Arto had been friends since they were small boys. They both came from intelligent and intellectually curious families and as children the two of them had shared their play and their thoughts in equal measure. As adults that state of affairs had not really changed except for their respective professions. Arto, like his elder brother Krikor, had opted for a career in medicine and had for the past twenty years been working for the police as a criminal pathologist. Çetin too worked for the police, but in the far less well-paid arena of detective in the homicide division. That the two frequently met over what was left of somebody's unwanted wife or inconvenient father gave them, in common with others who work in rather morbid professions, cause for some very cruel and grim humour.

Outside of work, however, the two could not have been more different. With nine children, a wife and an ageing father to support, Çetin lived the life of a struggling working-class Turk, albeit an educated one. His home was a crowded, reeking apartment in Sultan Ahmet, an area of the city that not only boasted most of the famous Istanbul monuments but also a large shifting population of backpackers, drug dealers, pimps and illegal immigrants. The thing that he drove—he rarely called it a car for it hardly warranted the term—was the same article he had driven since just after the birth of his third child. It was all in startling contrast to the opulence around him now. Arto, his rotund and jolly little Armenian friend, had not only done very well for himself professionally, he had married well too, which was why Çetin was now standing in this vast floodlit palace on the shore of the Bosporus. Seeing his host's wife, he raised his glass to her in greeting. He received a frosty smile from the lovely Maryam Sarkissian in reply. Not wishing to address the fact that she, he knew full well, couldn't stand his skinny scruffy Turkishness, Çetin chose to believe that her latest bout of plastic surgery was preventing her from welcoming him properly.

'Are you enjoying yourself or are you actually drowning your sorrows?'

Çetin turned around and found himself facing his friend. 'You want me to be honest?'

Arto smiled. 'As ever.'

'Well, this jacket isn't really me, is it?'

'No, but...'

'And...' Çetin sighed heavily. 'Look, Arto, I don't really fit in with this lot, do I? Maryam's just given me a look that said it all.'

'Oh, you should know not to pay any attention to Maryam,' Arto laughed, 'and besides, whatever you may think of the people here, they are all working for the project just like we are.'

Çetin looked down at the floor, apparently shamed by his friend's words. 'Yes, I know.'

'In order to get anything like this on track we need to get hold of money and that's what these people have. In abundance.'

One cursory glance around was enough to convince Çetin of that. There was a lot of money in that room, or at least the possessors of a lot of money. Industrialists, well-heeled professionals, old and venerable families—they were all here and, what was more, they were all very eager to get their cheque books out in support of this initiative that had first been put forward by Arto's brother Krikor. Drug addiction, or rather the fight against drug addiction, was, especially in view of the threat from AIDS plus the influx of some very dubious organisations from the former eastern bloc countries, becoming a grave cause for concern amongst certain sectors of Istanbul society. The police, as represented here by Çetin Ikmen, were noticing that more and more crimes were related to narcotic abuse, and doctors like Krikor Sarkissian, who had been involved with such problems for some time, had decided to take a lead in trying to address the problem. A first step was to try and secure funds for a dedicated advice and information centre at the heart of the 'trade,' the districts of Sultan Ahmet and Beyazit. And that was why Çetin, Arto, Krikor and all these smart folk were here now.

'Arto! At last!'

Both Arto and Çetin turned in response to this rather strident cry and found themselves looking at a tall, extremely attractive man in, Çetin quickly reckoned, his late thirties.

'Avram!'

Quickly, but with much affection, Arto hugged and kissed this man and then, smiling, introduced him to his old friend.

'Çetin, this is Dr Avram Avedykian, a most avid and enthusiastic supporter of my brother's project. Avram, this is my oldest and best friend, Inspector Çetin Ikmen.'

The two men shook hands.

'Inspector Ikmen as in police, isn't it?' the doctor said.

'Yes, sir,' Çetin replied in his best speaking-to-those-outside-my-usual-sphere-of-influence voice, 'we have, as you can imagine a vested interest in—'

'You don't have to call anybody here sir, Çetin,' Arto put in before his friend's awkwardness became a problem. 'We are all here for the same reason, all trying to help.'

'Oh. Right. Yes.'

Chastised, Çetin then looked down at the floor. It was a movement that even he found childish. Had it not been for the appearance of another man at Dr Avedykian's side the moment could have been embarrassing, but this man, possibly just slightly older than the doctor, was so arrestingly handsome that even a red-blooded heterosexual like Arto was quite lost in admiration.

Moving forward to greet this newcomer, he said, 'And you are?'

'Oh,' said Dr Avedykian, suddenly also aware of this man's presence, 'this is *my* best friend actually, Arto.' He moved the man forward to include him in the group and made his introductions. 'Dr Arto Sarkissian, this is Mr Muhammed Ersoy.'

The name was familiar to Arto. 'Oh, yes, Avram talks of you frequently, Mr Ersoy, and my brother Krikor has, of course, mentioned your name to me. You're very interested in his work, I believe?'

'Yes.' Muhammed Ersoy shook hands with his host in a casual, almost off-hand manner and then turned almost immediately to Çetin. 'I couldn't help overhearing that you are a member of our fine body of police officers.'

It was said in such a way as to imply a mockery of that force. Luckily, Çetin, who was accustomed to this sort of reception, rose only mildly to the bait. 'Yes, I am,' he said, 'but like yourself, Mr Ersoy, I am here tonight to support Krikor's initiative rather than talk about what I do.'

'Quite.'

A rather frosty silence followed which was only brought to a close by a change of topic on Arto's part. 'So,' he said, addressing the two newcomers, 'I hope that you gentlemen are going to be generous after my brother's speech tonight.'

'You can count on us,' confirmed Dr Avedykian lightly.

'Quite,' said his companion, still, for some reason, looking at Çetin.

It was at this point that an annoying beeping sound was heard. In response to this the two doctors and Mr Ersoy checked their jacket pockets and removed a varied selection of mobile telephones. As a man they all checked their machines muttering short phrases such as 'Not me', 'Not mine', and 'No'. Then they all looked around to see who might be in receipt of a message—until Arto, with a heavy I-am-so-accustomed-to-this sigh, reached inside Çetin's jacket pocket and removed the offending article for him.

As he pressed the 'receive' button and then handed the instrument back to his friend, he said, 'I do wish you'd get to grips with this thing, Çetin. It's not that difficult.'

The look of smug amusement that this elicited from Arto's other companions was not lost on Çetin. He made a mental note of their reactions for a later date as he turned away and spoke into the machine: 'Ikmen.'

Leaving his friend to get on with whatever conversation he was having on the telephone, Arto motioned one of the waiters over in order to offer his companions more drinks.

'Çetin does unfortunately get calls at odd times,' he explained, 'as do I and probably yourselves too.'

'We are all busy men these days,' agreed Dr Avram,

'which, in our case, is odd when you consider that we probably have more doctors than ever before.'

Muhammed Ersoy took a champagne flute from the
waiter's tray and smiled. 'Ah yes, my dear Avram, but
don't you also have oh so many more patients too?'

'Oh, well...'

'Now that those we have always considered to be the
traditional "poor" can have things like televisions, mobile
telephones and other instruments of information and com-
munication they are far more aware of what doctors can
and cannot offer them. Whereas in the past some nebulous
ache would be ignored, now they repair to the doctor just
in case that ache may be cancer or heart trouble or one of
the other ills they have seen mentioned on the television.'

Arto viewed his new acquaintance keenly. 'Do I detect
that you feel there is something wrong with that, Mr Ersoy?'

'Indeed I do.' It was said with an arrogance which
seemed to embarrass his best friend, who turned away and
busied himself looking at some of the other guests. 'Had
we, or rather people like us, not planted such ideas in their
heads then they would hardly have formulated them for
themselves and—'

'I'm sorry, Arto, I've got to go.'

It took a few moments for Çetin's words to register
with his friend. 'Eh?'

'I've got to go, Arto,' Çetin reiterated, 'right now.'

'Oh, is it, er...?'

'Yes.' With some difficulty Çetin folded his mobile
phone away and replaced it in his pocket. 'In fact I could
actually do with you.'

'Right.' Arto sighed and then squared his shoulders.
'Right, yes, of course. I'm sure Krikor can manage without
me. I'll just...er...'

He pointed in the direction of his brother and made off towards him.

'Something come up?' Muhammed Ersoy asked as he and Çetin stood alone, the latter rather tensely shuffling his feet against the pile of the carpet.

'Yes, sir,' Çetin replied absent-mindedly.

'Might I ask...?'

'No, I'm afraid you can't. We have our rules as I am sure do you in your work.'

Muhammed Ersoy shrugged. 'Ah, but I don't work, Inspector.'

'Then perhaps we should leave it at that then, sir?' Çetin observed. He saw that Arto was threading his way back towards him and he moved forward to join his friend.

# 2

WHILE THE DOCTOR attended to his part of the investigation, namely the corpse upon the bed, Inspector Ikmen and Sergeant Farsakoğlu looked around at the living quarters of the deceased. A cursory examination seemed to confirm the sergeant's earlier contention that this part of the house was a separate apartment. The main room contained the bed, a chair, various cupboards and bureaux plus a television; two smaller rooms led off from it. These were a rather opulent bathroom and a small, almost cupboard-like place that contained a refrigerator, a small sink and a work surface bearing an electric kettle.

As was his custom, Ikmen made straight for the fridge, one of his great fascinations at moments like this being with what his victim liked to eat. But as he went to pull the handle towards him, Sergeant Farsakoğlu preempted his curiosity.

'It's quite empty, sir, I've looked,' she said. 'Like the kitchen downstairs. Not a crumb in there.'

Ikmen raised one eyebrow. 'And yet someone obviously lived here.'

14

'Yes,' the sergeant replied. 'An Armenian gentleman, according to the grocers opposite. Although from the description we've had it seems unlikely that he is our corpse.'

Ikmen moved out of the kitchen and back into the main bedroom area again. 'No?'

'No. The man the old grocer described was middle-aged and very smart. You could not,'—she moved her head in the direction of the bed—'describe what lies there as either of those things.'

'You could, however,' the doctor put in from the side of the bed, 'describe our friend here as a user of hard drugs.'

'Really?'

Holding up a limp arm so that his colleagues could see it, Arto Sarkissian pointed to a number of small scars and sores on the inside of the forearm. 'These marks are scars left by repeated injections with a hypodermic syringe. They are typical of the damage habitual drug users inflict upon themselves. Untrained or desperate for their fix, they shove needles into any vein they can find. Needles, furthermore, that are not always clean, hence the sores.'

Farsakoğlu let her eyes drift slowly around what, with its expensive chandelier and very clean, tasteful furniture, was an extremely nice apartment. 'Users don't generally live in places like this, do they?'

Ikmen frowned. 'Don't be so sure. Addicts, like any-body else, can surprise you. Just because a man shoves heroin in his arm on a regular basis doesn't mean to say he necessarily lives in a slum. And besides, we don't yet know that this man did live here, do we?'

'No.'

'Perhaps when Cohen gets back from questioning the hotelier next door we'll know a bit more.'

While the doctor silently continued his investigations,

Ikmen walked over to the chest of drawers nearest to the door. He'd noticed its incongruity as soon as he came in. Although he had only really passed through the rooms lower down in the building, he had taken note of Farsakoğlu's observation that the house was almost totally without character. She had said that it 'lacked personal touches', a rather more typically 'womanly' observation from her than he was accustomed to, but he trusted her instinct nevertheless. And that was why the items on top of the chest of drawers appeared so startlingly strange: little crystal figures, about fifty of them, all arranged in neat rows across the top of the chest; animals, domestic items, little people, tiny houses, palaces, mosques. Each in its own way a dazzling work of art and, making up a collection of such magnitude, probably worth quite a lot of money too. A little evidence, so Ikmen mused, in support of the idea that the victim had not actually resided in this house. Small, portable and expensive things like these crystal figures rarely survived around the heavy and committed drug user. But then...

'Until I've done some tests I won't know for sure what killed him,' Arto Sarkissian said, thoughtlessly wiping his hands on the lapel of his dinner jacket, 'but I'd say it's pretty certain that it wasn't the drugs.'

Ikmen strode over to the side of the bed. 'No?' he questioned, looking into the face of what had once been a really quite nice-looking young man.

Gently but firmly, the doctor pushed the young man's head to one side, revealing to Ikmen's gaze a dark purple and red line around the base of the throat. 'I would say that he was strangled, possibly by ligature,' he said, 'which, if I am right, opens the door quite neatly to some very foul play indeed.'

'Mmm.'

'Get the place dusted, Çetin,' the doctor continued.

'I think that Farsakoğlu was quite right to have you called out here tonight.'

'I had a bad feeling,' the sergeant put in, looking over the shoulders of the two men at the sad little body on the bed. 'Not very old, is he?'

'Probably about twenty, I should think.'

Ikmen looked across at his friend and sighed. 'But he'd been a user for some time, hadn't he?'

'Oh, yes. Some of those marks on his arms are old and, if I'm right, he's probably got some more on his legs and maybe in his groin too. The longer they've been using, the more their veins start to collapse, which means that they have to go in search of sites in all sorts of improbable places. Very squalid.'

'And just the sort of information your brother would like to make a little more public.'

'Yes, on the basis that if those who are contemplating the habit knew about its more disgusting aspects, it might make them think twice. After all, who wants to die like this? Murdered probably for a couple of grams of heroin and left reeking in your own shit?'

Ikmen allowed himself a grim little smile. 'Perhaps we should have brought some of your brother's prospective sponsors out here to have a look?'

Arto Sarkissian pulled a comically shocked face. 'Oh, I don't think so, Inspector!'

'Bit too real, you think?'

'Absolutely.'

The door to the apartment opened to admit Constable Cohen. Ikmen greeted him with a nod of the head. 'Anything?'

Cohen shrugged. 'Not a lot. Mr Draz, the hotel owner next door, knew even less than the grocer about the man who lives here. He described him as middle-aged and quiet.

Keeps himself to himself. Didn't know how long he's been here but Mr Draz has owned the hotel for five years and our man was here when he came. Didn't know whether he was Armenian or not though.'

The doctor smiled. 'If a man has an expensive suit everybody usually assumes that he's either Armenian or Jewish, isn't that right, Cohen?'

'Some do, yes, Doctor. Except, that is, in my case.'

Ikmen, unable to join what was essentially a closed conversation, changed the subject. 'So what we've got,' he said slowly, as if fixing the information firmly in his mind, 'is a victim who is young, a user and who may have been strangled. This house, or rather this part of the house, may or may not have been his home. As far as we know the place is owned or rented by an older man who may or may not be Armenian and who we really do need to find now.'

'And the windows have been nailed shut.'

They all turned to look at Sergeant Farsakoğlu who had been minutely examining the casement.

'What?'

'These windows are all nailed shut, sir,' she said, 'and they've been painted over too. Some time ago by the look of it.'

'Have they indeed?' Ikmen replied. 'Well, quite a conundrum for my sergeant to get his teeth into when he returns to us tomorrow.'

The doctor put his gloves and stethoscope back into his bag and sighed. 'And another late night for me, I think.'

'Yes,' said Ikmen, 'we need to get going on this one fast.'

For those residents of Ishak Paşa Caddesi for whom high drama was a particular passion, the events of the rest of that night proved most absorbing. As well as the arrival of various ordinary police squad cars there was the added thrill of witnessing the entrances and exits of other people to and from the house. These included police photographers, forensic investigators and, just after midnight, a group of sombre individuals bearing a stretcher and body-bag. As this latter group and its grim cargo passed by the now considerable crowd of onlookers, those in that company of a more religious persuasion were heard to mutter 'Allah!' and turn away from this all-too-real manifestation of mortality.

Opinions varied regarding what may or may not have occurred in 'that house'. The police officers, as ever, were not in the least forthcoming about what was occurring and so theories abounded within the crowd. Mrs Yalçin, the grocer's wife, was particularly free with her ideas.

'I always knew that it wasn't quite natural for a man of his age to be living there all by himself.'

'Well, he is Armenian,' offered another elderly, heavily veiled woman. 'And you know that with Christians—'

'With Christians, what?' The voice was deep and, had it not been so thoroughly smoke-scarred, would have been almost operatic in quality. The two women turned to face the source of the voice and found themselves looking at a short, thin man wearing a dinner jacket that was several sizes too big for him.

'With Christians, what?' Çetin Ikmen repeated, shrugging his arms wide in a questioning gesture.

'Well,' said the veiled woman, 'you know, they're sort of...'

'They're different to us, aren't they?' said Mrs Yalcin. 'They don't make their men go through sünnet.'

'So not very clean.'

'Yes, and also they don't eat right which makes their women hot in the blood.'

'Which all means that they are far more likely than true believers to have lots of policemen turn up at their door?' Ikmen finished.

'Oh, yes.'

'Exactly,' agreed the veiled woman. 'My thoughts exactly.'

'And you know for a fact that the man who lives in this house is a Christian, do you?'

'Well...'

'From his clothes and his general look...'

'So he didn't tell you that he was a Christian, but you assumed so?'

'Well, er...No, I mean we rarely spoke. But he had a ring and...er...'

Ikmen's face resolved into a bitter scowl. The old them-and-us thing rearing its ugly head again. He'd seen it so many times, but it never ceased to anger him: the notion that 'we' couldn't possibly commit a crime and so 'they', whoever they happened to be at the time, had to have done it. Ignorant and dangerous assumptions. He turned a stern face upon the two old ladies and then proceeded to give them a small but to him familiar lecture.

'Keeping your opinions to yourselves may be rather a safer course of action at this time, don't you think, ladies? Making assumptions about people can be very dangerous, particularly when they pertain to a person's race or religion, and especially in view of the fact that you don't know what may or may not have happened in that house.'

A somewhat aggressive looking middle-aged man who had been listening in on the conversation quickly came to the ladies' defence. 'And what do you know?' he asked Ikmen. 'Who are you to tell people what to say?'

Ikmen smiled. He really rather enjoyed situations like this. 'I'm the officer in charge of this investigation, sir.'

'Oh.' The man moved, just slightly, away from where he had been standing.

The two ladies, however, became if anything, more animated. 'So, what has happened then, Officer?' asked the grocer's wife.

'Is he dead, that Ar—the man who lives in that house?' put in her companion.

'That is not something I am at liberty to tell you, ladies,' Ikmen replied, 'but if you would like to assist us in this matter I would suggest that the best thing you could do right now is return to your homes.'

'Ah.'

'Um.'

Arto Sarkissian, moving surprisingly rapidly for such a plump and uncomfortably dinner-suited man, ran down the steps of the house and into the street. Rapidly scanning the assembled crowd, his keen eye quickly caught Ikmen's and the latter excused himself to the ladies. He joined his friend.

'I want to bring the body out now,' the doctor whispered into Ikmen's ear, 'but I don't want this lot looking on when I do so.'

'All right.' He turned around in order to look for some sort of support and found that Farsakoğlu was at his side. 'Get hold of some of the men,' he said to her, 'and get this lot shifted.'

'Yes, sir.'

However, rather to Ikmen's surprise, she didn't act upon this immediately.

He looked at her questioningly. 'And? Yes?'

'Oh, it's, er...' She smiled, her face just very slightly red.

'Yes?'

'It's just...er...Did you say that Sergeant Suleyman is back again tomorrow, sir?'

'Yes, from his vacation. And?'

'Oh.' She smiled. 'Good. That means you'll have, er, more support.'

'Just get these awful ghouls moved for me, will you, Farsakoğlu? Now would be nice.'

'Yes, sir.'

She moved away, looking, so Ikmen could not help but notice, just a little bit too happy.

The doctor raised a wry eyebrow. 'She's a little keen, isn't she?'

Ikmen flung a much-needed cigarette into his mouth and lit up. 'I often wish,' he said wearily, 'and this is without any disrespect to the man, that my sergeant would be struck down by some sort of ugly virus.'

Arto Sarkissian smiled. 'I know what you mean. I assume that Farsakoğlu knows that he's married?'

'Oh, yes,' Ikmen replied sourly, 'everybody knows that he's married, especially Suleyman himself.'

'Oh.'

As Sergeant Farsakoğlu and a small squad of men attempted to disperse the crowd, both Ikmen and Sarkissian drew their jackets tightly around their bodies. There was a stiff wind blowing up from the nearby Sea of Marmara now that was distinctly autumnal in character.

# 3

FATMA IKMEN SLUMPED down on to the floor beside the telephone and stared, glassily, at the instrument. While half of her mind hoped that it would ring of its own volition, the other half wondered whether she should take the initiative and risk disturbing Çetin by calling him herself. He was obviously very busy with something which, she reasoned, could only be work. She imagined him all sleepless and tetchy, barking out orders from his untidy desk and squirming about uncomfortably in his dinner jacket. Then she looked down at herself, at her great, uncomfortably swollen belly and tried to put from her mind other reasons why he might have been out all night. The sort of women who would have been attending Krikor Sarkissian's fund-raising evening were not women like herself. Plastic surgery (like Arto's wife Maryam underwent so regularly), and for that matter surgery of a conventional nature, was common-place to them. That she was still living with these huge and wretched fibroids which had chosen to inhabit her uterus was more a tribute to her poverty than any fears she may have had regarding operations—although that was all part of it too, of course.

But then, what on earth would any of those lovely society women want with Çetin? Small, thin and, if she were perfectly honest, really quite ugly, her husband was hardly a catch to be boasted about within the salons of the rich and famous. He was middle-aged with no money, had too many children, few prospects and...and yet his charm was as undeniable as it was infectious. When he wanted to, Çetin could make a woman feel like an empress—he'd made her feel so on many occasions. Until quite recently. Until this fibroid business had started, bringing with it a great deal of pain, endless bleeding and absolutely no interest in sex. Dr Koç had said that it would all stop when her change began. As hot flushes and dry skin rolled in so the fibroids would shrink and, eventually, disappear. Fatma pulled a sour face. Well, that was something to look forward to anyway! She'd have a face like a lump of old leather but at least her stomach would be flat!

As she sat thinking these morbid and defeatist thoughts her youngest child, four-year-old Kemal, appeared from out of her bedroom, trailing a blanket behind him.

'Can I have a drink now, Mummy?' he asked.

'Yes, in a minute.'

'I'm really thirsty.'

'Yes, and I said that I'd get you a drink in a minute.' She eyed him miserably. It wasn't his fault that he was so young and full of energy and she was so old and tired. 'Mummy's not feeling very well and—'

'Poor Mummy!' With the sweetest will in the world he threw himself upon her in order to provide comfort, unfortunately landing on her fibroid-encrusted belly.

Fatma, squealing in agony but at the same time so appreciating his gesture, both held on to and pushed away her little one as he attempted to cover her face with wet early-morning kisses. 'Oh, Kemal, darling!'

'Fatma!' It was a man's voice, old and heavy with thick mucus.

Gently she moved her child over to one side so that he was sitting next to her and then whispered in his ear, 'It's Grandad, sssh!' Then, calling out in response to the voice, she said, 'Yes, Timür, what is it?'

'I'm afraid I've got that Greek under my bed again,' the elderly voice continued. 'He's driving me mad with his singing, as usual.'

Fatma sighed heavily. She frequently found herself in situations like this with her father-in-law these days. On top of the children and her own problems it was really too much. She would have to speak to Çetin—again. She took a deep breath before replying. 'He'll go if you ask him to leave nicely, Timür.'

'You think so?'

'Yes.'

'But how will he get out?' The old man sounded, as ever, genuinely concerned. But then that was all part of it, the fact that he now actually believed these things.

'He can easily climb out of the window and get down the fire escape,' Fatma continued, thinking all the time about how absolutely mad she would sound to someone outside the family.

'Oh, yes,' answered the old man, 'I'll ask him to do that then.'

'All right.'

And as she listened to the sound of Timür Ikmen gently inviting his guest, whose name she now learned was Nikos, to leave, Fatma Ikmen looked back at the telephone. But still it didn't, wouldn't ring.

Her eyes now stinging with tears, Fatma began to stand up, heaving with her the little springy body of her youngest child. She was, she thought, just like a big, fat miserable old goat. 'Come on,' she said to Kemal, 'let's get you that drink.'

The little boy smiled and hugged her neck.

Mehmet Suleyman entered his office looking smart, tanned and thoroughly worn out.

Ikmen, his eyes red and watery from lack of sleep, raised his weary head from the papers before him on his desk and grimaced. 'A vacation to mark down to experience, I take it, Suleyman?'

'Yes, sir,' the younger man replied, 'you could say that.'

'Sorry.'

Suleyman slid his briefcase underneath his desk and sat down. 'You're wearing a dinner jacket, sir,' he observed. 'Is there something I should know?'

Ikmen lit a cigarette and, once he had recovered from the heavy bout of coughing this precipitated, he said, 'I was at a fund-raising event over at Dr Sarkissian's last night.'

'For his brother's drug project?'

'Yes, although I wasn't there for very long. Almost as if to underline Krikor's efforts some young drug addict went and got himself strangled at a house down by the Topkapı Palace.'

'Oh. Any details?'

Ikmen shrugged. 'Some. Although there is a lot of work to be done which is why I am so very glad to welcome you back, Suleyman. Forensic are over at the house now, which is on Ishak Paşa Caddesi, but I'd like you to go over too. Get a feel for the crime.'

'Yes, sir.' Suleyman, almost in spite of himself, smiled. It was good to be back; despite everything he might say about the job when he was fed up, it was very good to be back.

'In fact, perhaps it would be a good idea if I get back over there myself too.' Ikmen stood up rapidly, in the way that he did when he was very tired and needed to motivate himself. 'You don't mind driving, do you? I think I'd have an accident if I did.'

'OK.' Suleyman took his keys out of his pocket and jangled them in his hand.

'Oh, and, er...' Ikmen looked down at the floor in a rather studied fashion. 'I should, er, perhaps warn you that young Sergeant Farsakoğlu may well still be on duty.'

'So?'

It was said in such obvious innocence that Ikmen was for a moment quite taken aback.

Suleyman, seeing his superior's confusion, asked, 'Why?'

Ikmen wasn't very good at tackling subjects like this and so, after a brief moment's thought, he decided that the best course of action would be to take the coward's route out. 'Oh, it's just that she's a bit keen, that's all. She tends to chatter on when you're trying to think.'

'Oh. I hadn't noticed that, but...' Suleyman shrugged. The fact that Sergeant Farsakoğlu was beginning to display an interest in him was probably, Ikmen thought, still quite unknown to Suleyman, which would be entirely in character. Over the years many women had been attracted to him without his apparent knowledge. But the subject died then and there as the two men prepared themselves for the day to come.

'There's something odd about this crime scene,' Ikmen said as he made ready to leave his office.

'Like?'

'Well, I'd really rather you saw the place yourself, without any preconceptions, before we talk about it. I came to the scene yesterday evening with a very tired brain, which may have made me deduce things incorrectly. You see what your fresh, vacationed brain can do with it and then we'll talk.'

'All right,' Suleyman smiled, 'although I can't promise that my brain is fresh after what can only laughably be called a vacation.'

Ikmen frowned. He had hoped, together probably with Suleyman's parents, that this latest vacation would help heal some of the wounds between his deputy and his wife. Poor Suleyman hadn't been happy about his marriage, which had been an arranged one, from the start. Five years on and with a very expensive break in Alexandria behind them, things didn't seem to be any better.

'Was it really that bad?' he asked.

Suleyman's smile didn't move, but his eyes became sad. 'It was worse.'

'I'm sorry.'

Suleyman sighed. 'I wanted to walk and talk, wander about on the Corniche, look at the little that remains of Alexander's city, but all Zuleika wanted to do was spend our money in the bazaars...' He shrugged. 'Well, anyway, shall we go, sir?'

Ikmen walked over and patted him affectionately on the back. 'Yes, let's get to work. To be honest, I could do with a drink, just to start my day off.'

In recent years Ikmen's once legendary habit of drinking during duty hours had been most ruthlessly curtailed. In an effort to clean up his subordinates, Ikmen's boss, Commissioner Ardiç, had done much to take what some used to describe as the joy out of the job. With Ikmen's drinking gone, only cigarettes, or so it appeared to him, remained as sources of pleasure during the course of the day—and there were rumours that Ardiç had plans for those too.

They moved towards the door and, in an attempt to alter the air of melancholy that had enveloped them, Suleyman changed the subject. 'And how are your wife and children then?'

'Oh, Allah!' Ikmen struck his thoughtless brow with the heel of his hand, 'Fatma! In all this madness I haven't even thought to contact her. She'll kill me!'

With rapid, fumbling fingers he reached for the mobile telephone in the inside pocket of his jacket. 'Now if I can just get this thing to work...'

The house on Ishak Paşa Caddesi had never had a number. Officially it didn't have a name either, although any letter addressed to 'The Sacking House' would have got to its destination without any problem. Quite whether the property deserved its name, no one now knew, but that the legend behind it survived did give the place a sort of notoriety, deserved or otherwise. The grocer had told Sergeant Farsakoğlu the old story.

'When the Ottoman Sultans ruled the Empire from their great palace of Topkapı, they were wont to collect numerous treasures, including many wives and concubines. Like so many with so much, they didn't actually always want all of them. Some of them would displease, if you know what I mean, in the bedroom and... Well, anyway, they had a very special way of disposing of those they didn't like: they threw them into the water just off Seraglio Point. It was the eunuchs that did it. They stitched the women up in sacks and then heaved them into the Bosporus. This house is called "The Sacking House" because at one time a maker of sacks lived in it. It is said that it was he who made the sacks into which the young girls were placed before being thrown to their watery graves. Whether the story is true or not, I don't know. But it used to be said that this was a wicked place and, as the Prophet Mohammed, blessings and peace be upon him, is my judge, I feel that given recent events that just might be so. Places, like people, can be evil, Officer, and this is one of them.'

Sergeant Farsakoğlu rubbed her tired eyes with her fingers and looked up once again at the time-scarred façade of the house. In the strengthening light of the morning, which was proving to be one graced with a little weak sunlight, it looked far more welcoming than it had done the night before. If it hadn't been for the two constables stationed either side of the front door, it would have looked like a perfectly normal dwelling for this part of the city. And if Farsakoğlu hadn't known that a young boy had recently met his death in there she, like most people, would have given the house very little thought.

But she did know, and she knew other things about this house too. She knew that the windows had been nailed shut in the room where the boy had died and that they had been like that for some time. She felt the strangeness of the place right through to her bones. Who, she wondered, lived in a house with no food, no books or papers—no little things, with the exception of some rather fine crystals, to mark the place as their own? It was almost as if the dead boy had been somehow materialised on that bed out of thin air—there was nothing except him and who he was, nobody as yet knew.

The grocer, who had been standing silently by her side during these musings, cleared his throat. 'Will that be all then, Officer?'

'Oh, er, yes, thank you for your help.'

He shrugged. 'It's nothing.'

As the grocer sauntered back to his shop a car pulled up and two men got out. As they approached her, the sight of one of the men made Sergeant Farsakoğlu's face redden. Quickly she put her hands up to her cheeks in order to cover their colouring, a movement not lost upon old Ikmen who was eyeing her most keenly.

'Ah, Sergeant,' he said, 'we're just going into the house for a bit. Forensic OK?'

'Yes, sir,' she replied, 'all very hard at work.'

'Good.' He lit a cigarette and smiled. 'You should be getting off home soon, you must be exhausted.'

'Yes.' She took a deep breath before addressing Ikmen's partner. 'Hello, Sergeant Suleyman,' she said, 'did you have a good vacation?'

His smile was such a beautiful thing to see that she found herself looking away as he replied, scared that he would see her reaction and know what she was feeling.

'Yes, thank you, Sergeant,' he said. Then, turning immediately to Ikmen, 'Shall we go in now, sir?'

'Yes.'

As the two men moved forward, Ikmen turned to Farsakoğlu and said, more as an order than a suggestion, 'Go home and get some sleep now, Farsakoğlu, there's nothing else for you here at present.'

And then they were gone, up into that strange house of death, one old and small and bowed down by the accumulated heaviness of time, the other so straight and tall and yet also, in his own beautiful way, marked by the passage of weary years. Perhaps, she thought, it was dealing with death which made them like that. Maybe if one looked upon it too frequently that was how one's eyes would end up looking—heavy and yet hollow, hurt in a way that only they could understand. But then again, if some of the more gossipy constables were to be believed, there was more than that at play in the case of Mehmet Suleyman. Cohen, who probably knew Mehmet better than most, had upon several occasions intimated that things were not entirely perfect between the sergeant and his wife. Not that this was any of Farsakoğlu's business. That she was so violently attracted to Mehmet was a source of great shame and anxiety. Whether the Suleymans were getting on together or not was immaterial to the fury with which Mrs Suleyman would react if she found out that someone else desired her husband. After all, the lady was Turkish and that was how a Turkish woman would react. She knew that was how it would affect her. If Mehmet belonged to her she would tear the head off any other woman who looked at him.

With heavy limbs and an even heavier heart, Sergeant Farsakoğlu started the long climb up towards the great monuments and home.

The room, seen now in daylight, was slightly larger than he remembered. But then with the body gone that was quite logical. For some reason that Ikmen had never been able to fathom, a dead body appeared to fill a room in a way that a live one just didn't. Perhaps it was the fear that touched them all in the presence of a corpse which made it seem like that? Despite the advances scientists had made in the study of death the process was still largely a mystery, and although Ikmen had no time for the notion of life after death, there was always something troublesome hanging around those who had recently died. The only thing that he could liken it to was a vague feeling of being observed.

But that had quite gone now and, as he watched Suleyman scanning the apartment for the first time, Ikmen was aware that now they could just be any two men looking around a room. Such was the transitory nature of tragedy.

'Did you find any drugs on the body?' Suleyman asked as he bent down to look closely at the numerous crystal figures on top of the chest of drawers.

'No, nor in the house either, I think.' Ikmen turned and called out down the stairs, 'Demir?'

'Yes?' replied a disembodied voice from somewhere down below. 'Any narcotics on the premises?'

'Not as yet.'

'Well, let me know if you find any.'

'I will.'

Ikmen, turning back into the room again, added, 'If forensic fail to find anything I think I might ask for the floorboards to be lifted. You know what users are like.'

Suleyman grunted his agreement.

Then the intrusive beeping sound that had brought Ikmen to this place the night before made itself heard again. Suleyman responded quickly and with practised efficiency, pulling his mobile telephone out of his pocket and looking carefully at its unresponding face. 'No, not me,' he said, 'must be you, sir.'

'I hate these things,' Ikmen mumbled as he pulled the screaming instrument from his jacket pocket. 'Now what do I...' Holding it helplessly for a moment, he could only scowl with relief when Suleyman leaned over and pressed the 'receive' button for him.

'Oh, yes, right.'

'Ikmen?' he said into the impossibly small mouthpiece. 'Yes?'

As Ikmen spoke into his telephone, Suleyman moved

back once again to the display of fine crystal. Some of the pieces, like the little model of the Sultan Ahmet or Blue Mosque, were very fine indeed. His mother was a devotee of such items, and he reasoned that these were, like hers, probably of either Polish or Czech manufacture. Principally of Turkish subject matter, they had for some time been produced in the former eastern bloc countries for the burgeoning Istanbul tourist market. Not that other, more local people (like his mother) didn't collect them too, but he found it a trifle odd to find such things in a house where just one man was reputed to live alone. Perhaps he was being rather small-minded about it. That men could and did appreciate beauty was a fact that went very much against the stereotype of the powerful, strutting Turkish male, yet it was a trait he recognised within himself. But since he was not like most other men that he knew, perhaps this pointed to a person of rather unusual tastes?

'Oh, well, at least we now know who owns this place,' said Ikmen as he turned the telephone off and replaced it in his pocket.

Suleyman looked up. 'Oh?'

'Just up on Divan Yolu, an import-export carpet place.'

'Oh.' Suleyman made no attempt to hide the gravity in his tone.

Ikmen laughed.

'I take it that you are not altogether enamoured of carpet men, Suleyman.'

'No I am not,' the younger man replied somewhat stiffly. 'I find their working practices extremely distasteful and not just because they cheat the tourists. When they go into villages offering to swap really beautiful antique carpets for that awful mass-produced rubbish that they hawk, it makes me mad. It's just blatant exploitation of the peasants who do not and cannot know any better.'

'It is also,' Ikmen said with more than just a small smile in his voice, 'quite legitimate business. As one whose whole apartment is covered with mass-produced rubbish I can, I'm afraid, sympathise with the desire to have something new and clean which will stand up to the tread of many heavy-footed children. Poverty, Suleyman, makes whores of us all. You are just fortunate that you have never had to, figuratively speaking of course, trade your arse for another week's rent. I've done it so often, I don't even notice any more.'

There really was no answer to any of this and Suleyman knew it.

'Anyway,' Ikmen continued, 'I'm going to get over there now and see if I can find out a little bit more about the mysterious occupant of this house. If he's a carpet man himself, I'll let you interrogate him. Your lack of empathy with his kind may prove useful.'

'Do you want me to drive you there?' Suleyman asked.

'Well of course I do, but you really are better employed here for the moment. No, I will walk,' Ikmen said with a rather regretful sigh. 'The unaccustomed exercise together with the moderately fresh air may even serve to wake me up—that or kill me. I'll meet you back here when I've finished.'

'I can come and get you, sir, if—'

'No, the journey back is downhill which even I can manage.' He left and, as silence entered in his wake, Suleyman began, for the first time, to feel some of the horror of that room. Although tastefully decorated, there was no way of ignoring the awful stained counterpane on the bed which was still rumpled in the shape of a human body. There was a smell too, only faint now, but perceptible: the oddly sweetish reek of death and human waste. With all the windows nailed shut there was no way for the smells to escape. The only consolation was that it was now autumn; this room in the height of summer would have been unbearable.

As he wandered thoughtfully from one part of the small apartment to another, Suleyman tried to build a picture in his mind of how and why the young victim might have come to this place. There were not, as yet, any signs that the apartment was frequently used for taking drugs, or dealing. The place seemed to be clean, both in the hygienic and in the drug-related sense, and so it was doubtful that the boy, who Ikmen had told him was a seasoned intravenous drug user, actually lived here. For some reason therefore, he must either have come of his own volition or been brought here for some purpose. Various scenarios came to mind. It seemed unlikely, but there was a chance he had come to the house to buy drugs or, possibly, to sell them. Just because people lived in nice houses didn't mean that they didn't do drugs, and buying them from other users was not unknown. Then again he could have come here for some reason completely unrelated to drugs. To attribute everything in a case like this to drugs was an error that was frequently made. Although enslaved by their habit, users had sides to their lives that were unrelated to their addiction. However, until the boy was identified or, indeed, until Dr Sarkissian had completed his examination of the corpse, most of these musings were pure speculation. At present all they had was a body that had died by strangulation and a very empty and featureless house.

In order to get a full picture, Suleyman decided that he

really ought to have a look at the rest of the house. Eerily, as he moved towards the entrance door of the apartment, he became aware of noise once more: the doleful arabesque singing from a woman outside, her words telling of an old love that had been lost many years before, the harsh, guttural call of a young simitci. As he walked forward, he tried to tell himself that all this was just a coincidence, but his blood, which now ran icy cold in his veins, failed to agree. And, as if to underscore the emotions in his blood, when he stood inside the doorway and looked at the lintel above his head and the posts at his sides, all the noises stopped once again. What he saw on those posts was not what he, or anyone else, would have expected to see; as he leaned his head towards them through the stillness of the renewed silence his blood, ever responsive, froze to a standstill.

The Galleri Turque was a slightly more upmarket carpet business than Ikmen was accustomed to seeing. Ensconced within a large, if vaguely dilapidated, Ottoman house, the Galleri reflected both its owner's sense of himself and of his aspirations. Almost the first thing that Mr Mohammed Azin, the owner, had said to Ikmen as the latter wheezed into his shop, was that both himself and his staff were fluent in French. This had absolutely no bearing on anything that was of interest to Ikmen, but it did not surprise the policeman. The Galleri Turque was, by its very name, obviously designed to appeal to Europeans and to the more snobbish (and moneyed) Turk.

Once the routine exchange of pleasantries had been got over and tea had been served, Ikmen, who was enthroned on the most ornate chaise longue he had ever seen in his life, got down to business. During the course of his conversation with Mr Azin, he became aware of the depth of gratitude he owed to his old French teacher.

'So how long have you owned the house on Ishak Paşa Caddesi, sir? '

'I inherited it from *mon père*, who died in 1975, so since then.' As he spoke, Mr Azin gently fondled several carpets, which were laid out, rather hopefully Ikmen thought, at his feet.

'And you have rented it out since?'

'No, I did live in the house myself until I moved to Sarıyer in 1982. I assume that in the light of this recent tragedy you have been into the house yourself?'

'Yes.'

Mr Azin smiled. 'Then you will know that the decoration and furniture, which was chosen by myself, is of the Louis Quatorze style. Mr Zekiyan has not, I understand, decided to change that, which is a tribute, I believe, to his taste.'

There was no false modesty here, but then carpet men were not renowned for that virtue.

'Mr Zekiyan is, I take it,' Ikmen asked, 'the current tenant of the property?'

'Yes, and as his name suggests, Mr Zekiyan is an Armenian *gentilhomme*.'

By pointing out this evident fact was Mr Azin in some way distancing himself from events at his house? Ikmen suspected that he was, but then this, especially in light of his altercation with the Ishak Paşa neighbours the night before, was no more nor less than he had expected.

'How long has Mr Zekiyan lived in your house?' he asked.

'Since 1982. He's a very good tenant. He always pays

his rent on the first of every third month and keeps the place neat and tidy. I have no complaints.'

'So you do check on the property from time to time?'

'Yes. About twice a year.'

'And Mr Zekiyan has paid his rent for the current period?'

'Yes. In fact that was the last time that I saw him, the first of October. He paid, as always, three months in advance, in cash.' Mr Azin smiled. 'It's very convenient, cash. And in these days of credit cards...'

'So you don't know why he might now be absent from the property?'

'No. He does have a job, quite an important one, I think. I don't know what or where.' The carpet dealer shrugged. 'But then, as a good tenant, he can come and go as he pleases. I do not require him to let me know what his plans might be. He pays the rent and is always polite and businesslike when he comes in here.'

'I see.' Ikmen paused briefly to take out a cigarette which Mr Azin, ever the perfect host, lit for him. 'Thank you. Now, as you know, Mr Azin, we are anxious to speak to Mr Zekiyan, hopefully so that we can eliminate him from our inquiries. It would, however, help us if you could give us a brief description of the gentleman, just in case he is elsewhere and unaware of recent events.'

Mr Azin, although still smiling, suddenly displayed what could only be called a little disquiet beneath his otherwise smooth exterior. 'Well...'

'Yes?'

'Well, er, he is...well, he is Armenian, isn't he?'

'Yes? And? What type of Armenian is he, sir? Is he fat, thin, short or tall—what?'

Mr Azin laughed nervously before retreating once again into his beloved French. *'Pardonnez-moi,* Inspector, but what can I say? He has those features like they have, the rather large nose and deep-set eyes, but...I suppose he must, you would say, be middle-aged by now, reasonably tall and...'

'But they all look rather the same to you, sir, is that the case?'

'Well. Well, yes, I...'

Ikmen closed his eyes and sighed deeply. This was not the first time he had come up against this: the invisibility of minorities, or rather his compatriots' tendency to ignore difference. There was also, he had to admit, a certain disquiet around Armenians, which pertained to events long since past and which he did not even dare to think about here and now.

'So what you're saying then, Mr Azin,' he said wearily, 'is that this Mr Zekiyan is just a typical Armenian.'

This seemed to please the carpet man who now smiled broadly. 'Yes!'

'Oh, good, that certainly does narrow the field. Now, about this separate apartment at the top of your house.'

'Separate apartment?'

'Yes. The one where we found the body. On the top floor.'

Mr Azin's face creased into an expensively sun-tanned frown. 'I don't know what you mean, Inspector. There is no apartment at the top of my house.'

'But on the second floor—'

'Oh, you mean the attic store!' Mr Azin's face broke into a smile of recognition. 'No, that's not an apartment, Inspector. That's just a storage area.'

This time it was Ikmen's turn to look confused. 'So

you have no knowledge of a bedroom, bathroom and small kitchen area in that space?'

'No. Although not having been up there for—'

'The attic store, as you call it, is not checked when you periodically go to look over the place?'

'Oh, no. There is, or as far as I was concerned, was nothing of interest there. Mr Zekiyan said that he had no use for the space and so...'

'And so,' said Ikmen with a sigh, 'he could do anything he liked with it without your knowledge.'

'Well, er, yes, I...' The carpet dealer leaned forward inquiringly. 'What has he done with it, Inspector?'

'Well, it's decorated in exactly the same style as the rest of the house, Mr Azin, and it boasts a rather nice bathroom and kitchen.'

'How extraordinary!' Mr Azin took out his own packet of cigarettes and lit one. 'How strange to do all that with one's own money in a rented property! I suppose I should thank Mr Zekiyan when I see him, it must have enhanced the value of the house considerably, don't you think?'

'I don't know, sir,' Ikmen replied, stubbing his own cigarette out in one of the nearby ashtrays, 'but if you do see Mr Zekiyan before we do, I must urge you to get in contact right away.'

'Oh, *naturellement*, Inspector. Yes, of course.' Mr Azin looked down briefly at his carpets once again and then turned back to smile at Ikmen. 'Is that all, Inspector?'

'That is all for now, sir, yes.'

Mr Azin picked up a very small, but nevertheless almost luminously beautiful kilim from the top of his substantial rug-pile. 'Then perhaps you would like to accept this little gift as a token of my esteem with regard to what you people do for our *communauté*.'

Ikmen, his face very straight, allowed himself only to smile inside. This situation was not foreign to him and his reaction was a practised routine. 'That's very kind of you, sir, but I'm afraid that I am not allowed to take gifts.'

Mr Azin smiled, labouring, Ikmen imagined, under the misconception that he was simply playing hard to get. 'Then what about one of the larger Herekes then,' he said pulling a much bigger carpet out from somewhere near the bottom of the pile. 'A floor covering fit for a sultan and so hard-wearing that your wife would—'

'Sir,' Ikmen reiterated with almost painful clarity, 'I am very flattered, it must be said, that you deem me worthy of such a gift, but I really must impress upon you that I am neither able nor inclined to take gifts from members of the public. It compromises my position.'

'You mean,' the carpet seller said slowly, as if trying to force this concept inside his own uncomprehending head, 'that you never take anything at all, for any reason?'

Ikmen stood up, making the point that he was going and going empty-handed. 'No, I do not, sir. If, as I imagine you do, you would like your name removed from any association with the house in Ishak Paşa, then I would suggest that you find another policeman to do that for you.'

Suddenly, Mr Azin's face was flooded with the high redness of real fury. 'That was not my intention at all and I resent the implication most strongly! I was sincerely and without any conditions making a gift—'

'Which was extremely generous of you,' said Ikmen in his best conciliatory tone, 'but that I cannot take it, sir, you must—'

'Well, you're the first policeman I've ever met who hasn't, Inspector,' Mr Azin said hotly, 'in fact I am quite lost in admiration for your fortitude even if I cannot understand it. You people earn so little!'

Ikmen shrugged. 'I'm a fool, but I'm a fool that can live with himself.'

'Oh, well...' Mr Azin replaced his carpets on to their pile and then rose to show his guest out. Ikmen bowed slightly as his host passed.

But as the two men moved towards the carpet-encrusted exit, Mr Azin suddenly had a thought. 'There is something else about Mr Zekiyan, Inspector...'

Ikmen creased his brows. 'Yes?'

'He wears a ring. It's in the shape of a cross.' He held up his little finger in order to demonstrate. 'Wears it on this finger here. It's quite unusual.'

'Oh?'

The carpet man laughed. 'Oh, yes. Diamonds and very large emeralds. Not the sort of thing that an honest man like yourself can afford even to dream about.'

'No,' Ikmen replied on a scowl, 'I don't suppose that it is.'

# 4

As NIGHT CLOSED in around the sleek, black Mercedes, Arto Sarkissian seriously questioned just what it was he was doing. Bars, however pleasant, were not his scene and having had just two hours' sleep (at his desk) in the last twenty-four, it occurred to him that perhaps driving was not such a good idea either. But then this meeting in the Mosaic Bar had not been his idea—like a lot of his other encounters with alcohol it had been initiated by his friend, Çetin Ikmen. The latter had phoned him some two hours ago, saying that he needed to talk, which they could quite easily have done at the station or, for that matter, at Çetin's home. But then the issue of Çetin's home was a vexed one at the present time. There were reasons why his friend didn't want to go back there; they were the same reasons, or rather reason, why Arto had not been to the Ikmen apartment for such a long time. As the thought hit him, the doctor frowned; his friend's father, Uncle Timür to him, was not a topic he suspected they would be discussing tonight even though he knew that really would be the best thing for Çetin.

Arto turned the car off the main Divan Yolu thorough-fare just before the large parking area in front of the Sultan Ahmet Mosque and negotiated his way down the brightly lit side street. Although the tourist season was now officially at an end, small streets like this still continued to reverberate to the sound of music and laughter, usually that of men, within its little Mediterranean-style bars. Having parked the car as best he could given the fact that the pavements were crumbling and there were numerous bags of litter on the road, Arto walked across to an establishment which boasted many multi-coloured lights around its door. The smell of cheap cigarette smoke and the sound of wooden counters being bashed down on to the surfaces of tavla boards assailed his senses as he entered.

Çetin Ikmen, still marvellously unresplendent in last night's dinner jacket, was sitting just inside the door nursing a glass of his favourite brandy. As the two men embraced in greeting somebody behind the bar put on a mournful arabesque tape; the miserable but sexy music of the great Ibrahim Tatlisas.

It was quite warm inside the bar, after the sharpness of the weather outside on the street, and so Arto had to wipe the steam off the lenses of his spectacles before settling down.

Çetin smiled as he watched his friend and, when the waiter came over it was the policeman who ordered the doctor's Coca-Cola—as ever knowing full well the mind of the other. It was only when the waiter had brought the drink that the conversation began.

Arto opened the proceedings. 'So you wanted to see me?'

'Yes.' Çetin lit a cigarette which, given the heap of butts that now resided in the ashtray, was definitely not his first. 'I want to know what, if anything, you've found out about our victim.'

Arto was used to rather global requests like this from his friend who had very little understanding of pathology. He smiled. 'Well, he is, as I suspected, around twenty years old, and rather overweight, which is a little strange for a drug addict, but...Cause of death was asphyxiation, strangulation by cord or ligature. Where, or indeed if, his habit played any part in this, I don't yet know. He was a long-term user with marks all over his body including the groin. I think we're looking at someone who had been an addict since childhood. The toxicology tests are not yet completed, but I imagine that the narcotic involved was heroin.' He frowned. 'There's also the fact that his limbs are somewhat atrophied.'

'What do you mean?'

'I mean that his limbs show signs of lack of use. It's a phenomenon that you sometimes see in people who are crippled or have been bed-bound for a considerable length of time.'

'So what you're saying is that he could have been in that room for a long period?'

Arto Sarkissian took a sharp intake of breath. 'That I don't know. It's possible. There are, however, no signs of his being forcibly tied to the bed or anything like that. And despite the atrophy he appears to have been quite normal— by that I mean not obviously crippled in any way.'

'Interesting. Any sexual evidence?'

Arto frowned. 'Why?'

'I'll tell you in a minute.'

'No. No signs of anal entry if that is what you mean. His penis was clean and, I should also add, uncircumcised, which would indicate to me that we are either dealing with a native Christian or a foreigner.'

'Yes, that could fit.'

His friend was being somewhat evasive. Çetin did this

when he wanted others to question him about something, usually when he'd been rather clever about discovering a particular fact. Arto took a small sip from his glass and then did what was expected of him. 'All right, Çetin, come on, what is it?'

'The missing tenant of the house is, apparently, a Mr Zekiyan.' He raised his eyebrows questioningly.

Arto shrugged. 'Well, the name is undoubtedly Armenian, but it isn't one that I know.' Then he added rather acidly, 'We don't all know each other, you know.'

Çetin waved a dismissive hand. 'No matter. But the uncircumcised state of the victim could possibly suggest a connection between the two.'

'Yes.'

'But, and this is what really chills my blood about the whole affair, there is evidence which you have just underscored, to suggest that the boy may have been imprisoned in that room.'

'You mean the windows?'

'Yes, but also the door too. This morning, Suleyman discovered that the door to the apartment had quite recently been padlocked. We didn't see it at first because the place from which the lock had been removed had been painted over. The paint was actually still damp to the touch. This indicates, I trust you will agree, that whoever did that did not want us to know that the door had at one time been locked. In addition, the landlord of the property told me that he had absolutely no knowledge of the apartment at the top of the house. According to Mr Azin, the landlord, the place should be just a plain storage area. This begs all sorts of questions about why Mr Zekiyan secretly constructed this area.'

Arto put his hand up to his head and raked thoughtfully

through what little was left of his hair. 'Which is why the issue of sexual interference interested you so much.'

'Yes. Although if there is no evidence to support that...'

'No, there isn't. Although we both know that there are many sexual acts which do not leave any visible signs.' He took a sip from his glass and then looked up gravely. 'So what are you doing to try and discover who this boy was?'

Çetin shrugged. 'The usual. I've circulated my initial rough description, plus I've got people searching through missing persons. I do fear, however, that the victim may have been from outside the city or even originally from abroad. So'—he said it quickly and with what he hoped was a stunning smile—'I'm going to enlist the services of Mrs Taşkiran.'

Arto suddenly wrinkled up his nose as if a bad smell had just assailed him. 'Oh, God!'

'It has to be done,' his friend continued. 'If we can circulate a portrait of the boy we are going to stand a much greater chance of obtaining a positive ID, particularly amongst those who can't read Turkish.'

'Yes, but...'

'Look, Arto, I know that you don't quite see eye to eye...'

Arto leaned across the table and lowered his voice. 'If she didn't insist upon touching them I could just about cope, but she treats corpses as if they are live sitters. Talks to them, even laughs sometimes. I feel like a fucking mortician when she turns up. She's fucking mad, if you ask me!'

Çetin laughed. 'She's an artist, Arto! They're all weird. But she is good, you have to admit, and if she gives us a decent likeness then we can start putting that about and, hopefully, get some answers.'

The doctor, floored by this argument, leaned back in his seat again and grudgingly muttered his assent. His friend smiled.

'It would also be helpful,' he continued, 'and I do really mean absolutely no disrespect here, Arto, if you could run the name Zekiyan by some of your—'

'I'll access the Armenian "network" if that is what you want, Çetin,' the doctor replied, his face a taut mask of distaste, 'if, of course, you will do something for me?'

'Name it.' Çetin raised his empty brandy glass up to one of the passing waiters and indicated that he would like another.

'I'd like you to give your father the care he deserves.' It was not said unpleasantly and, indeed, Çetin's reaction to his friend's request was not hostile in any way.

'My father is perfectly all right where he is now,' he said, smiling.

But Arto was not to be put off that easily. 'He's very sick, Çetin. And I know that that is very hard for you but—'

'He's an old man who has rheumatoid arthritis, Arto, of course he's sick.'

The doctor maintained an awkward silence as the waiter placed the brandy in front of Çetin, but as soon as the man had gone he continued his offensive. 'I'm not talking about his physical condition, Çetin, as well—'

'Are you a member of my family?' This time the policeman's tone was unmistakably harsh as were his eyes which bored into those of his friend. 'I don't think so.'

'No, but Halil—'

'Oh, you've been talking to my brother, have you?' Çetin leaned forward across the table and, in a move that was most certainly one of warning, wagged his finger underneath his friend's nose. 'Now, you listen to me, Arto, my brother may pay for me to care for our father, but his involvement ends there, do you understand?'

'Yes, but—'

'My family and I are perfectly happy to care for Timür for the rest of his natural life. And if my brother has a problem with that, he should come to me, don't you think?'

Someone behind the bar switched the Ibrahim Tatlisas tape for Europop. It was a particularly inappropriate change of tempo. With some difficulty, Arto went on, 'Yes, I agree. But, Çetin, you must understand that it is so difficult for people to talk to you about this. You will not or cannot acknowledge what is happening to Uncle Timür and I do understand that that is hard, but—'

'Hard!' The policeman laughed but without mirth and his eyes were shiny with unshed tears. 'You have no conception, do you?' He leaned forward still further so that the tip of his nose was almost touching Arto's chin. 'I don't talk about it, doctor, because I can't! And what is more I won't! My brother may have all sorts of most laudable ideas about getting me some help with Timür, but while he lives under my roof he will remain as he always has been!'

'But there are, I know, therapies and drugs that can alleviate behavioural—'

'The old man may have lost his mind, but at least allow him the dignity of dying without fucking his brain even further with your fucking drugs!' Çetin turned away quickly, pausing only to pick up his glass from which he now drank deeply.

A moment of silence followed, during which Arto had a chance to reflect upon what had passed between them and, in part, to regret his words. At least Çetin had finally admitted his father had a problem, but he was now very angry and extremely upset—which wasn't at all what his friend had wanted. Arto also realised, as he watched Çetin's face as the latter wrestled with his tears, that it would be stupid to press the point any further.

Arto took another sip from his drink before continuing along an entirely different track. 'So you will organise Mrs Taşkiran to come in?'

'Yes.'

'I suppose the sooner the better from your point of view.'

Çetin turned back to half face Arto and, wiping his dampened eyes on the cuff of his jacket said, 'Yes, if that's all right with you.'

'I've said so, haven't I?'

A small but perceptible smile passed briefly across Çetin's lips. 'Yes, and...and look, I'm sorry she's such a weird old—'

'I've watched people converse with the dead before,' Arto said, smiling a little too, although in his case it was out of relief at the passing of what had been a most awkward moment. 'Not many of them, admittedly, keep their pencils in the brim of their hat or wear army boots in the summer but then Mrs Taşkiran is nothing if not entertaining.'

'True.' Çetin took another sip of his drink before asking, rather sheepishly, 'And with regard to the Armenian...'

'I will ask around as I said that I would.'

Çetin looked down at the floor as he spoke. 'So you won't put that condition...'

His friend attempted to find Çetin's downturned eyes with his own. 'That wouldn't be very professional of me, would it? And besides, whatever I may have said before, I don't think that our friendship is about conditions, do you?'

'No.' Çetin looked up quickly and just as rapidly barked out what amounted to a get-out clause for his friend. 'You just got frustrated, right?'

'Yes.' Arto smiled sadly. 'Yes, that's all, Çetin. I've had a long and tiring day and I just got frustrated. In fact we should both really start thinking about getting home to bed. It's been a terrible twenty-four hours and I know that if I don't get some rest soon I'll be absolutely useless tomorrow.'

Çetin flung what was left of his drink down the back of his throat and then growled appreciatively. 'Yes. You're quite right there.'

Arto took out his wallet and threw enough money on to the table to cover their drinks plus a very healthy tip for the waiter. 'And to celebrate our leaving this place, have your drinks on me—together, as ever, with my love and my esteem.'

He said the last with, as was his custom, a slight note of amusement in his voice. Only Çetin would have known, and did know, that he meant every word he had said.

Wordlessly, for there was nothing more to say, the two men embraced before going their separate ways. But just after Arto got into his car and fired up the engine, he happened to look back at the front of the Mosaic Bar. With some dismay, he noticed that Çetin Ikmen was sneaking back inside.

It is easier to be pragmatic about one's dreams in the cold, grey light of a mid-October dawn than in the thick darkness of the small hours when they are actually happening. Although feeling quite calm and logical about it all now, the dream that Mehmet Suleyman had experienced in the middle of the night had caused him to wake, sweating and thrashing around in panic. Frankly, it was a miracle that he hadn't woken Zuleika Suleyman, who lay beside him, one that he had been very thankful for. She would, he knew, have read all sorts of things into his dream had he been obliged to tell her about it, things to do with his feelings about entrapment, some of which would have been quite accurate.

In the dream he had been in that apartment at the top of that house in Ishak Paşa Caddesi. Some things had been different, because he was in dream country. For instance he had seen a wardrobe where there was in reality none and there had been a panel of vibrant blue Iznik tiles across one of the walls. But apart from that it was the same, with the notable exception that he was alone in the room, sitting on that bed. Probably because in waking life Mehmet Suleyman was a very ordered, logical person, he knew that to panic in this situation would be pointless and so when he did finally rise from the bed, he moved around the room with a measured curiosity. As in life, the chest of drawers had numerous crystal figurines lined up across its surface, and when he walked over to the windows he found that they were indeed nailed shut as he had expected they would be.

It was the door that was to change the character of the experience. Unlike the real door, in the dream it was closed which, at first, simply aroused his interest. Since he didn't know what the door really looked like, when he approached it he found it quite blank and plain, unlike the rest of the ancient building. In addition, there was no handle. As he would have in real life, he tested the door with the palm of his hand to see whether it was spring operated. It wasn't. He pushed it again, but still it didn't give. It must be locked from the outside, but that was OK because there had to be colleagues beyond the door to open it for him should he ask. He opened his mouth to call to them and it was at that point the true nightmare began. Although he called and called, no sound came. He even, in an attempt to help his voice to emerge, pushed his hand down over his larynx to try to massage the damn thing into action. But it flatly refused to comply. He was quite dumb and perfectly alone in a room where someone had only just recently died. Weird and uncharacteristically superstitious feelings found fertile soil within the rising panic inside his mind. Then, just as if someone had either put out a light or closed the blinds across the windows, the room suddenly darkened.

Frozen in front of that terrible, unyielding door, Suleyman hardly dared to breathe as day became night. Lightly at first, and then with more insistence, something touched him on the back of his neck. He was certain that the touch was someone's fingers and, as they took a slightly stronger hold upon him, he remembered how the previous occupant of that room had died. It was then that, either by coincidence or via a supreme act of will, he came hurtling out of the dream and into the shaking, midnight reality of sweat and lingering fear.

At first, as his mind absorbed the far less sinister reality of his bedroom, he simply lay on his back panting. It wasn't and hadn't been real; he was safe; it was all over. But as the minutes passed he realised further attempts at sleep would be futile. He decided to get up and make himself a glass of tea.

The kitchen, although very tastefully fitted out, did not show any signs of recent use. Zuleika alone had been invited to the post-holiday meal and conversation session at her mother's house. It was an event which summed up the current state of the Suleymans' marriage. Not that his wife would have criticised him to her parents; she wasn't like that, she loved him too much to do such a thing. The tragedy was that he could not, despite his very best efforts, reciprocate her affections. Not that his lack of love for her was her fault; it wasn't even his. If there were any villains within the drama of this marriage it was their mothers, two very forceful women who were also sisters and who had many years previously decided that their children should marry. Had he been rather more forceful in his opposition to this arranged union it would not have happened, but then he, like his father, hated complications in his private life and had taken, as ever, the line of least resistance. As he turned on the heat underneath the kettle he could even recall how, just before the wedding, he had told his brother that he would, he felt, learn in time to love his cousin. He remembered how his brother had first laughed and then begged him to 'run away, right now, Mehmet. Now before it is too late!' But he hadn't listened to anything other than the drumbeat of his own sense of stupid, aristocratic duty. And where, ultimately, had that got him? Where he was now—sleepless, disturbed and lacking the benefits of a recently home cooked meal.

Not that the dream had been related in any way to his marriage. Or had it? Mehmet, although not prone to psychological introspection, realised that on one level the image of himself as prisoner was only too pertinent to his private life. But as he poured the boiled water on to the small pile of leaves at the bottom of the teapot, he cut off those thoughts to concentrate instead on the more immediate and, for him, less painful subject of the recently murdered young man.

Dreams, odd feelings and their relevance or meaning was usually much more his boss, Çetin Ikmen's line than his. Indeed, had he been asked by Ikmen about the value or otherwise of such experiences, Mehmet Suleyman would have declared them absolutely worthless. But now, on his own in the almost dark of the near dawn, things felt a little bit different. In spite of himself he wondered whether it had indeed been like the dream for the now dead youngster. Had the youth, alone in that room just as Mehmet's dream self had been, thought it all quite normal and safe until right up to the very end? Had he too, experienced a darkening in the room—a sort of signal of what was to come? A signpost to death and the reality that nothing existed beyond the end of all our lives?

He poured the golden tea out into a glass and then dropped one small cube of sugar into its depths. It hadn't been so long ago that he had existed safely inside his old beliefs. If you lived a good life Allah would provide a lovely perfumed garden complete with willing little slave girls in the next, far better existence beyond the grave. Even in the face of the early unnatural deaths upon which he had worked he had continued to believe that what Islam taught about death was in fact the truth. Exactly when that had all changed so drastically, he could not now recall. But there had, there must have been a moment when it all, for whatever reason, failed to make sense to him any more. Perhaps that too had more to do with his marriage than he cared to admit? It was very possible.

But as the watery autumn light flowed weakly across the tops of the buildings opposite his kitchen, all of these thoughts began to drift into a fog of irrelevance. Too tired to be really awake and yet still too unnerved to risk further sleep, Mehmet Suleyman watched the progress of the dawn with a glazed and hopeless blankness.

Bulent Gürdilek had been just fourteen when he had disappeared from his family's cramped little apartment in Beşiktaş. Although, when questioned about his son, Ahmet Gürdilek had given it as his opinion that the boy had, for some little time, been mixing in 'bad' company, he also felt that his son had not been unhappy with his lot. After all, Bulent had had quite a good job for a boy of his age helping out in his uncle's garage over in Karaköy. It was indeed his uncle who had first reported him missing when he'd failed to turn up for work one Thursday in August. There'd been a couple of reported sightings in the two weeks following his disappearance and then—nothing. His mother, it was said, was almost insane with the worry of it.

At sixteen a little older than Bulent, Aristotle Mavroyeni was a quiet and studious child with, according to his parents, his sights firmly set upon a vocation within the Greek church. When he had disappeared somewhere between his parents' apartment in Beyoğlu and his aunt's house in Sarıyer it had been thought for a time that perhaps he had unilaterally decided to enter into a monastic order rather earlier than his parents had planned. But when Aristotle failed to appear amongst the ranks of the local communities, his family's thoughts turned to more sinister explanations. Five months on there had still not been so much as a whisper about this boy.

By far the worst month for disappearances of young men so far that year had been July. Four boys had vanished in the first two weeks: one English tourist, two Turkish teenagers and the son of a Kurdish silversmith. Worrying it most certainly was, but not atypical. Youngsters frequently 'took off' during the summer months, usually following the sun and fun to the resorts of the south coast. When the season ended at least some of these would either come back or would contact their families to come and get them. It was a trend that also extended to girls, typically those who came from repressive families or who were faced with imminent arranged marriages.

In fact, the reality was that the majority of the young people who were reported as missing were eventually found. Those who had not gone south for the summer had often gone to live with secret boyfriends or girlfriends who, although routinely 'ruining' these youngsters with regard to their precious virginity, neither harmed nor killed them. The danger for these young people lay more with what their families would and did do to them when they returned from their little adventures. It was not unknown for an irate father to beat his immoral daughter to death in the wake of the latter's lost honour.

None of this, however, could detract from the fact that for a small but significant minority of these young people, the missing state did eventually resolve into homicide. The streets were not a good place to be for those with no money and little experience and, furthermore, they were full of enough pimps and drug dealers to make not falling into unwise practices very difficult indeed.

The young clerk whose job it had been to turn up this information looked at the latest pertinent missing report and frowned. On 28 September eighteen-year-old Bedros Mazmoulian had failed to arrive home after a party at a friend's house and had not, so far, been seen or heard of again. Bedros was a student at the university and his grandfather at least suspected that he may have had some experience with illicit drugs. More pertinent still was the fact the young man was Armenian. Inspector Ikmen had told the clerk to look out for this particular detail and, when he placed the files on his superior's desk, the clerk made sure that Bedros's details were on the top of the pile.

# 5

ARTO SARKISSIAN WAITED until the midday call to prayer had finished before leaving his office to join the two people who were waiting for him in the ante-room. Although only a minority of his staff members did actually respond to the call it was better not to be seen as conspicuously otherwise engaged when the legendary thousand muezzins of Istanbul invoked the power of Allah. Although still adhering to the principles of secular government as laid down by Atatürk in the 1920s there was now a significant minority within the country for whom Islam was rather more important than conventional politics. Some of these people had, in recent years, even obtained posts within the government and although the Turkish Republic was far from being an Islamic state like Iran or even the far more liberal Jordan, it was still as well for people who were not Muslims to adopt a low-key profile with regard to religion. Not that Dr Sarkissian was religious in any way, but as an Armenian he was nominally Christian. It also had to be admitted that, being of that race, problems with just about every other racial group in the region were not historically unknown to him. As he stood up from his chair he smiled across at his assistant, Selma Bilge, who had just finished reading the few notes her superior had written down during his recent conversation with Inspector Çetin Ikmen. They covered briefly some details about who was currently waiting for them in the ante-room.

'Shall we go then, Selma?' the doctor asked.

The young woman's face looked strained; she disliked this part of her job, he knew, which was why he had used a gentle tone to rouse her from her reading.

'Yes, Doctor. Do I need...?'

'No.' He smiled in a way that he hoped was reassuring. 'No, just bring yourself. I think that the more normal, for want of a better word, we look the better.'

He opened the door to allow her to pass and then followed her down the long, grey corridor that led to the ante-room and the laboratories beyond.

There were actually three people in the ante-room when the doctor and his assistant arrived. Two of them were, as he had expected, an elderly couple, probably in their seventies, both wrapped up rather extravagantly against what was, as yet, not a bitterly cold autumn. It was, however, their eyes rather than their clothes that caught the doctor's attention. In both cases, they were quite hollow; eyes that had seen not only what they did not want to see but what they should not either. During a long-ago visit to his cousin in Paris, Arto Sarkissian remembered seeing photographs of eyes like theirs in the pictures he had been shown of the Armenians the Turks had allegedly forced to march across Anatolia during the Great War, those terrible marches that had or had not happened according to who one was. Was it just a coincidence that this strange, sad little couple were Armenian too? Or was he slipping into the trap that he was aware so many of his fellow Armenians fell into—of giving themselves the monopoly on suffering?

The third member of the party was a young uniformed police constable who had, he suspected, been sent by Çetin Ikmen to bring the old couple to the mortuary. He nodded briefly in recognition of the policeman and then turned to the couple, extending his hand to the man as he approached.

'Professor and Mrs Mazmoulian?'

The old man took the doctor's hand and shook it as firmly as his trembling arm would allow. 'Doctor.'

The old woman, looking on, spoke in a small but surprisingly firm voice, her nervousness showing only in the small picking movements she made with her tiny fingers against the sleeve of Sarkissian's white coat. 'This is so terrible,' she said, 'so terrible, and yet we were both so relieved when Timür Ikmen's young boy told us that the pathologist was an Armenian. If that is Bedros in there I would hate to think that his body had been touched by unchristian hands.'

Noticeably, both the police constable and Selma Bilge turned away at this point. In order to cover his own embarrassment and to avoid further discussion of things Armenian, Arto Sarkissian concentrated on his own mild amusement at the notion of his friend Çetin being 'Timür Ikmen's young boy'.

'You worked with Dr Ikmen, I believe, Professor,' he said.

The old man smiled. 'Yes. His son is your friend, I understand. It was good of him to arrange for us to be here so quickly. You must tell him that when you see him. This morning, I just couldn't...'

His voice trailed off as tears entered the corners of his eyes—a signal, Arto felt, that what had to be done had to be done very quickly.

'Right,' he said, marshalling his most doctor-like air, 'in a moment we will go into that room there'—he pointed to a door at his right—'where I will ask you to stand beside the table on which the body is currently resting.'

'Oh, may I go blind if it is our grandson!' the old woman cried.

Her husband, shushing her gently, put a comforting arm around her shoulder and nodded his assent to the doctor.

'I will then remove the covering from the face,' Arto continued, 'which is when you may have as long or as short a time as you need to make your identification. Do you understand?'

In a voice that was already thick with tears the old man said, 'Yes.'

'And when you wish me to replace the cover, just either tell me, if you can, or raise your hand. Is that clear?'

'Yes.'

'Now,' he said, knowing of old that who was going to do what in situations like this was not always clear, 'is Mrs Mazmoulian coming in too?'

'I want to,' the old woman replied, 'but then I don't if you know what I mean. I cannot let Kevork go alone, Bedros was—is—the last part we had of our poor dead son and...'

'I understand.' Arto Sarkissian motioned to his assistant to move somewhat closer to the party. 'Miss Bilge will be on hand to assist you. Miss Bilge?'

The young woman, with a small smile, came and took the old woman's hand in hers. Then, without any further words, the old couple, the doctor and his assistant passed through into a room that was covered from floor to ceiling by stark, white tiles. The constable remained behind, sat down and lit a cigarette.

Although, by virtue of the fact that they were fitted, the

walls of the room were lined with sinks and work benches, everything that could distress those visiting, like instruments or trolleys laden with dishes and gauzes, had been removed. All that remained in the room, all that needed to be there, was a large metal table bearing an unmistakably human-shaped form covered by a white sheet.

Try as he might, and Arto could see that he was screwing every gram of courage up in order to cope with the coming ordeal, the old man just couldn't bring himself to stand by the table of his own volition. Like his wife and the attendant Selma Bilge, Professor Mazmoulian stood just inside the door, one hand held up to his nose against, the doctor imagined, the awful smell of preserving fluid. However, to allude to the fact that the old man might be afraid was not, the doctor knew, the done thing. It was therefore to Selma that he appealed, saying, 'Would you like to bring Mrs Mazmoulian over here, please, Miss Bilge?'

As he had suspected, as soon as the women started moving forward the old man followed; as the three of them got closer to the table, he even tucked his wife and the doctor's assistant behind his back. In this part of the world, as all four of them knew, a man protected his women whatever the cost.

Once all the actors in what Arto had come to think of as the identification drama had composed themselves, the doctor looked across at the old man and raised one eyebrow. 'Are you ready, Professor?'

The old man took in a very deep breath before replying. 'Yes. If you will please, Doctor.'

Arto gently folded the sheet downwards, finding beneath a face whose skin had sagged a little further since last he had looked upon it. This, though quite normal, made the young man appear slightly older, although when one really looked one could nevertheless see that he had been a good-looking boy. He had a strong, straight nose and his eyes, although closed, slanted upwards in long, smooth crescents edged by thick, dramatically curling lashes. Even the mouth was sweet, opened just a little as if gently inhaling the rarefied air of that terrible place. Someone, possibly Selma Bilge, had combed his hair, which though long and originally unkempt, now framed his face in dense, black waves. It made him, Arto felt, look so much more 'normal' than the wild, disordered drug addict that he had first seen in that strange apartment in Sultan Ahmet. But then that was often the way with bodies that were 'tidied up'.

He moved his gaze, gently lest he appear to be hurriedly curious, from the boy's face to that of the old man before him. There was no way of knowing from the blank look in his eyes how he was feeling or what he was thinking. Everybody behaved differently in this situation. During the course of his long career, the doctor had experienced people crying, tearing their own bodies and clothes in anguish, fainting, pleading to God for mercy and also having no discernible reaction at all—behaving, in effect, like those in a waking nightmare.

But when the old man did finally speak, it was in a voice full of strangled tension that seemed strangely inappropriate to the words. 'It's not him,' he said, 'this is not Bedros.'

His wife, whose head had until now been buried deeply against Selma Bilge's shoulder, crossed herself and murmured, 'Thanks be to God.'

'Are you absolutely certain, Professor Mazmoulian?' It was essential that Arto get either a definite yes or no on this identification.

'I am certain,' the old man replied and then, turning to his wife, he said, 'Am I right, Sylvie?'

His wife just glanced quickly at the body on the table before tilting her head backwards to indicate that it was not her grandson.

Arto Sarkissian replaced the sheet across the boy's face, thanking the couple for their time and effort. Even though the boy had not been their grandson, he could see that the identification had been a terrible ordeal for these tired, worried old people. What puzzled the doctor though, was that they did not seem to be relieved at all.

But then as he led them back out into the ante-room, Mrs Mazmoulian did partly explain this. 'I don't know what to feel now, Doctor,' she said. 'When Timür's boy told us there was a body here which could possibly be our grandson, I made myself face that awfulness. I prepared myself before God.'

'You think such things,' her husband added, 'when your children go missing. The night Bedros's father was killed, I knew. And like Sylvie I thought I knew again now. But I was wrong.'

'It could mean that your grandson is safe and well,' Arto said.

The old man smiled, but not out of happiness. 'Oh, I don't think that I dare to hope for that, Doctor.'

'Why not?'

'Because we know that our boy was involved in drugs and we also know that no good can ever come of that.'

'People can recover from addiction, you know,' Arto replied, 'with help and—'

'But Bedros isn't getting any help, is he, Doctor?'

'No, but...'

The old woman, who was once again picking nervously at the sleeve of Arto's white coat, said, 'Don't even begin to give us false hopes, Doctor. I know that you mean well, but...to hope is not a thing that Armenians dare to do. You must know that.'

'Yes, well...' Arto turned away, embarrassed yet again

by another reference to his race. 'I will leave you with the constable here who, I hope, will take you home?'

The young policeman snapped to attention at this, grinding a half-finished cigarette out on the floor as he rose. 'Yes, sir.'

'Good.' Arto shook hands with both the Mazmoulians and thanked them again. As he went to leave, however, the old man called him back again.

'Oh, Doctor?' His face was troubled in a way that it had not been before.

'Yes, is there something else?'

The professor shrugged. 'Only something you might find stupid.'

'I'm sure that I won't, but...If you don't want to tell me, I don't mind.'

'It's just that...' He looked at the floor briefly, then, snapping his gaze upwards again, he said, 'That dead boy in there is not Armenian, you know.'

'He isn't?'

Quite how the old man would know such a thing was beyond Arto, but he was interested nevertheless. 'How...?'

'Don't ask me how I know,' the old man continued, 'but I do know it for certain. As a man of science you probably will not accept what I have said, but...Look, call me an old fool if you like, but will you please promise to tell Timür's boy what I have said? He will understand.'

'Yes.' Even though he could in no way vouch for the veracity of the old man's feelings, Arto knew that Çetin would not only know what he was talking about but would also pay serious heed to it. Çetin was like that. Çetin , as everyone who had ever come into contact with the Ikmen family knew, had had a witch for a mother. 'Yes, I will tell the inspector when next I speak to him.'

'Thank you.'

And with that the couple moved soundlessly out of the ante-room, followed at a short distance by their young police escort.

When they had gone, Arto Sarkissian sat down with his assistant for a few moments. 'It doesn't get any easier, does it, Selma?' he said.

'No, Doctor, it doesn't.'

'This also means that Mrs Taşkiran is almost certainly going to come and do some sketching.'

'Oh.'

It was an 'oh' that spoke many volumes.

Arto smiled. 'When I find out when she's due, I'll book you in for a day's leave.'

'Thank you.'

Commissioner Ardiç had not had a cigar for a week when he went out to the house on Ishak Paşa Caddesi to see how Çetin Ikmen's investigation was progressing. It was not customary for him to go out to crime scenes but, in light of the fact that his doctor had recommended fresh air and exercise as ways of dealing with his constant nicotine cravings, he had decided that this was an activity that he was going to pursue in his new life as a healthy-living non-smoker. That the decision had not had the effect of making him a happy man was evident to all who witnessed his arrival. As he eased his large form from the seat of his BMW and up on to the high pavement beside the car, he swore in frustration at the lack of strong, willing constables to help him. That most of his staff were too frightened of him even to consider touching his arm lest their actions be misinterpreted was something that Ardiç either failed to understand or chose to ignore. The only one of his officers who was the exception to this rule was now lounging against the wall of the hotel next door to the crime scene; he did not help his superior for a different reason. To Çetin Ikmen, the sight of Ardiç struggling to move unaided from his car was always a comic treat that was just too good to miss.

'Hello, sir,' he said as the larger man puffed and panted his way towards him. 'To what do we owe the pleasure of your company?'

'I'm just checking...' Ardiç replied, speaking in rapid soundbites, 'that you are not...wasting your time...sitting about thinking...and contemplating nonsense.'

Ikmen smiled and then, taking a very full packet of cigarettes out of his pocket, proceeded to light up in a way that, had he done so in front of a woman, could have been seen as sexual harassment. 'Well,' he said, 'I must admit to being guilty of thinking, sir, as you know it is one of my weaknesses, but as for contemplating nonsense—'

'Oh, you know exactly what I mean, Ikmen!' his superior exploded. 'Moving away from the facts and into little private theoretical worlds of your own! Both you and I know that you do it and both you and I know that I don't like it.'

'But if it works?'

'And you can put that cigarette out while you're talking to me too!'

'Oh, but it's such a—'

'Just do it, Ikmen! And then let's get into this house and see what's been done, shall we?'

'If that will make you happy, sir.' Ikmen threw his almost pristine cigarette down on to the floor and ground it out with his foot. Several colleagues who were nearby at the time struggled to decide whether what they had just seen had been real or illusion. For as long as anyone could remember, Ikmen had never finished a cigarette until it threatened to burn the tips of his fingers.

As the two men walked towards the house, Ardiç barked out questions which he never let Ikmen have enough time to finish. 'So what have you got so far then, Ikmen?'

'Well, sir, we have the body, which I have described to you, and this rather strange house, and—'

'Do you have the tenant yet, this Armenian or whatever he is?'

'No, sir, Mr Zekiyan is still missing but—'

'Put out a description, have you?'

'Well, yes, Suleyman has faxed all districts and regions, but the man's landlord was rather vague as to his appearance and—'

'You've got the neighbours, haven't you?' In a gesture that, due in part to the large size of Ardiç's arm, seemed to encompass the entire world, he graphically described the scope of what he thought Ikmen should be doing with regard to questioning local people. 'Have them all in is what I say. People can often remember much more when they are actually with us than if you allow them the luxury of staying in their own homes.'

This was not an argument without logic, but for reasons rather different to those that Ardiç was referring to. People could be quite frightened when they came into the station—some so scared that they retreated into works of quite amazingly intricate fiction. In an attempt to circumvent this eventuality, Ikmen said, 'Mr Zekiyan did rather keep himself to himself, sir. I don't think that having—'

'Oh, for the love of Allah, Ikmen! It isn't that difficult. Look.' He'd spotted, much to Ikmen's chagrin, one of the men who worked on the reception desk at the hotel who was having a cigarette break outside. 'You there!' he said to him.

The man pointed to his chest.

'Yes, you,' reiterated Ardiç, 'come over here for a moment, will you?'

The man, who was probably in his twenties and rather moody, sauntered over and stood in front of the far shorter and definitely stouter Ardiç, his cigarette hanging casually from his lips. 'Yes?'

'You work in this hotel here?'

The man looked across at Ikmen, whom he had seen before and knew to be a policeman, and asked, 'Is he with you?'

'He is my superior,' Ikmen replied, 'Commissioner Ardiç.'

'Oh, right.' Then turning back to Ardiç he said, 'Yes, I work here. And?'

'I don't feel that your tone is entirely helpful, sir, but... Now look here, this house here, number...What is the number of this house, Ikmen?'

'It doesn't have a number sir,' Ikmen said. 'It's called "The Sacking House" on account of—'

'Yes, yes! That's quite enough.' Turning back to the moody man, Ardiç asked, 'An Armenian is known to live here, a Mr...'

'Zekiyan,' Ikmen put in.

His patience tried and stretched to the limit by the presence of the man's cigarette, Ardiç barked rather than asked, 'We need to know what he looks like, where he goes, things like that.'

'You're asking me?'

'I'm talking to you, aren't I?'

The man shrugged. 'Well, I don't know,' he said, 'he's a man about forty, dark. I don't know.'

'Oh come on, man!' Ardiç exploded. 'You live next door to him, you must know something about him! Does he wear suits? Does he have a car? What!'

'He does wear a very expensive ring,' said another, older voice.

Ardiç turned around to find himself facing an elderly little gentleman that Ikmen recognised as the grocer.

'Ah,' said Ardiç, obviously very pleased with himself, 'so here we have someone who does have eyes in his head. And what is this ring like?'

'It's in the shape of a cross made of emeralds and diamonds, right?' said Ikmen.

'Yes, sir, it is,' the grocer replied. 'I've noticed it many times when he's come in to buy water or bread or cigarettes from my shop.'

'You knew about this?' Ardiç asked Ikmen.

The latter shrugged. 'The landlord told me. I was going to tell you when—'

Ardiç turned back to the grocer. 'So what else have you noticed about this man?'

'Not a great deal, sir,' he said, 'except that he is quite polite. He has lived here for many years but then this being a tourist area one doesn't really get to know people as one did in the old days. The younger residents, like the Armenian gentleman, tend to live their lives really away from here. He comes and goes, I suppose to and from his place of business; often I don't see him for weeks. He is very smart though so he must have a good job.'

'Did he ever appear with anyone else, like a young boy, for instance?'

The grocer thought for a minute and then inclined his head backwards. 'No, although sometimes he would go into the house with another man.'

'Who was?'

'That I don't know, sir, and to be honest I paid it little attention. The youngsters don't like the old ways; interest from one's neighbours and suchlike. Not now.'

Ardiç harrumphed by way of reply and then, ignoring both the grocer and the hotel clerk, took Ikmen by the arm and started to walk him towards The Sacking House. 'I hope you can see from that, Ikmen,' he said, 'that getting talking to the people is vital. We learned some new facts there which I trust you will build upon.'

'Yes, sir.' Not even Ikmen would have dared to point out that he knew most of what had just been discussed anyway. Ardiç so rarely talked to the public that to discourage him with criticism would have been tantamount to stealing his finest hour.

Before the two men went inside the house, they both stood and looked at its façade for a few moments. Architecture was not one of Ikmen's particular passions, but as he looked up at the great metal-studded door, he had to concede that The Sacking House was a fine example of the Ottoman Mansion style. The wood, which was a warm, honey colour, had been well preserved and, although somewhat bowed by time and weather, it was really in a most remarkably good state of repair. The windows and sills were clean, as were the front steps, giving the whole place a well-kept and pleasing aspect. Indeed, and unusually for him, even Ardiç muttered that it was 'nice'.

But what made the outside of the house so pleasing took on a more sinister air inside. During the course of the almost thirty-six-hours since the forensic team had been given access to the house, not once had so much as half a fingerprint been found. Every cupboard, every work surface, even the bowl of the lavatory and the tiny shower-side soap-dish visibly gleamed from the application of either water or cleaning fluid. On closer examination it had, in addition, been revealed that not even the soft furnishings had escaped this treatment as settees, beds and chairs were found to have been purged of human evidence. Either the elusive Mr Zekiyan or someone else, as yet unknown, had been very careful to leave nothing of himself behind with that boy's body. Not that there was anything of the boy apart from himself evident either. It was reasonable to expect at least some accoutrements of drug usage around the body of a long-term addict like him, but nothing had so far been found. They'd even had the floorboards up in that awful little death chamber, but had discovered nothing beyond the bodies of a few dead mice. Either Mr Zekiyan, if that was indeed his name, had very expertly covered his tracks, or someone else had been in his house to do these extraordinary things for reasons that, at the present moment, could only be guessed at.

It was Ardiç who finally broke the reverie with, 'So do we have any idea about the identity of this dead boy?'

'I thought he might be the missing Mazmoulian child,' Ikmen replied, 'but the grandparents failed to make a positive on him this morning. I've asked Dorotka Taşkiran to prepare some sketches for circulation.'

Ardiç grunted his approval before adding, 'She's as mad as Sultan Ibrahim, that one.'

'Yes, sir.'

There was nothing to add to that so Ardiç changed the subject. 'I understand you think that the boy might be Armenian?'

'I did,' Ikmen sighed, 'although now I'm not so sure.'

'Why?'

'Because Bedros Mazmoulian's grandfather was very certain that the body was not that of one of his countrymen.'

Ardiç's face assumed a sour and at the same time exasperated aspect. 'I suppose he had a "feeling", did he?'

'That's it, sir.'

'Pile of rubbish, Ikmen! You're too susceptible to nonsense like that.' He turned and wagged an extremely rude finger in Ikmen's face. 'If the child is uncircumcised and was found in the house of an Armenian it is only reasonable to suppose that he was Armenian too. It's probably some personal vendetta thing amongst themselves.'

'I am investigating the community here in the city, sir. I'm not just—'

'Well, don't just do that via Sarkissian, Ikmen. I know you and how blind you can be to the idiosyncrasies of your friends. Sarkissian is an Armenian and could have a vested interest in all of this. I mean, I'm not saying that he would lie or anything...'

'Oh, no sir,' Ikmen smiled, 'of course not.'

'But you get on to it yourself, do you hear me? Have that sergeant of yours out and about amongst the buggers. Eh?'

'Yes, sir.'

'Right.' With a deep and he hoped cleansing breath in, Ardiç moved forward in the direction of the front door. 'Come on then, Ikmen,' he said, 'let's see this crime scene. I'm here to help so use me.'

'Yes, sir. Thank you, sir.'

As he followed his boss into the house, Ikmen just managed to suppress a somewhat ironic laugh.

Although the day had progressed thus far without incident, Fatma was far too wise to assume that it would stay that way. As she came back in from pegging the washing out on the balcony she surveyed the living room with some suspicion. Despite his infirmities, the old man could get about quite well and although the last time she had seen him he had been safely asleep on his bed, there was no guarantee that he would still be there now. Still, at least Kemal and Gul were playing quite happily. Although two years younger than his sister, Kemal could be a real torment to her at times and so it was nice to see that they were getting on for a change. It was going to be quite a shock to the little one when Gul joined three of her older siblings at school the following year. Then, Fatma suspected, Kemal would want to use his mother as his playmate which, though sweet in a way, filled her with dread. These confounded fibroids made bending and stretching, activities so essential to good play, almost impossible and she feared, even this far in advance, her youngest child's uncomprehending impatience with her.

But for now the children were settled and so Fatma decided to sit down for a few minutes and take some time to read the latest letter from her son Orhan who was studying medicine at Hacettepe University in Ankara. As ever, his missive started with greetings to every member of the family, all of whom were carefully named and credited in order of age and, she supposed, importance. Especial love and thanks were, of course, accorded to his father who had recently sent the boy a pair of winter shoes that he had obtained from his sergeant who had bought them on a whim and then discarded them. Not that Fatma believed that little story for one moment. Mehmet Suleyman, as well as being far better off than the Ikmen family, was a very kind young man who had almost certainly purchased the shoes with the vision of her poor cold student son in mind. But it was not good form to flaunt one's wealth to those less fortunate than oneself so he would never admit that, nor had Çetin or

Fatma questioned the action beyond thanking Mehmet very kindly for his gift. Fatma was just reading a little piece about a friend, who she noted was female and apparently sported the most gorgeous blonde hair, when the telephone rang. The two children looked up briefly from their play as their mother moved slowly across to the instrument and then went back into their own little fantasy once again.

'Hello?' Fatma said into the receiver.

'Hello, Fatma,' a familiar voice replied. It was Krikor Sarkissian, brother of her husband's best friend, Arto.

Fatma smiled. 'Krikor. It's nice to hear from you again. How did your fund-raising go the other night?'

'Hasn't Çetin told you?'

She sighed, heavily and with practised weariness. 'I think that this murder investigation he and your brother had to attend somewhat overtook events at the fund-raising, I'm afraid.'

'Oh, yes, of course. Well, it was very successful, thank you. It's a pity you weren't well enough to come.'

'I just get very tired, what with the younger children,' she said, preempting any awkward questions he might pose about her state of health. He was, after all, a doctor, but she was not only too embarrassed about the fibroids but also too bored with them to want to discuss them. She changed the subject. 'Çetin isn't here right now, he's at work.'

'Yes, I know. I haven't rung about that. It's about my project committee which, as you know, he is on.'

'Yes.' Out of the corner of one eye, Fatma saw something moving over by the television set. Her response to this, a banging sound in her head, was immediate.

'I'd like him, if he can,' Krikor continued, 'to attend a meeting of the committee tomorrow night to discuss just how we are going to proceed now that we have some money.'

'Oh, right, yes.'

She turned just in time to see the old man peer myopi-cally at the dials on the set, his open mouth dribbling long strands of drool on to the carpet below.

'We're going to meet at the house of Muhammed Ersoy who is, very kindly, going to provide us with dinner.'

'That's nice,' Fatma replied, now only barely going through the motions of her conversation with Krikor.

The old man gently tapped the television screen and then looked up at his daughter-in-law and smiled. 'Well, he's not in there, Fatma dear,' he said.

She smiled and then shushed him silently. He made vari-ous hand movements to indicate that he had understood.

'So if you could ask Çetin to ring me,' Krikor said, 'I'll give him directions, times and so on.'

'Right.'

For someone who supposedly made a living from lis-tening closely to other people, Krikor Sarkissian was being very insensitive to her distracted state. Once the main pur-pose of his call was over he proceeded to make conversa-tion which, though pertinent to the current situation, she found most upsetting.

'And how is dear Uncle Timür?' he asked just as the subject of his inquiry decided to dispense with his shirt.

'Put it back on! Put it back on!' Fatma hissed, aware that the children were viewing their grandfather rather worriedly. Then to Krikor on the telephone, 'Oh, he's fine, you know, apart from the aches and pains in his joints.'

Krikor, understanding that something quite vital was missing from her diagnosis, lowered his voice. 'And the other problem, Fatma. The, shall we say, psychological aspect.'

'Oh.' A vision of her husband's anger should she be discov-ered discussing this taboo subject rose up large in her mind.

As if to underscore Krikor's questioning, Timür Ikmen completed his shirt removal and then said, 'I had a son once called Halil. I think he must have died.'

Fatma put her hand over the receiver and said, 'No, he isn't dead, Father, he is—'

'You're not my daughter!'

'Are you still there, Fatma?' Krikor asked. 'Is everything all right?'

She removed her hand from the receiver. 'Yes, Krikor, I'm fine.'

'You know that there are physicians who specialise in the medicine of, er, ageing and...There is help available, drugs that can alleviate and quieten symptoms. If you like I can put you, or rather Çetin in touch with—'

'Oh, it's not that bad, you know,' she lied. 'He's quite manageable now.'

'Well, do please bear what I have said in mind, Fatma. Speak to Çetin. Uncle Timür was like a father to Arto and myself when Dad died and so the money side of the treatment would be no—'

'Oh, thank you,' she said, her face flushing hot with embarrassment, 'but it really won't be necessary, Krikor, I...'

'The Greek has told me,' said the old man, now starting to remove his trousers, 'that my other son may very well have some involvement with a fat-arsed whore. But I know that can't be true, because I only have the one son and he's dead.'

The trouser development was really rather more than Fatma could handle. Let Krikor think what he liked, she had to go. 'I'm very sorry, Krikor,' she said, 'but the children are alone in the kitchen and...'

'Of course, you must go and attend to them,' he replied, 'I apologise if I—'

'That's all right, Krikor, but...'

The old man's trousers had hit the floor.

'Goodbye!'

'Goodbye, Fatma, don't forget to—'

She put the phone down and with a turn of speed she hadn't known she was capable of rushed across the room and scooped up the old man's trousers in one smooth, seamless movement.

'Oh, for the love of Allah, Father,' she said as she pulled the trousers up over his tiny, stick-like legs.

The old man laughed; it was a high-pitched, almost girlish peal. 'You're very good with a man's trousers, girl, I will say! Do you charge very much for a fuck or—'

'Father!' She felt her face redden; the pounding in her head was becoming ever more insistent. Bad language from the old man was not exactly unusual but when he had been himself he had at least tried to be reasonably polite in front of the children.

'I have two hundred kuruş in my pocket for a girl who will—'

'Will you please be quiet, Father!' Fatma screamed, watching the children jump in fear as she did so.

For some reason that was apparent only to the old man, he quite suddenly became quiet again. Just like a compliant little baby he allowed Fatma to re-dress him and, his face now quite calm and composed, uttered not another word.

She was just about to take him gently back to his room when the silence was broken one last time.

'Fuck, fuck, fuck, fuck, fuck,' said Kemal.

Mehmet Suleyman left Çetin Ikmen at The Sacking House at about four-thirty and returned, alone, to the station and his office. Because Commissioner Ardiç had spent the best part of the day at the scene (indeed was still there now), Suleyman was more weary than he would be normally. Ardiç had wanted to investigate everything and everyone on site minutely which he had done in his usual bullying way. It was odd of him to show such a profound interest in what his officers were doing but then, hard as it was sometimes to credit, he had been a good policeman in his day. His summing up of the situation as 'bloody weird' had not been the most professional response, but it was apt.

In the relative calm of his office, Suleyman sat down and took out his notebook. Ikmen was famously a bit slack about paperwork, so it was up to him to record what had taken place that day. Not that there was a lot that was new. The house was still entirely 'clean' of all relevant evidence and all that the neighbours seemed to know about the elusive Mr Zekiyan was that he wore a very expensive ring. There was, however, one little item which was sounding a small but significant alarm bell in his head. The mother of a Mrs Toker who lived with her daughter in an apartment over the grocer's shop possessed a memory of the Armenian which she described as coming from 'very long ago'. Like her daughter, old Emine was a deeply religious, heavily veiled woman whose advanced years could only be discerned from the small gap in the charshaf which revealed her eyes and the heavy lines around them. Amid a welter of religiously inspired entreaties and oaths she had told Suleyman that 'very long ago' she had seen Mr Zekiyan, from time to time, enter his house with a child. That was all she had said but, probably because of Mr Zekiyan's purpose-built apartment, Suleyman and Ikmen had found this disturbing. No one else could remember seeing the child and old Emine had only ever seen it periodically, which begged the questions: who was that child and why had it been going into the house with the man? It had probably been quite innocent, but...The corpse of the young boy had shown no signs of sexual assault, yet the notion of Mr Zekiyan as one who was not quite 'right' would not seem to go away. The reality of that sinister apartment put paid to any feelings they might have had that he was entirely innocent. And as Dr Sarkissian had reputedly said at the time there were hundreds of ways in which people could obtain sexual gratification that did not involve penetration. That the dead boy's body had appeared untouched did not necessarily mean that he had not been abused. After all, there had to be a reason for his being there and a motive for his death and although sex was not necessarily in the frame, as it were, it could not be entirely discarded either.

Not that these musings had anything to do with the bald facts which were what he was required to note down now. He took several sheets of paper out of his drawer and fed one into his typewriter. He was just about to start typing when there was a knock at the door. 'Come in,' he called.

A short, unkempt individual who reeked of cheap cigarettes entered.

'Oh, hello, Cohen,' Suleyman said, 'what can I do for you?'

Constable Cohen, whose respect for Suleyman's more senior rank had never managed to overshadow the fact that they had once pounded the beat together, sat down neatly on the edge of the sergeant's desk and then smiled. 'Is it old Ikmen's birthday this week?' he asked.

'No, the inspector was born in December. Why?'

Cohen, rather disturbingly Suleyman thought, rummaged around in one of his trouser pockets for a moment before bringing out a small, brightly packaged box.

'This arrived for him today,' he said and, holding it up so that Suleyman could see, observed, 'looks like a present to me.'

'Well, if it's for his birthday it's very early,' Suleyman replied.

Taking the box from his colleague he examined it minutely. 'No sender's address.'

'No.'

Suleyman shrugged. 'I don't know, Cohen. Although why a friend or whatever would send a present to him here, I can't imagine.'

'Can I leave it with you then, Mehmet?'

'Yes. I'll take it round to his apartment on my way home. He's not coming back here tonight.'

'OK.'

'Right.' Suleyman very pointedly looked away from Cohen and addressed himself to his typewriter once again. Cohen, however, had other plans for his immediate future which did not include work.

'Er, Mehmet,' he said, 'um...'

Somewhat impatiently, Suleyman looked up again and said, 'Yes? And?'

Cohen smiled. He was used to this perpetual, if maddening, industrious trait in his friend. 'Me and some of the others are going to Çiçek Pasaj tonight if you're interested.'

'I don't think so.'

'Sergeant Farsakoğlu said that she might stay for one or two before...'

'So?' Using only two, albeit rapid, fingers, Suleyman typed the date and his name at the top of the page.

Cohen, who knew exactly how much or rather how little his friend knew of the pretty female sergeant's feelings, assumed his most casual air for what was to follow. 'Because she's got breasts like Agri Dağ and because she's got the raving hots for you.'

'I beg your pardon?' Now Suleyman did look up from

his work and with an expression so full of offence that Cohen almost laughed.

'You must have noticed, Mehmet?' he said. 'Her tongue almost touches the ground when she sees you. Some of the younger men and, I must be honest, myself too were very disappointed when it became apparent that she was only interested in you. I mean I could have given that some serious attention myself—what with that hair and those thighs...'

'Cohen!' Suleyman's face was red with either anger or embarrassment or both, not that the constable was impressed by his outburst.

'Yes?'

'I don't want to hear this kind of prurient gossip, thank you! I am, in case you hadn't noticed, a married man, and Sergeant Farsakoğlu is a very intelligent and virtuous officer! Such silly rumours could damage us both if they were allowed to circulate!'

'Avcı's been taking wagers on where and when you'll get together.'

'Then Avcı can just damn well give them back then, can't he!' There was fear in Suleyman's demeanour now. His job was everything to him and he knew very well that rumours of this sort could and did kill people's careers. In the arena of sexual relations at least, Turkey remained, he knew, a very Muslim country and for a married man to take a virgin's honour was, well...

'You can tell that lot on the ground floor,' he said, meaning the little bunch of constables with whom his friend associated, 'that if I hear any more of this, I will tell Ikmen who will, as you well know, devise the kind of punishment only he can originate.'

Cohen's face paled just a shade, but enough for Suleyman to see his apprehension. 'You mean...'

'Oh yes,' Suleyman said, really rather enjoying the application of power, if only by proxy. 'Your duty rosters will come from the pen of Shaitan himself. And if you think that constables can never be assigned to duty during post-mortem investigations then think again!'

'You wouldn't!'

'I wouldn't, but Ikmen...'

'You—'

'Don't say it, Cohen!' Suleyman said moving close in upon the little man's face. 'It was very trusting of you to tell me how you feel about doctors and post-mortems and all the procedures that go with that but unless this business stops right now, I will use that knowledge and—'

'I understand,' Cohen said hurriedly.

'Good.' His anger at least temporarily spent, Suleyman turned once again to his typewriter and tapped out the location of the crime scene.

'I suppose you want me to—'

'Just go, Cohen, before our friendship is irretrievable.'

'Yes, er...' Cohen, unusually, stood briefly to attention before departing, 'sir.'

'Goodbye.' Suleyman, searching the keyboard (or so he wanted Cohen to think) for the right letters, listened to the sound of the other man leaving the room. When the room was silent again, he let his head plunge forwards into his hands. He didn't need this. What he hadn't said, indeed couldn't say to Cohen, was that if rumours of this sort were going around it was only fair that he alert Sergeant Farsakoğlu to their existence; which wasn't going to be easy. There was also the problem of what he should do if the rumours proved to be true. If Sergeant Farsakoğlu did have the hots for him he was going to find looking her in the face again extremely difficult. Especially in view of the fact that he had the hots for her.

# 6

LOOKING AT THE thing closely, as he was now, was fascinating. Crystal, when it was finely cut like this, was such a clean, but at the same time deeply complex medium. Reflecting the entire visible spectrum was quite a feat for any substance and, as he stared into its depths, Çetin Ikmen wondered whether the experience he was having now was like being under the influence of psychotropic drugs. It was an interesting notion and not entirely out of place considering the recent discovery of so many similar little crystals at The Sacking House site. Was it possible that the young addict had used these in order to heighten his narcotic experiences?

This little miniature was, however, although quite unaccountably, his own. Carved, he could see, from one single rock or lump of crystal, it was a most intricate and delicate little cage. Fashioned after the style of those domed birdcages seen on the pavement outside tourist shops in the south coast resorts, it even contained a little canary suspended on a tiny golden swing in the middle of the model. And even though he had never really paid heed to such fripperies as ornaments before, he had to admit that the cage was both clever and pleasing. Quite why he was now in possession of it was another matter.

According to Suleyman the little package had arrived at the station sometime during the previous day. Ikmen and Suleyman had searched exhaustively for some indication either inside or outside the box that might give them a clue as to where it had originated. But there was nothing—even the postmark was illegible. All they or rather Ikmen, alone now that his colleague had gone home, possessed was this pretty little model which was, either by accident or design, extremely similar to those still in the upstairs apartment of The Sacking House. Was it just a coincidence or was there something rather more sinister behind it? Nobody that he could think of would send him such a thing and anyway why would anyone send him a present? It wasn't his birthday or even that of Fatma or any of the children.

He looked at the postmark again and decided that a trip to the Forensic Institute might prove instructive. If he knew where it had come from he might be able to work out who had sent it, and even if it proved to have come from a relative or friend he could easily justify the time and resources spent: the similarity to the other models was just too close. What, if anything, did it mean? If someone connected with the crime had sent this to him then what was he or she trying to say?

Assuming that the locked apartment had been some sort of prison for the dead boy, the symbolism of the caged bird was clear. The old Turkish custom of paying to release caged pigeons and thereby obtaining a blessing for setting something free also crossed Ikmen's mind. Death could, under certain circumstances, be seen as a freedom: from worries, woes, pain; in the case of the boy, a release from the hell of drug addiction? But all of this was based on the assumption that whoever had sent this to him had intimate knowledge of the crime, which was something, as yet, he did not know. He could be jumping to conclusions. It wouldn't be the first time. And yet...And yet there was, for want of a better analogy, a smell about this small development that just wasn't right. It wasn't a strong 'smell' and if someone told him tomorrow that the package had in fact come from some forgotten cousin in Kars, he would not be exactly surprised. But...

The sound of the front door opening and closing roused him temporarily from his reverie. He put the little model down on to the coffee table and then lit a cigarette. Just one more before bed, although as to whether he would sleep or not...

'Still up, Dad?' said his daughter Çiçek as she came into the room, discarding her high-heeled shoes and rubbing her aching ankles as she went.

'Yes.' He turned to look at her. Unlike him she was tall and pretty, her hair tied tightly into an elegant chignon, her long black coat flattering her slim figure. He smiled. 'Good trip?'

'Amsterdam,' she replied as, throwing her coat over one of the chairs, she collapsed on to the settee beside her father.

'See the "ladies" selling their "wares" in the shop windows, did you?'

She cast him an acid look. 'I saw the inside of Schiphol Airport, as usual.'

He laughed. 'Join Turkish Airlines and see the world.'

Çiçek bristled under her father's gentle teasing. It betrayed her extreme youth. 'Captain Lazar said he'd take me to Oxford Street next time we go to London,' she said.

'Oh, you want to be careful of pilots, girl! What with all their money and the glamour...'

'Oh, Dad!'

'Well.'

Çiçek closed her eyes for a few seconds and then, pushing an imaginary hair away from her face, she changed the subject. 'How is Grandad?'

Ikmen sighed before replying, 'OK.'

She looked down, not wishing to meet her father's eyes. 'Except that he isn't.'

'Çiçek!' It was not said in an angry way, but more as a warning.

Under normal circumstances she would have challenged him on this, but she was far too tired and so she simply shook her head in something between lack of understanding and despair.

'I'm going to bed now,' she said, hauling her long, slim form upright.

'You don't want a last cigarette with your old father first?'

She smiled. 'There was a problem with the refuelling at Schiphol which took three hours to fix. It was very boring. I smoked for a small country. Can't you hear it in my voice?'

'No.'

She bent down to kiss him lightly on the top of his head and, without another word, left the room.

Ikmen ground his cigarette out in his ashtray and went back to looking at the miniature. But then, finding that his tired brain would just not think in any coherent fashion, he too got up and walked slowly towards his bed.

Although quite fearless when it came to dealing with people, Dorotka Taşkiran had always treated motor cars with the respect that, in all probability, they deserved. She had, in other words, never learned nor even wanted to learn to drive. Living where she did, however, over in the distant suburb of Polonezköy, this did mean that in order to get into the city she had to take first a taxi, then a ferry and then, depending upon her final destination, usually a bus or a dolmuş too. Her appointment this morning at nine with Dr Sarkissian at the mortuary had meant leaving her home before the sun had even vacated its bed. It had been a wet and windy dawn which had not, sadly, discouraged Dorotka from standing outside on the ferry—she loved to look at the numerous palaces and gardens that lined the shores of the Bosporus—it had done little for the state of her hair. Strange hat notwithstanding, when she approached Arto Sarkissian and powerfully shook his hand, she looked not unlike a woman with her head inside a huge, grey storm.

As was her custom, she asked to be taken to see her 'sitter'—as she liked to term anybody, living or dead, whom she was sketching—right away and so Arto led her down the long central corridor towards the small room where the body of the dead boy lay. As she strode along beside him, Arto periodically stole small but embarrassed glances at her. She was, he always felt, someone who irresistibly invited second looks.

Dorotka Taşkiran was not really an 'official' police artist. There were several of those but, whenever Çetin Ikmen needed work of this sort done, he always employed this strange old woman as opposed to any of the others. This sprang from the high opinion he held of her work. She alone, so Ikmen said, could capture the 'soul' of a subject, although quite what he meant by that, the decidedly unaesthetic Arto Sarkissian could not imagine. All he knew was that she liked to talk to her sitters in a way that he found particularly disturbing and that on this occasion she had what appeared to be a dead bird attached to the brim of her hat.

When they arrived at the designated room, Arto put on all the lights and uncovered the face of the corpse while Mrs Taşkiran removed a large selection of pencils, brushes, paints and sketch pads from the small suitcase she carried for this purpose. Arto, who had, as promised, given his assistant the day off, asked whether the artist would mind if he stayed in the room in order to sort through and replace recently cleaned instruments. She gave her permission with a regal wave of one hand and then, drawing a stool up to the side of the trolley on which the corpse lay, she bent low over it and peered into its face.

'Well, you're a soft little thing and no mistake!' she said, skittering but not touching her fingers across the top of his features. 'You've a very fine nose there and a pretty rather girlish mouth.' She turned away quickly to address Arto Sarkissian who was cringing over by the sinks. 'He was strangled you say, Doctor?'

'Yes, although there are signs of drug abuse on the arms. The samples are still at the lab, but I suspect that the narcotic involved was heroin.'

She tutted and shook her head. 'Shame.' Then with one swift movement of the wrist she grabbed hold of the edge of the sheet and whipped it right off the body and on to the floor.

'What are you doing!' Arto cried, running over to the trolley and picking the sheet up off the floor. 'You're only supposed to be drawing the face!'

Ignoring him completely, the old woman took one of the body's hands in hers and held it up closely to her eyes. 'My goodness, but you've got soft hands, boy!' she said and then, pushing roughly past the outraged doctor she performed exactly the same procedure with one of the feet. 'And these are like little babies' hoofs too!' she exclaimed.

'Mrs Taşkiran, I insist that you—'

'Oh, come, come, Doctor,' she said, almost with humour in her voice, 'neither of us is a Muslim and so their dictates regarding opposite sexes attending to bodies don't apply to us.'

'That's not the point!' he said, hastily shuffling the sheet over the top of the torso. 'You have been asked to draw the face and only the face and that is what you must do!'

She shrugged. 'If you wish,' she said in a way that showed that she was totally unabashed. 'If you will be rigid on these matters.'

She then opened one of her sketch books and, as she bent low in order to look closely into her 'sitter's' face, Arto Sarkissian took a few deep, hopefully composing breaths. It was all very well for Çetin Ikmen to send this crazy person over to the morgue but he didn't have to either talk to her or supervise her work. Not that, probably, her antics would have worried the inspector; he could, at times, be quite as strange himself. To inflict such oddity on others, however, was not really on and the doctor determined to speak to his friend about it when next they met.

'Your skin is quite flawless, dear,' said a voice that looked, from where Arto was standing, to be emanating from the creature that adorned her hat. This, followed by the sound of graphite moving across paper, told him that, speaking or not, she had at least started the work that she had been contracted to perform.

Partly reassured that she wasn't going to do anything else that was too peculiar for a while, Arto returned to the bench and the pile of instruments arranged around the sinks. He did from time to time keep half an eye upon what the woman was doing, just in case. Not that he could really criticise her unless she did something absolutely outrageous. Mrs Taşkiran did this work for love rather than money—which was, of course, another reason why Çetin Ikmen was so keen on her stuff. But then, Mrs Taşkiran—whose last exhibition had, Arto recalled, been entitled 'Forest Mummies' and had consisted of a load of mummified moles and rats mounted on card—didn't exactly need cash. A lifetime resident of the pretty Polish refugee village of Polonezköy, Dorotka was the daughter of two Polish doctors of some note and had married well into good Turkish Republican money. Skilled as she no doubt was as an artist, her large cushion of wealth had to take more than a little blame for her obvious howling insanity. That, and of course the nature of the place to which her parents had come. Although far more scarce than they had been during the Belle Epoque when Dorotka's parents had lighted upon the shores of the Bosporus, Istanbul could still produce some startling eccentrics: like the old Ottoman general, now long dead, whom Arto could remember from his childhood. He had fought most bravely during the First World War despite suffering from the delusion that both of his legs were made from glass. Every morning, it was said, his men had to lift him on to his horse taking great care neither to chip nor shatter his legs. It was, Arto had thought even then, an eccentricity—like Mrs Taşkiran's dead bird, like the city itself—almost palpably tainted by the typically Stambouline obsession with sorrow and frail mortality.

'It is my opinion,' she said, resurrecting Arto from his thoughts, 'that this dear boy was quite a pampered little soul.'

'Not all those who take drugs are on the street.'

'True. But I do know quality when I see it and I see it very clearly here,' she continued. 'Those hands of his are barely touched by the lines of time and his feet have not for a long period, if ever, climbed up and down our lovely seven hills.'

Rather than dignify her ramblings with a reply, Arto took a handful of clamps and placed them in rows inside a drawer.

For a few moments following this exchange, the two of them worked in silence until, and addressing the corpse rather than the doctor, the old woman said, 'It is a little known fact that Atatürk once graced our little Polonezköy with his presence. My mother was just pregnant with my brother at the time. But my father sent her away anyway when the great man came. Just in case his eyes should light upon her and...He was like that, our beloved Ghazi, bless him. Poor mother always said she wished she could have just danced with him once. If I believed in heaven, which I don't, I might like to imagine my mother and Atatürk waltzing in the afterlife, dressed in evening clothes, of course.'

It wasn't easy to concentrate on anything much with all this nonsense going on, but Arto Sarkissian was grateful that what he was doing now was at least quite boring and mechanical. During the course of his time with her the doctor was vouchsafed many things about Mrs Taşkiran —second hand of course—some of which he already knew and some that he didn't. Principal amongst these facts was the origin of the little bird on her hat. She had, apparently, throttled the poor thing just that morning and was using her hat to transport it home for mummification. She liked it, which was just as well, because he doubted whether anybody else would find it attractive.

A rather interesting story about how she had once taken Çetin Ikmen out to dinner, at McDonald's, had just begun when the telephone in the corner rang. Arto picked it up and, having murmured his name into the receiver, recognised the voice of Dr Deminsan who was in charge of forensic testing.

'I have those toxicology results for you,' she said in that cold I-am-a-woman-and-a-professional manner of hers.

'Oh, yes,' Arto answered in a similar, but masculine vein. 'And?'

'Your victim was loaded with pethidine,' she said.

Arto creased his brow, partly in response to what Dr Deminsan had said and partly because Mrs Taşkiran now appeared to be sharing a joke with the corpse. 'Pethidine? Are you sure?'

'Of course I'm sure, Dr Sarkissian,' that same icy voice insisted. 'I did the tests myself. I'll put the report in the internal post or, if you wish, we could meet in about an hour.'

Time spent in Dr Deminsan's company tended, in Arto's experience, to make one feel a little inferior. He opted therefore for the former suggestion and, with a short word of thanks, put the telephone down again. This toxicology information was both perplexing and unexpected and, for a few moments, he just stood motionless by the bench, thoughtfully stroking his chin. Dr Deminsan's results were raising all sorts of questions in his mind, questions that were, in reality, the province not of himself, but of the investigating officer. When Mrs Taşkiran had finished her work, he would have to call Çetin Ikmen and explain all this to him. His friend was not a medical man and so the significance of this discovery would need to be outlined for him. And, as he watched the old woman rendering the face of the stranger in their midst in lines of graphite, he found that he was suddenly almost irresistibly drawn back to her and her sitter.

Seeing his movement, the old woman looked up from her work and smiled. 'He's really very lovely, isn't he?' she said.

'He was a handsome youth,' the doctor agreed.

'It is the preserve of the rich to be so,' she continued, her hand flying deftly across the paper, 'good food, clean and warm conditions all one's life. I was a great beauty myself, in my day. Had I been poor, it would have been a different story, but—'

'You think this boy was wealthy?'

'Oh, undoubtedly. As I said before, his hands and feet haven't seen a lot of service, even for one as young as he. I have, as I expect you have too, worked on children much younger than this whose skin is already wrinkled by sun and wind and work.' She looked up briefly from her labours, her nose creased slightly in disgust. 'Street urchins and the like, you know.'

And, usually, drug users too, he thought. But then that was just it really, wasn't it? Given his telephone call from Dr Deminsan, could this boy still be considered a drug addict in the conventional sense? And if he wasn't then what was he? As he watched Mrs Taşkiran put the finishing touches to her sketch Arto Sarkissian realised that he could not answer either of those questions.

As soon as Mehmet Suleyman entered the office he knew that the time had come. Ikmen's deeply thoughtful face said it all. Now was review time, when everything that had been discovered so far would be looked at and a strategy for moving forward decided. Unlike most other detectives, Ikmen kept all the salient facts regarding cases he was working on almost exclusively in his head which meant that very soon he would blurt it all out in one long and really quite impressive stream.

Suleyman did what was expected of him and sat down and waited. Ikmen as ever, began by taking a deep breath in.

'So, Suleyman,' he said, 'where are we now then?'

This was the sergeant's cue to give an account of what he had done in the last few days. 'Well, sir, I've circulated a description, such as it is, of Mr Zekiyan to all forces in Turkey and I'm in the process of checking the major ports and air terminals. I'm having a list drawn up of all known addicts, some of whom may also be dealers, in the Sultan Ahmet area and Sergeant Farsakoğlu is currently with a man who has stated that he wishes to confess to the crime.'

Ikmen raised an eyebrow. 'Know his name?'

'Well, Cohen told me that it was Lenin, but...'

Ikmen laughed. 'Oh, yes, I know him,' he said, 'he regularly dosses in a doorway near my apartment. The children call him Red Ahmet. I haven't a clue as to his real identity, but his declamation of the Communist Manifesto is something to behold.'

'So, he's just a...'

'Mad person, yes, Suleyman. When I've finished here, I'll go down and see him and sort it all out. Anything else?'

'I'd like to talk about the house.'

'OK.' Ikmen lit a cigarette and settled back comfortably in his battered leather chair. 'Let's talk it all through, shall we?'

'Yes.'

'Right. The boy died, according to Dr Sarkissian's calculations, at around about ten p.m. on the evening before the day he was discovered. He died by strangulation via a cord or ligature. We know that the boy used drugs because of the track marks on his arms although I am still waiting for the toxicology report on that as well as Mrs Taşkiran's portrait of the boy for the papers and others.

'Now, we know that the house was rented out to a man called Zekiyan who is, as yet, nowhere to be found. It seems, but until we find Mr Zekiyan we cannot really know for certain, that he actually created the self-contained little apartment at the top of the house for some reason and, further, he failed to tell his landlord about this. We think this man is probably Armenian and there is a strong possibility that the dead boy is also of that race.'

'Didn't Professor Mazmoulian disagree with that though, sir?'

'Yes, he did, Suleyman, and I am taking his opinion into account even though Commissioner Ardiç says that I am a fool to do so.'

'Well, the boy was uncircumcised and—'

'Ah.' Ikmen smiled. 'Yes, that is so, but to assume that he is Armenian just because of that may lead us into error. He could originate from almost any ethnic group which does not practice circumcision—or even, perhaps, one that does.'

Suleyman looked shocked. 'You mean that he could even have been Turkish?'

'Yes. Why not?'

'Well, because of his uncircumcised state.'

'It's a possibility you find shocking, I feel, Suleyman. And because you are a traditionalist Turk I can see that you would. But it is something I feel that we cannot afford to close our minds to.'

'Yes, but—'

'Anyway...' Ikmen held up his hand to silence his deputy. Further discussion of this detail at this very early point in the investigation would do nothing more than embroil them both in a largely unresolvable argument. 'So, in the absence of Mr Zekiyan and with no witnesses beyond the woman who first reported the unlocked state of the property, we only have the house and the boy as significant sources of evidence at the moment.'

'There was also the testimony of the old woman, Emine, who remembers seeing Zekiyan with a child some years ago.'

Ikmen inclined his head in recognition. 'True. And I will come to that in a moment. But for now, the house. What can we say about that, Suleyman?'

'Well...'

'Well, basically we have a clean house, don't we? No fingerprints, no mess, no food or drink, no items of clothing or toiletry. Just furniture, some household equipment, including a recently used and emptied vacuum cleaner, and a dead twenty-year-old.'

Suleyman frowned. 'No fibres from the carpets or soft furnishings then?'

'A few. Forensic are working on it now.'

'So it looks like whoever killed the boy cleaned the house afterwards.'

Ikmen scrunched his cigarette out in his ashtray and then lit another. 'Yes. Which means that he must have been quite busy that night. He must also have had to dispose of quite a bit of stuff too. Unless he never ate and walked around naked there would have been food and clothes to get rid of and perhaps other, more personal items, too. My theory is that he did all this in the early hours of the morning, although I can't see how he could have done it without transport.'

'He must have had a car then. There is space for one to the right of the property if I remember correctly.'

'Possibly. Unless he cleaned and removed everything the previous day, knowing what he was going to do.' Ikmen sucked thoughtfully on his teeth. 'He obviously went to a lot of trouble.'

'Well, he doesn't want to be caught, does he?'

'No. And yet'—Ikmen reached down into the drawer of his desk and pulled out the crystal miniature he had received the previous day—'he is an exhibitionist. This figure comes from the same series as the ones in the top apartment. I compared them this morning before I came in.'

'You're saying you definitely think that this was sent to you by the killer?'

Ikmen shrugged. 'I have no evidence to suggest that it wasn't and as you know I do not hold with serendipity. I know that a lot of people have these things but I don't personally know any of them. Friends or relatives would have included a note of some sort and besides there is no reason to send me a present at this time, especially one like this that would not appeal to me.'

'So,' Suleyman began slowly, 'if that is the case then what we are looking for is someone who doesn't want to be caught and yet wants you to know that he is still around?'

'Who wants me to know that he is cleverer than me,' Ikmen corrected. 'He has presented me with a puzzle, which I must say intrigues me, and now he wants me to know that he is around to enjoy my perplexity.'

'You are, I must say, sir,' Suleyman said, 'ascribing a lot of significance to an act we do not know to be suspicious.'

Ikmen shrugged. 'What else can I do? Until we know who this boy is and or get some sort of grip on a motive we have to explore every angle, however tenuous.' He picked up the miniature and held it up. 'We know that the boy was locked into that apartment for some reason and this is a cage. Cages might imply imprisonment for some time and with those atrophied limbs of his...'

'Atrophied limbs?'

'Yes, I thought I told you. Dr Sarkissian has observed that the boy's limbs are sort of withered, underdeveloped for his age. Like those of a cripple or one who has been bed bound.'

'But why was the boy imprisoned?' Suleyman said. 'Drug connection? Yes, maybe. But then what about old Emine's sighting of Zekiyan with a child all those years ago? OK, sexual abuse doesn't have to be obvious and if this man has a history of "liking" children...'

'Could have just been a nephew or niece,' Ikmen replied,

'and our boy was hardly a child, but it's a fair point. Some of those needle scars on his body were very old and extremely numerous. He must have got the drugs from somewhere and if Mr Zekiyan or whoever, maybe even this other man Zekiyan has occasionally been seen with, had been supplying him for some years, it may well be that sex could have been involved at some stage. I've got Dr Sarkissian looking into the darker side of the Armenian community which may or may not turn up something.' He put his hand up to his mouth and frowned. 'There are a couple of kiddie-fiddlers I could check out.'

Suleyman sniffed his disgust, a gesture that was not lost upon Ikmen.

'Don't worry,' he said, 'I won't ask you to talk to them.'

'So where do we go from here then, sir?' Suleyman asked, quickly changing the subject to one that his mind would not shrink from.

'Well,' Ikmen said, 'as soon as Mrs Taşkiran finishes her portrait of the boy, which should be very soon now, I will circulate that to the papers and to other forces. I'll check out the kiddie-fiddlers while you handle the drug angle. A trawl of local contractors who could have carried out that work at the top of the house might be useful too. I think it would also be instructive to send a few men out to some of the refuse dumps and try to find out whether a large number of quite nice clothes or food have recently been deposited. Refuse men are usually quite sharp with regard to nice rubbish.'

Suleyman, who had been writing all these points down on a piece of paper, said, 'OK.'

'I must also remember to ask Arto Sarkissian where he thinks this Mr Zekiyan might have bought his Christian ring. I expect we're talking the Gold Bazaar here, but such an unusual piece might have to have been purchased at a particular place—maybe somewhere the Christian clergy go. Anyway. In addition we must not, I feel, forget one other aspect that neither of us has mentioned, other than obliquely, before.'

Suleyman looked up and shrugged. 'Which is?'

'Well, lest we forget, Suleyman, we do have rather a lot of our friends from over the Black Sea living in the city at the moment. Friends who are, at least nominally, Christian.'

Suleyman pulled a face. 'The Beyazıt branch of the Moscow Mafia, you mean.'

Surprised and also rather pleased that his normally straight-laced deputy should make a joke, Ikmen said, 'Yes, and that's really rather good, Suleyman. Well done. Indeed, our Russian friends could possibly be involved. Where there are hard drugs they do tend to follow.'

'Yes.'

'They do have a penchant for such trade as well as, of course, selling us their bleach-blonde women.'

'Hah!' exclaimed Suleyman with disgust. 'The Natashas.'

Ikmen laughed. 'Yes, bless them. Every street corner should have one and in my part of town, of course, it does. My wife's sister spits at them. But—'

Suleyman's telephone trilled into loud and intrusive life.

'Excuse me please, sir,' the younger man said as he moved to pick it up and then, announcing his name into the receiver, he listened with what Ikmen observed was a grave expression. Several seconds later, his face now alarmingly white, Suleyman threw the receiver, still connected, down on to his desk and started to run out of the room.

'What the hell is—' Ikmen started to ask.

'It's your friend Lenin,' Suleyman shouted as he approached the top of the stairs, 'he's taken Farsakoğlu hostage down in one of the interview rooms.'

It is well known that, in general, male police officers are of the opinion that their female counterparts are not really capable of dealing effectively with acts of violence. They do not always, however, express such opinions in public. Constable Cohen on the other hand did not let such sensibilities hold him back. As Ikmen approached him, demanding to know what was happening, he was very free with his opinions.

'What that silly woman thought she was doing with that nutter, I don't know. I mean—'

'What, exactly, is the position, Cohen?' Ikmen asked as he, Suleyman and three other officers stood outside Interview Room Number Five.

'Well, she was asking him some questions, sir, and—'

'You were in the room with her?'

'Yes. But then he, this Lenin, gets all sort of agitated and the next thing I know he's got her round the throat. Across that table like a—'

'You did, I take it, attempt to stop him, Cohen?'

The little man drew himself up to his full height and pulled his shoulders just very slightly backwards. 'Oh yes, I...But have you seen the size of him? All that hair and those great big hands and shoulders like a lion...'

'Yes, well.' Ikmen, rather roughly, or so Cohen thought, pushed past him and opened the door on to a scene that looked not unlike a still from a rather bad Egyptian movie. Over in the far cigarette-butt-strewn corner, an extremely tall man of quite staggeringly filthy hairiness was holding the very pretty neck of Sergeant Farsakoğlu tightly between one vast finger and thumb. Under the powerful spell of her own fear, the young woman's eyes had widened to a degree that made them look as if they could almost encompass the room and, as she caught sight of Ikmen, they became if anything even bigger. As the man's eyes contacted with Ikmen's, he reacted by pulling the woman still closer in to his chest and grunting.

Despite furious, hissing entreaties from his rather more than usually agitated deputy, Ikmen thrust his hands very casually into his pockets and then smiled at the man in a warm and friendly fashion.

'Well, Vladimir Ilyich,' he said, 'it's a great pleasure actually to meet you in the flesh. What can I do for you?'

The man simply carried on staring.

Ikmen shrugged and then took a cautious step forward. 'I understand you claim to have murdered the boy in Ishak Paşa Caddesi?'

'She won't believe me. She laughed at me,' the man said, inclining his head towards his hostage. His voice was cracked and scarred by too many nights spent under the open sky.

'Well, now,' Ikmen said, 'it's not really up to Sergeant Farsakoğlu, is it? If you have committed this very serious crime then I think you should offer your confession to a rather higher authority, don't you?'

'I could snap her neck in a second if I wanted to.'

Ikmen acknowledged this statement with a small bow and, at the same time, he moved just a fraction closer to the scene. 'I'm sure that you could, sir. But wouldn't you rather talk to me about all of these issues first? I am an inspector of police and I am therefore much more important than the sergeant there.'

'Yes?'

Ikmen could now feel Suleyman at his back—a rather tense presence which he sincerely wished was not there. Vladimir Ilyich Lenin was not, he could see, the sort of man one would want to antagonise.

Ikmen took his cigarettes out of his pocket and offered one to the man. Strangely, he declined, although that was probably more because (so Ikmen thought) he didn't want to loosen his grip upon Farsakoğlu than because he didn't actually want one. Ikmen, for his part, lit up and once again smiled warmly.

'I often see you around and about in Sultan Ahmet,' he observed. 'You speak to people about your politics and—'

'They never listen! They neither understand nor deserve the concept of world revolution. You have to fight if you want equality. Blood is what it's about! You don't get anywhere unless you have the guts to spill blood.'

Ikmen took one step nearer. 'Was that why you killed the boy in Ishak Paşa?'

'I put my knife to his throat, yes.'

'Why him?'

The man laughed. 'Why not? I don't have to justify myself to you! When they come to write the history of this time, it will be my name that will live on to frighten the children, not yours.'

'Indeed. However, the killing or maiming of a woman is, don't you think, another matter?'

'Not if she works for a fascist system.' And then noticing that Ikmen had, somehow, crept closer to him, the man said, 'And you can stay where you are too or I'll have the both of you.'

'If you let Sergeant Farsakoğlu go you can willingly have me in exchange.'

The man laughed. 'You are joking, aren't you?'

'No.'

'Well, isn't that brave!' he said, turning the head of his hostage around to face him. 'He must really like you, girly, just like I do!' Then, obviously highly amused by all this, he started to laugh into the woman's terrified face—

an eerily unnerving development that made absolutely no
sense to anyone else in the room apart from the man. It
also signified, despite Ikmen's best efforts, that his instabil-
ity was if anything escalating.

As the man laughed, Ikmen was aware of the fact that
Suleyman was no longer at his back, but when he did finally
register that his deputy was now standing beside the man,
it came as almost as much of a shock to him as it did to
the hostage-taker. With what could only be described as
spiteful intent, Suleyman jammed his pistol up against the
side of the man's head and then exhorted him, for his own
good, not to move. The laugh died on the man's dirty lips
as quickly as it had been born.

'Take your hands from my colleague's throat,' Suleyman said through rapid gulps of air, 'and do it slowly.'

'Are you going to kill me?' the man sneered. 'Blow my
brains out across her lovely face?'

'If necessary,' Suleyman replied. 'If you move in a way
that I don't like I will not hesitate.'

'I'd do as he asks,' Ikmen put in, 'and then I promise
that I will listen to you. And I will not laugh, Vladimir
Ilyich, you have my word on that.'

Although at first the man's movements were too small
to really see, it slowly became apparent that there was a
slight decrease of pressure on Sergeant Farsakoğlu's throat.
As if to signal this, she coughed a little and then moved her
neck just fractionally to one side.

'But why should I believe you?' the man asked Ikmen.

'Because I give you my word,' Ikmen replied, 'and
because my word both as a man and as an officer of the
law is not a thing lightly given. It's about honour, Vladimir
Ilyich, which is, I know, as important to you as it is to me.'

Although nobody in that room could even begin to

guess at the man's thoughts, he did at least appear to give this speech some consideration. In fact, as Ikmen watched him, he fancied that he could almost see flickers of inner conflict moving across the tramp's fine, if filthy, features. Now that he was looking at him properly it occurred to Ikmen that this man, though obviously deranged and confused, had an air about him that had definitely not been engendered on the street. Was it the odd flash of confidence or the sculpted nose? The occasionally sophisticated use of words? Or was it just Ikmen's own preconceptions that assumed anybody who had the wit even to consider complicated political and philosophical concepts had to be someone of substance? It was intriguing and, although he was nervous for Farsakoğlu's safety, Ikmen was aware of an excitement within himself at the prospect of actually getting to grips with this man's mind.

'I'm waiting,' Suleyman said and, as if to emphasise his point, clicked the safety catch off.

'I could die and become even greater than I have been in life,' said the man slowly.

This was a dangerous and not unexpected development which Ikmen countered immediately. 'But if you die, Vladimir Ilyich, how will you know whether or not we tell the people lies about you? Perhaps to us you are not the great revolutionary you know yourself to be? Perhaps we will demonise and abuse your memory?'

The man grunted and then once again, appeared to drift into some deep thought process.

Ikmen, afraid of what might result from this further hiatus, held his hand out to the man and said, 'Give me back my girl, Vladimir Ilyich. She's nothing to you and everything to us. Show us that you can be that brave.'

His fingers were only just lightly touching her neck now. And as the man's eyes fixed upon Ikmen's face he moved them just that little bit further outwards and then pushed the woman into Ikmen's waiting arms. As she barrelled forwards into Ikmen, Farsakoğlu let out a small but still half-strangled cry.

Suleyman, in one swift movement, kicked the man in the shins and then pulled him by his hair down on to the floor. 'Face down, hands behind your head!'

Two of the observing constables, including Cohen, ran forward to offer assistance. Somewhere, somebody shouted, 'Fucking bastard!'

As the scene behind Ikmen and Farsakoğlu became one of arrest there was a very real danger that things would get very ugly. Policemen don't like it when one of their own is attacked and with a woman involved that dislike can easily turn into outright fury. As Ikmen attempted to turn away from the shaking woman he became very aware that if he didn't do something very quickly traditional Turkish machismo would explode around him.

'Cuff him and sit him on a chair, Suleyman,' he said and then, turning to the one constable who had not gone over to the prone man, 'and you, take the sergeant here upstairs and ring the hospital. I want her fully checked out by a doctor and then sent home.'

'Yes, sir.'

Gently, he placed Farsakoğlu into the arms of the constable and then walked up to his deputy who was still standing over the man with his gun pointed at his head. 'Get him up and cuff him, Suleyman.'

'Oh, but, sir,' Cohen said, 'can't we just...I mean, you go out and then...He's a total bastard!'

'Get him up, cuff him and put him into a chair!' Ikmen reiterated to his colleague.

Suleyman, his breath still coming short and heavy, looked up into the eyes of his superior, who did not like

what he saw there. There was fury, real and tangible murderous intent. It was not like Suleyman, not at all. And
with the others clustered like a small but dedicated lynch
mob around him, they formed a tableau that Ikmen found
both repellent and disturbing.

Drawing himself up to his full, diminutive height, Ikmen
did something he had never done before—he threatened his
sergeant in public. Something had to be done to break this
potentially murderous spell that had overtaken them all.

'Sergeant Suleyman, I am ordering you to raise that
man, cuff him and put him in a chair! Failure to comply
with my order will result in you being placed on a charge
and relieved of duty!'

'Oh, sir,' Cohen exclaimed, 'you wouldn't—'

'Oh, yes, I would and will, Cohen!' Ikmen looked at
each of the men in the room in turn, ending with Suleyman
whose eyes were as hard as diamonds. 'If any of you so
much as breathes at that man in an inappropriate or violent
manner I will be utterly merciless!'

Suleyman, who had only now found his voice, said, 'Sir...'

'Don't even think it, Suleyman!' Ikmen held up a warning finger. 'This man is ill.'

'He's a fucking nutter!' a large constable named Gülügölü
muttered.

'Yes, that's quite right!' said Ikmen. 'A nutter and
therefore not responsible for his actions! Now get him
up, cuff him and put him in that chair there'—he pointed
to the appropriate place—'and then go and pray to Allah
that I don't assign you all to some hellish duty in the
mortuary!'

With Cohen's help, Suleyman raised the now shaking man
up from the floor and then put him, in cuffs, into the chair.

'You were going to kill me, weren't you?' the man said

as he looked up into Suleyman's now quite immobile face. 'I know you're a killer, I can see it in your eyes.'

'That's quite enough of that, Vladimir Ilyich,' Ikmen said, attempting to catch hold of yet another potentially explosive situation.

But then yet again, quite inappropriately, the man laughed. 'I'd rather his violence than your false understanding,' he sneered.

'What do you mean?' Ikmen asked.

'I mean, policeman, that you can't even begin to understand me. I mean that you're calling me a madman is something you do for yourself, not me. I mean that you know nothing'—he spat copiously down at Ikmen's feet—'not even the fact that one of your own is a blood-crazy killer.'

And then he laughed again, but this time he didn't stop.

# 7

DRIVING AWAY FROM the central areas of the city felt not unlike extricating oneself from a huge monster. As well as experiencing rapid urban development over the past twenty years, Istanbul had also suffered a massive rise in population, which had both pushed property prices up and filled the streets, particularly in the more central districts, to bursting point and sometimes beyond. Even at this time of night—it was now eight o'clock—the streets around Taksim Square were choked with traffic and, as Arto Sarkissian moved the car forward, by the centimetre at times, he could feel weariness at it all emanating from the silent man beside him.

As they drew level with the Republican monument, a tall, blonde whore tapped on the window and smiled. In this part of town it could be either male or female, but whatever it was it was quite insistent about selling its wares to at least one of the middle-aged men in the car. Çetin Ikmen, who had not spoken since Arto had picked him up from his home half an hour before, muttered 'Fuck off!'

under his breath and then turned away from the window, his head sunk low into the depths of his coat.

'Oh, so you are alive then?' said his friend as he manoeuvred the car away from the 'girl' and beyond the confines of the monument.

'I really tried to be understanding of that man,' Çetin said, lighting yet another cigarette.

'He was insane, Çetin,' Arto answered. 'What did Dr Halman say about him?'

'She said,' and here he quoted the psychiatrist's words verbatim, 'that he was "suffering from paranoid delusions of a persecutory nature coupled with an underlying political obsession". It took four of my officers to hold him down while she gave him that injection in his arse.'

'And how was he after that?'

'Quiet. He'll stand trial for the assault on my officer, you know.'

'Well, yes.'

'But it's not right, Arto! He's mad and...' He looked out of the window once again, his face set and exhausted. 'My officers were like a pack of animals with him. Even Suleyman. It was appalling. I told them he was ill but—'

'You lot don't like attacks on one of your own, as well you—'

'I will not tolerate barbarity!' The policeman turned and looked hard at the side of his friend's face, the lights from a gaudy café reflected in his furious eyes. 'I know of officers who would turn their faces from what nearly happened today but I will not! I thought that Mehmet Suleyman was the same.'

'Perhaps he too fosters a secret desire for the lovely Sergeant Farsakoğlu.'

'Oh, don't be absurd!'

They passed the next few minutes in silence and as the car finally extricated itself from the knot of traffic strangling Taksim Square and headed off down Inönü Caddesi, Çetin took to concentrating on the wide sweep of darkened Bosporus that now stretched out in front of him. To his left crouched the huge floodlit whiteness of the Dolmabahçe Palace; a rococo fantasy which had been built in the last century by the civilised and gentle Sultan Abdul Mejid. This monarch, who had sadly died at the early age of thirty-nine, had done much to direct the eyes of the Turks towards the West. Not only had his palaces been of Western, or rather more specifically French design, but he had also played a large part in reorganising and modernising the armed forces along European lines. He had, in addition, been open to the idea of democracy for his people. That Atatürk, who went so much further than Abdul Mejid, indeed who took upon himself the task of pulling his country back from the brutal excesses of Abdul Mejid's son Abdul Hamid, had lived and died in Dolmabahçe too was one of those strange little historical facts which sometimes made the inspector believe that certain things were just meant. Mere synchronicity did not describe this phenomenon adequately. There was an order in the universe which ensured that certain things of a symbolic nature took place in a certain way. It was, he thought, perhaps a method whereby some higher power, whatever that was, taught humanity its hard lessons.

Two Bosporus ferries hooted their mournful horns in almost perfect unison and Çetin looked across from the great French palace towards his rather humbler birthplace on the Asian shore. Üsküdar, or Scutari as it had once been called, had for several generations been the Ikmen family's native district. It was the place from which his great-grandfather had been taken by agents of the wicked Sultan Abdul

Hamid to his death at the hands of the imperial executioner on Galata Bridge; it was also the place to which his father had once brought his strange and exotic European wife. Because his mother had come from Albania, Çetin was strictly speaking half European himself; this was an 'honour' that most Turks could in a spiritual sense claim because of Turkey's geographical location, yet he had always felt that it was rather more marked in him. The urge to modernise and rationalise his world was both strong and evident in him, yet that wild, independent and at times irrationally superstitious streak of the insular mountain dweller remained. It was a split that caused some confusion in his life and, at times, some pain too. Were he truly a rational, modern man, he would at least listen to his wife's anxieties and difficulties with old Timür. Once again, earlier that evening, she had attempted to speak to him about it, and once again he had silenced her with the hard eyes and upheld warning finger of the unchallengeable Turkish male. But that was not a subject he wanted to consider now or indeed ever, and so as the car turned out of Inönü Caddesi and on to the coastal road, he moved his thoughts on to other subjects.

'So run this pethidine thing past me again, will you, Arto?' he asked his friend.

After beeping his horn at the car in front, Arto Sarkissian replied, 'It's quite simple, Çetin.'

'To you, yes.'

'Well...Look, pethidine is a synthetic form of heroin. Its principal use is in the alleviation of pain during childbirth. Like any drug, it possesses the potential for abuse but as an actual street drug...I have never heard of or experienced it being used as such. Some medics have been known to "experiment" with it, but beyond the medical sphere it is, I would say, really rather difficult to obtain.'

'But doctors, nurses and the like could get hold of it?'

Arto creased his brow in doubt. 'They could, but it wouldn't be easy. Drugs of that order are highly controlled. People have to sign them out and they would only be issued to those in positions of authority.'

'So if our boy were a nurse or a medical student...'

'It's possible, but...' Arto sighed deeply, 'in this case no. What with the atrophied state of his limbs, plus...well...'

Çetin turned to look at his friend who was obviously wrestling with himself.

'Well what?' he asked.

'It was actually something that the truly fantastic Mrs Taşkiran said.'

The inspector laughed. 'And what did that old maniac tell you?'

'She said that the boy's hands and feet were remarkably soft and—unused, I suppose you'd say, for a person of his age. She gave it as her opinion that he had the hands of an aristocrat. I must admit that I paid her words very little attention until pethidine was mentioned and I started to think along the lines you've just mentioned.'

'Meaning?'

'Meaning that if our boy were a nurse or a medical student he could not have had atrophied limbs or hands that were soft and unused. Those people work very hard. I know, I've been there. As well as mucking in on the wards even your academic work involves, figuratively, rolling your sleeves up. You can spend days in laboratories getting all sorts of foul and corrosive substances on your hands. Mine were just like leather by the time I had completed my studies—indeed they still are.'

'And so were the boy's hands soft and unused as you put it?' Çetin asked.

'Have you ever looked at the hands of people who have suffered brain damage at birth?'

'No.'

'Well, they are quite interesting in that they are not only very soft, because of course they do not and cannot do anything, but they are also almost completely unlined too. I tell you that when I first saw this phenomenon it made me rather rethink my opinion of the value of palmistry. However, when Mrs Taşkiran had gone on her eccentric way—you did, just digressing a bit here, get her sketch, didn't you, Çetin?'

'Yes, yes!' his intrigued friend said impatiently. 'And? The boy?'

'Well, as I said, when the old woman left I had a look at his hands myself. And'—he turned his eyes away from the road for just a second in order to emphasise his point—'they were just like the hands of those damaged people. Plump and smooth and almost completely unlined.'

The room in which dinner had been set for that evening was not strictly speaking a room at all, rather it was a conservatory. Its almost completely glass-constructed walls looked out directly on to the blackness of the darkened Bosporus below, allowing what little light that emanated from the water, together with the stronger illumination from passing ships and ferries, to shimmer up into the area giving the dining environment a luminous, shifting quality. Around the long polished mahogany table set with shining silver cutlery and candelabra, tall and luxuriant indoor plants provided the only privacy, in the absence of blinds, that the room possessed. Passing ferry and ships' passengers could, at least theoretically, see what was going on inside. They would probably also be quite jealous of the luxury being paraded therein.

At various points amongst the lush foliage tall, ceramic charcoal-burning stoves were sited, an archaic but totally apt form of heating for an apartment in this household. For, as the eyes of these few early guests of Mr Muhammed Ersoy were gradually discovering, his house, great though it was, boasted little in the way of modern artefacts. There was a small but discernible hissing noise beneath the general conversational hubbub that indicated the presence of gas as opposed to electric lighting. The uniforms of the maids consisted of long skirts and high-necked blouses topped off by thin veils which almost completely covered their faces. And then, of course, there was their host, Mr Ersoy himself.

Dressed in a long black coat of the high-necked Stambouline variety that had been popular at the end of the last century, his tall, slim frame was flattered by narrow black trousers and an abundance of gold finger and neck jewellery. On his head, and at odds with Atatürk's strict dictates regarding headgear, he wore a bright red fez, the vibrant colour of which was reflected on the patina of his dense black hair. To say that he looked dashingly dramatic was an understatement and even though his friend, Avram Avedykian, who now followed Ersoy into the room, was equally if not more handsome, the Armenian paled almost into invisibility beside this stunning, past-times vision. His entrance, which was 'performed' with arms outstretched in greeting, drew many admiring, or perhaps shocked, gasps from the small knot of male guests who were clustered, drinking chilled champagne, around one of the stoves.

'My God!' exclaimed the far more soberly dressed Krikor Sarkissian, 'You are quite the thing tonight aren't you, Muhammed!'

'I like to dazzle when I entertain,' replied Ersoy, smiling, 'and in view of the fact that we have collected so very much money for your marvellous project I feel that we must celebrate as well as plan for the future.'

'Well, you have certainly made a stunning start, Muhammed,' said a small, bespectacled man who was one of the most prominent divorce lawyers in the city.

'Thank you, Murad,' said the host, bowing in acceptance of his guests' appreciation, 'but my appearance is not the only surprise I have for you all tonight.'

'Oh, what might—'

'You will see!' Ersoy teased. 'Won't they, Avram?'

The Armenian only moved his mouth in a suggestion of a smile and then muttered, 'Yes.'

It was then that the arrival of Krikor's brother Arto and his friend Çetin Ikmen was announced. Turning to greet the two newcomers, Muhammed Ersoy was faced with rather plain and, in one case almost scruffy, men, both of whom looked rather shocked.

'Ah, Inspector!' Ersoy exclaimed, reaching his hand out to Ikmen with a smile. 'I am very pleased to see you. I felt that perhaps we got off to rather a poor start the last time that we met. But maybe we shall be able to have a proper talk this time.' Then, turning to Arto and shaking his hand he added, 'I do hope that you will ensure his mobile is switched off tonight.'

'I'm afraid that I'm always on call when I'm working on a case, sir,' Ikmen answered. 'And as you probably know, I am heavily committed at the present time.'

'Oh, but of course,' Ersoy exclaimed, 'the boy in Sultan Ahmet. A terrible thing.'

'Yes.'

'Are you—'

'I cannot divulge any details regarding on-going work, sir,' Ikmen interrupted.

'Oh, no, of course not.' Then, turning to one of the nearby maids, he said, 'Could you please offer these gentlemen a drink?'

The girl, who was carrying a large silver tray bearing numerous champagne flutes, glided over to where the men were standing and offered them refreshment. As he removed one of the glasses from the tray, Ikmen watched, fascinated, as the liquid light from the Bosporus bounced and reflected up into the seemingly endless strings of bubbles in the glass.

'How much money does this character have?' he asked Arto when Ersoy had gone to greet yet another new guest.

Avram Avedykian, who had been standing unnoticed at his elbow, laughed gently.

Embarrassed, Ikmen stuttered, 'Oh, er, I'm sorry. Your er, friend, er...'

'That's all right, Inspector,' the handsome Armenian smiled, 'most people at some time or another become insatiably curious about Muhammed's wealth. And in answer to your question I have to say that I don't know how rich my friend is. I doubt he even knows himself. When one is multiply asseted, it is always difficult to tell. Muhammed owns a shipping company, a publishing house and a string of hotels on the south coast. He has it all.'

'Unlike,' Arto Sarkissian put in, 'humble doctors like ourselves, Avram.'

Çetin Ikmen laughed the thick and mucus-filled chortle that only a heavy smoker can produce. 'If you doctors are humble, I don't know where that puts me!'

'In the gutter, as ever,' said a new but familiar voice.

Turning round, Çetin Ikmen found himself looking into the slim and intelligent face of Krikor Sarkissian. The two men embraced affectionately.

'It's good to see you again, Çetin,' Krikor said. 'Let us hope that this time both you and my brother will be able to stay with us.'

Ikmen shrugged. 'You hardly need us to help carry through your plans, Krikor. You have the money, the backing...But I hope that we can stay anyway, if only to experience'—and here he looked around the room with obvious wonder—'yet more of Mr Ersoy's whims.'

'Muhammed is quite a showman, isn't he?' Krikor observed.

'Either that or completely barking mad!' Ikmen replied, still staring at the fabulous apartment with rapt eyes.

Arto Sarkissian drained his champagne in one large gulp and then, turning to his friend, said, 'Actually, Çetin, now that we have two other doctors here, why don't you ask them about pethidine?'

'Oh, yes. Arto and I were talking earlier about where and how one might obtain this substance.'

'Pethidine?' Krikor inquired. 'Why?'

'Well, er,' Ikmen said, 'I can't actually...'

'Oh, I see,' Krikor said, understanding almost instantly. Then, addressing the younger Armenian at his side, he asked, 'Pethidine—synthetic heroin, is it not, Dr Avedykian?'

Caught just as he was about to take a sip of champagne from his glass, Avram Avedykian merely grunted his assent. 'Mmm.'

'Its main application is in the field of obstetrics,' Krikor continued, 'as an analgesic. Very powerful, very effective. Add anything to that, Avram?'

The younger man, having swallowed his mouthful, now spoke. 'No,' he said, 'but then I'm male surgical, so what would I know?'

'We all employ pain control of one sort or another, and, theoretically, we may use any drug we like provided it is appropriate and sufficient to the pain.' Krikor added, 'I mean what do you use for your patients after, say, prostate removal?'

Avram Avedykian laughed, but softly, in a mildly embarrassed fashion. 'I don't really think that these gentlemen want to be discussing prostate surgery.'

'But what do you use, anyway?' Krikor insisted, a smile firmly present on his face.

'Well...if pain is severe, we employ morphine. For lower levels of discomfort we may use any number of products which, er, are currently, er...'

'Like what? Voltarol, coproximol? What is your preference, Doctor, and what quantities do you employ? I'm interested.'

'But getting back to pethidine,' Arto Sarkissian interrupted, 'have either of you ever, you in particular, Krikor, come across it as a street drug?'

'Well...'

'Certainly not in my experience,' said Avram Avedykian and then, moving to bow lightly to the other men, he smiled as he added, 'But I am sure that if anyone does know it is Krikor. I will leave you with him while I meet some of our other guests.'

And then with a wave he walked off in the direction of a Greek priest the Sarkissian brothers recognised as one Father Nicos Pangulos.

When he had gone, Krikor Sarkissian nodded his head sourly in the direction of his retreating colleague. 'He doesn't improve.'

'You really shouldn't tease him like that though,' his brother scolded.

'Well..."

'Would anybody,' Ikmen asked, 'care to tell me what you two are talking about?'

Leaning close in to the policeman's ear, Krikor Sarkissian whispered, 'Dr Avedykian has the unfortunate reputation for being rather more interested in his relationship with Muhammed, who is admittedly a delight, than he is in his patients. I have heard it said in some quarters that he has even, on occasion, underprescribed, in error I suppose, causing his patients considerable distress. It is, in my opinion, indefensible.'

'That is all only hearsay,' his brother added.

Krikor rolled his eyes in disbelief. 'Look, I know that you like him and that you were very good to him when he was struggling with his studies, but—'

'I think, Krikor, that you are allowing your personal distaste at the notion of an Armenian homosexual to cloud your judgement about him. He is a very good—'

Ikmen, pleased that his initial assessment of the two men's relationship had been confirmed, said, 'Oh, so they, Ersoy and your friend are—'

'But to return to pethidine,' Arto said in a loud and obvious voice, 'have you ever seen it on the street, Krikor, or...'

As the sound of drinking, soft music and laughter grew amidst the small groups of men gathered about the warm stoves, servants were scuttling to and fro in the kitchens beneath the great house. For those, like Ikmen, who did not know Muhammed Ersoy very well, a great treat was in store. Those armies of minions had spent all day preparing not a dinner but a feast of eight beautifully presented gourmet courses. It was to be, and indeed had been designed to be, not just a meal but an experience.

By the time the fourth course had arrived, been consumed and the dirty dishes taken away, the guests who were rather more spare in stature, like Ikmen, were beginning to feel really rather uncomfortable. Although individually quite small, each dish had been incredibly rich and the combination of delicate fishes, piquant morsels of red meat plus a garnish of buttery filo pastry had rendered quite a few of the guests virtually immobile. Not so, however, Muhammed Ersoy who was, despite copious quantities of Chablis, Côtes du Rhône and champagne, quite as lively and entertaining as he had been at the beginning of the evening. In response, however, to a whispered request from Krikor Sarkissian, he did eventually catch the mood of the party and announced a short hiatus in the banquet for, he said, smoking purposes.

Ikmen and Father Nicos, plus two or three other men the policeman did not recognise, did not have to be asked twice and lit up immediately. There had been a time when the whole party would have burst into joyful flames, but as Ikmen sadly acknowledged, Turkish habits were changing in line with more European mores, at least within the confines of the upper classes.

Ersoy, who was leisurely unwrapping a large Havana cigar, turned to Krikor Sarkissian and said, 'So, I understand it is your opinion that we should site this centre of yours in Beyazıt.'

'That's right, Muhammed,' the older Sarkissian agreed. 'In the very belly of the beast, as it were.'

Krikor smiled. 'We must go where the problems are at their most acute. The area is heavily populated by those involved in the drugs "world" including many of those young people we particularly wish to target.'

'It's very good, isn't it,' their host said to the table at large. Many heads inclined in agreement. 'However, utterly supportive as you know that I am of this project, Krikor, I must, I feel, express one very significant reservation.'

Several faces around the table, including Krikor's, frowned.

Ersoy smiled. 'It is simply,' he said, 'that I sometimes wonder whether abstinence is quite right for us.'

Father Nicos placed his cigarette delicately in his ashtray and then asked, 'Quite right for who, Muhammed?'

'Well, for Istanbulis of course,' Ersoy replied. 'Whether we are Turks, whatever they are, Greeks, Armenians, Venetians, all of us who live in this city are bound by the irrefutable fact that we are Istanbulis and'—he laughed a little, his eyes flashing just briefly in the direction of Avram Avedykian—'as such, we are not known for our dedication to simple living.'

Krikor shrugged. 'All large cities are, by virtue of the variety of pursuits available within them, wicked.'

'Ah, but don't you think that our city is so much more so?' Ersoy paused briefly to light and puff upon his cigar.

'Well...'

'I mean,' Ersoy continued with much enthusiasm, 'we have such a marvellous history of it, do we not?' Then warming still further to his subject, 'For example, just take one Byzantine ruler as a template. Theodora. What was the mighty Empress Theodora?'

Father Nicos rather obviously cleared his throat.

Smiling, Ersoy reached out to touch the cleric's hand in a gesture of reassurance. 'Yes, I know that you old Phanars are immensely sentimental about your emperors, Nicos, but in reality you must know what Theodora did?'

'Yes, well...'

'She was a tart! Or at least that was how she started out.' Then Ersoy elaborated quietly so the servants would not hear: 'She was selling her body when she was still a child and, so rumour of the time has it, was capable of taking on multiple lovers in a variety of orifices. She was also, and this is pertinent to what I have been saying, most enthusiastic about her work.'

'Your point being?' Krikor asked.

'My point is that be it sex or drugs or food or whatever, the average Istanbuli is utterly devoted to his or her chosen vice and so to change that—'

'Is not—or should not—the pursuit of purity be the goal of a civilised and evolving society?' Arto Sarkissian offered. 'Vices like drug addiction, like the selling of sex, can and do breed disease and, as a man of science, I have to believe that disorder and disease run quite counter to the survival of our species.'

'In your medical sense, I suppose I can see that,' Ersoy said with a smile, 'but from a historical point of view your argument is somewhat spurious, Arto. We have always absolutely wallowed in vice here in the city. The Sultan Ibrahim, if you recall, was addicted to murder and would routinely kill passing subjects from his eyrie in the Topkapı Palace. Most of our sultans in the last century were addled with drink and the only one who wasn't—'

'Old Baba Hamid,' put in Ikmen, sourly. He knew the story of this particular despot well.

'As you say, Inspector, Abdul Hamid, the Damned,' Ersoy said. 'He was quite inordinately devoted to power which was why, my dear Çetin, he incarcerated his again drink-addled older brother Murad in the Cirağan Palace for twenty or whatever it was years. We've always been ruled and guided by the weak and vice-ridden and we are still here and will continue to thrive. In a sense vice is what we know, what we are comfortable with.'

'So,' Krikor Sarkissian said, not without some ire in his voice, 'what you are saying is that what I am attempting to do with the development of the centre plus all the good work and money that you have all put in is utterly pointless.'

Ersoy's bright red fez vibrated in time with his laughter. 'No, not at all, Krikor. And if I caused offence to you I apologise. I merely wished to point out, and this is only my view, that the task you have set yourself is a very difficult one.'

'I know that,' Krikor replied.

There was a slight atmosphere of unease in the room now. It was well known that Krikor Sarkissian was utterly devoted to his drugs project and to have its value called into question, before it had even been built, was not really what any of the men around the table wanted to hear. Muhammed Ersoy being, like a lot of very wealthy people, a law unto himself did however have to push his point just that little bit further. In order to do this he engaged the services of Çetin Ikmen.

'You deal with crime on a daily basis, Inspector,' he said, turning to the small, heavily smoking policeman. 'What do you think?'

'About vice?' Ikmen asked.

'About addiction in all its myriad forms. Do you think, as I do, that it is an essential and almost genetic part of the Istanbulis' psyche?'

The Inspector took in a deep breath before replying. 'I don't know, sir. Having only ever worked here, I have no other cities or countries with which to compare. What I do know, however, is that where these things exist, violence and sometimes even death can and do follow.'

'You're saying that vice, addiction and suchlike breed the homicides that you investigate?'

'In a significant number of cases, yes.'

'And is that so with regard to the case that you are working on now?' Ersoy's eyes twinkled mischievously as he asked.

Before Ikmen answered, Avram Avedykian cleared his throat in a very obviously embarrassed fashion.

'I can't, as you well know, Mr Ersoy, say anything about any of my current cases,' Ikmen replied.

Ersoy dropped his beautiful gaze in mock humility. 'Oh, yes, but of course. I apologise yet again. But—'

'You will be able to glean all the details that the public are permitted to have in tomorrow's newspapers,' Ikmen continued, 'together with an artist's impression of the victim.'

'Oh, how interesting!' Ersoy exclaimed, 'And is it—'

'Muhammed!'

Ersoy turned quickly and, or so Ikmen thought, angrily to face his partner whose face looked a little strained.

'Yes, Avram,' Ersoy said in a tone of only just controlled annoyance, 'what do you wish to add to this?'

'You said earlier that you had a surprise for us. Don't you think...?'

'Oh, yes! Yes, of course!' Then, clicking his fingers in the direction of one of his waiting servants, he said, 'Yıldırım, would you please bring the artefact?'

'Yes, sir,' the menial murmured and, with a small bow to his master, left the room.

'You're all going to just love this!' Ersoy exclaimed, positively oozing enthusiasm.

As the men waited for the arrival of Ersoy's surprise the party broke into small and subdued conversational groups. Ikmen, who was seated beside Arto Sarkissian, turned to his friend and in a voice even lower than the other guests said, 'Mr Ersoy possesses some rather challenging views, doesn't he?'

Arto Sarkissian smiled. 'Muhammed is somewhat eccentric, but then he is related—if distantly—to the former royal family.'

'How so?'

'His great-grandfather, General Damad Ferid, was married to one of the Sultan's daughters.'

'Which sultan?'

Arto thought for a moment and then said, 'I've a feeling Krikor said it might have been Murad.'

'Crazy Murad in Ciragan?'

'Yes, although I don't suppose that his daughter was mad or "drink-addled" too, and anyway the old general was quite howling enough for both of them.' Moving still closer to his friend, he whispered, 'Damad Ferid was one of those who was in charge of directing the campaign against the Arabs in the 1914–18 war.'

'Which we lost.'

'Yes, and that was due partly at least to the fact that the Ottoman troops were led by cruel and clueless aristocrats like Ferid. Muhammed is quite restrained in comparison to his forebears. Both his father and his stepmother committed suicide some years—' He stopped, his eyes widening. 'Will you look at that,' he said, pointing towards the top of the table.

Ikmen duly looked up and he too was both amazed and dazzled by what he saw. On the place-setting in front of Ersoy was a large and seemingly golden samovar, its front and sides moulded into shapes representing large, ripe fruit.

A murmur of appreciation went up from the assembled company. Ersoy acknowledged this with a bow of the head and then, standing up, he tapped his fork on the table in order to call for silence.

'Gentlemen, if I may have your attention...' Putting his hand on top of the samovar he turned towards Krikor Sarkissian and smiled. 'I should like to donate this samovar to your project, Krikor, if I may. It is solid gold and should fetch a good price. I've had it for many years and used it with pleasure. But now I would like you to have it.'

'Oh, but, Muhammed,' Krikor exclaimed, obviously

embarrassed at this theatrical if generous show of largess, 'you can't possibly give us something so valuable.'

Ersoy held up one hand in order to silence him. 'Please, Krikor, it is nothing. You need funds, I have funds and besides'— he stroked the side of the article and smiled, a little sadly— 'what use can an old man like me have for such a thing?'

Father Nicos, who was probably around seventy, laughed. 'Old? Muhammed you—'

'My dear little man,' Ersoy said with more than just a hint of patronage in his voice, 'I was forty earlier this week. Before the advent of modern medicine people rarely lived beyond the age of forty. Almost all of the pharaohs died before they achieved that age. It is the biological first call to an appointment with the grave. Why on earth do you think that women rarely produce after forty? And'—here he smiled broadly—'why, further, do you think that they are really quite hideous to us after that time?'

Several of the men, including most significantly the divorce lawyer, Murad, laughed heartily in agreement.

Ikmen however, did not laugh.

'And so,' Ersoy continued, 'I do hope that you will accept this gift, Krikor. You will, I know, use the money that it brings wisely.'

'Well,' Krikor Sarkissian began, 'what can I say? Of course I will accept, but how I will ever thank—'

'Use it well and you will have thanked me enough,' Ersoy said and made to sit down. Before he did however, he added one more point which he seemed to be addressing to Arto Sarkissian. 'Oh, and in case prospective buyers are interested in its history, this samovar, you can tell them, was purchased by my late father from one of our impoverished princelings. The man claimed, so my father said, that it came from the Kafes apartment of his palace and...'

The sound of cutlery smashing down into porcelain put a premature end to Ersoy's exposition. The offender who, it turned out, was the rather heavily inebriated Avedykian, looked up briefly and then muttered an embarrassed, 'Sorry.'

A thin smile played around Ersoy's lips as he gave Avedykian's shoulder the lightest of touches. 'Perhaps now would be a good time to switch to water,' he said and then, turning to the other members of the party, he declaimed, 'Anyway, whatever it is and wherever it comes from you are most welcome to my samovar, Krikor. And now'—he clapped his hands dramatically and then sat down—'let us get back to the serious business of eating.'

As one of the servants moved the samovar to a safe place behind its new owner, fresh and exciting dishes started to arrive at the table. When he thought that the conversational noise had reached a level sufficient to cover his words, Ikmen turned to Arto Sarkissian again.

'What is a Kafes apartment?' he said, hoping that nobody in the immediate vicinity could hear.

'Oh, Çetin!' his friend exclaimed. 'Don't you know?'

'Would I be asking you if I did?'

Arto Sarkissian groaned. 'Well, it's the place where the old Ottomans used to place their rivals in order to keep them out of the way. The sultans used to put their younger brothers in the Kafes so that they wouldn't be a threat.'

'So it was...'

'It was a sealed apartment containing all the things—food, women, drink—that would please the "extra" princes until such time as the sultan died or there was a palace coup. It replaced the earlier, more barbaric custom of fratricide, although that is a moot point because, as you can imagine, when a prince came out of the Kafes after God knows how many years of incarceration, he was not much good for anything, much less high office. There's a Kafes in the Topkapı, you must—'

'Arto,' Ikmen said slowly and thoughtfully, 'is this scenario not reflecting other, more recent events in our lives?'

'No.' But then knowing his friend as he did, Arto Sarkissian suspected that perhaps it should. 'Why?'

'Our boy was sealed up in an apartment that was not unpleasant, wasn't he?'

Arto Sarkissian sighed heavily. 'Yes, possibly, but...Oh, come on, Çetin! All this Kafes thing happened a long time ago!'

'True. Yes.' But then Ikmen's grave expression disappeared as quickly as it had arrived. 'It was just a thought. Just a—I suppose you'd call it a disturbing little connection.'

'But hardly pertinent, Çetin. This is the twentieth century.'

'Yes, but our boy's soft hands and—'

'From my point of view, Inspector,' his friend said, looking down at the small dressed quail that had just arrived in front of him, 'I'm going to start getting some advice about brain damage. Hands like that are rare outside that group and this being Turkey it is still possible that those who cared for the boy did not register him. Some people can be very ashamed of such things. I've been giving it some thought tonight and it could be that either a sympathetic or acquisitive doctor may have been supplying the pethidine to keep the boy quiet. Such patients are notoriously agitated.'

'But it wasn't the pethidine that killed him.'

'No, Çetin, I don't know who killed him or why he was killed. That is your job. What I do however know is that the boy was not being kept in a Kafes and, quite honestly, I think that the notion is eccentric even by your standards. Kafes implies, remember, vast amounts of time spent in one place and we don't, as yet, have a clue as to how much or how little time the boy had spent in that room. I must remember to keep you away from Muhammed in the future, he's had a very bad effect upon your reason.'

Ikmen looked briefly around the room and then inclined his head in agreement. 'Probably, but with all this luxury and—'

'Can we eat now?' his friend asked tetchily. 'And not talk about any of this again until we are back at work?'

'OK.'

But when he started to address the meal again, Çetin Ikmen realised that he didn't really have much of an appetite. The quail's poor naked little body looked just too close to how it had been in life, which repelled him. Ikmen pushed the tiny body uninterestedly around his plate and then, with very bad form, lit another cigarette.

# 8

THE ONLY TWO men who were not fishing off the side of the Galata Bridge appeared to be rather enjoying the bright if cold morning. To their left rose the old districts of Sultan Ahmet, Beyazıt and Eminönü; their gigantic imperial mosques glinted, against the unseasonable blue sky. To their right Beyoğlu and Galata were already frantically at work, their close-packed thousands making their daily crust in either legal or nefarious ways. All this, together with the busy waterways both before and behind the bridge made for a most invigorating and interesting scene—one that would naturally give two friends reason to pause.

Not that these two were friends. On closer inspection it was apparent that the notion was, if not impossible, certainly rather unlikely. The younger and taller man was both handsome and well groomed, in his fashionable and flattering camel-coloured overcoat. By contrast the older man, whose wild grey hair stuck out at unplanned angles from underneath his woollen cap, not only looked but indeed was really very dirty. As if to emphasise this point, as the younger man began to speak, the older one rubbed the ash from his homemade cigarette into the thigh area of his rumpled trousers.

'I'm looking for someone who sells something called pethidine,' Mehmet Suleyman asked his companion.

The man, whose voice was thick with the guttural tones of the Georgian race, said, 'What's that?'

'It's an opiate like heroin. I know no more than that.'

'Never heard of it,' the man replied. 'I can put you in touch with some very considerable Lebanese gold.'

Suleyman flicked his head backwards to indicate his lack of interest.

'No. I want pethidine, nothing else. Will you run it by a few people?'

'Well, I can do, but—'

'Pens! Pens! New and working ballpoint pens!' A tiny, gnarled old man pushed one malodorous hand containing three or four chewed-looking pens right up into Suleyman's face.

'Pen, effendi?' he said. 'Nice new pen for your office?'

Allowing just the ghost of a smile to waver across his lips, Suleyman reached inside his coat, took out his wallet and placed one crisp, new note into the man's hands. In return he received what was probably the least awful of the group of pens plus some very embarrassing thanks and prayers for his eternal good health.

When the old one had gone, Suleyman continued, while the other man looked and smoked out to sea. 'Pethidine can easily be tracked down in hospitals.'

'Then perhaps you should try looking for it there then, Mr Suleyman.'

'I understand, Mr Djugashvilli, that some people in the line of business practised by your associates do sometimes liaise with elements within the medical profession. Doctors of, shall we say, rather dubious morality?'

The man, Mr Djugashvilli, at least on this occasion, drew his breath in sharply. 'Oh, I think you'll find that's a bit outside my line of work, Mr Suleyman. I can of course, for a consideration, find out who might have interests in that direction.'

Suleyman smiled. 'And I could interest my friends in vice in those two extraordinary girls you've got working out of Ayvansaray.'

Mr Djugashvilli scowled. 'Understood.'

'So I can leave that with you then, can I, Mr Djugashvilli?'

'You can,' he replied wearily. 'Mind you, I could get the girls to do you a free—'

'I don't think so,' said Suleyman, now minutely examining his fingernails.

'I'll see you around then, Mr Suleyman,' Djugashvilli said, pushing himself away from the side of the bridge and moving off into the hurrying crowds.

'Goodbye, Mr Djugashvilli,' Suleyman said as the man disappeared.

Strictly speaking, Suleyman should, now that this exchange was at an end, have returned immediately to his office. But it was such a lovely sparkling morning that he was loath to do so. Besides there was a lot that he had to think about now, much of it confusing and, quiet though his office usually was, the atmosphere at the station as a whole was not really conducive to considering deeply troubling issues.

As he watched a ferry pull up to the Princes Islands pier, he started to make a short inventory of his current concerns. Firstly there was the pethidine. The discovery that this had been the drug of choice of their murder victim, and not heroin as expected, had come as something of a shock. Ikmen, he felt, had not really fully understood what this meant when Dr Sarkissian had told them the previous afternoon. Despite the doctor's entreaties to the contrary, the 'old man' kept on insisting that anything and everything of a narcotic nature could be considered a street drug. And in part he was right: anything could be abused. But because pethidine was a synthetic drug designed specifically for medical application, its street use, if it happened at all, would be of a rather specialised nature. Suleyman reasoned that pushing it must have some sort of connection with doctors and/or hospitals—hence his meeting with the odious Mr Djugashvilli.

It was odd, though, that Ikmen had been so dense on this subject. He was usually very quick to grasp the significance of things. But then, in his defence, yesterday had not been a good day for Ikmen—or for Suleyman himself come to that. He looked down briefly at his elegantly gloved hands and then shook his head in disbelief. What on earth had possessed him to become so brutal with that lunatic, poor old Vladimir Ilyich Lenin? Of course he knew the answer to that question as every other officer in the station probably did by this time—the presence of Cohen at any event being rather more effective than broadcasting information on the television news. And after all that fine work he'd put in to conceal his lust for Sergeant Farsakoğlu too! No one would have, could have guessed—until now. He'd even threatened Cohen when he'd told him how everybody was laughing because Farsakoğlu had the 'hots' for him. Part of his anger had, of course, been motivated by terror. That she desired him had never occurred to him and, if the truth be known, that knowledge really rather alarmed him. While Farsakoğlu had been just a distant and impossible fantasy, he had felt quite safe within his own private lust. But now? How was he ever going to be able to look her in the face again? And, more importantly, what was he going to write on his incident report about the Vladimir Ilyich Lenin incident?

'Enjoying the sunshine?' a familiar voice asked.

Turning, Suleyman found himself looking into the inexpertly shaven face of his superior. 'Hello, sir,' he said, 'I didn't expect to see you here.'

Ikmen shrugged. 'I tried settling down in the office, but my hangover was so bad I had to get some air.' He lit a cigarette. 'So why are you here?'

'I've been putting the word around about pethidine with one of our Black Sea friends actually, as you suggested.'

'Oh.'

A moment of uncharacteristically awkward silence passed between them until Ikmen finally said, 'I was at Dr Krikor's project meeting last night. I got a bit smashed.'

'Oh. Right.'

'Arto did however take some time to explain the pethidine thing further to me. And...well I suppose that putting the word out on the street won't do any harm. I do now think though that the possibility of its being on the street, in the conventional way, is slim. But well done anyway for getting on to it so quickly and...You have, I take it, related its use to doctors, hospitals and...'

'Yes.'

It was the closest Suleyman knew his boss was going to get to acknowledging that he was doing the right thing. He was not surprised, however, when Ikmen completely changed the subject. 'He, Arto that is, is looking into the possibility of our boy being brain damaged.'

Suleyman frowned. 'How? Why?'

Ikmen shrugged. 'It's complicated. He's coming over later today. I'll ask him to explain it to you himself.'

It was not like Ikmen to put anything off until later; it indicated to his deputy that there were still issues from the previous day that needed addressing.

'Look, sir, I—' he began.

'In the meantime, Suleyman,' Ikmen interrupted, 'I have a little confession to make to you.'

'Sir?'

Ikmen smiled and, thankfully, with some of his old familiar warmth. 'I didn't just come down here to get some relief for my hangover.'

'No?'

'No.' He reached into the pocket of his thin summer-weight jacket and pulled out a small and rather elegant box. 'I came here to think about this too,' he said and, taking the lid off the box, revealed a crystal miniature.

'Another one?' Suleyman said.

'Yes.' Ikmen slipped two thin fingers into the box and pulled the model out. 'And what do you think that it is?' he asked, holding the thing up to the glittering morning light.

Suleyman squinted. 'It's the Topkapı dagger, isn't it? From the imperial treasury?'

'Yes,' Ikmen replied, 'and together with the little bird-cage that started my unlooked-for collection, I do believe a picture may be beginning to form.'

'How so?'

'Well, the dagger comes from the museum, doesn't it? And there is also a cage there too.'

'You mean the Kafes?'

'Yes.'

Suleyman looked doubtful. 'That's rather a tenuous connection, isn't it, sir?'

'The subject of the Kafes came up, quite by chance, at the dinner I attended last night. I pointed out to Dr Sarkissian that there were some similarities between that old custom and the way in which our boy was incarcerated and, indeed, in the way that he died, by ligature or bowstring as the old Ottomans called the cord they would insist upon strangling their betters with. The doctor told me, of course, that I was quite mad, but...unless I am very much mistaken, someone may be pointing us in the direction of the museum. Now whether that is because the perpetrator is actually connected to the museum or whether it is just to point out the connection with this Kafes phenomenon, I don't know.'

Suleyman turned back round to look at the shining surface of the Bosporus and bit his lip. 'Kafes would imply that someone held the boy for a long period of time and we don't know whether that is so. He may have been just one in a succession of lads who...Have you managed to speak to your connections in the...' He suddenly looked awkward, almost embarrassed. 'You know, the men who...'

'The kiddie-fiddlers? No, not yet, Suleyman. That could well be my task for today actually. I must also start checking up on outlets for this crystalware too.' He paused, deep in thought. 'Perhaps I'll delegate that.' But I do also want some action on the museum which I would like you to take charge of. Take five or six officers and get over there as soon as you can.'

'And do what exactly, sir?'

Ikmen started to look exasperated, but then his features softened into a smile. Suleyman was quite right, it was all a bit tenuous. 'Find out who works there, where they live and what they do. Look specifically at people employed in the harem complex. The director is a very accommodating soul, he'll help you. Oh, and see if any of these people are known to care for sick or disabled relatives.'

'Why?'

'Think of it as a favour to Dr Sarkissian.'

'Oh. OK.'

Ikmen looked at his watch and then sighed. 'We must

get on,' he said, 'or time will get the better of us. Not that it makes a lot of difference to me.'

'Why?'

He laughed, but without much mirth, before replying. 'Because, Suleyman,' he said, 'our host last night was of the opinion that anybody over the age of forty should really be dead anyway.'

Suleyman looked shocked. 'But that's absurd!'

'Not,' said Ikmen, waving a cautionary finger at his deputy, 'if you look at it in Darwinian terms.'

'Eh?'

'Oh, don't worry about it, Suleyman,' Ikmen sighed, 'it's really not that important.'

The boy's face, even with the eyes closed and despite the slight plumpness around the jawline, was quite beautiful. Mrs Taşkiran may be, in Arto Sarkissian's opinion, as mad as a sackful of bats, but she could certainly sketch far more expertly than anyone he had come across before. Under her skilful hand the boy looked quite compelling and really very distinctive too. It was quite amazing what even his trained eye could miss, like the small, pale but perfectly crescent-shaped little birthmark underneath his jaw. Arto thought, and he had to smile as he did so, that perhaps it was this little detail that, albeit unconsciously, Professor Mazmoulian had reacted to when he declared that the boy could not be Armenian. To be Armenian and branded as it were with the symbol of everything Turkish would indeed be unfortunate. Despite anything that he may say or even think to the contrary and even though his best friend in the entire world was a Turk, Arto knew that there was far too much blood between the two races for true peace ever to be declared. The forced marches of literally millions of his countrymen across Anatolia and into Syria during the cruel summer of 1915 had put paid to any true fellow feeling for ever. Not that he could ever mention such things—the Government was quite clear upon that subject: Armenian Massacres and all stories thereof were quite unfounded. And indeed even he had to admit that concrete evidence on the subject was scant, but...But then what was known was that some at least of his countrymen had given the Empire cause for concern at that time. Almost certainly some Armenian subjects of the old Ottoman Empire had colluded with the Russian co-religionist enemy. Again, if for different reasons, Arto Sarkissian could not mention this in a public place either. But then, not unlike this poor unknown boy, the doctor rather fell between two stools when it came to nationality. Although by blood and religion an Armenian, the Sarkissian family's lack of suffering in the past sometimes made things difficult for them within their small, select community. By virtue of wealth or connections or perhaps both, the Sarkissians had escaped the ravages of Ottoman wrath both during and after the Great War. Like, at the moment, this boy, it left Arto and his relatives in a place that was neither truly Armenian nor really Turkish. It left them, in effect, open to abuse from both sides. And even though he had promised Çetin Ikmen that he would speak to his community about the elusive Mr Zekiyan, he suspected that, known or not, murderer or not, they were very unlikely to tell him anything about the man even if they knew. Not wearing the sacred badge of past suffering was an offence for which few were readily forgiven.

Of all his acquaintances, only Avram Avedykian, whose family had been in much the same position as his own, could really understand. He too at times expressed doubts about where, or even if, he fitted into the grand scheme of things in this cosmopolitan but still essentially Turkish city. Just prior to his qualification as a doctor, he had been particularly worried about what people—Armenians and Turks, for different reasons—would make of an Armenian doctor working with almost exclusively Turkish patients. Krikor, Arto felt, had been quite unjustly hypercritical of the younger man's struggles—difficulties that had once been his own, and Arto's too for that matter. He made a mental note to call his younger friend soon and then, in an effort to distract himself from such morbid thoughts, turned the dead boy's sad picture aside in favour of the sports pages of his paper. It was then that his telephone rang.

He picked it up. 'Arto Sarkissian,' he announced into the receiver.

'Is that Dr Sarkissian?' a voice replied in English.

Quickly switching into what was his third language, Arto said, 'Yes. Who is this?'

The voice possessed one of those strange American accents that Arto understood to originate from the south of that country. 'My name is James Hunter, Dr Sarkissian. I work out of the German Hospital here in Istanbul. I was given your name by Dr Tercuman.'

'Ah, yes!' Arto acknowledged enthusiastically. 'You are the neurologist!'

'Yes I am.' The voice was relaxed, lazy even, and it oozed, as was so common with Americans, the sort of confidence other races could only dream about attaining. 'I understand,' the American continued, 'that you've got a little problem with a boy.'

'Yes. I suspect that perhaps he might have been brain damaged.'

He could hear the American smile in reply; he would have been prepared to swear to it. 'Well, bring him over and let me have a look then, Dr Sarkissian.'

There was obviously a misunderstanding here. 'Dr Hunter,' Arto said, 'you do understand, I hope, that the boy we are speaking of is dead.'

'Oh.'

'Dr Tercuman did not, I think, explain. I am a pathologist, Dr Hunter. My subject is dead.'

'So why do you want to know whether he has brain damage, Doctor? I mean, if he's dead...'

'It could be important to a current police investigation.'

'Oh, I see.' Hunter sighed heavily. 'Well, if you could bring him over to me here at—'

'But he is dead, Dr Hunter!' Arto reiterated. 'I would need to get permissions from all sorts of people in order to move him now.'

'Well, if you give his relatives a call and—'

'The boy is what you call a John Doe, Dr Hunter. He has no relatives. It will be very difficult. Could you not come here?'

'Well, that depends upon what type of equipment you've got there, Doctor. I mean I could probably do some surgical investigations over at your place, no problem. But if you want me to look at neurotransmitter levels or scan I suspect I'll have to do that here. Are there any obvious outward signs like Downs features?'

'Not Downs features, no. Some atrophy of the limbs and, for a subject of his age, his hands and feet are remarkably soft and unlined. You know in that way—'

'Appendages like that don't necessarily indicate brain damage, Doctor,' Hunter said with, Arto detected, a patronising note in his voice. 'There can be many reasons why

that may have happened. Lack of social and emotional stim-
ulus, or even just good old-fashioned idleness.'

'I would rather that you check him out anyway, Doctor.'

'You gotta feeling about it, yeah?'

'There are problems, yes.'

Hunter sighed heavily. 'OK then, Doctor. I'll come
along and have a look. But I'm not promising anything.'

'That is OK.'

'All right then. I'll get over to you at the end of my
shift. About five?'

'That would be very kind.'

'You're very welcome. I'll see you then.'

'Thank you and goodbye, Doctor,' Arto said. It wasn't
easy putting into words what he felt about his most recent
subject. Brain damage may or may not be the answer to that
nagging troubled feeling he had about the boy. It was, however, the closest he could come to elaborating his feelings of
'wrongness' about the whole thing. Even before the boy had
been murdered, perhaps even before he had first started taking or been given drugs, maybe right even from the very
beginning of his life, there had been something not quite right
about this boy. Perhaps it was simply because nobody, as yet,
knew who he was? But then he'd dealt with unknown bodies
tens of times before. This was the first time he had felt like this.
Could it be because of all the differing theories that people
were coming up with about the boy's identity? Again, this was
not unknown in cases like this. So what was different?

What was different was that everyone who expressed
an opinion was so sure that they were right. The evidence
gleaned so far seemed to suggest that the boy was Armenian and yet Professor Mazmoulian was certain that he was
not. To Mrs Taşkiran, he was a pampered aristocrat, definitely, but to Arto himself the idea that the boy was brain-

damaged or lacking in some way, would not go away. It was almost as if his cold, dead flesh had some way of making people perceive it in different ways, which was utterly absurd, except that...

Except that what they were all doing was trying to make sense of something mysterious, which was, after all, only human nature. And considering that each human being makes sense of the world in his or her own individual way it should only be natural that opinions differed. But he just couldn't believe that. For some reason it seemed more sensible to Arto Sarkissian to believe that the boy was closer to the blank slate of the infant than the fully rounded person possessed of nationality, class, religion and so on. And as a cipher he almost seemed to be consciously waiting for others to place an interpretation upon him.

Looking across at the door behind which he knew the body was stored, Arto Sarkissian shuddered. It wasn't that the boy's form was now emptied of soul or spirit or whatever, it was that it had never been full to start with.

Blind Attila was, almost uniquely amongst those with his disability, afforded neither help nor sympathy by those of his neighbours who really knew him. Admittedly, he was only blind in one eye and he did, even amongst the poorest classes in his native Beşiktaş, possess the reputation of existing in the filthiest set of rooms in the quarter, but neither fact was really why he was regularly treated with contempt. It was solely because Attila had served the kind of prison sentence that had extended from his youth right up until almost the present time. And considering that he was now seventy years old, it spoke volumes about the seriousness of the crime that he had committed.

As Ikmen entered the squalid little hovel that passed for Attila's sitting room, he fancied that just being there with the old man was tainting him in some way. But then that sort of disgust was standard, if not normal, around those who had sexually abused children. The fact that Attila's crime, the buggery of a twelve-year-old boy, had occurred when Ikmen himself was but a small child, did not detract from the odium in which his host was held.

'Can I make you a glass of tea, Mr Ikmen, or...' The old man moved in a bizarre fashion, shuffling nervously from foot to foot in a way that was not unlike the movements of those on psychiatric medication. Not, of course, that Attila, his little eyes sparkling with low cunning, was mentally ill in any way. Had he been so there would perhaps have been some sympathy for his plight. But Attila was as sane, if not more so considering he had spent so much of his life inside prison, as anyone on the street could hope to be.

Ikmen waved a dismissive hand in reply. 'No, thank you, Attila,' he said, 'this is not a social call.'

'Oh,' the old man replied. 'So...'

In an effort to limit the amount of time he spent in this man's company, Ikmen came straight to the point. 'I need to know, Attila, whether any of your lot are into imprisonment. Whether anybody you know gets a particular kick out of holding kiddies hostage, boys that is.'

Attila looked down at the floor before murmuring. 'Oh, I don't associate with any of that kind any more, Mr Ikmen. I have learned my lesson.'

'Which is why, I suppose,' Ikmen replied, 'you've been seen around and about with an innocent like Huseyn Akdeniz.' He put his finger up to his mouth in a gesture indicating deep thought. 'Now, how many little boys was it that he got to—'

'We met inside, Mr Ikmen, in Imrali, you know that.'

'Which is why you should know better than to associ-ate with him now that you're out, Attila.'

The old man lowered himself stiffly into one of the greasy armchairs. 'We don't do anything,' he said.

'Recalling past triumphs whilst having a convivial wank is not doing nothing, Attila.'

'We don't—'

'Look,' Ikmen said impatiently, 'just dispense with the poor old man shit and tell me what's going on in your perverted little community. I need to know who gets off on imprisonment and whether they're inclined to do it over long stretches—with the same child that is.'

'But I don't...'

Ikmen leaned menacingly over the front of the chair and stared deeply into the old man's rheumy eyes. 'Look, I know that you know everyone, Attila. You're famous for knowing everyone.'

'There's Lame Ali from Beyoğlu, but he's been inside for six months now. He kept a boy for six months once before he killed him—hammer blow to his head.'

'Yes, I remember that, vaguely,' Ikmen replied. 'Now tell me about people I don't know, Attila, people on the outside, in the open as it were. Active. Out of prison, free—in the place where you are now provided you act nice and tell me everything I need to know.'

'Well...'

'Yes?'

Outside, on the street, the midday call to prayer started its sensuous, high-pitched entreaty.

'You'd better tell me the truth,' Ikmen said, pointing at the old man's nicotine-stained windows. 'The route back to Imrali is very short and Allah is listening.'

'Well, it's just a rumour,' the old man started, 'but...'

'But what, Attila?'

The old man looked around before he spoke as if he were checking that they were not being overheard. 'I don't know who, you understand, Mr Ikmen, but there is apparently some action around a crippled lad in Sultan Ahmet. He's not imprisoned as such but he's kept quiet with drugs, that's usual, and—'

'Usual to keep lads quiet with drugs? What drugs?'

Attila shrugged. 'I don't know, Mr Ikmen, but drugs have been used like this for some time—or so I've heard since I've been out and...anyway, it's Sultan Ahmet. They say it's the boy's brother, you know, who—'

'Where in Sultan Ahmet? Do you know?' Ikmen felt his skin freeze as he said the name of the district, every sense on the alert to what the old man had to say.

'Oh, I don't know where he is, Mr Ikmen,' the old man replied, licking his lips in a repellent fashion as he spoke. 'But the word is that if you go and stand beside the Gate of Felicity in the Topkapı Museum just before it closes—'

'Have you been?' He placed his hands heavily on Attila's shoulders as if he were about to shake him. 'Have you seen—'

'Oh, no, Mr Ikmen, no!' the old man said, bringing his own hands up towards Ikmen's, fear streaming from his wide-open eyes. 'No, I have never been, I assure you! All I know is what I tell you! You go and stand at the Gate of Felicity until the brother comes and—'

'How will this brother recognise you?'

'Oh, he will know one of us, Mr Ikmen,' the old man said and then, turning his eyes down to the floor again, 'we are, as you can see, the most pathetic and sad little creatures in Allah's garden of humanity.'

'All right! All right!' Ikmen pushed himself away

from the old man's chair and then took something small and, to Attila, unrecognisable out of his jacket pocket. 'If Suleyman is already at that museum, I'll...' Ikmen held the mobile telephone up to the light and, with a somewhat tense expression on his face, punched in a number and then waited for the thing to ring.

'Oh, it's one of those—' the old man began.

'Shut up, Attila!' Ikmen snapped, realising that the silence he was currently experiencing was due to the fact that he had not pressed the 'send' button. 'Fuck it!' he added as he pushed the button home and then, the tone now active, his face relaxed just a little.

As it buzzed loudly in his ear, Ikmen turned away from the old man and moved a little closer to the window. Reception was supposed to be better there.

'Suleyman,' said a crackly voice at the other end of the line.

'Are you at the museum yet?' Ikmen asked, his voice strained with tension.

'No, I'm just—'

'Well, don't go, do you hear?'

'Why, sir?'

'There's been a development,' Ikmen said. 'Just stay where you are until I come.'

'Oh. OK. Can—'

'I'll be with you as soon as I can, Suleyman. Stay where you are! OK?'

'Right.'

Ikmen pressed the 'call end' button and then turned to face the old man in the chair. His eyes were, strangely Attila thought, really rather full of merriment.

'So, Attila,' he said as he moved back across the room, brushing from time to time against some unpleasant item of furniture, 'you think that your lot look a bit different to the rest of us, do you?'

'Yes, I do, Mr Ikmen, but...'

'But?' Ikmen, his eyes wide with innocence, shrugged, as if inviting further questions from the old man. 'But what, Attila?'

'But...I mean, I...Do you want...'

Ikmen smiled and then, leaning over the old man, said, 'Yes, I want, Attila. I want you to come back with me to the station.'

The old man's face turned a most alarming shade of grey and he clutched his chest, which would have been quite worrying for Ikmen had the latter not been so totally contemptuous of his host. 'Ah...'

'Not that you'll stay there for very long, Attila.' Ikmen smiled very broadly and added, 'Just long enough for us to brief you about what we want you to do up at the museum this evening, beside the Gate of Felicity.'

❋ ❋ ❋

She had, she estimated, been staring through the grille into that cell for a full ten minutes before the man inside so much as blinked. Usually prisoners would occasionally get up and walk around like caged beasts or, at the very least, utter some oath or shuffle about petulantly on their beds from time to time. Such statue-like immobility was both unusual and unsettling in the extreme.

Turning to the rather nervous-looking duty constable, she said, 'What did you say the doctor gave this man?'

'I don't think that you're supposed to be here, Sergeant,' he answered guardedly, 'not before he comes up in court.'

'Yes, I know that!' Farsakoğlu replied somewhat tetchily. 'But I'm interested. What...'

She didn't finish her sentence, but not because of the unhelpful attitude of the constable. A very familiar, sometimes even dreamed about figure was walking down the corridor towards her and, as he got closer, Sergeant Suleyman's face resolved into the same mask of embarrassment as her own.

'Oh, Sergeant Farsakoğlu,' he said as he drew level with her, 'what, er...'

'I was just...' She stumbled and then, unable to speak further, inclined her head in the direction of the cell. 'The prisoner?'

'Lenin.'

'Yes.'

'Yes.' He looked down at his shoes, but not before he had noticed the smirk that was building on the constable's face. 'You know, Sergeant, that you're not supposed to—'

'Yes,' she said, also now looking down at the ground. 'I—'

'Actually, neither of you is supposed to be here,' interrupted the duty constable, projecting just about as much authority as he could have hoped to muster—until he muttered 'sirs' apologetically at the end.

Suleyman smiled. 'Of course, you're right, Constable.' Then, turning back to Farsakoğlu, he motioned her forwards with his hand. 'I think we'd better...'

'Yes,' she agreed and with one last not particularly forgiving look at the constable she made her way towards the stairs.

In an effort to appear as normal as possible Suleyman asked his companion about the prisoner.

'Well, he's very quiet,' she replied, her face showing obvious signs of inner conflict. 'He's rather like a stone, in fact, completely unmoving and silent.'

'It bothers you, doesn't it?'

Just before she reached the stairs she turned to face him. 'Yes. He's obviously very ill, like the inspector said. I mean if he wasn't the doctor wouldn't have given him so many drugs.'

'We, or perhaps more accurately, I did a very bad thing treating him like that,' Suleyman said, his head hanging low across his collar-bones.

'You didn't have a lot of choice though, did you?' the woman replied by way of mollification. 'He really meant business with me.'

'I went too far. It was totally unprofessional.'

'But you were afraid, weren't you? I mean for...' and then realising that she had gone too far she just muttered the last word under her breath, 'me.'

Suleyman's response to this was to raise his head again and sniff very obviously. 'Yes, although not in the way that others might interpret such an act, not romantically or... As a colleague, I was afraid for you. I would have done the same for any colleague.'

'Yes.' The disappointment in her voice was so marked that all he could do by way of response was to remain completely silent. To do or say anything else would have been far too dangerous.

Luckily, however, the mood changed considerably as they both started to move upstairs, for Ikmen appeared on the top landing.

'Is that you down there, Suleyman?' he called.

'Yes, sir.'

The relief with which he responded must have been so evident that Ikmen caught on to it immediately.

'Are you all right, Suleyman?'

'Yes.'

Farsakoğlu, who was walking ahead of Suleyman, came into Ikmen's view first—a sight which elicited a small 'Oh' from the man above.

'Sergeant Suleyman is just behind me, sir,' she said in a voice that sounded both tired and vaguely tetchy too.

'Good.' Then, when he saw Suleyman, Ikmen smiled and said, 'I've got some real treats in store for you, Suleyman.'

'Oh, yes?' Suleyman looked up and, seeing his superior's evilly grinning face, smiled. 'Anything to do with cancelling my museum investigation?'

'Everything to do with that, Suleyman,' Ikmen said, 'plus a kiddie-fiddler in Interview Room Three.'

'Oh! What...'

'Now don't you turn up your nose at this, Suleyman,' Ikmen cautioned. 'Old blind Attila may yet solve this case for us so you just hold your prejudices close to your chest for now.'

Level now with his boss, Suleyman looked down at the shining if bloodshot eyes of Ikmen and then moved his head slowly from side to side. 'But a kiddie—'

'I know I said that I wouldn't expose you to one of his kind, Suleyman, but this could really be something here. This—'

'You have a lead of some sort on the unknown boy?' Farsakoğlu interrupted.

'Yes we do, or rather we may do, Farsakoğlu,' Ikmen replied. 'One that both you and Suleyman are going to have to help me to explore.'

Dr James Hunter was, sadly, just as Arto Sarkissian had imagined him to be. Tall, blond and muscular, he dressed in the same confident but casual way that he spoke, which was in stark contrast to Arto's own besuited state. Not that he wasn't a pleasant man, he was; and furthermore, the deeper he and Arto delved into the ramifications of what or what not might be the dead boy's condition, the more the Armenian was impressed by Hunter's obvious enthusiasm for his subject. It was just that medicine practised by a man with this sort of relaxed image was very rare within the confines of the rather conservative Turkish medical establishment. Doctors still dressed and behaved very much as doctors had always done and were meant to do; this 'doctor as friend' or even equal kind of approach was something that was completely outside Arto's experience.

As they both leaned across the trolley upon which the boy's body lay, Hunter, his brow creased in deep concentration, muttered a short 'mmm'.

'Beyond the atrophy and the smoothness of the hands and feet there are no outward signs that point in either direction,' Arto said.

'The limbs may be withered but they're not twisted,' Hunter replied, 'which would rule out cerebral palsy.' He looked up and smiled mischievously, 'That, Doctor, would be one of the usual suspects vis-à-vis brain damage.'

'OK.'

'The problem is,' Hunter continued, 'that now the boy is dead even if I were to examine his brain in detail we might still be left without any firm conclusion.'

'How so?'

Hunter straightened up to a height that was so far above that of his colleague that Arto had to strain to look into his face.

'Well, just say for argument that I found no neurological signs of brain damage in this subject's nervous system.'

'Yes?'

'What would that tell us, do you think, about the status of his brain?'

Arto thought for a moment, feeling like a schoolboy: disadvantaged and frightened of saying the 'wrong' thing. 'Well...'

'It would or could,' Hunter said, smiling in his rather flashy and vulgarly confident way, 'mean absolutely nothing at all. Some conditions like Tuberous sclerosis show no specific structural defects in the brain tissue at all. People can and do have it but, *post mortem*, it is almost impossible to detect.'

'So what you are saying is...'

'What I'm saying, Doctor, is that I could do all the tests under the sun on your kid here, but unless something very obvious like CP were to show up, I couldn't make a safe diagnosis either way with regard to brain damage.' He bent down again and gently picked up one thin, white limb. 'This could be social in origin, know what I mean?'

Arto shrugged. In theory he knew what Hunter was getting at, but...

'I read a report of a guy in Las Vegas had limbs like this. He belonged to some nutso religious cult that never went outside their house. Mind you, he weighed nearly five hundred pounds so...Do you have any background on this kid?'

'We found him in what had been a locked apartment at the top of a house in Sultan Ahmet. As I told you before, he was full of pethidine, which he had been taking or which another had been giving him for some long time. Cause of death was strangulation which had occurred the day before we found him. Quite how long he had been in the apartment, we do not know, but the investigating officer thinks it may have been some time. There is no sexual evidence but—'

'Could be a Genie.'

Arto frowned. 'A what?'

'Of necessity I had to study some psychology when I was training. A little girl called Genie was used as a classic case of deprivation. Basically this child, who was discovered in the seventies when she was thirteen, had been hidden in a back bedroom since she was a toddler. Her father, who was completely wacko, tied her to a chair, hit her if she cried, stuff like that. Whether she was ever normal, we will probably never know, mainly because of the paucity of language she has managed to develop since.'

'Were there any physical symptoms also?'

'Atrophy, like this; probably some other stuff too but we only ever touched on the subject briefly.'

Arto Sarkissian thought for a moment, his fingers resting lightly upon his lips. 'By other stuff you mean...'

'Vitamin D deficiency due to lack of sunlight which may precipitate rickets. Pressure sores due to long periods spent tied or held in some way to a bed or chair...'

'But my boy doesn't have either of those signs,' Arto said, looking once again at the prone body upon the slab.

'True,' the American conceded, 'although I guess if the narcotic strait jacket were strong enough he could move around a little without actually being able to get anywhere which could account for the lack of bedsores. But then all this is just speculation, Doctor, your boy may or may not be a Genie. I simply brought the subject up in order to illustrate just how many possibilities there are in a case like this. Brain damage is just one of them.'

'I see.'

'Have you tested for Hep B?'

Arto frowned. 'Pardon?'

'Hepatitis B, have you tested for that?'

'No.'

Hunter shrugged. 'Might not be a bad idea. In my experience it could point in two directions in this case. One it could indicate that his pethidine was administered amateurly, on the street, although I've never actually heard of it on the street myself. And two it could mean, seeing as you don't know who the kid is, that he might once have been in institutional care, like a mental asylum or something.'

'One I can understand,' Arto replied, 'but two?'

Hunter smiled his knowing casual grin once again. 'In places like that, Doctor, they all fuck each other, those that aren't impotent that is.'

Arto felt himself blush and, in order to hide his embarrassment, looked down at the floor. 'Oh, I see.' Then, changing the subject quickly, he asked, 'And the smoothness of the hands and feet?'

'That can be a feature of particularly Downs subjects. In cases of deprivation it's also possible, but I wouldn't lend it too much credence or you might be accused of sorcery.'

Arto Sarkissian smiled. Yes, the old palmistry connection—compelling if too much on the margins of pure science.

'One thing it does tell us though,' Hunter added thoughtfully, 'is that it's unlikely, with hands and feet like this, that the boy lived on the street.'

'The pethidine evidence does make him an unusual addict,' Arto agreed.

'Yes,' said Hunter, 'and it does beg the question about where he obtained the drug and also why he doesn't appear to be vit. D deficient. Somebody who knows what he's doing. An educated druggist or graduate in pharmacology...'

'We have thought about doctors and medical staff,' Arto replied, feeling quite pleased that he was, at least this time, one step ahead of the American. However, all that ensued was a small but definitely unsettling silence.

'Not that anyone in our profession would do such a thing,' Hunter said, his face suddenly masked with seriousness.

'Oh, of course not, Doctor,' Arto agreed, a little taken aback by the sudden vehemence of his guest's tone. 'And it would not, of course, be very ethical of me to make inquiries in that direction, would it?'

'No,' said Hunter, 'it wouldn't. And if I were you, Doctor, I would just stick to your routine pathology work from now on and leave the police to deal with theories of this kind.'

The atmosphere in the room had now changed from that of companionable co-operation to one of almost hostility. 'Yes, but if I were just to start by attempting to trace a drug to an institution—' he began.

'I've told you what I think, Doctor,' Hunter said, 'and whether or not you pass that on to your police colleagues is up to you. But I'd leave it at that.'

'Ah.' Arto had come up against this 'all doctors together' kind of attitude before. Never before, however, had it been put so obviously to him. 'But...'

Hunter held up one warning and final hand. 'That is all I have to say on the subject, Doctor,' he said. 'You can expect my bill in about a week.' With that he turned on his heel and left the room.

# 9

THE GATE OF Felicity was the point where, during Otto-man times, those who were royalty or who were intimately connected with same parted company with those who were not thus blessed. It marks the start of the Inderun or inner part of the palace beyond which lie the Petition Room where the Ottoman Grand Viziers would consider requests from individuals for favours from the Sultan and the Treasury where the largess of the old Empire is still lovingly stored. It is therefore a place that is equally evocative of both the splendours and the cruelties and inequalities of absolute rule. It is also a place where large numbers of tourists are usually gathered. On this occasion, however, there was almost total silence in this area—a late afternoon in October not gener-ally being a busy time for any part of the Topkapı complex. Closing time had also just been announced.

However, beneath the great, soaring portal of the gate, standing directly under the huge gold and green tuğra or signature of the Sultan, one figure still remained. Small and stunted, it was a man of advanced years and, from the way that he shuffled his feet ceaselessly against the ground, either considerable nervousness or impatience too. With his stained and ill-fitting clothes he was unlikely to be a tourist, so it would have been reasonable to assume he was one of the great army of cleaners that periodically descend upon the palace. But assumptions can often be wrong: Blind Attila the paedophile was no innocent cleaner.

Not that Attila was actually about his usual perverted business. A young and seemingly innocent couple who were walking in the gardens in front of the Gate made certain of that. Although the aim of the exercise was to make the paedophile contact that Attila was hopefully going to meet here believe that the old man was indeed a 'customer', Sergeants Farsakoğlu and Suleyman were on hand to make sure that as soon as the location of the intended victim was discovered, the police and the police alone would take charge of whatever was found.

As the two younger people sat down on a wall some distance from where he was standing, the old man pulled his thin coat tightly about his shoulders and blew warm breath on to his cold, bare hands. He didn't know whether this strategy was going to work any more than the bastard who had bullied him into doing it. Ikmen! What a son of a whore! Were it not for him, Attila would be curled up comfortably in his chair now with a glass of tea in one hand and a magazine in the other, peering one-eyed at what he shouldn't. After all there was no proof that the rumour he had received about this supposed paedophile contact within the museum was true. Within the circle many stories about lush young things on offer abounded; some sprang from reality and others just from wishful thinking. But then he only had himself to blame for telling Ikmen in the first place. If only he hadn't allowed his fear of another prison sentence to open his big stupid mouth! He hadn't, after all, actually done anything wrong since he came out of prison. He'd thought about it on many occasions but...

'Good evening, Uncle.'

The old man turned until he found himself facing a short man in early middle age carrying a large yard broom.

'Good evening,' he replied, then, blowing on to his hands again, said, 'Cold.'

'Yes,' the other responded. 'You do know that we're closed now, don't you, Uncle?'

'Yes.'

'This means,' the man continued, as if speaking to one who was rather slow, 'that you should be making your way back towards the entrance.'

'Yes, I do know that,' Attila said, still not moving.

'Well, then...' The man gestured impatiently, urging the older one to shift himself.

'Um...'

'Listen, old man, I...'

'Er...'

Something between recognition and sudden dawning passed between the two men. It wasn't so much a meeting of minds as a change in the atmosphere around them. They both, simultaneously, knew. This was not a phenomenon that was unknown to Attila who, despite his years in prison, knew how the 'system' worked. The younger man, in response to this, first smiled a little and then leaned his yard broom against the side of the gate and put one hand up to his mouth. 'Ah.'

'Ah, indeed.'

'So you were waiting for...'

'You?' the old man asked.

The younger man's face then hardened rapidly. 'It'll cost a filthy old goat like you twenty million.'

'And if I wasn't a filthy old goat?' Attila asked.

The man simply shrugged in response, then added, obviously mindful of the young courting couple still lingering in the gardens, 'Just walk with me, like we're friends. I'll have your money when we get to the place, before, if you know what I mean.'

It would have been very easy and was indeed most tempting for Attila to ask at that point where the place was. But when one is wearing a hidden microphone under one's clothes one must be careful not to arouse suspicion. This man was a lot younger and stronger than Attila and, in addition, not the pleasantest person he had ever met. If he were clever, Attila could still guide his police masters to the intended destination and besides, the young officers would be following him for at least part of the way.

'Will I need to be thinking about getting a bus or dolmuş to where you—'

'No, we can walk,' the younger man said, then, sneering, added, 'provided you're up to it.'

'For what I want, I think I can make the effort,' Attila countered.

'Good,' his new companion replied, 'well, let's do it then.'

Attila smiled, but not with the full heart he would have put into this expression had this not been a police operation.

Ikmen had already smoked half a packet of cigarettes within the cramped and airless confines of his car. Not that he allowed this to prevent his lighting another when he heard that Attila and his new companion's destination was somewhere quite near to the museum. Constable Avcı, although a smoker himself, fanned the fumes away from his face in what he hoped was an obvious manner. But Ikmen, his ear pressed tightly to the side of the radio that connected him to Attila's microphone, didn't so much as flinch. This was all far too serious for him to be worried about other people's reactions to his smoking.

The car was parked just outside the museum up on one of the grass verges opposite the small row of tourist-trap shops by the main entrance. There were always, even out of season, lots of vehicles lurking around this area and so it was a logical and unobtrusive place to be especially if one wanted to observe people coming out of the Topkapı. The only possible problem with this was if Attila and friend exited by another way, although this was unlikely as every employee had to be security checked before they left and the principal post that dealt with this was at the main gate. And besides he did have officers at the other, less well-known exits too. On a personal level that was not, however, the point. Ever since this whole thing had blown up when he went to interview Attila earlier in the day, Ikmen had been in a state of high tension. What with discovering a possible connection between an imprisoned boy and the Topkapı Museum, followed by the frantic activity involved in both getting permission to perform the operation and then persuading Attila to take part, the day had so far been one of almost gut-wrenching anxiety. If it worked, and from the conversation he had heard pass between Attila and the other man it seemed that they were on to something, that was he knew no guarantee that this scenario was in any way connected to the Ishak Paşa murder. But if it were he wanted to be there, in at the 'kill' when whatever was going to happen happened. If a living child were imprisoned for immoral purposes by this as yet unknown man, Ikmen wanted to be absolutely certain that he wasn't mixed up in his murder too, first. Vice could and probably would do whatever the hell

they liked with the man after Ikmen's questioning of him—
'after' being the operative and most important word.

As he had been doing on and off for nearly an hour,
Ikmen casually moved his eyes in the direction of the massive palace entrance, his face silhouetted against the light from
the shops opposite. Through a cloud of what to Avcı was
an impenetrable wall of smoke, he at first squinted and then
peered hard at two figures, one tall, the other tallish, that had
just emerged, side by side, from beneath the darkened portal.

'That looks like the two sergeants,' he said, 'side by side.'

Avcı who, like most police officers, was not above a
good bit of gossip, smirked.

'That'll be enough of that, Avcı,' his superior reprimanded
him, then, changing the subject rapidly, observed that, 'This
means that Attila and friend cannot be far behind.'

'Yes, sir.'

They both watched in silence as the two officers,
Farsakoğlu and Suleyman, walked past without so much as
a glance in their direction, seemingly wrapped up entirely
in each other's conversation.

'I couldn't do that,' Avcı said once they had passed by.

'Do what?' Ikmen asked.

'Not look in the direction of people that I know. I just
don't think that I could help myself.'

Ikmen smiled. 'And that is why you are a constable
and they are sergeants, Avcı. Think about it.'

Several further seconds of silence then passed before
someone else appeared at the gate, but unlike the youthful
sergeants he was not an edifying sight. Old and shambolic,
a thick woollen hat pulled down over his forehead, Attila
cut a figure that was both nervous and disreputable. The
man at his side was no more savoury to look upon, but he
was a good deal younger and, as the pair drew level with

the car, Ikmen could see that he had one of those leathery, well-weathered faces that characterise those who spend much of their lives out of doors. Keeping his head down in order to avoid any accidental contact with Attila's eyes, Ikmen murmured, 'Don't look at the car,' as the old man passed—a pointless mantra, of course, but one which appeared to work as the pair moved on without incident.

Once he was certain that the men had cleared the car, Ikmen looked up and watched as they passed up the road and then crossed over to the right-hand pavement.

'I think they're moving up towards the Aya Sofia,' he said, indicating that the area around the great Byzantine church might be their destination. And, as if to confirm this, the two men rounded the corner and made their way in that direction.

'Shall we go now then, sir?' Avcı asked, his feet poised over a theoretical selection of control pedals, even though he wasn't actually driving.

'I'll give it a count of ten,' Ikmen said, 'that old ponce Attila never could move very quickly.' And then, smiling grimly, he added, 'If he could he'd still have the same number of eyes as the rest of us.'

The route from the museum to the top end of Yerebatan Cad-desi follows a slight incline which, though not actually a hill, can be rather taxing for those who are old or particularly unfit. Attila, who came into both of these categories, was not there-fore feeling at his best when he and his companion passed by the entrance to the massive Byzantine cistern complex which gives its name to this particular street, the Yerebatan Saray. Constructed during the reign of the Emperor Justinian, the Yerebatan Saray or underground palace was built originally to store water for the nobles of old Byzantium and was and remains a miracle of early engineering technique. The apartment building just one block down from this amazing structure, which was to be Attila and the man's final destination, was of a quite different order. Built during the late nineteenth century, in the twilight of the old Ottoman civilisation, its heavily stuccoed facade was blackened both by time and by the thick sooty deposits which cling to all of Istanbul's buildings and which come from the dirty brown coal the city is obliged to warm itself with during the winter months. The entrance to the building was dark and smelt strongly of stale urine.

For several seconds, in an attempt to catch his breath, Attila leaned heavily against one of the portals while the man plunged into the darkness beyond in order to locate the time-operated light switch. Somewhere a baby cried and a drunken- or drugged-sounding voice exhorted the baby or someone else to 'Shut that fucking noise up!' The atmosphere was not unlike that in Attila's own humble building but, because this was for him unknown territory, his heart beat faster anyway.

The man, who was now illuminated by the weak bulb above his head, motioned for Attila to follow him which, with a sigh of weariness, he did.

'It's only one flight up,' he said as the old man drew level with him, 'at the back. Think you can make it?'

'Yes.'

'Think you'll be able to perform when you get there?' he taunted Attila, his eyes full of the sort of contempt people usually reserve for lower life forms.

Attila nodded his assent. Fortunately the man didn't see the look of fury and hatred in his eyes as he did this; besides, as soon became apparent, his mind was already on other things.

'I'll take your money here,' he said, holding out one grubby paw for his cash.

But Attila, knowing of old how these things work, threw his head backwards in a gesture of refusal. 'Not until I've seen what it's like,' he said.

'It's young and it's gorgeous and its arse is just for you,' the man snapped. 'What more do you want?'

'I want to see him first,' Attila persisted, 'just a glance and then you'll get your money, on my word.' And, by way of underscoring this point, he put his hand inside his jacket pocket and took out the large roll of used bank notes with which Ikmen had supplied him.

The man's greedy eyes expanded as what amounted to thirty million lire hove into view.

'You've a lot of money there for such a useless old tosser,' he said. 'Where'd you get it?'

'Is that your business?'

The man shrugged, slightly offended at this sudden show of pique. 'No.'

'Then shut your face and take me where I want to go,' Attila countered. 'I'll give you your price when we get there.'

The man turned and started walking up the stairs. Attila, quite rightly in all probability, surmised that if things did not go the way the inspector had planned, this man would probably take all his money off him as soon as he entered the apartment. But he followed him anyway. What else could he do? Whichever way he looked at it, he was probably going to take a beating from someone in the very near future—if not this man then the police themselves if they didn't get the result that they wanted.

The man opened the door to the apartment with a key that looked almost as greasy as the lock which it turned. He then switched on a light and illuminated a dingy room which was entirely bereft of furniture with the exception of a bedroll upon the floor and a television in one corner. There was a smell of unwashed human flesh about the place and of doors too long shut against the same.

'Come in then,' the man said, standing to one side so that he could push the door shut on Attila as he passed.

'Where's the boy?' the old man asked, stoically hovering in the doorway.

The man flicked his head in the direction of a door at the back of the squalid living area. 'In there,' he said, 'in the bedroom.'

Still standing inside the open doorway, Attila took the money out of his pocket and started to count it in front of the man's eager face. Then, temporarily giving in, the man moved into the room and said, 'I'll go and get him ready.'

He disappeared into the bedroom and Attila, conscious that he could easily be relieved of his money in front of the open door, shut it.

For the next few minutes the only sound he heard was that of his own pounding heart. The bleakness of the apartment, the awful overpowering smell and the generally hostile demeanour of the man would even under normal circumstances have been enough to unnerve him, but with the added pressure of not knowing what the police planned to do—or when—it was almost insupportable. In addition he was terrified of what might happen once the police did arrive. People like this man, basically pimps, were notorious for their violence towards those who crossed them and although Ikmen had assured him that it would be all right he rather doubted that.

'You can come in now,' the man said as he re-emerged from the bedroom.

Attila moved slowly forward, his twenty million lire held

out in front of him. Just before he passed, the man snatched it out of his fingers. He began counting immediately.

'You'll find it all there,' Attila said, crossing the threshold into a room that was even more squalid than the other. 'It's...'

But he didn't finish the sentence, the words died on his lips as he beheld what was before him. Even in his wildest imaginings, or rather his worst nightmares, he could never have dreamed of such a thing. In fact his disgust, for disgust was the only word that he could use to describe his feelings now, was so great that he began to wonder about himself, about whether he was indeed the true pervert he had always believed himself to be. This was...this was...

A knock at the front door of the apartment temporarily broke his reverie. The man leaned forward into the bedroom and muttered, 'Probably just the kapıcı,' before pulling the door shut behind him, leaving Attila alone with what lay silent and unmoving as stone upon the litter- and faeces-strewn bed.

❀ ❀ ❀

'I'm sorry to disturb you, sir,' Ikmen said, briefly flashing his ID card in front of the startled man's eyes, 'but we have reason to believe that a criminal we are currently tracking is here in this apartment.'

The man's eyes, almost goggling out of his head, told the policeman everything he needed to know.

'You don't mind if we just take a look around, do you, sir? We won't trouble you for long.'

'But—'

'Thank you,' Ikmen said as he, plus six other officers including Suleyman and Farsakoğlu, pushed past the man. 'Constable Cohen will attend to you while we look,' he added. 'Cohen?'

'Yes, sir.'

'Attend to Mr, er, what is your name?' The man simply stared.

'Look after this man, will you, Cohen?'

'Yes, sir,' Cohen replied, taking up a very firm stance in front of the now closed front door.

'All right everybody,' Ikmen said, 'spread out. Every room, please. He's got to be here somewhere. You come with me, Suleyman.'

The two men walked straight ahead towards a door that directly faced the front entrance. The others moving to right and left of them busied themselves with the kitchen, bathroom and sparse living area. Not that the man standing in front of Cohen was watching them; his eyes were firmly fixed upon Ikmen and Suleyman—a fact not lost upon the older detective.

'I think that you and I may have struck gold here, Suleyman,' he said as he pushed the door open to reveal first the trembling form of Attila and then the one item of furniture in that room, the bed.

It was when his eyes lit upon the bed, or rather upon what was on the bed, that Ikmen's previously jocular mood disappeared.

The boy, who was moving rhythmically to and fro across a lake of what appeared to be his own faeces, could have been anywhere from twelve to sixteen years of age. Naked except for a thick leather collar studded with spikes like those worn by Anatolian sheepdogs, the sparse dark hair on his body giving the lie to the bleached blond mat on his head, he looked up with the vacant eyes of one who is either drugged or simply beyond all emotion. The thick, pustulous track marks upon both his arms and legs confirmed the former theory, yet the latter was undoubtedly true too. Even assuming that the child had been in this situation for only a few short days the circumstances of his imprisonment were so vile that it was easy to see how he could die from inside. As the boy moved, a thin trickle of blood came out from somewhere beneath his rear end and Ikmen, his eyes pinned in horror to the scene before him, heard Suleyman gamely trying to suppress a heave behind his back.

Slowly he turned his head towards Attila. 'Did you?' he growled.

The old man's first response was to piss his own pants, after which he said softly, 'No, I never, I swear...'

'Bring me the tenant of this apartment, will you, Cohen,' Ikmen shouted out into the living area.

With some difficulty, principally because the man was so reluctant to move, Cohen shoved, cajoled and pressed his charge a metre or two forward and, when he stopped, persuaded him to make the rest of the journey towards the bedroom using the barrel of his pistol.

'You can stop searching now,' Ikmen called out to the rest of the officers, 'Suleyman and I have found what we were looking for.' Then, turning towards the cowering man at his elbow, he said very quietly, 'Is this your doing, sir?'

'It's not...' the man blurted. 'It was the old bastard. He...Wasn't me...'

'You're sweating very heavily for an innocent man,' Ikmen observed, 'especially for an innocent man who does not, surely, yet know what is in this room.'

'I...'

Ikmen's hand shot forward like a streak of light and latched itself firmly on to the man's hair.

'Look inside, sir,' he said, 'and tell me in your own words what you see?'

'I...it's...'

'Allah protect us!' Farsakoğlu, who had just arrived at the doorway, cried.

'Well?' Ikmen asked the man once again. 'What do you see here? Tell me?'

The man opened his mouth to speak but no sound would come out of him except for the small cry of pain that he uttered as Ikmen pulled still harder on his hair.

'It is an abomination in there!' Ikmen was shouting now, right into the man's red and terrified face. 'That is what it is, sir. It is the most foul and disgusting abuse of a child that I have ever seen in my life!'

'I...'

'And you will, you have my absolute promise, spend the rest of your revolting life in prison for it!'

'But I...'

'Don't even begin to...' Ikmen's one free arm was now raised high up in the air, above the man's head, ready to strike and, as it hung suspended, the man cringed in preparation for the blow he was certain was about to come. Not one of the officers, he knew, would come to his aid now and, dull soul that he was, he realised in that moment that the collective will of the policemen present was for their superior to strike him down where he stood.

'Oh, effendi, I...' He closed his eyes in preparation for the blow as the whole room seemed to hold its breath.

But when it didn't come, when Ikmen slowly and with an effort of will that was so great that there were tears in his eyes, lowered his arm, it was almost worse than if he had hit him. Had he done so it would have provided a catharsis for that moment which now it lacked, leaving only unresolved, raw hatred in its place.

'Sir...' Suleyman began gently.

'Get an ambulance for that boy in there,' Ikmen said, quite altering the direction of his efforts. 'Tell them we actually want a doctor to attend.'

'Yes, sir,' Suleyman said and took his telephone out of his pocket.

Then, looking at Farsakoğlu, Ikmen added, 'And you, Sergeant, stay with the boy until it comes.'

She nodded and then, not without some nervousness, entered the room, pushing past the old man who now stepped out into the living area. Ikmen, as had been agreed with Attila earlier, surveyed the old man with a jaundiced eye before instructing Avcı plus one other younger constable to take him down to one of the cars. Then, posting another man at the front door, Ikmen and Cohen took the owner of the apartment into the only room that had chairs, which was the kitchen. This, it turned out, was as filthy as the rest of the apartment and Ikmen cautiously wiped the chair he chose to sit on before he actually sat down at the table. Pulling another chair away from the crockery-filled sink, Cohen placed it opposite his boss and then pushed the cringing man down into it.

After spending a few moments looking around the grease- and nicotine-stained little room, Ikmen sat back in the chair and folded his arms. The man before him, who was breathing in a very laboured fashion, muttered something that Ikmen couldn't hear and then fell silent.

'So,' Ikmen said, his face still a mask of bald fury, 'let us start at the beginning, shall we? What is your name?'

'I, I, I want a lawyer, I...'

'Yes and you are entitled to have one, I know. But'—Ikmen leaned across the table so that his face was as close as it could be to that of the man—'it will go better for you if you co-operate now.'

'I must have a lawyer! You can't—'

'I can do anything I fucking well like at the moment!' Ikmen roared. 'You are lucky still to be in one piece after what we've found here today!'

The man put his head down and sniffed. 'Yes, I...'

Ikmen banged one fist hard down upon the table top and shouted, 'Name!'

The man mumbled something neither Ikmen nor Cohen could hear.

'Louder!' Ikmen ordered. 'We didn't quite get that, did we, Constable Cohen?'

'No, sir.' Then, shouting into the man's ear, he said, 'Speak up when the inspector asks!'

The man raised his head just a little and mouthed, 'It's Halil Tekin, my name.'

'Halil Tekin.' Ikmen said it slowly as if savouring the individual sounds in his mouth. 'Halil. Same name as my brother, that. Coincidence.' He raised one eyebrow and looked as if he were about to smile but then didn't. 'Except of course that my brother is an honest, normal sort of a man and you are not.'

'Effendi...'

'You are, unless I am greatly mistaken, some sort of pimp, are you not, Halil?'

'No, it...'

'Do you deny that I have just discovered a naked and I believe under-age child in your bedroom with a known paedophile?'

'No, but...'

'And, further, that the child in question appears to have either used or been given some sort of intravenous drug?'

Halil Tekin put his head down once more and then muttered the word lawyer yet again.

'Oh, yes,' Ikmen replied, 'you can have one of those.

I've said that you can have one of those but I am afraid I'm going to put a condition on that.'

As quickly as it had fallen, Halil Tekin's head rose once again, 'But you can't do that, it's...'

'Not quite legal?' Ikmen smiled for the first time since he had entered that apartment. 'No, it isn't, Halil, I agree. But'—and here he reached out and once again grabbed the man by the hair of his head—'nobody really cares a great deal about that sort of thing right now.'

'But if—when it goes to court my lawyer will say that you—'

'Your lawyer will be very lucky to get you to the court alive, Mr Tekin,' Ikmen spat, 'and as for legal niceties, you tell them to that boy whose life you've probably ruined.'

'All right! All right!' Tekin raised his hands up to where Ikmen held his hair and then laid his fingers around those of his captor. 'Let me go and I'll tell you—something.'

Ikmen let go of the man's hair and then sat back in his chair once again. 'Right. That's better.' And then, sweeping one hand in front of his body, he asked, 'And so?'

Halil Tekin took in a deep breath and then said, 'The kid's not Turkish.'

'Oh, which makes it all right, I suppose!'

'No, well, yes, well—look, it's...' Tekin flung his hands up in the air and then sighed. 'He's Russian—I think, I don't know, foreign. He was on the game anyway and—'

'Is he an addict?'

'Well...'

'Is he or isn't he?'

'Well, he wasn't, but...'

Ikmen leaned over the table once again, piercing the man's face with his hard eyes. 'But what?'

'But...Look, I think that I really do need a lawyer for—'

'Did you put the boy on to drugs? Was it you caused all those track—'

'He didn't like it, OK, the sex with the old men and that and...Look, I'm not a monster or—'

Cohen, unable to control his feelings any further, suddenly laughed in a high-pitched staccato.

Ikmen, who did not appreciate this sudden interruption, snapped, 'Be quiet, will you, Constable!'

'Yes, sir. Sorry, sir.'

Then, turning back to the man in front of him, Ikmen said, 'Well, Mr Tekin, you were saying?'

'Well...' Tekin bit down hard on his bottom lip and then licked the sides of his mouth with his tongue. 'Look, I just wanted to help him cope with it and...'

'Yes?'

Suleyman entered the room and silently indicated to Ikmen that the ambulance was on its way.

'Well...'

'I've not got all night, Mr Tekin,' Ikmen warned and then added, ominously, 'even if you have.'

Suleyman leaned back against the door frame and looked on, his face a picture of disgust.

'If the kid was drugged up, it didn't bother him so much. He was always willing to take it, wanted it. Put his arm out to take it every time I went in to him.'

'It being?'

'Well, I don't know, I...'

'Oh, come on!' Ikmen exploded. 'You must surely know what you were giving him. You must at least have known what you were buying?'

'No, I didn't!' He looked around the room at all three of his tormentors, his eyes pleading for understanding. 'Honest! I—'

'That's total crap!' Ikmen exploded once again. 'Push-ers don't just sell any old—'

'Didn't get it from a pusher! Like I said, the kid's not bad, I didn't want to harm him and so...'

'And so what, Mr Tekin?' Ikmen asked. 'What did you do? Ask the pharmacist for some advice about how to deal with anal pain or—'

'No!' Tekin was almost crying now, his eyes wet with tears and barely controlled terror. 'No. No, I got it from a doctor.'

'A doctor?'

Ikmen and Suleyman exchanged a brief but, to them, meaningful glance.

'Yes,' Tekin said, 'a proper one too, in a hospital.'

'How on earth did you get a doctor...'

Tekin put his head down again and said, 'It's a man I know. He knows this doctor.'

'Who is?'

'I don't know! Just a doctor! Some rayah, so he says.'

'And your friend?'

'What about him?'

'He is?'

'He's not my friend, he's just this man.'

'What is his name?' Ikmen asked.

Tekin ran his fingers shakily through his hair. 'I don't know—Mehmet.'

'Mehmet who?'

'I don't know, I...He works doing this and that and...I don't know, I just see him sometimes.'

Ikmen leaned back into his chair again and sighed. 'So,' he said, 'let me get this straight. You have been, for the past—how long?'

'I don't know, some months maybe.'

'Some time. For some time,' Ikmen continued, 'you

have been pimping for this child who you have been sedating with some unknown drug that you have procured from Mehmet who does this and that, who gets said drug from a doctor who is not a Muslim.'

Tekin leaned forward on to the table and put his head into his hands, 'Yes. Can I see a lawyer now?'

'All in good time,' Ikmen replied, 'all in good time. Just one more question for now and then we'll see.'

'Yes?'

'Which is,' Ikmen said slowly, 'whether or not this is the only boy that you keep like this?'

'The only...'

'Yes,' Ikmen said, his voice now strangely bright and light once again. 'Whether you pimp for other boys in locked rooms or not, Mr Tekin. But,' he warned, 'think carefully about what you say in answer to this, because if you lie to me, I will know and that will make me very angry. That will make me turn you over to some other officers I know who will not be so lenient with your revolting little life.' He leaned across the table and smiled. 'Well?'

Suleyman sat down on the wall beside Ikmen and wordlessly draped his coat across the older man's shoulders.

'It's cold out here, sir,' he said, 'you don't want to catch a chill.'

Ikmen, his eyes heavy with weariness, smiled. 'You sound like my mother.'

Suleyman shrugged. 'What will happen to Mr Tekin now?' he asked.

Ikmen lit yet another cigarette and let the smoke out of his mouth on a sigh. 'If he's telling the truth, he'll be handed over to vice. I can't do much with him if he hasn't actually killed anyone.'

'Do you think that he is telling the truth?'

'That the Russian—or whatever he is—boy is his only business venture?' He shrugged. 'I think that it's more than possible. Besides I can't see how a squalid little pimp like Tekin could be involved with someone like our dapper Mr Zekiyan, do you?' He turned round and with a sweep of his hand invited his colleague to look up at the drab tenement building behind. 'I mean, look at this place? Look at Tekin and his operation? Our boy didn't have an arse like a war zone like that poor kid up there, did he?'

'No.'

'Both lads were kept locked up but that is about the sum total of the similarity between the two. I do, however, want to have some blood tests done on Tekin's boy.'

'In case the drug involved is pethidine?'

'Yes. Presence of pethidine plus Tekin's testimony about a bent doctor might indicate that one of our medics is selling on the sly to anyone for any reason. And if he's been supplying to this Mehmet character, then why not to nice Mr Zekiyan also?'

'This means, of course,' Suleyman said, 'locating this Mehmet somehow.'

'Yes.' Ikmen sighed again, heavily. 'If it is pethidine I'll liaise with vice for some more time with Tekin; if not...' He shrugged again, this time just slightly. 'No movement on our search for Mr Zekiyan, I suppose?'

A woman with alarmingly bleached blonde hair stopped briefly in front of the officers and lifted up her skirt to reveal a distinct lack of knickers. Suleyman, his face a blank slate, waved her on her way.

'No,' he said, 'nothing as yet. I'm starting to wonder whether he actually exists.'

'Well, I think that it's safe to assume that Zekiyan is not his real name,' Ikmen replied, then added, in a slightly more upbeat tone, 'Perhaps we'll have a shot at locating the maker of his famous ring tomorrow. Dr Sarkissian has given me one or two names of possible outlets in the bazaar.'

'Yes.' Suleyman took a small packet of sweets from one of his jacket pockets and popped one into his mouth. 'So where does this leave us with regard to a connection to the museum, then?' he said. 'Or the little crystals?'

'I don't know,' Ikmen said, his voice again quite devoid of all hope. 'Perhaps the connection is less obvious than an employee of the Topkapı. Perhaps it's symbolic? Perhaps it's totally unconnected? I don't know.'

They sat in silence for a few moments, each lost in his own thoughts. When Suleyman did eventually speak, however, Ikmen knew exactly what he was about to say.

'Sir...'

'Yes, I know, we can all behave like animals at times, including me.'

'I...'

'I'm not proud of what I almost did to that man, you know,' Ikmen said, 'but I was just so outraged by the sight of that boy. I mean, I've got sons of that age myself and...'

'We all wanted you to hit him, you know that, don't you?'

Ikmen sighed. 'Yes. But in the end I couldn't. It's not right. There is and can never be any justification for violence against another, whatever that other might have done. Self-defence is the only reason why one person should ever strike another. Had I made physical contact with Mr Tekin I would have been the one to suffer and not him. It would have gone against everything I believe and hold valuable and he just wasn't worth it.'

'I don't feel good about what I almost did to that poor madman,' Suleyman added.

'And quite rightly,' said his superior, 'he, unlike Mr Tekin, is hardly responsible for his actions.'

'You think that Tekin is sane?' Suleyman looked at his boss with wide, almost shocked eyes.

'Why not? To use a young boy's body in order to make money is a rational act for a man living in these conditions. Unlike our friend Lenin, he's not doing what he does because of some deluded belief, but because he wants to. I can't see that he cannot be judged as fully competent under the law.'

'I can see that, but'—Suleyman looked down at his hands and sighed—'but look, it can't possibly be normal to do what he did to that boy.'

'What is normal?' Ikmen asked. 'When somebody, like old Lenin, who is right out there mentally presents himself to us, we know that that is unusual. To define what is mad is easy, but to try and do the same for normality is almost impossible. Tekin has done something that could be judged as normal within the context of his lifestyle. There are two ways out of poverty, not just in this city but globally, and they are the legal way, through education, skills and what have you, and the illegal way, like this. We don't like and cannot understand this way because it is outside our frame of reference. My father, though never wealthy, never for a moment allowed my brother or myself to consider that ways to advancement other than through hard work even existed. Tekin's father, his peers, his family, are probably of quite a different order.'

Suleyman shrugged a vague agreement to all of this and then said, 'Yes, I can see that, kind of. But...But look, sir, going back to old Lenin—'

'About whom you feel tremendous guilt.'

Suleyman put his head down. 'Well...Look, what, if anything, can we do for him now?'

Ikmen patted his colleague affectionately on the knee. 'He will be tried but with the evidence from the psychiatrist taken into account. I'll do what I can for him also. I expect they'll send the poor bastard to one of those dumps they call a "mental hospital," shove him into a chemical cage and then forget about him for a few decades.'

'A bit like our boy in Ishak Paşa isn't it?' Suleyman said, softly. 'Perhaps he was mad too?'

'Perhaps.' Ikmen rubbed his eyes with his fingers and then groaned with tiredness. 'I can't think about much now, I'm too exhausted.' He looked up and smiled. 'Old age coming on.'

'No!'

Ikmen held up his hand to quell any protest from his sergeant and then slowly rose to his feet. 'We must get back to the station now,' he said, 'clear up the events of this evening.'

'Yes.' Suleyman, standing also now, stretched his arms out wide and yawned.

Ikmen lit another cigarette from his existing butt and then gave Suleyman back his coat. 'By the way,' he said, as casually as he could, 'I thought that that little act you performed with Farsakoğlu at the museum was most convincing. Young couple and all that.'

Suleyman, feeling his face flush with embarrassment, turned quickly to one side. 'Oh. Good.'

'I'd just be a bit careful you're not too convincing in front of certain other people. You know what gossips some people can be.'

'Yes, I...' Suleyman turned back towards Ikmen again, his face telling the latter just about everything he needed to know about how his sergeant felt. But not being at all good in situations of this kind, Ikmen simply patted him on the shoulder and then changed the subject.

'I didn't tell you about my rather unusual dinner last night, did I?'

'You told me that you got very drunk.'

They started walking back towards Ikmen's car which was parked in front of one of the small, dingy backpackers' hostels opposite.

'Well,' Ikmen said as he casually stepped out in front of a slowly meandering donkey cart, 'that was hardly surprising given the opulent eccentricity of my surroundings.'

Suleyman, pulling his boss back a little in order to allow the animal and its burden to pass without incident, said, 'Oh?'

'Yes, we met at the house of a Mr Muhammed Ersoy who is, I am told, one of the wealthiest men in the city. He's certainly pledged a lot of money to Krikor's cause.'

Suleyman, uncharacteristically, snorted as if he had a bad smell under his nose. 'I find that hard to believe,' he said sourly, 'with his reputation.'

Despite being in the middle of the road, Ikmen suddenly stopped and looked with a sudden recognition at his deputy. 'Oh yes, I suppose you would know him. He's one of your lot, isn't he?'

'If you mean, sir,' Suleyman replied, rather haughtily Ikmen thought, 'that Mr Ersoy and myself both come from old Ottoman families, then yes. But as for knowing him...I know of him but that is all.' Then, looking nervously in the direction of an oncoming car, he added, 'Don't you think we should get out of the road now'

'Oh, er, yes,' said Ikmen and moved forward at what was still a somewhat too leisurely pace to accommodate most Turkish drivers.

Suleyman, who was much more wary in such situations, took the matter into his own hands and, taking him firmly by the elbow, propelled Ikmen towards the pavement just before the car crossed what had been their path.

Ignoring, as was his wont, this recent brush with oblivion, Ikmen, once on the pavement, took up the conversation again. 'And so, Mr Ersoy?' he puffed.

'Muhammed Ersoy belongs to the class of person that still believes itself to be essentially Ottoman,' Suleyman said, 'He has no time for the common man and has enough money to live within the illusion that the common man doesn't even exist. That's why I'm so surprised that he is interested in Dr Sarkissian's project, which is essentially aimed at the dispossessed.'

Ikmen shrugged. 'Well, he's been very generous. Although whether that has more to do with the interests of his "friend" Dr Avedykian, I don't know.'

Suleyman raised his eyebrows a little. 'He's still with Avram Avedykian?'

'Yes. Why?'

'They've been lovers since they were at school, which has to be twenty-five or more years ago. With all the money and privilege Ersoy had I would have thought that would have finished years ago.'

Ikmen smiled. 'You lot certainly know a great deal about each other, don't you—considering that you, by your own admission, only know "of" the man.'

Suleyman pulled a sour face. 'He was in the same year at school as my brother. He bullied him. Being so much younger than Murad, I was only aware of his difficulties via playground gossip. He never spoke of it himself until much later on and I was far too small at the time to do anything about it myself.' He raised one hand and made a small space between his forefinger and thumb. 'Ersoy, with all his money and his pampered lifestyle, made poor Murad feel about this big for most of his time there.'

'He certainly is very rich.'

'And completely untouchable too,' Suleyman added.

As he unlocked the door of his car, Ikmen asked, 'How so?'

'Well, money or not, his life has been tragic. I mean, I don't like the man, but—'

'You mean his father and mother committing suicide?'

'Stepmother. His own mother died when she was having him. He was spoilt almost beyond belief from then on, as you can imagine.'

'But his father remarried?'

'Yes.' Suleyman leaned across the top of the car, his chin in his hands. 'The second Mrs Ersoy, who was some sort of relative, bore his father a second son who, if I remember correctly, also died—I don't know how. But it was after that that old Mr Ersoy and his young wife decided to destroy themselves.'

Ikmen sighed. 'Poor Muhammed then.'

'Indeed.'

Ikmen climbed into the car and then leaned across to unlock the passenger door. As Suleyman opened the door and slid himself into the seat, Ikmen added, 'You lot certainly do live tangled personal lives, don't you? Every time I hear anything about what is left of our old aristocracy it's like listening to an account of life in the Seraglio.'

'It's because,' Suleyman explained, his head now leaning down towards the floor, 'unlike you, we still partially live back there in the days of duty and power and the importance of dynasty. We do things like marrying our cousins in order to preserve our old ways and keep all the money in the family.' He looked up and smiled, sadly, 'But it weakens the line in the end, as we now know, which is why so many of us are crazy or suicidal. Exotic things happen to exotic people for perfectly logical reasons.'

Ikmen lit a cigarette in order not only to fulfil his craving but also to cover his embarrassment. Suleyman's unwanted wife was, as he knew, also his cousin. 'But the old sultans only ever mated with slaves,' he said, 'and so this marrying-in phenomenon...'

'Is comparatively recent, yes. You see, it's er...' Suleyman stumbled a little as he found the right words. 'When Atatürk told us that we were all no longer Ottomans but Turks, many in the old order couldn't really, um, get behind this new nationalism. People like the Ersoys, my parents and others are still Ottomans in their minds.'

'I remember Ersoy saying something about "Turks, whoever they are". Something like that.'

'Exactly,' Suleyman said, 'which is why supporting a drug project for people who are, essentially, Turks is so out of character for him and why you're probably correct in thinking that Avram must have been behind this move. Muhammed Ersoy probably feels that many of the lower orders deserve nothing more than a good beating. Since the Lenin incident, I now fear that part of my own self must feel the same.'

'Ah, but you had a lovely excuse!' Ikmen answered and then almost immediately regretted his words.

'Yes, I did,' Suleyman replied, 'but as you have indicated before, sir, that is not something that we will talk of again. Sergeant Farsakoğlu's honour is as safe with me as it would be with a eunuch.'

His eyes almost deliberately hard and dead, Suleyman then turned away and looked out into the street. Ikmen fired up the engine and thanked his luck that he was the poor, shabby peasant that he was.

# 10

HAVING A BROTHER-IN-LAW in the building trade was not proving to be the advantage Cohen had thought that it might in his lonely search for the contractor who had done that conversion work on the top apartment of The Sacking House. That he had actually volunteered for this duty made his singular lack of success so far all the more galling. There were literally hundreds of companies who took on such work, not to mention the more unofficial outfits who tended to be of the here today, gone tomorrow variety. Not, in all likelihood, that the work on The Sacking House could be included under the latter category. The craftsmanship, even to his untrained eye, was very good and so the chances of a disreputable contractor being involved were slim. But that didn't make his task any easier. With only 'sometime after 1982' as a guide to when the work had been carried out, plus the hundreds of possible names still remaining before him in the telephone directory, it looked like he was going to have a particularly frustrating time in the hours or even days to come. That his brother-in-law, Nat, had shaken his head in disbelief when he had outlined the task ahead had not boded well either. In Nat's opinion, if you didn't have dates, job specifications and possibly even receipts too, most builders that he knew would just laugh in your face.

Cohen wrote down the names of the next three companies to be contacted on a sheet of paper and then paused to light a cigarette. The frantic and disturbing events of the previous evening had left him tired and washed out. Sleep after all that horror with the poor imprisoned boy had eluded him until the early hours of the morning rendering his usually very sharp brain sluggish and unwilling to shift itself into work mode.

'You look as if you need a very strong cup of coffee.'

Cohen turned his head and saw the smiling face of Sergeant Farsakoğlu looking down at him. She looked almost as tired as he did, if much more attractive.

He hid his lust, as usual, behind a slick comment. 'I feel like a rat has just dragged its claws across the surface of my brain and then died in my mouth,' he said.

She laughed. 'That is a most inventive way of describing what I imagine must have been a bad night's sleep, Cohen,' she replied. 'Almost artistic.'

'Well...' he shrugged. 'Could you sleep after all that business yesterday evening?'

Farsakoğlu sat down in the chair beside him with a sigh. 'Not terribly well, no. If you remember I actually accompanied the boy to the hospital.' She turned away briefly, 'It was vile.'

'Yes, well, um...'

She turned back again and then smiled. 'So you're telephoning builders again today.'

'Yes.' He stubbed his cigarette out in his ashtray and

then sighed. 'Hundreds of them, I expect. Unless of course I get lucky straight away, which I won't.'

'It's unlike you to be so despondent.' She eyed him closely for a few seconds and then added. 'Is there anything else I should know about?'

'No. Thank you, Sergeant.'

He turned away and addressed himself very pointedly to his work.

'OK,' she said, 'but if there is anything…well…' She stood up. 'I'd better go and finish my report, I suppose.'

'Yes, right.' He looked up and smiled. God, she was sexy! 'Thanks for your concern anyway.'

'Right.'

She moved back to her desk leaving Cohen alone with both the hated telephone directory and his thoughts.

Of course there was something else that was wrong, apart from recent events. But then…But then that was not something he could talk to her or indeed any other woman about. Come to think of it talking about this to other men was a bit of a problem too. Had he not been possessed of such a reputation amongst his colleagues perhaps his current predicament would have been easier to bear, but…

When one has been known and admired as a prolific womaniser for most of one's adult life, any change in that situation can come rather hard. Although Cohen had been married since the age of nineteen he had never let that fact or indeed his rather short stature and dishevelled appearance hold him back from the most ardent pursuit of other women. Jokey charm, of which he possessed copious amounts, had always seen him through. The knowledge that women love a man who can make them laugh had successfully taken him to many bedrooms and had, quite frequently, resulted in his being asked back again. Until this year.

Whether it was because now he was on the 'wrong' side of forty-five or just a patch of ill fortune, Cohen didn't know, but the fact was beyond dispute. Women, it seemed, didn't want him any more. The rebuffs and even in one notable case the cruel sound of mocking laughter were hideousiy painful for him to bear. Even his long-suffering wife, who had for so many years pleaded with him to leave other women alone and attend to her, had lost interest. He'd tried to find a little comfort in her arms the previous night when he found that he couldn't sleep, but she, like all the lithe little girls that he still so desired, had just sent him on his way, back to his customary couch, flinging her curses in his unfaithful wake.

It was, Cohen would have been the first to admit, his own fault. Had he bothered to try and be faithful to Estelle he would now, in his middle years, have both a friend and a lover with whom he could take comfort as the lines overwhelmed his face and the loose skin around his middle began to sag. His wife was, after all, ageing like himself and, unlike the pretty little tarts he hankered after, unable to point mocking fingers at his inadequacies.

As he turned back to the telephone directory, Cohen tried not to consider where his current sad situation now left him. But even as he was reading the number of the next company out to himself, still his mind persisted in wandering into unwelcome and rather pathetic avenues. No lovely Sergeant Farsakoğlu for him! No. Rather the odd dirty magazine hidden beneath his uniform, smuggled surreptitiously into his apartment under cover of night. Pictures of girls, naked if he was lucky, or more likely scantily clad like the ones on those 'naughty' calendars that grace the walls of garages or workshops—the fantasy fodder of the common, unfulfilled man.

He shook his head as if to try and loosen the unwelcome thoughts from his mind and then picked up the telephone receiver and began to dial the previously rehearsed number. Halfway through dialling, however, he suddenly stopped and after a short pause replaced the receiver. A thought had occurred to him which, if he were right, might just make all this telephoning a completely redundant pastime. If he were wrong, of course, he would have wasted valuable investigative time, but...but the more he thought about the kitchen of The Sacking House, or more accurately what was on the wall of the kitchen the more he was convinced that he just had to be right.

Big or particularly attentive companies often gave things away to valued customers: little gifts like calendars; calendars often of girls in swimwear and little else and...

Like one shocked from behind by an electric charge, Cohen leaped from his chair and started running out of the room.

Sergeant Farsakoğlu, who had only moments before spoken to a very dour and sluggish version of Constable Cohen looked up, confused, at this sudden whirlwind of activity.

'Cohen, what are you doing?' she said as he almost flew past her desk. 'You have work to do for the inspector and—'

'And that's just what I am doing,' he replied and then added with a most unprofessional wink, 'I've had a bit of a thought, see. Bye!'

And then he was gone, leaving behind him only an open telephone directory and the ghost of some previously unsettling thoughts.

Dr Avram Avedykian opened the door of his apartment on to a face and figure that he had not expected to see.

'Arto,' he said, 'how nice to see you! What are you doing here?'

'Oh, I was just passing,' the older man replied, 'just thought I'd see if you were in.'

'Well, it's my late shift today so you're in luck.' He stood slightly to one side in order to admit his guest. 'Come in.'

Avedykian led the pathologist through into a lounge characterised by very angular and sparse black furniture. Having now seen the home of this man's lover, Arto Sarkissian could not help but be impressed by the difference in taste that his friend exhibited.

'Sit down,' Avedykian said, indicating several large leather settees. 'Can I get you some refreshment? Tea perhaps, or coffee?'

'Coffee would be very nice,' Arto said, easing his large frame down upon one of the seats.

'Medium sweet, right?' his host asked.

Arto smiled. 'Yes. As ever I strive but fail to completely dispense with sugar.'

Avedykian laughed as he made his way towards the kitchen, leaving Arto, for the moment, alone with his own thoughts.

His excuse for being there, 'just passing' had, of course, been a lie. There was a definite reason why he was here now and it had very little to do with either a social call or any overwhelming desire to discuss things Armenian. However, there was one part of the reason he was there that could, possibly, touch upon their shared nationality. But that was going to have to wait until Arto had broached the 'other' subject with his younger friend.

As he looked around the expensively furnished room, Arto found himself feeling pleased for the way that his friend had come so far since he qualified. It had to be at least fifteen years since he had bolstered and encouraged what was then a very nervous young man through his final exams. Avram's actual tutor had been a rather unsympathetic Turk, and, in part at least, the older man had taken on both that role and the role of counsellor too. So very unsure and afraid that his nationality might preclude advancement, Avram had not been an easy man to encourage. On more than one occasion, Arto would arrive at Avram's parents' house only to find the young man in tears. And although Arto had, on several occasions, gently suggested that Avram might obtain more comfort from a 'special' friend or girlfriend to help him through, Avram's sharp retort that that person was Turkish and would not therefore understand had struck a familiar chord in his mind. To be fair, Çetin Ikmen had always tried to understand, but he couldn't any more than Avram's 'best friend' could, the man he only later discovered was the fabulous Muhammed Ersoy.

'So, to what do I owe the pleasure of your company?' Avedykian said as he came back into the room bearing two very tiny coffee cups.

'Do I need a reason to see an old friend?' Arto asked as he took one of the cups out of his host's hand and placed it on the coffee table.

Avedykian sat down and then shrugged his gym-toned shoulders. 'No. But I do know that you are very busy at the moment.'

'OK, OK!' Arto said with both a sigh and a smile. 'You've got me, Avram. You know me too well.'

'So you came for a reason? So what?' He laughed. 'It must be something that is of interest to both of us.'

'Look, Avram, I want to run something by you, something you may find difficult. I have a problem which...only another doctor can understand. And seeing that we are both doctors and Armenians...'

'Whatever you're trying to say, Arto, you might as well just come out with it,' Avedykian replied, his frowning face nevertheless belying his somewhat light tone of voice.

Arto smiled. 'Oh, all right. It's like this. But only between ourselves.'

'Whatever it is, it will go no further. Now come along, Arto, it's obviously bothering you.'

'This case I'm working on—'

'The boy in Sultan Ahmet.'

'Yes. Well, do you remember discussing the drug pethidine with Krikor the other night?'

'Yes.' Avedykian raised his coffee cup up to his lips and sipped. 'Your point being?'

'Our victim was loaded with the stuff when the police found him. In addition, we are, or seem to be, coming to the conclusion that he had been in that building, where he was found, for some time. The pethidine together with no obvious signs of vitamin D deficiency is leading us, or rather me, to the conclusion that the boy might have been, or his keeper might have been, supplied by someone in our profession.'

'Oh.' Avedykian moved just slightly in his seat and then added, 'So?'

'Well, my first urge,' Arto continued, 'was of course to make some inquiries myself. I mean I'm rather better placed than the police to do this particular thing. I could, for instance, speak to pharmacists about whether any drug stocks have gone missing or unaccountably become low over a length of time—'

'Hold on! Hold on!' Avedykian held up one hand in order to silence him. 'You're saying that you suspect someone...?'

'Oh, no, no! And originally I wasn't even looking at doctors as such. I was thinking about merely tracing a drug to an institution.'

'But?'

'But?'

'But what changed, from your original aim simply to pursue lines of inquiry about drugs?'

Arto sighed. 'It was last night that it all became a little too close, shall we say.'

'Oh?'

'Çetin Ikmen was instrumental in bringing to light a most nauseating case of paedophilia, the details of which I will not distress you with. However, it would seem that the boy in this case, who was, by the way, an obvious drug user, had been obtaining his supplies via a third party, from a doctor.'

'Ah.' Avedykian put his hand up to his mouth and then just as rapidly took it away again. 'You know this for certain?'

'I can't see why the man Çetin arrested, the boy's pimp, would lie, given his current situation.'

'And so you think...'

'I think it is possible that we have a doctor out there who is selling opiates to people that he shouldn't.'

Avedykian put his coffee cup down on the table and lit a cigarette. 'And so? I mean, have you come to me for—'

'I've already been pressured by one colleague to curtail my involvement in this.'

'A victim of the professional Mafia.' Avedykian smiled. 'Well, I must confess, Arto, that were I in your position, I would probably hand all this over to your police colleagues. You and I both know what happens to doctors who inform on or investigate other doctors. You remember Dr Yahya, the anaesthetist, and his alcoholic consultant?'

Arto sighed. 'Is it Iran or Pakistan where he works now?'

'I don't know. But wherever it is, it's a very long way from being a top-rate anaesthetist in Istanbul.' He reached over and placed a consoling hand upon his friend's knee, 'Like this other doctor said, I'd leave it to the police. You have a good career and a good life here in the city and—'

'But that's not all,' Arto said gravely. 'Were that it, I might just be able to walk away, but...'

'But what?' Avedykian's tone was suddenly edged with a hardness, a tension that had not been present before.

'But they're saying that this doctor is a Christian.'

'Who, the Turks?'

'Well, the pimp and—'

'Bastards!' With one smooth but violent movement, the younger man stood up, his face an almost motionless mask of rage wrapped around his cigarette. 'They're always trying to implicate us! Murder, robbery, fucking rape of their women!'

'Now...'

'Has anybody bothered to investigate or question this pimp's story? No! The same old thing!' Avedykian's eyes, which darted about across the room fixing upon nothing in particular that Arto could see, were almost aflame with fury. 'Ninety per cent of the time we are invisible and then suddenly along comes a crime and bang!' He whacked his hand down hard against the back of his chair. 'It is us, the outsiders, the rayahs. Not even the Jews, but—'

'Look, Avram—'

'And now I suppose you and I and every other Armenian, or, if the Turks are feeling so inclined, every Greek practitioner in the city will be—'

'Avram, I came for your advice,' Arto said, almost shouting to be heard above his friend's sudden fury, 'and, off the record, to warn you as a friend that an investigation of this type may be about to occur. But...'

'But what?' his friend asked, his eyes revealing little of what Arto had always assumed was their mutual affection.

'But I don't see the value of ranting like this about something over which neither of us has any control. And besides,' Arto added, 'nationality and career status aside, surely what this really has to be about is one boy who is dead and another who is a completely ruined drug addict. I mean, personal allegiances aside...'

'Yes, I'm sorry,' Avedykian said, deflating almost as quickly as he had become aroused. 'But don't you see that it is always us?'

'No, I don't think that that is so,' Arto answered. 'I'd be lying if I didn't say there were problems, but...Look, the fact that there is a doctor out there who is doing this who is also a Christian cannot be disputed until we know otherwise. And it could be otherwise, but until the police have—'

'So you're saying that you approve?'

'I don't so much approve as recognise that this may become a reality.' Arto looked up at his still obviously disturbed friend and smiled. 'I just wanted your views upon my future involvement.'

'I think that you must make up your own mind about that, Arto.' Avedykian sat down again and then stubbed his cigarette out in one of the ashtrays. 'I cannot really, in all conscience, advise you either way. As I've said, I think it may be difficult for you professionally. But on the other hand I, at least, would feel a little happier about things if there were to be an Armenian on the case. But...'

'But what?'

'But if they, the Turks, if they really want...'

Arto leaned forward and looked deeply into his friend's troubled eyes.

'With Çetin Ikmen in control, those investigated can be much more certain of a fairer hearing than with anybody else. And anyway, with powerful friends like you have'—he purposely refrained from mentioning Ersoy—'plus your innocence, you personally have nothing to fear.'

'And all the other Armenian and Greek doctors, what of them?'

Arto shrugged. 'Well, same thing, if they are innocent.'

'And if one of them is not?'

Arto squinted for just a second, as if not understanding the question. 'Eh?'

'If one of our colleagues is guilty?'

'Then he will face the full force of the law,' Arto replied, anger rising as he understood what Avedykian was implying. 'And quite rightly too—or am I missing some underlying message about another internal Mafia here, Avram?'

His friend looked away in the direction of a large and empty black bookcase.

As soon as Fatma opened the front door she knew that something was wrong. Çiçek, who generally spent her days off either asleep or out shopping with her friends, was standing in the hallway, her normally perfect hair awry, her face grey and strained. Shooing the two younger children hastily into the living room, Fatma put her heavy bag of vegetables down on the floor and, without even thinking to take off her shoes, went over to her daughter.

'What's wrong?' she said. 'Are you sick?'

'No, I'm fine,' Çiçek replied, looking far from it. 'It's Grandad.'

Fatma put her hand wearily up to her head and sighed. 'What's he done now?'

Çiçek looked down at the floor as she spoke. 'Just after you left he came into my room, naked. He said that the Greek had stolen his clothes and that I had to help him look for them.'

This was not an uncommon occurrence and although unpleasant was generally quite quickly and easily resolved. This time, however, there had to be something more.

'And?' she asked. 'Was that it?'

'I went to his room and, of course, found his clothes. But then...' She looked up and Fatma noticed that there were tears in her daughter's eyes. 'But then he started touching me, Mummy. Making suggestions that a grandfather shouldn't make to a granddaughter. It was disgusting, and I was scared, which I know is silly given his age, but...'

'No, I can understand that,' Fatma said, putting her arm gently around her daughter's waist and hugging her tightly.

'I don't suppose you'll understand the fact that I called Bulent home to help me though, will you?'

Fatma shook her head slowly in disbelief. Oh, she understood all right, but she wasn't very happy about her son being called away from his place of work to come and deal with this. Her father-in-law was slowly but surely beginning to disrupt the lives of the whole family.

'Is Bulent still here?'

'He's in with Grandad now. I'm sorry, Mummy, I just couldn't cope.'

'You did the right thing,' Fatma said, patting the girl encouragingly on the back. 'I'll speak to your brother's employer if necessary and explain. Don't worry.' And then turning back to pick up her shopping she added, 'This has got to stop though. Ow!'

As she'd bent to pick up the bag something, or so it seemed to Çiçek, had either clicked in her mother's back or more likely something in her stomach was hurting her. When she moved closer however, Çiçek caught sight of the blood running down her mother's legs. It was then that she knew exactly what was wrong.

Placing an arm around her mother's shoulders she said, 'You know you really must get something done about this, Mummy.'

Fatma turned an agonised face towards her daughter. 'But there's no time, what with—'

'You've been having bleeds like this for ages; it's not right.' Taking her mother's hand away from the bag, she said, 'Come on, let's get you to the bathroom before Bulent comes back out.'

'Oh, yes.' Her mother suddenly panicked lest one of her sons should see her in such an undignified position. 'Yes, quickly!'

Blood was clearly visible trailing on to the floor as the two women scuttled quickly into the bathroom. Çiçek made a mental note to clear it up as soon as her mother was organised.

As she sat, gasping in agony, on the side of the toilet, Fatma said, 'If only your father would listen to me when I talk about Grandad and how he is.'

'It's hard for Dad to come to terms with.'

'Krikor Sarkissian has offered us help with your grandfather, but your father won't have it.'

Çiçek made to leave so her mother could have some privacy. 'Don't you think that if you explained to Dad how you really feel, how ill you really are...'

'It's not for men to know such things,' Fatma said with a dismissive wave of her hand. 'He knows about the...' Even with her daughter she couldn't bring herself actually to name the hated fibroids. '...The things.'

'But he doesn't understand, does he?'

'No, he's a man.'

'But if you told him the truth he might change his mind about Grandad. He might accept some help.'

'No, I don't think so, Çiçek.'

'But it must be worth a try, Mummy.' It was so awful seeing her mother like this, especially since Fatma's agonies were not, unless something was done very quickly, anywhere near an end. It was this thought that made Çiçek say what she did next. 'Well if you won't tell him then I'll have to.'

'Oh, but Çiçek, it will cause so much trouble!'

'No, it won't. Dad loves you and I'm sure that if he was given the choice between alleviating your suffering or continuing to delude himself about Grandad he'd see sense.'

Fatma sighed. She wished that she could be so certain about where her husband's priorities lay right now. Ever since the old man had started to become confused almost two years before her husband had slowly but inexorably become quite a different man. Before, apart from going to work and the occasional night out with male friends, he had rarely been away from the family home—not like he was now, out Allah alone knew where sometimes at all hours of the night. But then when he was home he was rarely communicative. Oh, he still said that he loved her, he said it a lot, but he didn't show it any more. Instead he used what little time he had at home to pander to the old man's delusions; that or laying down the law as he saw it to the rest of the family. It was almost as if he too had become a different character and one, furthermore, that Fatma found she could not really sympathise with.

'Please leave me now,' she said to her daughter as she felt the tears well up in her eyes.

'All right,' Çiçek said but, as she started to open the bathroom door, she added, 'I am going to tell Dad though, about—you know.'

Tired and miserable almost beyond endurance Fatma Ikmen waved a dismissive hand in the air. 'You do what you will,' she said. 'I can't think any more.'

❋ ❋ ❋

Çetin Ikmen sighed heavily before looking up, rather sternly, into his friend's anxious eyes.

'I think that you're pushing forward with this doctor connection thing rather ahead of the known facts,' he said. He was trying to deflect Arto Sarkissian's somewhat fixated pursuit of this topic in as diplomatic a way as possible.

'Yes, but...'

'We don't even know whether the boy we found last night was taking pethidine or not, do we? And until the analysis on his blood is completed we can't know it.'

'Well...'

'And even if he was we don't know whether the doctor who was supposedly responsible for supplying him also supplied our victim. I'd need to go out with the revolting Mr Tekin in pursuit of this Mehmet character, if he indeed exists, in order to try and establish who this doctor might be. And besides'—Ikmen paused briefly in order to light a cigarette—'it wasn't the pethidine that killed our boy. Personally I think that the chances of a doctor strangling our victim are slim. Your input is really at an end here, Arto. It is my job to pursue the investigation now and it is my belief that only a vigorous pursuit of connections relating to our elusive Mr Zekiyan will—'

'But Çetin, learning never stops when it comes to pathology!' Arto said, his eyes shining with almost unrestrained enthusiasm. 'We are all human and so sometimes we miss things. I mean it wasn't until I saw Mrs Taşkiran's sketch that I became aware of that birthmark underneath the boy's chin!'

'Indeed, and evidence like that could be pertinent, I

agree. But to look upon every member of one's profession as a potential—'

'Yes but, people aside, if I could just trace the flow of a substance to perhaps a particular institution and—'

'Oh, Arto!' Ikmen threw himself backwards into his chair and then brought one tired hand up to his head. 'Where on earth are you going to start? We don't even know whether this doctor even came from this city. All we know is that he might be a Christian and I can understand how that might be troubling for you but—'

'It could even be a friend!'

'Oh, so you really think that your friends have secrets of that order, do you?'

The doctor looked stricken. 'Anyone can have secrets. Everyone has things they would rather others didn't know.'

'Yes, I accept that. Your friend Avedykian being one of them.'

The doctor studiedly, or so Ikmen thought, ignored this reference and continued, 'And in our profession one has to be absolutely, almost unreasonably, clean. It's hard— and yet for me to do something about it—'

'Then don't get involved! You've given me a précis of Dr Hunter's thoughts which I will bear in mind. But now, please, let me do what I am paid to do and take it from here. I—' The telephone interrupted him. 'Hello, Ikmen.'

Arto Sarkissian, his head bowed in contemplation of his clenched hands did not listen in to his friend's conversation. He knew that what Çetin had said was right but that didn't mean that he had to be happy about it.

Despite all the dire warnings he had received from fellow professionals regarding his getting embroiled in a possible malpractice case he still couldn't help but feel that he should be 'in' there somewhere. Professional solidarity was one thing but where lives were involved Arto could not just let things take their course without comment. And his recent altercations with both Hunter and Avedykian had, if anything, made his resolve even firmer. Things like this, if leaked into the public domain, could not help but undermine confidence in the entire medical profession and, because his job was also his overriding passion, Arto felt personally as well as professionally concerned. If a doctor was out there selling drugs to vulnerable people he needed to be stopped—now. Tomorrow or even one hour's time might prove too late for God alone knew how many desperate people. If his brother, whose speciality this was, had taught him anything about addictive behaviour it was that not infrequently one exposure to the narcotic of choice could be enough—especially where powerful opiates were concerned.

'Well.' Çetin Ikmen put down the telephone receiver with what looked like a satisfied expression on his face. 'Call him a dirty little dog if you must, but that Cohen has more of a brain in his head than most of the other constables put together.'

Arto looked up with a query stamped across his plump features.

'Cohen may have found something,' Ikmen explained, 'regarding who might have done that building work on the top apartment.'

'Oh?'

'Yes.' Ikmen smiled, pleased by what he saw as good thinking on the part of one of his junior officers. 'When Cohen first went into that house he noticed a calendar in the downstairs kitchen. It showed pictures of scantily clad girls...' Both men shared a brief but significant smile. 'Well anyway,' he continued, 'although he didn't take much notice of it at the time it occurred to him earlier this morning that perhaps it might be of some use.'

Arto frowned. 'How so?'

'Well, sometimes firms like building contractors or car dealers or whatever give such things out to their customers.'

'And had that happened in this case?'

'It appears so, although as Cohen just said when he tried to ring the telephone number on the calendar it came up as a dead line—the calendar *was* dated 1982.'

'Shows initiative on Cohen's part, although it's a shame the result was so negative,' Arto replied.

Ikmen shrugged. 'Not necessarily so,' he said, 'Cohen's going over to the address of the place now. Maybe they've simply changed their number. He might just find something out anyway. The builders who worked on Mr Zekiyan's apartment, provided they can remember the job, could very well add something to our scant knowledge about the man and his doings. Who knows?'

'Well, let's hope so anyway.'

'Mmm.' Ikmen's face, as it often did at times of strain or trouble, suddenly darkened quite dramatically. 'We do need something in order to open this case up. There's not been so much as a whisper with regard to our victim's identity, and with Mr Zekiyan seemingly disappeared into thin air...'

Arto, looking down at the floor once again, said, 'I have put the name around.'

'Yes, I know,' his friend replied, 'and it is appreciated. I know that you find such things difficult.'

'So where is Suleyman today?' Arto said, changing the subject rapidly from things Armenian to things most decidedly Turkish.

Ikmen smiled inwardly, if sadly, at his friend's awkwardness. 'He got a call from one of his informants. He is, I believe, headed out towards Beşiktaş.'

'You don't know...?'

'Oh, no,' Ikmen replied, 'they never say what it's about over the telephone. Suleyman just got up and went. Informants are transient creatures; if they ask for a meeting, it usually has to be right away. They never know, you see, who might be watching them.'

Several moments of silence followed, during which both men considered the implications of what Ikmen had just said. To the doctor the notion of going alone to meet somebody who was probably a criminal was terrifying, whereas to Ikmen it was, or so his impassive expression seemed to suggest, just routine.

'You know that that hepatitis B test that I had done on our victim's blood came back negative,' Arto said, retreating once again into what was familiar and therefore safe to him.

'No, I didn't,' Ikmen replied.

'What it means,' Arto continued, 'is that the possibilities of our boy being a street user are now, if anything, even slimmer.'

'I think that we established that he was no typical user some time ago, didn't we?'

'Yes. However...'

'Atypical and unidentified. Held captive, or not, by a faceless Mr Zekiyan who may, or may not, be sending little crystal models to me. Quite a conundrum.' Ikmen smiled as he lit another cigarette from the burning butt of his previous smoke. 'A challenge which, were I ten years younger, I might appreciate.'

Arto shrugged. 'We all get old, Çetin. It's just the way things are.'

'Well, you try telling that to Muhammed Ersoy,' Ikmen replied and then both he and the doctor laughed.

The nameless man who, for reasons that only he would ever appreciate or understand, presented himself to the world under the sobriquet of Vladimir Ilyich Lenin, opened his eyes slowly. The policeman currently guarding him had gone now. Not wanting to communicate with this person, Vladimir Ilyich had successfully pretended that he was asleep when the man had come in with the bowl of awful slop that passed for food in this hell hole. And, although he knew full well that the bowl would contain only foul, unidentifiable muck, he did give his 'lunch' just a brief glance before finally tossing it on to the pile of similar matter in one corner of his cell. Not, of course, that this was going to be the worst food that he was destined to experience in his very dark and uncertain future. The morning guard had said that he was down to be transferred to prison at some point in the next few days and prison was, as everybody knew, even dirtier and the food less appetising than in this place. It was, he thought, typical of the punishments meted out by fascists to the honest working classes. Such places hadn't ever existed within good socialist states.

As he sat up, he looked towards the small grilled window that showed him only the feet of those who walked and talked in the 'real' world outside. Sad people all, or so he thought, blissfully unaware of how oppressed they really were, bought for the price of their nice warm city boots. But then that was what was so very clever about how this state, or indeed any oppressive regime like France or the USA, manipulated people's most basic needs. Warm a man's feet and you can unfreeze his heart, give a man a meal and he'll do your bidding with a smile on his face. It was a message that was as depressing today as it had been all those years ago when these concepts had first entered his consciousness at university.

'Nothing changes,' Vladimir Ilyich muttered bitterly as he wound his single blanket around his thinly clad shoulders. In trying, so he thought, to change the world for the better, it seemed to the man that he had achieved little beyond his own degradation. And even though he knew only too well that this was often the lot of revolutionary thinkers, there was a part of him, the larger part, which knew also that unlike them he did not have the facility to bear it. It was disappointing in a way; he would have liked to aspire to heroism on that scale. But...He put his head down and frowned. On the street, however cold or squalid his life might have become, there had always been the possibility that one or two people might have learned something from his words. It wasn't much but it had been enough—until, for reasons he could now only guess at, he had formed that connection between certain events that had occurred in a certain street and a rumour of a killing in that place.

Whole days and nights would come and go without him being aware of them. Only occasionally, like now, would he actually know where he had been and what he had done. Once he had found himself suddenly in another city without a clue as to how he got there or why. That had been very frightening: like waking into the darkest reaches of a nightmare.

He could have killed the boy. Even with no memory of the child, that could, chillingly, be the case. He vaguely remembered someone running at him. Perhaps that figure had in fact been the boy? Perhaps his mind alone had made the figure a man? Anything, after all, is possible for a man who can travel seven hundred kilometres but still think that he is in Sultan Ahmet.

He hadn't let on to the psychiatrist that he knew what she was giving him. He rubbed his right buttock as he recalled the sting of the injection. A standard depot injection of a chlorpromazine-based drug. An anti-psychotic.

The man smiled. He knew all the names they had for what they called madness; they couldn't fool him.

He could, however, fool them. It was because the drugs hadn't worked the first time that he had managed to get out on to the street originally. His long since dead father had told the doctors that his son was too strong for them but they hadn't listened. And their ignorance had played right into his hands, just as it could now, provided he thought it through properly.

Vladimir Ilyich opened his curious and unclouded eyes wide and then surveyed his squalid domain with a slow, sly smile. There was no way that he was going to prison either now or in the future. There was no reason why a big strong man like him had to. That was no place for a creature of the people. And for what reason? Taking some silly girl by the neck in order to get his point across. It was so out of proportion it was absurd! Something would have to be done and he already knew that basically he had only one option left.

However, even as he threw off his blanket and surveyed the long, sinewy extent of his arms he knew that it was going to take every gram of his passion. Every tiny centimetre of his heroism.

But then for a someone who had once travelled seven hundred kilometres like a dead man was this such a massive task? Well, was it?

Vladimir Ilyich lowered his head slowly towards his hands, laughing softly.

'I've got documentation for everything,' the man said, swinging his arms wide to encompass his large stock of refrigerators and microwave ovens.

'Oh, good,' Cohen said as he moved around to face the small, rotund person at his elbow.

'Do you want me to get them? I've got everything: shipping receipts, bills of sale...'

'No.' Cohen smiled while the man just looked confused. 'Thank you, sir. I'm not actually interested in any of your stock.'

'No?'

'No. I've come about another matter actually. I understand that this premises was once owned by a firm of building contractors called'—he pulled the folded-up calendar out of his pocket and read—"Kayseri Architectural Services".'

The man frowned whilst looking with some disapproval at what was depicted on the calendar. 'Yes? Why?'

It was a somewhat defensive reply; Cohen wondered why. In order to make things run a little more smoothly he put the calendar back in his pocket.

'We need to speak to someone from this company about some work they did back in 1982.'

'Why? Did it fall down?'

'No. No, it's nothing to do with any fault or wrongdoing on the part of this company. The work I'm talking about is actually very good.'

'Oh.' The man, who had been sweating rather more profusely than was normal for a cool day in October, wiped his brow and then quickly touched the gold maşallah that hung around his neck. 'Oh, well, praise be to Allah for that.'

'Do you know something, sir, of this company?'

'Actually'—and here he laughed in what looked very like a relieved way—'the truth is I used to run that company myself, officer.'

'Oh?'

'Yes, until 1990 when I moved into electrical goods

supply. Would you like to come into the office? I'll have the boy bring tea.'

Cohen smiled in that wonderfully gracious way that only he and Ikmen could successfully pull off without slipping into obsequiousness. 'That would be most refreshing, sir,' he said. 'Thank you.'

The man, a Mr Kemal, Cohen learned as the former led him through a confusion of white goods, worked in an office that was literally plastered with photographs of the holy Muslim city of Mecca. As they entered the small room, a woman whose face was covered by a silk scarf scuttled out into what Cohen imagined must be the yard behind. As she left, Mr Kemal instructed her to 'send the boy with tea, two'. Then, squeezing behind a small but heavily laden desk, Mr Kemal sat down while Cohen placed himself on a three-legged stool opposite.

'And so?' the man asked, proffering a gracious hand for Cohen to begin.

'The property we're interested in, sir, is an old Ottoman place called The Sacking House. It's on Ishak Paşa up in Sultan Ahmet.'

Mr Kemal frowned. 'We were doing a lot of work on properties like that then, people turning them into hotels and suchlike,' he said, 'and 1982 is a long while ago.'

'Yes, I know.'

'And I only ever surveyed the sites myself. However...' He paused briefly to shuffle with a few papers, and when he had apparently found what he was searching for, he looked up again. 'I'll just get my brother in here. He might remember it...'

'Thank you.'

Mr Kemal punched a number into his mobile telephone and then sat back to await a reply. 'My brother actually did some of the work and so...' He smiled as someone apparently answered. 'Oh, Selim, could you come to the office please? There's a police officer here who...No, no problem, just something about an old job...OK, OK...Thank you.' Mr Kemal put the receiver down and then smiled. 'He will be here in a moment. Marvellous instruments, these mobile telephones, are they not?'

'Yes.'

'I'm thinking of getting into that myself. They are so popular it's impossible to make a wrong move with them.' He offered Cohen a cigarette from a small wooden box which the officer, gratefully, took.

'You seem to have your eye very firmly upon popular trends, sir,' he observed.

'Oh, you have to! I had a building company for many years, as you know, and during the time that I had it I made a good living. But with the coming of the tourists everybody wanted to get involved and so I reasoned that for a small operator like myself it would be better to get out before I was pushed. A lot of foreigners came in too.' He waved a dismissive hand. 'I expect you know all about that. Spanish builders taking over the south coast resorts and so on. People will always need refrigerators and ovens and this trade has been good to me. And if Allah wills the same will apply to mobile telephones also. After all, we each of us have one now, do we not?'

Cohen, who had not, as yet, joined the Turkish mobile telephone boom, smiled. 'And from the appearance of your old calendar, you too have changed quite a lot over the years, Mr Kemal.'

His host lowered his eyes as he answered. 'Ah, yes, the...er...'

'Girls with not much on,' Cohen offered.

'Yes. Well, I was a young man back then...It was a good day when I rediscovered the religion of my fathers; it put a lot of things into the right perspective, if you know what I mean.' He looked up and smiled. 'Do you, er, believe yourself or—'

'You wanted to see me?'

A man of about the same age as Mr Kemal but far slimmer entered the office and walked up to the desk. Cohen, who had not wanted to get into questions regarding whether or not he 'believed' in anything, inwardly sighed with relief.

'Ah, yes, Selim.' Mr Kemal greeted his brother with a slight nod of the head. 'The officer here is asking about a job that we did back in 1982.'

The second Mr Kemal drew his breath in sharply and then sat down on the edge of his brother's desk. 'That's a long time ago. I don't really think...'

'It was up in Sultan Ahmet,' Cohen explained, 'a top floor conversion of an old Ottoman property on Ishak Paşa, called The Sacking House. It backs on to one of the walls of the Topkapı.'

Selim Kemal pursed his lips as he very obviously wracked his brains. 'Mmm.'

'The man we think you may have done the work for is said to be Armenian. He—'

'Quite a posh type?'

Cohen leaned forward a little. 'Yes.'

'Mmm.' Selim Kemal took, without asking, a cigarette from his brother's box and then lit up.

'Well?' Cohen asked, a little more impatiently than he should have.

'Yes, I think I do vaguely recall the job you're talking about,' Selim Kemal replied. 'Some sort of little apartment?'

'Yes, that's it.'

'We did some plumbing up there, a bathroom, I think, and—'

'About the man,' Cohen continued. 'Do you remember anything about the actual man who asked you to do this work?'

Selim Kemal shrugged. 'Not a lot beyond the fact that he was posh. Didn't know anything about his being Armenian, but...Had a sweet little boy there though.'

Cohen frowned. 'A little boy?'

'Yes.' Selim Kemal smiled, exhibiting numerous broken teeth. 'The customer's son.'

'Mr Zekiyan had a son?' Cohen had to ask just to make absolutely certain. Artisans had, he knew, the well-deserved reputation for being rather vague and not just when it came to estimating costs.

Selim Kemal shrugged once again. 'If that was the man's name then that was his son, yes. It was because of him that we had to try and be quiet.'

'What, Mr Zekiyan or—'

'No, the boy!' Selim Kemal puffed three times rapidly on his cigarette and then dragged what was left over to the corner of his mouth with his tongue. 'The little one wasn't well—don't know what with—his father didn't talk that much; well, not to us. The boy was laid downstairs on a couch, his eyes closed for most of the time. He looked very sick, which is why it all sticks in my mind so. You don't see posh people at home sick too often, do you? I mean if they're that ill they usually go to hospital. Come to think of it...' he paused briefly, looking up through squinting eyes at the ceiling, 'that was the place where I had that disagreement...'

His brother snorted sharply. 'You had so many, Selim, which one are we talking about here?'

Acknowledging his sibling with only a passing glare, Selim Kemal then looked back down again, at Cohen. 'There was one day,' he said, 'when I noticed that the boy was awake. It was mid-summer, very hot, and the men and I were eating watermelon on the front steps. The little one looked parched and seeing as his father wasn't about to get him a drink I went in and started to prepare a slice of melon for him.'

'And?'

'Well, I gave it to him and I don't actually remember what happened next except that suddenly his father was there shouting at me. He was furious, which I couldn't understand seeing as how I was only helping the poor child.'

'Do you know why he was so angry at you?' Cohen asked.

'No. Just went on about not talking to his boy. Didn't want him mixing with peasants, I suppose.' He smiled a little sadly. 'As you've probably guessed, Officer, we're from the mountains and...'

His brother cleared his throat in a very obvious fashion.

'Some people can be a bit, you know, about that sort of thing.'

'I don't suppose you can describe this boy at all, can you?' Cohen asked. 'I know it's a long time ago.'

'He was little. About four years old, maybe. Black hair.'

'He didn't wear a crucifix, a Christian symbol on a chain?'

'Couldn't tell you. He might have done. I didn't notice.'

Cohen scratched his head and sighed. 'So what you're saying is that the little boy was just simply a—'

'An ordinary little lad, yes.'

'Did he speak, do you remember, to you?'

Selim Kemal considered this for a few seconds and

then lifted his eyebrows. 'I don't know. I can't remember. Can you tell me what all this is about, Officer?'

'We're trying to trace the boy's father,' Cohen replied. 'He may have some information regarding an investigation we're pursuing at the moment.'

'Oh.'

'Is it a serious thing, this investigation?' the owner of the shop asked.

'Well...' said Cohen, continuing in his best official voice, 'I can't really tell you anything about that at this point in time, sir.'

'Oh, that's all right, Officer,' Mr Kemal said, barely able to contain his plump enthusiasm, 'only there has been a murder, so I've heard, up in Sultan Ahmet and—'

'I do remember that he had a mark underneath his chin, the little boy,' Selim Kemal, who had been seemingly lost in thought during the previous exchange, interjected.

Cohen turned to look at him. 'What kind of mark?'

'I don't know, but it was a livid red, a bit like a cut. It bothered me at the time and I think I might even have told the other lads about it.'

'Straight and bleeding or healed up? What was it like?' Cohen asked.

'It was curved,' Selim Kemal said. 'Like someone had flicked a knife around the bottom of his chin. It was, if I'm not mistaken, a crescent.' And then quite suddenly he smiled. 'Just like on our national flag, I suppose. Strange really, don't you think?'

# 11

SULEYMAN DIDN'T GET home until quite late that night. Zuleika had already gone to bed and, despite the fact that the opera singer who lived opposite was still practising her scales, she appeared to be asleep.

For his part, although tired, Suleyman himself was not sleepy. His second meeting in so many days with the repellent Mr Djugashvilli had been a disturbing experience and what with having to go back and relay all that had happened to Ikmen afterwards he was now in a state of weary wakefulness. He went into the living room and sat down with the full intention of switching on the television but, once ensconced in a chair, he found that his mind was far too preoccupied with the events of the day to bother with either films or soap operas.

Although he had known that a lot of the people who came across the Black Sea from the former Soviet Union supported themselves in Turkey by performing less than legal tasks, the full scale of the thing had not really come home to him until now. It was well documented that the women of Russia, the 'Natashas,' sold their bodies in order to pay for their keep, but that so many young men did it too had shocked him. In the light of recent events it shouldn't have, but he had seen the case of that sad boy up on Yerebatan Caddesi as an isolated incident, which it was, he now knew, most decidedly not.

Mr Djugashvilli, whom he had met at the Beşiktaş ferry station, had not been specific about the nature of his information until he and Suleyman had been close to their destination. This place, which was entered via a doorway next to a tyre shop somewhere in the back streets of Beşiktaş was, so Mr Djugashvilli warned, 'unpleasant'. It was, he continued, the abode of three boys who sold themselves for sex, one of whom had some sort of story to tell about a doctor.

Only two of the boys, who looked about eighteen or twenty, were at home in their cigarette-butt- and sweet-wrapper-strewn home above the tyre shop when Suleyman and his informant entered what passed for their living area. There was a pungent smell of damp about the place which, even now, Suleyman could easily recall. And where the wallpaper had peeled away from the walls he noticed that the boys had stuck pictures of scantily clad male models, some arranged in very suggestive poses.

The boy they had come to see, a blond blue-eyed character, gave his name as Ilya; more than likely it was a false one. Despite the bone-chilling cold he had been wearing only a pair of jeans and a tiny singlet vest, which from Suleyman's point of view was useful as it allowed him to see the very numerous track marks on the boy's arms.

When Ilya had finally settled down with a cigarette to tell his story, partly via Djugashvilli and partly in his own halting Turkish, Suleyman was struck by both the reek of body odour that came off him and by the almost sensual way in which he addressed him. It was almost as if the boy were trying to tout for Suleyman's 'business', which either said something disturbing about how he was coming across to the boy, or meant that Ilya just couldn't help doing what he did best.

Several days before (Ilya couldn't be specific on the date which was not surprising given his drug habit) he'd brought a client home. This customer, a smart middle-aged man carrying a briefcase, had behaved rather strangely. After acceding to his sexual demands and taking his fee, Ilya had gone to the bathroom in order to, as Djugashvilli translated, 'fix himself up'. He was just about to inject himself when this man followed him in and placed a hand on to the boy's arm to stop him. Angry at first, the boy shouted at him to leave him alone but, not understanding his Russian words, the man persisted. After a short struggle, he tore the hypodermic from Ilya's hands. However, rather than fling the thing away or even use it himself, the man went over to his briefcase, took out another hypodermic and clipped the needle from that one on to Ilya's syringe. Then he took a bottle of what Suleyman assumed must have been surgical spirit out of his case and rubbed the boy's arm down with some of this on a ball of cotton wool. At this point the man pointed to himself and said the word 'doctor', after which he expertly and, according to Ilya, with great gentleness, drew the liquid heroin up into the needle and then slipped it almost painlessly into the boy's vein. Ilya thought that the 'doctor' had said something about coming back in order to give him something else, he didn't know what, at some time in the future.

It was all very vague and not, so Suleyman thought, directly connected with the pethidine that he had told Djugashvilli to keep a watch out for on his part of the street. Yet it was a link, albeit tenuous, with the notion of doctors doing things that they shouldn't. And, though Ikmen had not expressed any tremendous interest in this development, he had said that perhaps they should try to think about ways to follow it up—without of course telling Dr Sarkissian, who it seemed had developed rather an obsession with the subject of doctors acting unprofessionally.

One thing that seemed to be sticking in Suleyman's mind, however, was a detail that the boy Ilya had included in his rather poor description of the man. This 'doctor' was uncircumcised. Although, as a Russian, Ilya was in that 'untouched' state himself, not many of his customers in this principally Muslim country were, which was why this 'Turk with a foreskin' had registered so forcefully in his mind.

Could it possibly be that this man and the doctor who had supplied the drugs to the lad on Yerebatan Caddesi were one and the same? Or even, at a far darker, not to mention controversial level, could it be that the smart and obviously prosperous Mr Zekiyan of Ishak Paşa was in fact a doctor, but under a different name? And if so had he both supplied and injected the boy who had died in his house? An unspoken assumption that Mr Zekiyan and the supplier of the boy's drugs had not been one and the same person had almost unconsciously taken hold somehow and yet, as Ikmen had acknowledged just before Suleyman left him that evening, assuming that the boy had been in that house for some time, the Armenian had at least to have known about his habit. And if he knew could he not also have been involved too? It was a new, but at moments an almost overwhelming notion.

Suleyman's thoughts were abruptly curtailed by the insistent beeping of his mobile telephone. Taking the instrument out of his jacket pocket he pressed the 'on' button and said, 'Suleyman.'

'I'm afraid I've some bad news for you, Suleyman,' Ikmen said, his voice cracked with tiredness.

Suleyman instantly felt his heart race. 'Sir?' he asked.

'There is no way that I can soften what has to be said and so I'll just say it. The prisoner who called himself Lenin was found dead in his cell about half an hour after you left this evening.'

'But...how?' As the veins in his head attempted to cope with the increased blood flow he felt his skull begin to throb with a dull ache.

'He committed suicide,' Ikmen said baldly and then added. 'Look, I know how you felt about him and I also know that this is only going to increase your sense of guilt but—'

'How could he do that? They take everything that could be used off them down there.'

'If a man is determined, he will find a way, Suleyman.'

The next few seconds passed for Ikmen in silence, but for Suleyman in a cacophonous jarring of thoughts, impressions and fears. Had the man committed suicide directly because of his arrest or in a fit of delusion? What had he been doing presenting himself to the police anyway? Why had they even entertained the notion of questioning a delusional man in the first place?

'Suleyman?' Ikmen asked. 'Are you still there?'

'Yes, sir.'

'Do you want me to come over?'

'No. No, that's all right, I'm...Look, how...I'm sorry, I don't understand. I mean, how...'

'Did he do it?' Ikmen asked. 'Do you really want to know?'

Once again the silence came; this time, Suleyman was attempting to deal with his own fears. He was, or so he felt, in part responsible for the man's death.

'Yes,' he answered quietly, 'yes, I do.'

He heard Ikmen sigh deeply at the other end of the line. Then Ikmen said, 'He cut his wrists.'

'But there was nothing...' Suleyman stammered. 'There can't have been anything in his cell to...'

'He used his teeth,' Ikmen said, a discernible tremor in his voice.

'Oh...Oh...' The picture that this painted in Suleyman's head was so disturbing and so abhorrent that for a moment he thought that he might be physically sick.

'You do have to remember that he was extremely ill,' Ikmen added. 'I mean, no normal person could possibly do such a thing.'

'No.'

'Look, if you want to talk, Suleyman...'

'No.' That was just what he didn't want to do. It was talking, this talking, that was building pictures in his mind that he did not want to see. And besides, what would discussing it all change? The man was dead and that was fact and nothing could change it.

'No, I think I'd like to be alone for now,' he said, 'I'll see you in the morning, sir.'

'As you wish,' Ikmen replied.

Suleyman switched off the telephone and then sat quite unmoving for a while. It was going to be a long night now for the three of them: just him, the horrifying pictures in his head, and his guilt.

'Mad people usually end up killing themselves.' It was said as a statement of fact rather than an opinion and it was one, furthermore, that Commissioner Ardiç believed to be irrefutably true.

'There will still have to be an investigation,' Ikmen said. 'I mean, just the simple fact that he had been dead for so long before he was found merits some sort of inquiry.'

'The custody officers are at fault,' Ardiç replied. 'I'm having the lot of them into my office at midday. I'm not happy about this, you know,' he added, 'but I also acknowledge that it was probably inevitable.'

'Nobody does something that terrible without being absolutely desperate,' Suleyman muttered from behind his unusually messy desk.

Ardiç, who hadn't really taken any notice of the younger man until now, turned to look at him. The bloodshot eyes and pale face spoke volumes about the kind of night Suleyman had had.

'I don't know why you're taking this so hard, Sergeant,' the Commissioner said. 'After all, you only restrained the man, quite rightly, after he had performed a violent act. And, as I have said, he was howling mad.'

'Which is why he shouldn't even have been here in the first place! Why Sergeant Farsakoğlu was even interviewing him...'

'It was her decision and so perhaps she is the person you ought to ask.' Although his words were quite logical and were said in a manner that was not directly confrontational, anyone looking at the sharp light that now danced in Ardiç's eyes would know that he was not best pleased. 'Anyway, I think that for the moment you have rather more pressing concerns than a dead madman. The Ishak Paşa victim still lies unclaimed in the mortuary and you are not, as far as I can see'—here he turned to face Ikmen— 'any closer to a solution to this crime. Am I right?'

Ikmen sighed. 'Where there are no protagonists obviously in evidence and also in the absence of any sort of identification on the victim, investigations tend to take on a rather shifting quality.'

Ardiç eyed his far more erudite inferior with a suspicious eye. 'Meaning?'

'Well, sir, what it means,' Ikmen continued, 'is that as evidence comes in to us we have to take time to review what it means in the light of what our thoughts and opinions have been in the past. We have nothing upon which to "hang" any of this stuff and so we are confined to speculation based upon the few facts that we do have.'

'Mmm.' Ardiç cleared his throat and then sat down on a chair in the corner of the room, pulling his coat protectively about his shoulders. 'So what are you actually doing?'

'Just before you came in, sir,' Ikmen said, 'I was considering a new piece of evidence that came in from one of my constables yesterday afternoon. Having tracked down the building company who converted the top floor of The Sacking House, this constable, Cohen, discovered from one of the employees who remembered the job that the tenant had a boy in the house back with him then, in 1982.'

'So?'

'The tenant, the one we know as Mr Zekiyan, said that the boy, who was about four at the time, was his son.'

Ardiç frowned. 'Which links in with our victim how?'

'Well, the builder noticed that the child, who was unwell at the time and who lay for the whole period unmoving on a couch, had a crescent-shaped cut under his chin. Not only does this correspond to a faint mark that Dr Sarkissian found in exactly that position upon the corpse but it could also mean, given the age of the child then and the age of the victim now, that the child and the victim are one and the same. Scars and birthmarks do often fade over time, you see.'

'So what you're saying,' Ardiç said, 'is that you believe that this Zekiyan character has murdered his own son?'

'Not necessarily, but—'

'His own son who, presumably, would have been known by many people during the intervening fifteen years?'

'It had always been a possibility that this man imprisoned the boy for some reason. Given the facts that the locked apartment was created soon after Mr Zekiyan moved to the property and that the boy's limbs were atrophied this is, fantastic as it seems, a possibility. I mean, why put him in what must, given the amount of pethidine in his body, have been a chemical straitjacket unless you wanted to keep him quiet and unmoving?'

'But for fifteen years? Why?'

Ikmen shrugged. 'That we don't know. Dr Sarkissian, however, has a theory that the man may have hidden the boy away because of some embarrassing defect that he had. It does happen. However, we can't even now be certain that the boy was Zekiyan's son and I am inclined to think that I must also investigate unsolved missing persons files from 1981 and '82. Just in case.'

'You think that the child might have been kidnapped?' Then, seeing that Ikmen was taking a cigarette out of his packet, Ardiç added, 'Don't even think about doing that in my presence, Ikmen.'

With a scowl, Ikmen replaced the cigarette and, a little tetchily, continued. 'There is no evidence of sexual interference on the corpse but then people can be spirited away for reasons other than—'

'You still cannot, I take it, trace any person with this tenant's name?' Ardiç asked.

'No. But it might well be a pseudonym.'

'I see.' Having seen smoking materials so near at hand

had made Ardiç suddenly even more irascible than normal. This translated physically into his biting his nails for the remainder of their conversation. 'So what of this drug you seem to think some doctor might have been supplying? Where, if anywhere, are we with that?'

'As yet there is no evidence to suggest that pethidine is circulating on the streets. However'—here Ikmen looked across at Suleyman who was miserably considering the pile of papers on his desk—'Suleyman was yesterday in contact with a young rent boy who claims to have been helped to administer heroin to himself by a customer who told him he was a doctor. This man, like Mr Zekiyan, was tall and middle-aged and, as one would expect an Armenian to be, uncircumcised.'

Ardiç sniffed as if he had a rather unpleasant smell under his nose. 'Did this man sell this prostitute any drugs?'

'No. Although he did say that he might come back later with "something".'

'The boy is Russian, sir,' Suleyman added, 'and didn't really understand whether the man meant that he was going to return to help him inject himself or in order to give him something.'

'So you're saying,' Ardiç reasoned, 'that this Mr Zekiyan, as well as being the boy's father, may also be a doctor.'

'It's possible,' Ikmen replied. 'We have always assumed that Mr Zekiyan and the supplier of the drug were two different people, but if the boy had been imprisoned in that house for such an enormous length of time then it is safe to assume that Mr Zekiyan at least knew about the drug use if not ordered and even administered it himself. And both his wealth and apparent breeding could well be consistent with the status of a doctor.'

Ardiç sighed. 'Well,' he said, 'I suppose you'd better ask Sarkissian about queer Armenian doctors then, hadn't you?'

'I have plans,' Ikmen said, smiling at his superior's direct-
ness, 'along those lines, yes, but without the doctor's help.'
He shrugged. 'It may all be absolutely nothing, but together
with the case of that boy up in Yerebatan Caddesi—'

'Yes! What did happen about that child? He was on
drugs, wasn't he?'

'The lab phoned this morning to say that the drug was
heroin. There is, as you know, information to suggest that
an unscrupulous doctor may be involved in that case too.
But I have to rely on vice to pursue that particular medic,
if indeed he is different from the Beşiktaş case. In a sense I
hope that they are one and the same—it'll save me time.'

'But then neither he nor the doctor who injected Suleyman's boy may be involved at all.'

Ikmen inclined his head to signify his agreement. 'True.
But the notion of Zekiyan as a doctor does make some
sense, we know the Beşiktaş client was uncircumcised, and
the Yerebatan pimp said his doctor was a Christian.'

'Yes. Yes, I suppose so.' Ardiç sighed. 'Just try and up
the pace a bit is all I ask, Ikmen. Whether we know who
he is or not, I want this boy buried as soon as we can now.
Sarkissian's done all that he can.'

'Not knowing whether or not the boy is Muslim does
present some problems,' Ikmen said.

'And with that Lenin person also,' put in Suleyman.

Ardiç stared at him with little compassion. 'Well, you
can leave the latter case to me,' he said. 'You just concentrate on the boy. Unsolved homicides translate into very
unfavourable crime statistics and also undermine public
confidence, which is, as you know, never high.'

All three men became quiet at this point. There were
and had always been stories about the Turkish police, what
they did and did not do. What happened when people

ended up in their cells could, Ikmen knew, be rather unpleasant. That his prisoners, irrespective of their alleged crimes, did not, on his orders, ever suffer such fates, did not make the general impression of the force any better. And that the madman Lenin had died whilst nominally under his aegis was something that he knew was not just going to go away.

Ardiç stood up and, to Ikmen's relief, made ready to take his leave. 'All I ask, is that you don't get too psychological about all this, Ikmen. You know what I mean?'

'Yes, sir.'

'All right.'

As he opened the door to leave, Ikmen took a cigarette out of his packet and prepared to light up. 'I'll get back to you as soon as I have more information.'

'You do that.' Ardiç closed the door behind him just as Ikmen flicked his lighter into action.

'I thought he would never go!' he said to Suleyman as he breathed in his first lungful of smoke. 'I was absolutely drooling for a smoke.'

Suleyman, who always ignored all of Ikmen's speeches on the beauty of smoking, sighed, 'So where do we go from here then, sir?'

Ikmen, who had now pushed himself back in his chair and placed his feet up on his desk, smiled. 'I have the names of two gold merchants who regularly fashion jewellery and religious artefacts for the Christian clergy. I was going to ask you to make some inquiries over there about Mr Zekiyan's unusual ring but I think I'll do that myself.'

'Oh?'

'Yes. I've not been to the bazaar for some months which is most remiss of me considering that it is always such a good source of gossip.'

'Yes,' Suleyman agreed, 'it is. So what do you want me to do?'

'I'd like you to arrange an appointment to see Dr Avram Avedykian.' Ikmen opened one of the drawers in his desk and took out a sheet of paper covered with what appeared to be names and telephone numbers which he threw across to Suleyman.

'What's this?' Suleyman asked.

'It's a contact list for all those on Dr Krikor's committee. You'll find Dr Avedykian's direct-line number on there.'

Suleyman took a few seconds to locate this information after which he looked back across at his superior again. 'You can't surely think that Avram Avedykian has anything to do with the death of our boy.'

Ikmen smiled. 'As an Armenian doctor who is known, amongst certain circles, to be homosexual, he cannot be discounted. Think of him as a start if you like. Besides, I get the feeling that Dr Sarkissian may be worried about his friend's reputation should all this doctor thing explode around us. I have no reason to suspect Avedykian.'

'Yes, but...'

'Dr Sarkissian has given it as his opinion that doctors with secrets can be vulnerable—he wants to check pharmacy drug stocks, which is a mite previous, I feel, and a little excessive, but then he is obsessed. However, about secrets he may have a point. You and I know about Avedykian's relationship with Ersoy, as do all of his posh, sophisticated friends, but I don't suppose that his employers are aware of it. And men like that, with something to hide, often know of others who live under the same predicament.'

Suleyman made a rather sour grimace. 'I'm surprised that someone like you, sir, can think that just because the man is homosexual he must know everybody else who is like that.'

Ikmen laughed. 'Dr Sarkissian accused me of something similar only the other day. But no, I don't think that, Suleyman. What I do know, however, is that people who are vulnerable in any way tend to attract others as friends. And also, it has to be said that Dr Avedykian probably does know more homosexual men than you or I.'

'Well, yes, I suppose if one moves in those...'

'Exactly!'

'However'—Suleyman looked down at his hands and then rubbed his tired brow—'what I'm supposed to ask Dr Avedykian is...'

'You put it to him that you have received information regarding a doctor who is becoming involved with both drugs and male prostitutes. Tell him that an investigation is pending, which is true, it will have to happen, and that as a friend—'

'I was never Avram Avedykian's friend, sir!' Suleyman exclaimed. 'He is considerably older than I am and, if you recall, he stood mutely by while Ersoy bullied my brother.'

'If you would just listen for a moment, Suleyman,' Ikmen said as patiently as he could. 'As a friend, I, not you, am sending him prior warning that this might become a scandal, and if he knows anything about such a person he should both alert us to what that person has done or who he is and distance himself from him. You should point out that if his name were dragged into anything like this, even if he is innocent, it could harm the good opinion the public currently has of Dr Krikor Sarkissian's drug project.'

Suleyman's face resolved into a picture of shock. 'But that's...'

'Completely unethical? Yes,' Ikmen said, 'it is, isn't it? But it is also exactly what you old aristocrats do for each other, isn't it?'

'Well, I don't!' Suleyman answered furiously.

Ikmen laughed again, amused by his deputy's self-righteousness. 'Yes, I know that you don't, Suleyman, and neither do I. But in order to get Dr Avedykian either to contact somebody he shouldn't, like young Ilya, or maybe someone who knows the boy, or do something panicky himself, we need him to think that we have his interests at heart. After you have spoken to him, I will arrange to have him watched—probably from tomorrow—he and Ilya. That should be time enough to discover his intentions.'

'But what if he really doesn't know anything about any of this?'

'Then he will behave completely normally and will have nothing to fear. However, if he does start meeting people with whom he has panicky conversations, we will know. I mean, how else in a country like Turkey are you going to find out where these people are? Folk are guarded about that sort of thing. Look upon Avedykian as I do: a resource we cannot afford to ignore.' Ikmen stubbed his cigarette out and then immediately lit another. 'Well, come on then, ring him up,' he said, 'do like the Commissioner told us and don't waste time.'

As Suleyman picked up the receiver, somebody knocked at the office door.

'Come in,' Ikmen called out.

'Hello, sirs,' Cohen said as he entered the office, then seeing that Suleyman was on the telephone he lowered his voice and said to Ikmen, 'Something came for you.' He placed a small and to Ikmen familiar box upon the inspector's desk. 'This.'

'Ah,' Ikmen said and then, peering down at the front of the package, he read, 'Kadıköy.'

'Kadıköy?'

'The postmark,' Ikmen explained, 'the first one of these I've been able to read, although the photographic boys reckoned at least one of the others came from Bebek.'

'Oh,' said Cohen, suddenly realising what was being spoken about. 'Is this another of those...'

'Yes, I think so,' Ikmen said as he roughly pulled the little package apart. 'Another crystal for my ever-growing collection, I believe.'

'It's fucking strange, all this,' Cohen observed as Ikmen removed something shiny from the wrapping paper. 'It's like somebody's having a game with you or something.'

'That is exactly what is happening, Cohen,' Ikmen said as he placed the article on the surface of his desk. 'Now what do you think that he's trying to tell us with this?'

Cohen bent down to look properly at the miniature, which appeared to be that of two small men or boys joined at the shoulder.

'Well, it's two little men, isn't it?' he said. 'Joined up.'

'I can see that!' Ikmen said tetchily. 'If I'd wanted you to state the obvious I would have said so. No, what does it mean, Cohen? What is it saying to you?'

'Well...' Sucking on his lips, Cohen bent still lower in order to consider the item and then announced, 'Well, it's two little men, isn't it, joined...'

'I can see,' Ikmen said with a frustrated sigh, 'that symbolic thought is not really your strong suit.' Then with a wave of his hand he concluded, 'Go on, out now, I need to think about this myself.'

Cohen duly moved towards the open door leaving Ikmen bending very closely over his desk and Suleyman smiling into the telephone.

Once again, this model was most exquisitely fashioned. The figures even had tiny carved facial features and, although devoid of sexual organs, they did have really very powerfully moulded chest muscles. They were undeniably male.

He heard the click of a telephone receiver being replaced and, looking up to see that Suleyman was indeed now free, he asked, 'And?'

'Dr Avedykian will see me when his clinic finishes in an hour.'

'Good.' Then, beckoning his deputy across to his desk, he said, 'Will you come and look at this, Suleyman? Tell me what you think.'

Suleyman got up from his chair and made his way over to Ikmen's desk, looking all the while at the model in front of his superior's face.

'Oh, another of those things, is it?' he said. 'What this time?'

Ikmen looked up at him and smiled. 'Well, I know what I think it is but I want your opinion.'

He held the miniature up for Suleyman to see. The harsh neon from the lighting strip above seemed to crash through the figure, scattering its numerous colours in each and every possible direction.

'Well, it's Gemini, isn't it?' Suleyman said. 'You know, the astrological symbol, two little joined-up men, the twins.'

'Exactly,' Ikmen said, 'and twins being siblings...'

'Or as in this, more specifically brothers?' Suleyman offered.

'Indeed! And if we put this together with our other little presents...'

'The caged bird and the Topkapı dagger.'

'We get?' Ikmen encouraged.

Suleyman, his inspiration suddenly drained, just simply shrugged. 'I...'

'The old sultans used to put their brothers into cages in the Topkapı,' Ikmen said, his eyes shining.

'Yes, but...'

'This boy was imprisoned, possibly, for fifteen years.'

'Yes, yes, I can see what is being indicated here,' Suleyman said a tad impatiently, 'but why make this particular comparison? I mean brothers were put into the Kafes because they were a potential threat to the ruling—'

'Exactly!' Ikmen cried. 'What he is saying is that this boy was a threat to him in some way. He therefore hid him away because of that threat!'

'But just a moment,' Suleyman said, 'this is a very Turkish thing we're talking about here, isn't it? And yet this doctor and even the boy we think are Armenians. Mr Zekiyan is Armenian, the boy is uncircumcised, we're looking into the lives of doctors who are Armenian...And anyway, why kill the boy after all that time? Why not just kill him at the beginning? To hold him like that for so long must have been difficult.'

'Well...' Ikmen scratched his head, 'yes, but...'

'There appears, I must say, sir, to be some sort of incongruity between what we are looking for with regard to this doctor who may or may not also be Mr Zekiyan and the messages you are receiving from this unknown source. I mean, if this doctor who is helping boys to take opiates or providing boys with them is one and the same as Mr Zekiyan, then all this Turkish stuff would appear to be meaningless. And even if they are not one and the same, we are still looking, until we have evidence to the contrary, for someone uncircumcised, possibly Armenian.'

'Oh, I accept that the two events could be totally unconnected,' Ikmen said, 'and that with the boy prostitutes we are even quite outside our remit. But it is the supply of opiates to young boys that...I cannot help feeling that our boy, strange though we think his case is, cannot be an isolated incident. And if Dr Sarkissian's correct then with pethidine we are definitely in the arena of the medical profession.'

'But the boy I went to see was on heroin.'

'The two are, if I'm right,' Ikmen replied, 'almost identical in effect. If this doctor could get hold of one then he could get the other too. It's my understanding that doctors can prescribe differing analgesics as and when they wish. And if a doctor, whether Mr Zekiyan himself or not, were supplying to either himself or another, then it is possible that the temptation of trading may have occurred to him—particularly if he moves within circles where sex is for sale.'

'I see. And as for the little models here?' Suleyman said, looking at the example upon Ikmen's desk.

Ikmen shrugged. 'If all this Armenian doctor connection is so much coincidence, then they could signify the type of Kafes-style scenario we have discussed. Unless we explore each and every hunch and avenue then we cannot hope to arrive at anything approaching a solution.'

Suleyman picked up the little model and held it up to the light. 'For things that are so shiny these certainly do appear to cloud the issue.' He looked down at Ikmen with a grave face: 'Makes you wonder whether they really do come from our murderer, doesn't it? You can buy these in almost any tourist shop in town, apparently. After all, we have no proof other than the fact that there were a lot of these in that apartment.'

'About which who could know but our reclusive Mr Zekiyan?' Ikmen asked. 'He didn't exactly have the neighbours round for cocktails and he was only ever seen a few times with one other man and a child.'

'Whom he didn't like workmen talking to,' Suleyman added.

'No.'

They remained wrapped up in their own thoughts for a few moments until Ikmen finally broke the silence. 'Well, you'd better get out to Dr Avedykian anyway. If the traffic is bad it could take you an hour.'

Suleyman sighed. Precisely why he was going out to see this doctor, this long-ago tormentor of his brother, and what that would achieve, he knew that both he and Ikmen were perilously unsure. It was a meeting that could prove to be very difficult indeed.

Ayşe Farsakoğlu shouldn't really have been anywhere near her place of work. Had a doctor examined her, it is almost certain that she would have been judged unfit for duty. She had not as yet that day spoken to anyone of her own volition. Quite simply, she was in a state of shock.

She hadn't herself actually found the remains of the poor madman who had so suddenly and violently taken his own life in his cell the previous afternoon. She had however seen him shortly after he had been discovered, while his face was still smothered in gouts of his own blood. Indeed the cell had been quite awash with gore; she felt it was going to be absolutely impossible for her to forget the sound that her boots had made as she literally waded her way over to the body.

Had he not been arrested, would he, as the psychiatrist had said, still at some unspecified point have committed such a savage act upon himself? She, the psychiatrist, had been of the opinion that his self-destruction had been imminent anyway due to what she had termed an 'incongruity between his delusional persona and that of his new reality'. What Ayşe thought she meant by this was that Lenin's view of himself as 'Lenin' had been breaking down even as he had entered the police station in order to confess to that crime that he could not, surely, have committed. He had said, she clearly remembered, that he killed the child by stabbing it, which did not in any way tally with the actual cause of death.

None of this, however, could, as far as she was concerned, detract from the fact that his suicide had followed very quickly after his attack upon herself and his subsequent harsh treatment at the hands of her colleagues. Even under the auspices of the enlightened Inspector Ikmen, those who attacked officers were generally given very little quarter. His food would have been disgusting and, stripped of his shoes (removed lest he try to hang himself with the laces) she knew that, especially in his wildly disordered state, he would have been both frightened and desperate—and with good cause. When he died he had done so in the knowledge that he was shortly to be transferred to prison to await trial and, having seen the inside of several of those institutions herself in the past, Ayşe knew that someone like Lenin would not have thrived.

She did not know how long she had been sitting on one of the low walls that partially encompassed the car park when Mehmet Suleyman stepped out of the station and walked towards his vehicle. It would be too simplistic to say that his appearance woke her from her dismal reverie, indeed when she approached him her eyes were still glazed by the conflicting thoughts and feelings that raged within her mind. The sight of him, or rather the desire for him, did however at least galvanise her into some sort of activity.

'You do know,' she said as she approached him, 'what has happened?'

His eyes, which exhibited both fear and weariness, darted about him nervously as she approached. 'Yes,' he said, 'I know. But I can't talk now. I'm just on my way out.'

'But I need to talk to somebody.' She moved forward as if to touch him, but seeing him flinch she pulled back and said, 'I need to talk to you.'

He slid his key into the lock of his car door. 'Why me?'

'Because you were involved too.' Then she added quickly, 'What other reason could there be?'

Not meeting her gaze, he shrugged. 'None that I can think of.'

'Right.'

'I can't talk now. I've got to go and meet somebody.'

'Well, later then! After work.' Her eyes started to weep uncontrollably, as if possessed of lives of their own. 'Please, Mehmet!'

He cast yet another quick glance around before replying and then said with a sigh, 'All right, all right, I'll meet you.'

Her whole body, or so it seemed to him, appeared to soften with relief. 'Where? And when?'

Nervously he chewed on his bottom lip with his teeth as he tried to think of a place where they would not be observed.

'I sometimes go to the Vitamin for my evening meal,' she offered, 'I've never ever seen other cops in there in the evening.'

He tried to think of an alternative that might prove even more discreet, but couldn't, so he nodded his assent.

'I'll be there from about seven,' she said. 'Will you...?'

'I'll be along when I can,' he answered. 'The way things are at the moment I cannot give you an exact time but if you wait I will be there. I will not let you down.'

'I know,' she said, and then looking down at the floor, 'You're very good to people, you're a good—'

'I really have to go now, Sergeant,' Suleyman said, cutting off what he was finding a most embarrassing moment. 'I will see you tonight as we have discussed.'

'Yes, thank you, Mehmet,' she said as he got into his car and fired up the engine. 'I will, I promise, wait for you.'

When he had gone, she went back and sat down on the wall once again where she promptly returned to her previous coma-like state. Cold as it was and without even the benefit of her coat which she had left at her apartment, she sat quite perfectly still right up until Commissioner Ardiç's secretary came to tell her that her boss wanted to see her in his office.

❀ ❀ ❀

'As you can see,' the gold merchant said, indicating the pane of his door with a sweep of his hand, 'I do accept all the major credit cards.'

'Yes,' said Ikmen a trifle impatiently, he'd already been through this routine once with the proprietor of the previous shop, 'but if we could just get back to the issue at hand?'

'Oh, yes, yes!' said the merchant, turning once again to the large leather-bound ledger on his counter. 'Zekiyan was the name, was it not?'

'Yes.'

'And a crucifix ring in emerald and diamond.'

'Yes,' Ikmen once again confirmed, this time with a tired sigh.

'Mmm.' The merchant turned the pages slowly, running one finger down each section as he went. 'I have quite a number of customers for this type of item.' He looked up with a smile. 'Christians.'

'Many of them clergy, right?' Ikmen asked, looking as casually as he could at two ropes of gold that must, he reckoned, be each one metre in length.

'Oh yes. Even patriarchs,' the merchant replied with an almost dismissive wave of the hand. 'Others too, of course. Like your Armenian gentleman and more recently people from er'—here he faltered a little, smiling in an embarrassed sort of way— 'across the Black Sea, if you know what I mean.'

Ikmen laughed. 'Our Russian friends who presumably pay in cash?'

'Well, yes, often.' The merchant looked most pointedly back at his ledger and then muttered almost underneath his breath, 'American dollars.'

'Oh how surprising!' Ikmen said with more than a little irony in his voice.

'Not, of course, that there is anything wrong with that,' the merchant added quickly, 'I mean as far as the honest trader is concerned money is money and provided it is not counterfeit...'

Ikmen placed one hand firmly on to the merchant's fingers and said, 'Look, it's not, I know, any of your business where they get the money and besides, I'm not here about that, am I? If you could just look for Mr Zekiyan?'

'Of course! Of course!'

As the merchant trawled through both the old ledger and hopefully his own memory too, Ikmen took some time to look again at his surroundings. These gold emporiums had always fascinated him. Not one either to wear or even desire jewellery himself, it had always amazed him that so many outlets for this stuff could survive all closely packed together in what was not, if one took the whole population into account, a wealthy city. But then Islam, as well as Christianity, could be quite intensive with regard to these things. What with wedding rings, 'Maşallah' talismen to protect, particularly the new-born, plus the blue boncuk beads to keep the 'eye' at bay, not to mention the custom of giving one's wife a gold bangle for every year one had been married...This latter tradition together with the knowledge that Fatma only possessed two, filled Ikmen with momentary guilt and so he turned his mind away from the subject.

There were the tourists too, of course. Gold was relatively cheap in Turkey and that, together with the reputation the bazaar had for fine workmanship, attracted them. And as for all the shops being herded together in one quarter of the bazaar, well, that was traditional which, in a way, made it even more appealing to those from outside the city. It must seem, or so he supposed, quite charming to those who did not come into regular contact with it. During the course of his one and only sortie out of the country, which had been to London back in the 1970s, just the mere mention of the words 'Grand Bazaar' had, he recalled, evoked from his audience a plethora of words like 'exotic', 'exciting' and 'mysterious'. That he had felt much the same about Oxford Street had for some reason elicited considerable mirth.

'Well,' said the merchant, rousing Ikmen from his gold-edged cogitations, 'the man that you name is not amongst my lists of regular customers. I will look to see whether there is a ticket for a commission of a bespoke item, but if you have no idea when he might have purchased it, such a search may take me some time.'

'Would you only make such an item to order?' Ikmen asked.

'Not always,' the merchant, who was an elderly, white-haired man, said. 'Both emeralds and diamonds are popular stones and so it is possible the gentleman may have just seen the item in the window and then come in to purchase it. With more unusual or less popular stones I would have to raise an order.'

'So if he bought it from the window there would—'

'Only if he paid by credit card, unless it was very recent, would I have a record. And then if the credit transaction was a long time ago...'

Ikmen sighed. This was, he felt, rapidly turning into a waste of time. Without even an approximate date of purchase and with the possibility that the elusive Mr Zekiyan could, especially if he paid by cash, change his name at will, it was like looking for a bus ticket on an overflowing desk in the dark.

There was, however, one other name that he could try, although it was an unlikely, not to mention mischievous connection on his part. He thought, after a few seconds' consideration, that he might as well give it a go.

'Does the name Avedykian mean anything to you?' he asked.

The merchant smiled. 'Oh yes, we do a lot of work for that family. Sevan Avedykian is, as you, Inspector, must know, a noted lawyer and with his brother in the church—'

'Do you know Avram Avedykian, a doctor?'

'Mr Sevan's son? Oh yes, he has been many times to our shop with his mother. Why?'

'Oh, just asking. What sort of things do they...'

'Oh, ladies' brooches, chains and suchlike. Nothing for men as I recall.' He leaned forward a little conspiratorially across the counter. 'With the exception of Mr Sevan's brother they are not a religious family.'

'No?'

'No. Dr Avram is very good to his mother though, buys her a lot of nice things.'

'Oh, does he?'

'I could check to see what they are and with regular customers it will be a little easier but,' he sighed, 'it will still take me some time. I mean I will have to get back to you.'

'That's all right.' Ikmen smiled and then, taking a small card out of his wallet he placed it on the counter. 'If you just ring me on this number?'

The merchant took a pair of spectacles out of the top pocket of his jacket, put them on and then peered myopically at Ikmen's card. 'Mmm,' he said as he held it away from him and then, looking up, added, 'Dr Avedykian isn't in any sort of trouble, is he?'

Knowing as he did that gold merchants possessed an almost legendary reputation for gossip, Ikmen replied, 'Oh no. It's just a little discreet inquiry; this being a police matter, it would be best kept between ourselves.'

'Oh, but of course,' the merchant oiled, 'naturally.'

'So you'll get back to me on the Zekiyan thing, the crucifix ring?'

'If Allah wills,' the merchant said with a slight bow.

'Then I will leave it with you,' Ikmen replied, mirroring the old man's obeisance with one of his own.

When he stepped out of the shop, Ikmen paused for a few moments in order to gather himself for the assault upon all senses that occurred when one entered any of the main thoroughfares of the Grand Bazaar. Standing to one side as he was now, the shoppers, sightseers, hustlers and pickpockets that passed in front of him seemed to constitute an almost solid being with an intelligence quite separate from that of its little human constituent parts. A thing bent only upon its prime function: to consume, seemingly without thought.

In order to fortify himself against the coming fray, Ikmen lit a cigarette. As he inhaled his first, almost orgasmic lungful (unusually he had chosen to abstain whilst in the gold shop), he found that his thoughts almost unconsciously turned to Avram Avedykian. Suleyman was probably with him now, feeling very awkward and maybe even stumbling over his words, which was natural given the very difficult task he had been assigned. And in truth, even to Ikmen in the clear light of the almost outside world of the bazaar, any connection between this man and any wrongdoing did seem absurd. Here was a kind man who bought his mother jewellery, cared about the underprivileged and who also, for his pains, put up somehow with that admittedly charming perfumed dandy Muhammed Ersoy. That such a man could lower himself so far as to sell drugs or even associate with those who did, whether or not those involved were of his 'kind', was hard to believe. Arto Sarkissian, he thought, would probably be quite angry when he found out what he had done vis-à-vis Avedykian, not to mention why he had done it. That his motives were both of an investigative and in a way altruistic nature would—

'If I did not know you better, I would be most suspicious at seeing one of our fine officers outside a very high-class gold shop.'

The voice, which was as smooth and cultured as the most perfect pearl, was instantly familiar.

'Hello, Mr Ersoy,' Ikmen said as he turned to face the man who was dressed, this time, in the height of businessman chic.

The man in the elegant three-piece black suit smiled. 'So are you buying or just looking, Inspector?' he said.

'Men like me can only look, sir,' Ikmen replied with a shrug. 'My wife would that it were otherwise.'

'I expect that if you allowed yourself to, shall we say, forget your own personal code of ethics for a while, things could be somewhat different.'

'Well...' This very forthright allusion to the fact that some policemen took bribes, caught Ikmen temporarily off balance.

'But then,' Ersoy continued smoothly, 'Krikor has told me that you are just not like that. It is a quality that is, if detrimental to your personal finances, most noble and laudable in this naughty old city of ours.'

'Yes, well,' Ikmen said, 'perhaps it is a function of my having had a European mother. Perhaps I am not the kind of genuine Istanbuli that you outlined at your recent dinner party.'

Ersoy laughed. 'Oh, so you remember my little tirade, do you?'

'I enjoyed it very much,' Ikmen said, not in any way deviating from the truth.

'Well, I'm flattered,' Ersoy said, to all intents and purposes meaning it too. 'Let me buy you a coffee. Çetin, isn't it?'

'Yes.'

'And please call me Muhammed and not "sir". It really does make me feel most awfully gauche when you do that.'

'Well...'

'As you know, there's a Han just around the corner here.' Ersoy reached out and touched Ikmen's elbow. 'Please do let me treat you? We can watch the old men play tavla and I may even have a narghile which will make you with your lovely Western cigarettes look most frightfully modern and enlightened by comparison.'

Ikmen laughed. Despite, or perhaps because of Ersoy's peculiarly excessive opinions, not to mention his turn of phrase, he couldn't help but be amused by his company. 'Yes,' he said, 'coffee would be very nice.'

'Then let us go,' said Ersoy, gently propelling Ikmen forward via his captive elbow. 'Acknowledging, of course, that coffee even of the finest variety could in no way ever be considered a bribe.' Then, bending low towards Ikmen's ear, he whispered, 'That was the right thing to say in front of all these people, wasn't it, Inspector? I would so hate for any of them to get the wrong idea.'

'Suleyman... Suleyman...' Dr Avram Avedykian muttered the name several times to himself rather than to his visitor who just stood and looked at the doctor as if the man were a little unhinged.

'The name is familiar,' Avedykian said. 'Do I know you at all?'

Suleyman, who although irritated was quite relieved that at least some reason for this muttering had become apparent, said, not without some cruel relish, 'Not me, sir, but my brother may be familiar to you. Murad Suleyman?'

'Oh, Murad, yes.' Avedykian smiled that gentle smile of his which was also, Suleyman felt, vaguely dissolute too. 'He was a clever boy, wasn't he? What is he doing now?'

'He manages a hotel,' Suleyman replied, 'in Bodrum.'

'Oh. Oh, well.' It was obviously not the sort of profession Dr Avedykian felt warranted further discussion and so once he had ushered Suleyman into the chair opposite his own he said, 'So, you wanted to talk to me about something, Sergeant?'

'I'm actually here on behalf of Inspector Ikmen, sir,' Suleyman said, 'but the matter is somewhat delicate...' He looked pointedly across in the direction of the secretary who sat at her desk in the corner of the room.

'Oh,' said Avedykian. Turning to the woman, he said, 'Miss Emin, could you possibly give the officer and myself a moment please?'

The woman smiled. 'Yes, Doctor, of course,' and then, pausing only to pick up her handbag, she left the room.

Once the door had closed behind her, Avedykian cleared his throat and said, 'Well, Officer, how may I help you?'

'It is how I might help you actually, sir,' Suleyman said, 'or rather how Inspector Ikmen...'

'Oh. Well.'

In lieu of actually launching into the rather difficult points that he had to make, Suleyman just sat for a few moments, smiling. It was a tense silence and one which Avedykian eventually filled by saying. 'Can I offer you tea or a cigarette or...?'

'No, no thank you, Doctor. Look'—Suleyman noted briefly that Avedykian had now moved slightly back in his chair—'we have reason to believe that a doctor, we don't know who, is associating himself with certain young men who, shall we say, sell themselves.'

Avedykian reached into his top drawer and took out a packet of cigarettes. 'Oh, I see. Do you have any idea as to the identity of this doctor?'

'No, and in the normal course of events it is not the kind of subject with which we would concern ourselves.'

'But?'

'But the physician involved also assisted, so we have been told, this young man to administer heroin to himself. Which, as you can appreciate, is a somewhat more serious matter.' Suleyman sighed in order to give himself a little more time to organise his thoughts. 'In addition we have received intelligence from a quite different source that a doctor is also selling heroin to these people, these male prostitutes. Now, whether these physicians are one and the same person, we do not know, but—'

'I am not sure,' Avedykian said, lighting a cigarette

and then blowing out the match afterwards, 'how this might concern me?'

Suleyman had been expecting this but found that he was nevertheless not as prepared for it as he might have been. 'Well, sir, it is as I said before somewhat delicate. But if I tell you that my brother Murad was sometimes quite frank with regard to your relationship with Muhammed Ersoy, which we gather is still current...'

'Meaning I suppose that because I lead a certain type of lifestyle...'

'We will be investigating, or rather officers other than ourselves will be doing so and they will almost certainly be approaching those who run our hospitals here in the city. They will be looking closely at whom people associate with and so—'

'Are you saying that I am under suspicion, Sergeant?'

'No, Doctor, that is not what I am saying. However, what I or rather Inspector Ikmen is preparing you for is an investigation which may bring to light certain aspects of your private life that you would rather your employers—'

'Are you threatening me!' His reaction appeared to Suleyman to be totally out of proportion to what was being said and for a moment it quite took the policeman back.

'Because if you are,' Avedykian continued, 'I—'

'Nobody is either threatening or judging you, Doctor, quite the reverse in fact! What we are saying is that perhaps in the light of this you might want to place your private life on hold, as it were, for a while. Perhaps even disassociate yourself from others, particularly in your profession, who—'

'We don't all know each other, you know! You talk as if there existed some sort of cabal whereby we—'

'Sir, with respect,' Suleyman protested, 'I know that that is unlikely to be true but you must see that for those of like minds it must be only natural to associate to a certain extent. And given your involvement with Dr Krikor Sarkissian's drug project, the inspector is only too aware that anything even remotely touching upon the misuse of substances in relation to practising physicians—'

'But why me?'

'The doctor who injected the young Russian boy was, so the boy said, a Christian, of which there are a finite number in this city, and since the inspector counts you as a friend he wished to warn you that—'

'But you only have this little tart's word, and besides how did he know—'

'The man was'—here Suleyman chose the words very carefully—'intact, shall we say. Which, as you know, is unusual in a nominally Islamic city like ours.'

Avedykian paused before replying. His fingers, Suleyman noticed, were shaking around the butt of his cigarette, 'Oh, I see,' he said, 'but did the boy identify this doctor in any other way? I mean did he say that he was of any particular race or describe how he looked or...'

'He said only that the man was untouched and gave a general description. This doctor spoke to him in what he imagined must be Turkish but seeing that he is not very fluent in our language himself...'

'I see.' Avedykian wiped the corner of one of his eyes with his finger and then forced a smile which stopped very obviously at his mouth. 'So is the inspector asking whether I might know of any person who might fit this description?'

'Well, if you do think you might know then that could be useful. I know that it is difficult for people in your profession to take such a step, as it is in mine. Policemen, like doctors, do tend to protect each other. But in a serious case like this...'

'Oh, of course it would be totally unethical of me not to...Not, of course'—here he suddenly laughed, a thin and nervous braying—'that I can enlighten you in that direction.'

'No,' Suleyman replied, 'I didn't think that you could. But please do bear what I have said in mind and do also take the inspector's warning to heart. This is going to happen and, after all the good work you have put into Dr Krikor's project, it would be most unfortunate if your name were to be unjustly smeared at this juncture.'

'Yes.' Avedykian looked down at his fingers for a moment as if minutely examining his nails before saying. 'And what do you think, Sergeant, personally, I mean?'

'Think?' Suleyman asked, genuinely confused by the question. 'About what, sir?'

'About a doctor who is also...About somebody in my position, doing what I do and being...'

'That is your own personal business.'

'Tell me then...' Avedykian stood up and started to pace slowly up and down behind his desk, raking his fingers through his thick, black hair as he went, 'how would you feel if I were operating upon you?'

'Well, you are a doctor and I would, I suppose like most people, trust you to know what you are doing.'

'You wouldn't feel the need then to take a blood test after I had meddled around inside your reproductive organs?'

Realising finally just exactly what he was talking about, Suleyman reacted with anger. 'If you're talking about AIDS, then I must say that I resent the implication that you think me so small minded. As my doctor, whatever your proclivities might be, I should hope that you would take as many precautions against that eventuality as all rational people.'

'But if you knew that I didn't?'

'If I knew that you didn't then I would not consult you in the first place. But with your reputation...'

Avedykian laughed. 'And what reputation would that be, Sergeant?'

'Well, as a noted consultant.'

'Not as Muhammed Ersoy's dirty little rent boy then? Or perhaps as the man who once laughed at your brother? I do know that you remember that, you know. I can see what you feel about me written in your eyes.'

Suleyman, his face as straight and impassive as a becalmed sea, stood up as if ready to take his leave. 'If that is your opinion then there is little that I can say to alter it. And in part you are correct, in that I can and do remember how Murad felt about you and Ersoy and your friends. But it was all a very long time ago and it would be foolish as well as unprofessional of me to allow such childish misdemeanours to colour my judgement now.'

With just a ghost of a smile remaining on his tired face, Avedykian shrugged. 'I cannot argue with that even though I find it hard to believe.'

'Well...'

'But anyway, you can tell Inspector Ikmen that I appreciate his concern for me and that I will take his words into consideration.' He shuffled some papers on his desk in what seemed to Suleyman an unnecessary fashion and then sat down upon his chair once again. 'And now, Sergeant, if you will excuse me, I do have records to update.'

'Yes, of course.' Suleyman gave a small bow in the doctor's direction. 'I will leave you to your work.'

'Thank you.' Avedykian, who was now to all intents and purposes engrossed in his work, simply waved one hand rather than look at Suleyman as he left. Had the doctor done so he would have seen the expression of extreme distaste that now lay across his recent guest's features. It was a look that, together with Suleyman's recently revived antipathy for his host that explained why the policeman went, not out of the hospital, but downstairs to the office of the pharmacy department.

'You say that your mother is European,' Ersoy said, gently fingering the lip of his tiny coffee cup. 'From which country does she come?'

'From Albania,' Ikmen replied with what seemed to Ersoy a taut smile.

'Oh. As I expect you are aware a lot of the wives of our former rulers came from Albania.' And then he added with a twinkle in his eye, 'As slaves originally, of course.'

'Yes.'

'Does she still speak the language?'

'My mother died when I was ten years old,' Ikmen answered.

'Oh, I'm very sorry. Might I ask...?'

'I find it a little hard to discuss actually, Muhammed, if you don't mind.'

Ersoy smiled, but in a manner that indicated some warmth and sympathy. 'I apologise,' he said with a slight bow of his finely structured head. 'Believe me, my interest is not in any way prurient. I am myself motherless, my own mama having died giving birth to me.'

'Oh,' Ikmen replied, 'how unfortunate. I am sorry.'

'Ah, but don't be, my dear man! I never knew her and so the loss for me was not like your own. When one's mother has never held one or wiped one's tears from one's eyes one is unaware of and therefore shielded from such feelings.'

'So you were raised by your father?'

'Yes and, of course, by a succession of nurses. My father did eventually marry again, but that...Well, it didn't exactly work out, shall we say.'

Ikmen was only too aware of what had happened to Ersoy's father and stepmother but, realising from the man's demeanour that this was probably a very difficult subject for him, he held his peace and returned to sipping his coffee.

'So, are you working here in the bazaar today or did I catch you purchasing a little trinket for your mistress?'

Ikmen laughed, amused by Ersoy's almost inevitable assumption that he had to be a womaniser. 'If I could afford a mistress I would be unable to buy her presents as well, which would, I believe, make me a rather poor prospect.'

Ersoy smiled. 'Yes, wealth does have its advantages, but also its disadvantages too.'

Ikmen could not at that point think of any and said as much. 'Like what?'

'Like the fact that people try to take advantage of one. Like the fact that the rich, like anyone else, can become bored and when we do'—he took a long, cool suck on his narghile pipe—'it is so much more devastating. I mean, imagine how it would be if even the relative luxury of fighting for existence were taken away from you? It is like that all the time for us. There is no challenge, nothing one ever has to pit one's wits against.'

'It all sounds very attractive to me,' Ikmen observed. 'In fact I was, I admit, quite envious of you when you presented that samovar to Krikor the other night. I don't know what it is worth but I should imagine that the sale of such an item could make quite a considerable difference to a project like ours. I could not even begin to dream about handing over anything valuable—not that I do actually have anything—and then not even miss that item.'

Ersoy shrugged. 'I have other family heirlooms. Some more and some less valuable than the samovar.'

Ikmen paused a little before continuing the conversation. This was because a thought had reappeared in his mind which he wanted to express in a way that did not sound odd or out of place. Evoked possibly by the mention of Ersoy's samovar or by the almost crystalline glitter of jewellery around him earlier, the little models he had been receiving and his strange thoughts about cages had once again sprung to mind. This time, however, they were accompanied by the thought that his colleague, Suleyman, was probably with this man Ersoy's lover right at that moment. It was a connection between fact and ideas that momentarily made him frown.

'Is everything all right?' Ersoy, seeing the look upon his guest's face, inquired.

'Oh yes,' Ikmen answered, smiling. 'Am I right in thinking that your samovar came from a prince's Kafes apartment?'

'Yes.' Ersoy took another long drag from his pipe and then released the smoke with luxurious slowness. 'Why?'

Ikmen shrugged. 'I just find it a very alien and rather excessive concept.'

'I don't know why,' Ersoy protested. 'I admit that Kafes does represent a rather unpopular aspect of our past but for one whose ancestors, presumably like my own, routinely veiled and incarcerated their women, your attitude is a little pious, don't you think?'

'You think then,' Ikmen said thoughtfully, 'that the putting away of those found inconvenient, threatening or, in the case of women, who are property to be guarded is a correct thing to do?'

Ersoy smiled. 'I sense that you might be goading me, Inspector.'

'Not in the least!'

'No?'

'No, but...'

Ersoy laughed. 'It's all right, I'm not offended in any way. In fact I do think in the main that you are right. Incarceration of another human being is largely indefensible. However, I do not know where this leaves you, as an officer of the law, with regard to those detained for their criminal activities.'

'Well...' Ikmen took in a deep breath before replying, a movement which acknowledged that this aspect was one that required at least some thought. 'I suppose that comes down to the greater good. If you have one person who represents a threat to others, even if that threat is only potential, then you may justify his incarceration for that reason.'

'Ah, but who decides when and for how long such incarceration may apply?'

'Well, judges, in some cases doctors...'

'In other words, people like ourselves,' Ersoy said, his eyes seeming to shine with the increasing challenge of their argument.

Ikmen gave a small, doubtful sigh. 'No, I'd disagree with that. These people are experts.'

'Yes, but they are only people, as you have said. It is only because the state is set up in such a way as to legitimise certain types of expertise in certain situations that they make these judgements instead of people like you and me. And'— Ersoy held one finger up in order to silence what appeared to be a move to protest on Ikmen's part—'over time the character and position of those who make such judgements changes. In the old days it was the Sultan and possibly his Grand Vizier, now we have, as you have said, judges and doctors. So, I put to you, what is the difference?'

'Doctors and suchlike are trained to make such decisions in an organised and dispassionate way. The sultans who put their relatives in the Kafes were driven only by greed or the will to power or perhaps both.'

Ersoy leaned back in his chair, looking both relaxed and amused. 'And doctors and judges are not motivated by such drives?'

'Well...'

'It is my belief that we all have somebody in our lives whom we would rather was not there, Inspector. Our reasons may be personal; we may for example fear for our own safety or reputation should certain people be permitted liberty. I mean the psychiatrist who permits the psychopathic killer to remain at large will be far more concerned about what people may think of his judgement than he will be about public safety. It all comes down to selfishness in the end.'

'So is there,' Ikmen asked, 'or has there ever been someone whom you would rather was not around?'

Ersoy smiled. 'That is a very leading question, Inspector—given what I have been told are some of your thoughts on your current case.'

'Oh?' Ikmen, intrigued, asked with a gesture of his hand. 'Please explain?'

'Well, I am aware, Inspector,' he said, 'that a theory has been advanced by yourself regarding imprisonment in connection with your young victim.' As Ikmen looked at him with rising sternness, Ersoy smiled. 'How do I know this? Like myself you are not one of the Armenian community, Inspector, and so you are not privy to their gossip. But what we do know is that those within the minorities do all know each other whatever they may say. And, as I know you are aware, I have as it were an "in" with such people myself.'

'Then,' Ikmen replied tautly, 'I will have to speak to my associates about this gossip, won't I? There are certain things that people should not discuss, particularly with those on the outside of an investigation.'

'Oh, I am sure that what was said was done so in good faith.'

'Yes, but...' Ikmen took another sip from his cup and then lit a cigarette. 'You have not, however, answered my question, have you, Muhammed?'

Ersoy smiled. 'No, I merely made you rather angry with your friends the Sarkissians, which was not kind, was it?'

'I don't know what your motivation was, but... Well,' Ikmen said, his eyes firmly fastened on to the man's seemingly ever-smiling face. 'Is there anybody that you would rather were out of the way?'

'Is there anybody that *you* would rather hide from view?' Ersoy replied, inadvertently flagging up the rather troubling vision of Ikmen's demented father in the mind of the policeman.

Annoyed at himself for thinking such a thing and at Ersoy for raising the subject in the first place, Ikmen repeated his question with even more vigour, 'But I am asking you, aren't I, sir, is there anybody—'

'Well, of course there is! I would not be human if I didn't have any enemies, now would I? We all have people in our lives whom we would rather be without. Some of my so-called friends are the most reprehensible freeloaders, people who routinely prey upon rich men like myself, but...'

'But to actually put them away is not, obviously,' Ikmen said, 'something that you would ever seriously consider.'

'But of course not!' Ersoy laughed again, 'Even for an old-fashioned boy like myself that would be almost too exotic. No, we just don't do such things any more, do we? We are far too civilised, far too Turkish.'

'I didn't think,' Ikmen observed, 'that people like yourself considered that you were Turkish?'

Ersoy reached out and touched Ikmen gently on the knee, 'Oh, but that is just a pose!' he teased. 'Some people, particularly some young men, find it rather attractive, but...of course in reality we are all, have to be, Turks. We live by Turkish laws, we read and write in Atatürk's Turkish alphabet. I lead my personal life in tune to rather older rhythms but that does not affect how I relate to the world when I drive through the gates of my home.' Then moving his hand away from his slightly cringing guest, he said, 'Do I sense that you might actually be starting to believe in my playful posturing, Çetin?'

Ikmen smiled. 'Your somewhat challenging views, real or not, combined with the shock of discovering that you, a civilian, have been privy to my professional thoughts is a little disquieting.'

Ersoy's face suddenly became grave and he said, 'Oh, I do apologise most humbly.' Then he took another long pull on his narghile and sat back contentedly with his eyes closed. 'But then I must admit to some fascination with whoever may have committed this crime. If as my dear friend Avram whispered to me only yesterday, the perpetrator might have incarcerated this boy for some years, I, as one who relishes both the compulsive and bizarre sides to life, must admit to an overwhelming curiosity about the details of all this. And most real Istanbulis will, I am sure you will find, secretly harbour such emotions also.'

Some old men wearing thick woollen caps and the incongruous suit jackets that so many country peasants favour came and sat at the table next to Ikmen and Ersoy, one of them grabbing a tavla board from beside the serving counter as he went. Ersoy, or so Ikmen felt, smiled rather indulgently at this sight.

Whilst Ersoy was thus temporarily otherwise engaged, as casually as he could, Ikmen took the latest crystal model he had received out of his pocket and placed it on to the table. The reason why he did this was not entirely formed in his brain. It wasn't as if, even despite his rather odd opinions, he looked upon Ersoy as anything other than an admittedly gossipy eccentric. Indeed, in doing this he was even, if obliquely, exposing this man to even more juicy information about the case, which, especially in light of the breach in security via one or other of the Sarkissians, was definitely not the right thing to do. But he just, for some reason, couldn't help himself.

Looking back, Ersoy quickly detected the little model with his gaze and then smiled. 'A little purchase of yours, Inspector? I didn't think that you had been buying today?'

'No, I haven't,' Ikmen replied simply. 'It is just something about which I would appreciate your opinion.'

Ersoy, frowning now, leaned forward and picked up the Gemini figure between his long, slim fingers. 'Twins,' he said, 'if I am not much mistaken. May I ask why...?'

'Just wanted to know what you thought of it,' Ikmen said with a shrug. 'As a man of obvious taste.'

For a few seconds Ersoy looked at the item, turning it around from time to time in order to view every surface. 'Well, it is pretty,' he said, 'and if pretty pleases you it is nice on that level.'

'Not your kind of thing, then?' Ikmen asked.

'No.' Ersoy placed the miniature very carefully back upon the table. 'A little too bourgeois for my taste, if you don't mind my saying. It brings to mind things that ladies of a certain class might collect.'

'Ladies like?'

He smiled. 'Well, ladies who, shall we say, have not always been accustomed to the money that now they possess. My late stepmother, whom my father chose from an outlying and financially embarrassed branch of our family, would probably have been charmed.'

'You would never then desire such an item?'

'Myself?' Ersoy laughed with what seemed to Ikmen to be genuine derision. 'Oh, I should think not, Inspector, no!' And then, moving his head across the table towards Ikmen, he added, 'A lover of men I may be, Inspector, but despite anything that you may have heard to the contrary we do not all behave like middle-aged matrons.'

Ikmen smiled. It was really quite difficult, despite his poses and views, to dislike this man. 'Anybody who thought that you were anything less than the most perfectly cultured gentleman would be a fool, sir,' he said, meaning every word.

'I will treasure that remark, Çetin,' Ersoy replied, also meaning what he said.

'But I fear I must be on my way again now,' Ikmen said, rising from his chair. 'Thank you very much for my coffee. It was most pleasant.'

Ersoy bowed his head in recognition. 'We must enjoy each other's company again.'

'Indeed.'

Ikmen had just started to move off through the crowded tables when Ersoy called him back. 'Oh, Çetin,' he said, 'you have forgotten something.'

Turning, Ikmen saw that Ersoy was holding something aloft, something small and shiny, something that, where the light caught its surfaces, reflected all the colours of the rainbow.

'Ah.' He made his way back to the table and put out his hand for the model.

'You don't want to be without the little brothers,' Ersoy said as he placed the crystal into Ikmen's palm.

'You know,' the policeman said, 'everybody I have shown this to has been of the opinion that these two are boys. And yet without obvious genitalia...'

'Oh, but in small boys it is hardly more than a tiny worm, is it not? Hardly big enough to represent on such a tiny thing.' And then he added with a smile, 'Unlike myself as a small child, of course. I was, as I am now, quite beautiful and absolutely huge too. But then, as you have implied yourself, I am a gentleman and as such I am immune from all base imperfections.'

And with that he turned, his eyes ablaze with playful wickedness, in order to hail the waiter, apparently careless now of Ikmen who stood alone save for his little figure and a good deal of puzzled amusement.

# 12

THE VITAMIN RESTAURANT, although not the most famous eating house in the Sultan Ahmet district, which has to be the once lauded Pudding Shop of old hippy legend, represents nevertheless fairly good Turkish eating which is not too crazily priced for what is essentially a tourist area. Numerous *bains marie* containing such delicacies as köfte, mixed vegetables, pilav and potatoes in various guises, bubble away from early morning until late at night providing sustenance for customers both foreign and domestic. The decor, which consists of a few tourist posters on plain walls, is as unobtrusive as the clean but functional chairs and tables at which the diners sit.

Although beer is offered for sale, the habitués of the Vitamin rarely get intoxicated and, with the occasional exception of a tourist who arrives drunk, raised voices are not frequently heard within its walls. Loud television noise is however, another matter, particularly when the national football team is playing. On this occasion, however, it wasn't, which, as far as Ayşe Farsakoğlu was concerned, was no bad thing. The usual parade of mindless game shows, one of which she was now half observing, was bad enough, but at least she knew that nobody would run into the street and start yelling if a couple from Altinkum failed to win a microwave oven.

Exhibiting little enthusiasm for either television or food, she moved what was left of her mixed vegetables around her plate with a small cube of bread. Every so often she would look over towards the door, her eyes apparently searching for something or someone, the identity of whom the restaurant owner and his employees were probably spending the odd moment speculating upon. Although they didn't know her name, she knew that they observed her rather more closely than some of their other regular customers. As a representative of the law, if female, her presence—particularly when, like now, she was in uniform—was not completely welcome. While she was there the drug dealers, the whores and even some of the more nervous tourists would pass on by the Vitamin. And seeing as there were a lot of the above types in Sultan Ahmet her effect upon business could be, she knew, quite profound.

With just a slight smile at the owner and his cohorts, Ayşe turned away from the door and started looking up at the television again. Like the proverbial stopped clock which only starts ticking if you look away from it, as soon as her attention was caught by the latest model of Mercedes car Mehmet Suleyman arrived beside her.

'You have already eaten, then,' he said, looking down at her plate before taking his place on the chair at her side.

'Yes. I didn't know...'

'It's all right, I'm not hungry.' He sighed as he settled back into his seat, rubbing his eyes with his fingers.

'Bad day?' she asked in a tone she felt, or rather hoped,

those sitting close by might take for the concerned expression of a loving wife.

He simply shrugged but it was eloquent enough.

'Can I get you a drink?'

'No, that's OK,' he said with a wave of his hand. 'I'll go up and get myself something in a minute. I should really go back and help the inspector as soon as I can. He's going to look at old missing persons files tonight. He gets like this... You said you wanted to talk?' He moved his head forward a little as if to indicate that she should start this and soon. It was not the gentle, sympathetic conversation that she had played over so many times in her head—the one that finished with him putting his arm around her shoulder and then, amid the anonymity of a deserted side street, kissing her hard and full upon the mouth. But then real life was like that, endlessly disappointing.

'I feel really bad about that poor Lenin man,' she said as she tried to avert her eyes from the restaurateur who was casting a rather sly and suggestive smile in their direction.

'Yes, I knew that,' her now, she felt, really unsympathetic companion confirmed. 'I too feel responsible.'

'Yes, but you didn't interview him in the first place, did you?' she said with a sudden vehemence that surprised even her. 'I mean it was quite obvious from his appearance that he was completely insane! He was dirty, wild-eyed, rambling. What on earth can I have been thinking of?'

Mehmet shrugged. 'You are not alone, believe me, in wondering why you took him in for questioning. I've pondered it myself and I must confess that I wasn't sure you were right to. But I've finally come to the conclusion that you had no choice, really. He confessed to a very serious crime, Sergeant. One that for all you knew—'

'But we always get crazy people in to confess after a

murder has occurred! And besides, the insane sometimes do it even when they haven't in order to get a free bed, especially at this time of year. How desperate, given the state of our cells, is that!'

'Look.' Suleyman leaned across so that they could both lower their voices. 'It was I who formally arrested him, wasn't it? It was I who nearly beat him up, if you recall, too. And by attacking you he—'

'But he was mad! Like the inspector said, he couldn't help himself.'

'Oh, so you think that I should have just left him to throttle you?' She looked down at her hands, a little shame-faced, or so he thought.

'No...'

Suleyman sighed again as he watched her delve inside her jacket pocket for a cigarette. 'Sergeant, I feel as terrible about this as you do, I can assure you. And, probably like yourself, I cannot altogether accept what the psychiatrist said about his violent death being an inevitability. His arrest and his imminent transfer to prison acted as catalysts. They must have...'

'Commissioner Ardiç has really savaged the custody officers.' She put the cigarette into her mouth and lit up. 'But it isn't their fault! They didn't start this thing. It was me!'

'Sergeant...'

'Hüseyn, you know the one with the squint, completely blanked me when I spoke to him this afternoon! They know.'

'Now listen to me!' Suleyman said, attempting to modulate his voice through tightly gritted teeth. 'You are not solely at fault here. Everyone—you, me, the custody officers and even Ardiç himself—has to take his or her share of the guilt for this man's death. I accept that he should never have been in a police station in the first place and that he should not then have been arrested. But those men down there in the cells should have kept watch over him! Dr Halman had already given it as her professional opinion that the man was insane and, as we all know, people who are irrational can and do perform desperate and excessive acts. Hüseyn has not, believe me, anybody to blame for his dressing down other than himself!'

Ayşe, her hands plus cigarette raking through her tangled hair, sighed miserably. 'But if that is the case then why do I feel like this?'

'Because someone you have been involved with and felt bad about has died,' Suleyman said, a little more calmly and quietly. 'And because you have allowed Hüseyn to get to you.'

She turned to look at him and then instantly wished that she hadn't. Even worn out he looked so good.

'You sound, Mehmet,' she said, daring for the second time that day to use his first name, 'like you have come to terms with what has happened.'

He smiled. 'Oh, I haven't, I can assure you of that. If you knew me you'd know that I am almost without equal when it comes to absorbing guilt. But I have to go on, do my job and concentrate on the issues at hand. And I can't do that if I'm hung up on what I did in the past.'

'No.'

She stopped talking for a few moments after that, seemingly concentrating solely on her cigarette and an advertisement for perfume on the television.

'Look...' Suleyman began.

She turned quickly as if pulled around to face him. 'Yes?'

'I really will have to get back to the inspector now. But...' He smiled again but, as was so typical of him, with rather sad eyes. 'Look, let me drive you home and we can, if you want, talk some more in the car. There's no one about to get the wrong idea and I'd rather be certain that you're home and OK before I leave you.'

She put her head down again and in an attempt to cover up the disappointment she felt at his obviously merely friendly gesture, she said, 'That's very kind.'

He put one hand just briefly on to her shoulder and then drew it away almost immediately. 'You're welcome,' he said and then stood up to go.

Ikmen sat at his desk and looked down at the large sheet of paper before him upon which he had constructed a considerable spider graph. He allowed himself a brief smirk as he contemplated what was essentially a throwback to his school days. Suleyman had achieved very little up at the hospital apart from angering Dr Avedykian and the chief pharmacist who, apparently, had insisted upon every permission in the book before he would allow anyone to view his records. He was quite correct to do this, particularly since no evidence yet existed to connect Avedykian or any other doctor at the hospital to any specific crime...

Cohen, who had come into the office in order to give the inspector a glass of tea, looked at the spider graph over Ikmen's shoulder and said, 'What is that, sir?'

'It represents,' Ikmen replied, 'a rather feeble attempt on my part to prevent my brain from exploding.'

'Eh?'

'In the absence of Mr Zekiyan and with zero identification on the boy we are still, sadly, at the speculation stage on this case. I am therefore using this device'—he swept his hand across the surface of his work with a smile—'to help me organise my various lines of inquiry.'

'And has it? Helped, I mean?' Cohen asked.

'No, not really,' Ikmen replied. 'I'm hoping that when Suleyman comes back he can organise it for me. He has a far more logical brain than I. I have it in mind to go and dig about in the archives and look at some unsolved missing persons, but I'm hoping that he can provide a logical reason for my not doing so.' He turned around to look at the constable. 'What do you think, Cohen, about all this, I mean?'

'About the diagram?'

'No, about our dead boy in Ishak Paşa.'

Cohen moved around to the front of the desk and then pulled a chair over so that he was sitting in front of Ikmen.

'Well, if you want my humble opinion, sir, I think that it would be unwise for us to discount the notion that the boy the builders saw all those years ago and this corpse are one and the same. And if the kid was this Mr Zekiyan's son then there could just be something in the old missing persons' files that could tie in.'

'Yes,' Ikmen murmured, 'I was afraid that you'd say that. What I don't understand, however, is how all these little models I keep getting link up with the case—if indeed they do. I mean they seem to point to a very Turkish kind of scenario and yet if all the players are, as we believe, Armenian...'

Cohen shrugged. 'I was always taught to stick to the known facts, sir. We have a dead uncircumcised body which has got to be that of a Christian, if you ask me. I think myself that he very well could be this Zekiyan's son, although...'

'Although what?'

'Well...' He wrinkled his brow in what Ikmen imagined was deep thought. 'Well, it does seem a bit of a problem for your missing persons thing if the father of the kid was also his captor, as it were. I mean, in that case he wouldn't have been reported, would he?'

Ikmen thought about what was a really very valid point for a few moments. Then he said, 'Unless the two of them went missing together. Dr Sarkissian has advanced a theory that the boy might have been brain damaged or shameful to the family in some way.'

'Then why not just send him to an institution? People do.' He sighed. 'Usually either the very poor who can't afford to have kids who can't work or the very rich who can't handle the aggravation.'

Ikmen smiled. 'You're making some very interesting points tonight, Cohen,' he said. 'Are you finally going for promotion?'

Cohen laughed. 'No, or at least not deliberately, sir. Like you I'm just trying to pick my way through all these ideas and somehow make them sensible in view of the few facts that we have. There's no need these days as far as I can see for anybody to be locked away unless there's something weird going on—unless you live out east of course, but then they just don't know any better, do they?'

Ikmen grunted his agreement.

'But then again perhaps sex is involved somewhere along the line here. I know that the kid didn't show any signs of it, but...I mean we know that some doctor is selling drugs to at least one kid on the game and may even be doing so to others too.'

'Yes,' Ikmen replied, 'the medical profession never seems to be too far from view. Talking of which'—wordlessly he offered a cigarette to Cohen, which the latter accepted, and then lit up himself—'can I ask you rather a personal question please, Cohen?'

'What, about my health?'

'No. No, about your...er...' Here Ikmen stumbled a little, unsure how to phrase what he wanted to say. 'About your nationality.'

'Well, I'm Turkish like you.'

'No!' Ikmen clicked his tongue tetchily, more at his own inability to find the right words than at Cohen. 'No, about your being Jewish in an essentially Gentile culture.'

'Oh.' Cohen looked ahead in a rather nonplussed fashion, puffing deeply on his cigarette. 'Yes. Well. What do you want to know, sir?'

'Well...' Ikmen wanted to sound Cohen out in the light of what Ersoy had told him about the Sarkissians. Although it had always been said that those in minority groups sometimes, as in the Sarkissians' case, talked out of turn amongst their fellows and indeed and perhaps quite rightly possessed support networks and systems that were all their own, Ikmen was interested to discover if this was a general trait or one that was peculiar to the long-persecuted Armenians. 'Look, I do have my reasons for asking this, which I cannot tell you, but...Do you ever sort of talk about things, I mean amongst yourselves and only to each other?' The expression on Cohen's face, which was one of deep distrust, was proving very difficult to ignore. Ikmen sighed. 'Look, my question doesn't actually relate to Jews, it's about Armenians.'

'Oh.'

'Well?'

Cohen shrugged. 'You know as well as I, sir, that we all have our own little sections of the city and our own clubs and places of worship and suchlike. And yes we do talk perhaps a little more freely amongst our own than we do to others, but then I expect that you lot do that too.'

What Cohen was saying was not something anybody could argue with. 'Yes, I...'

'Not being religious myself means that I probably seek out other Jews less than most people.'

'But would you give your Jewish friends sensitive information about the job?' Ikmen asked. 'Even if you knew that they were interested or involved in some way?'

Cohen frowned. 'Well now, sir, that would hardly be right, would it?'

'No pressure, no accusations, just the truth—which will,' Ikmen added, 'go no further than myself, I swear. I do need your insight really quite badly.'

For a moment Cohen chewed thoughtfully on his lip. This could either mean that he was considering what was being asked of him most carefully or he had never really considered the dilemma before.

Just before he answered he lowered his head. 'To be honest I think I'd find it quite hard to be in the position you've indicated, sir. Luckily it's never happened, but if my family or a good friend were involved, I'd have to take myself off that case or whatever. The pressure would just be too great.'

'The pressure of your knowing what they might need...'

'No.' Cohen smiled. 'No, the pressure from them, my friends and family, the community I live in.'

'So what you're saying,' Ikmen said slowly, 'is that as a member of a minority you...'

'You can have a duty to put them first in some cases,' Cohen answered a mite sheepishly. 'It's why I always steer clear of things involving Jews. I do the odd bit of translation for those who only speak Ladino as you know, but...Look, sir, I always put the force first, it's what being in the police is about. And if there's a risk that I might be compromised then I say so and get out, at least I would do if that ever happened to me. But if you're talking Armenians...'

'Yes?' Ikmen leaned forward across his desk. 'What about them?'

'Well, they're a little bit more different, aren't they?'

Ikmen frowned. 'What do you mean?'

'Well,' Cohen stubbed his cigarette out in Ikmen's ashtray and then looked down at the floor once again. 'Well, like I know that Dr Sarkissian is a friend of yours and...not to speak out of turn or...'

'Yes?'

'It's like it's to do with their past and that.'

'All the blood there is between their kind and my own, perhaps?' Ikmen inquired. 'Speak freely, Cohen, there is no one about to hear us.'

Cohen looked up and smiled, faintly. 'To be honest, sir, yes. A lot of them—well, the ones that I've met, but not including the doctor of course— they, some of them, can be a little bit sort of closed on themselves, can't they? Act like they've got stuff to be bitter about.'

'Which maybe they have.'

Cohen looked at Ikmen with a good deal of surprise on his face. This was not a topic that one could usually discuss with a Turk—the Government didn't like it—and even with other Jews it wasn't easy. 'Yes, well, whatever,' he said, strangely embarrassed. 'But then I don't know many of them very well. If you really want to know more, sir, it might be better if you ask Dr Sarkissian.' Then seeing the odd look upon his superior's face, plus finally realising just why and how this conversation had moved from bad doctors into the arena of race, Cohen added, 'Unless, of—'

'Dr Sarkissian is entirely outside any suspicion of this or any other kind,' Ikmen said gravely, 'so please take any connection you may have made between him and this conversation and expel same from your mind.'

'Er...'

'I do believe,' Ikmen continued, 'that this conversation is now at an end, and further that it is no longer in or even anywhere near to your brain.'

Cohen cleared his throat and then placed a serious expression upon his face. 'Right.'

'I do thank you, however,' Ikmen said, 'for your views on what you have now completely forgotten, Cohen.'

'That's all right, sir,' Cohen replied, getting up from his seat and beginning to move towards the door. 'Any time you want to talk about anything that you shouldn't, which you haven't, of course, but if you did...'

'Just go,' Ikmen said through slightly gritted teeth. 'Oh, and if you see Sergeant Suleyman...'

'Shall I just ask him to go straight down to the basement, sir?'

'I think that that would be a good idea.'

Cohen left the room and Ikmen sighed. After all this time the missing persons' files even on those still unsolved were going to be rather sparse. Basic details were all that were usually retained which meant generally one or two sheets summarising the salient facts.

Not that the missing persons' files were totally occupying Ikmen's brain at this point. What Cohen had said with regard to Armenians had been interesting, if troubling. The constable had, or so it seemed to Ikmen, been implying that this particular minority group was in some way a 'special case' even compared to other non-Turkish communities. Because of their somewhat chequered, not to mention controversial, career in this part of the world, they had now at the latter end of the twentieth century found themselves either by circumstance or design quite apart from others. Unlike the Jews they possessed no homeland upon which to focus their hopes and aspirations or even to escape to should life away from their own kind become too difficult. They had an ancient and, to Ikmen's ears, fiendishly difficult language plus a very old and theologically complex faith but...but rise through the ranks of whatever profession they chose, as some of them undoubtedly did, they could and would never be the same as other people, as he himself. Perhaps Cohen was right and it was all that terrible blood—alleged or real, it hardly mattered—from long ago 1915 that set them so radically apart. Or perhaps it was something else, something that had always been there, something that he in his small way with his friend Sarkissian had always sought to challenge: distrust.

Because they were different they had, as Cohen had indicated, other internal allegiances that were difficult, if not impossible to ignore. The old sultans, either through wisdom or out of fear, had always advanced the careers of talented Armenians, securing their loyalty via immense amounts of money and gold—the only things that could override the fierce nationalism that some of them seemed to possess. At the time this had made a lot of sense; the Armenians tended to be ambitious and possessed considerable skill in those areas that pious Turks traditionally felt were beneath them, like commerce and politics. Quite correctly the Sultanate had advanced them. However, when that institution was finally overthrown in 1908 it didn't take long for those who felt that some minorities had been unfairly favoured to move against them.

Ikmen looked down at his hands, noticing how his fingers were moving nervously, apparently without his volition. This subject always made him nervous. That none of his family, or none that he knew of, had taken part in any of the actions against the Armenian 'traitors' did not alleviate the guilt that this old event always made him feel. Not that that was pertinent now, of course. What mattered was the extent to which he could or ever had been able to trust his oldest and dearest friend. Ardiç had always, in his blunt and prejudiced way, criticised Ikmen for allowing the doctor access to all and any information that he might require. Indeed Ikmen had on more than one occasion laughed at the archaic misgivings of his superior, locked as he seemed to be into a world that had now, thankfully, long since departed.

But Ikmen was not laughing now. As he stood up to make his way towards the basement he felt both guilty and sad that this was no longer the case. Even laid back little Cohen understood about conflicts of interest, about putting the force first or getting right out of a case. And if Cohen could understand that so could anyone, especially someone who was both highly intelligent and a friend. It was a disappointment that Ikmen had never even considered that he would have to contend with. It was one that made him very sad.

Çiçek Ikmen placed her water glass back down on to the table and then smiled at her mother who was just finishing the last scrap of her vegetable stew. The younger members of the family, having finished their meals, had headed off to the living room or their bedrooms, leaving Çiçek alone with her mother and teenage brother, Bulent.

'Do you have any idea when Dad may be home?' the young woman asked, her eyes a little tightened around the edges by anxiety.

'Your father is very busy just now,' her mother replied, looking across at Çiçek's brother Bulent's still almost full plate. 'I do wish that you would finish that,' she said to the teenager. 'You're far too thin.'

'Dad was very thin at my age,' the lad replied defensively. 'I've seen photographs.'

'Your father was and is a man who would far rather smoke than eat,' Fatma said, eyeing the boy narrowly, 'which is not what you should be doing.'

'No, well...'

Ignoring what had just passed between her mother and brother, Çiçek returned to her own particular concerns. 'It's just that I don't like leaving you on your own with Grandad...'

'I have Bulent,' Fatma answered.

'Yes,' Çiçek said, giving her teenage brother a hard look that was not, her mother felt, entirely justified, 'but I would rather Dad were back before I leave for the airport.'

'If Allah wills it then it shall be so,' Fatma said with what Çiçek viewed as nauseating fatalism. 'And anyway,' her mother continued, 'you have to go to work whatever, don't you?'

'Where are you off to tonight?' Bulent asked his sister, his slightly sulky mouth just hinting at the envy he felt for her.

'London.'

'Stopping over?'

'Yes.'

'Uh.' He grunted as he placed his almost full plate into the sink and then said to his mother, 'I'm going for a cigarette with Grandad.'

'Oh, but your food...'

'I don't like it, Mummy,' he said as he headed quickly out of the kitchen. 'Sorry.'

When he had gone, Çiçek turned once again to her mother and said, 'So you honestly want me to feel confident with only him'—she angled her head in the direction in which her brother had just departed—'to protect you?'

Fatma smiled. 'Oh, he's not a bad boy, really,' she said, 'and he did come from his job as soon as you called when you had trouble the other day.'

'Mmm.'

'And anyway, Grandad will be going to bed very soon now. Bulent will help him and then he will be no more trouble until the morning when I will, if Allah is merciful, have your father's help for a little while before he goes to work.'

Çiçek smiled and then sighed. 'All right,' she said, 'but I would like to call Dad just before I go if he's not back by then. Have you spoken to him yet about the fib—'

'Oh, so London, is it?' Fatma said very quickly. 'Isn't some young pilot taking you shopping there?'

'Captain Lazar said that he might, yes. But returning to—'

'Your father went to London when you were very small, back in the 1970s. Some police visit. He liked it very much, your father.' Fatma looked up into her daughter's concerned face, her own eyes filled with both pleading and threat. Her health was not a topic for conversation either now or at any other time. Çetin had known all along about the fibroids and what they meant and how they could be dealt with. To go on at him about the pain would, Fatma felt, be utterly pointless. She didn't want, was afraid even to have a hysterectomy and besides with no money the whole thing was largely academic. So to worry him further and make him feel even more impotent and guilty about her than he already was seemed to Fatma almost like cruelty. Not that she could expect a liberated woman like her air hostess daughter to appreciate her care for her largely absent husband.

A few seconds of silence passed as Çiçek absorbed

what her mother's expression was conveying to her. Then she said brightly, 'OK, Mummy, have it your way, only—'

'I think that will do, Çiçek,' her mother said, raising one hand in order to silence the girl. 'Now, about this captain, what was his name?'

Çiçek smiled. 'It's Lazar, Mummy.'

'Oh, is he...' She didn't finish the sentence, but a daughter could easily fill in her mother's personal obsession.

'Married?' Çiçek obliged. 'No, he isn't, Mummy.'

'Ah!' Fatma raised one questioning eyebrow. 'And...'

'And yes I do like him and he likes me too,' Çiçek replied.

Fatma smiled. 'And the handsome captain is taking you shopping?'

Çiçek shrugged. 'I hope to have a very nice day in his company, perhaps I might even get to know him better.'

'Oh!'

'But...' Çiçek raised a warning finger, feeling at this point that she should really try to stem her mother's vaunting enthusiasm.

'But what, my love?' her mother asked. 'I mean all of this does sound very hopeful and I know that at your age you must be starting to—'

'Mummy!'

'Well!'

'I'm not exactly ancient yet.'

'I had three children by the time I was your age,' Fatma said firmly.

'Oh, yes,' her daughter said with some irony in her voice, 'that must have been marvellous on what Dad used to earn in those days!'

'We managed! And anyway at least your father has always had a job.'

'People will persist in killing each other, won't they?' Çiçek said mischievously and then added, even more wickedly, 'But then that's just as well for us, so—'

'Oh, for the love of Allah!' her mother exclaimed. 'We don't need to talk about your father and myself, do we? We know that story. What I want to know about is this Captain Lazar. What is he like?'

'Captain Lazar is thirty, lives with his parents in Bebek—'

'Lovely area that,' her mother put in, obviously impressed.

Çiçek, for whom the adult realities of either having or not having money had yet to override notions like love and physical attraction sighed. 'Can I go on?'

'Oh, yes, yes.'

'Captain Lazar is tall, good looking, very charming and...' She stopped.

'Yes,' the older woman said, 'he is tall, good looking, very charming and...?'

Although Çiçek did put her head down as if in shame when she answered, her eyes were sparkling with something that Fatma recognised as the look the girl's father gave people when he was being particularly evil.

'And he's Jewish,' she said simply. 'Captain Lazar, who is a friend, is Jewish.'

Sexual difficulties or problems have never been easy topics of conversation amongst men. Although far from being a coarse individual, Arto Sarkissian was nevertheless just as likely to laugh at a ribald joke told by some over-sexed young mortuary attendant as the next man. Impotence, premature ejaculation, masturbation and even adultery were all fair game in the casual world of jokes and apocryphal stories. Real life, on the other hand, was quite another matter.

And it was precisely because real life was quite another matter that neither Arto's closest friends nor even his own brother Krikor had any idea that Dr Sarkissian the pathologist and his lovely wife Maryam had not slept together for nearly ten years. It had started originally as a short-term measure after Maryam's hysterectomy—she had been both very sore and depressed for some time afterwards. When, however, it became apparent that the hormone replacement therapy her gynaecologist had given her after the surgery did not suit her, finding a treatment that did began to obsess her every waking moment. All she talked about was what she had been given this time and how she felt on it followed by questions about what she should do if or when she had to discard this treatment and try another. And until something was found there was also the problem that her hormone-starved body had started to age rapidly. It was then that the plastic surgery had begun. Now, ten years down the line, Maryam had still not found a drug that suited her, but the plastic surgery had continued and indeed increased in order to preserve the wonderful beauty that Maryam had always possessed.

One side effect of all this surgery was, however, that even when Maryam wasn't actually post operative, her scars were too painful to be touched. This Arto knew to be both understandable and correct. Maryam was five years older than him and at fifty-eight her skin was getting to the stage when it could take no more. Not that he could tell her so—her looks were everything to the childless Maryam Sarkissian.

To tell her would be to kill her. And Arto, despite this

trouble and heartache, for all that he occasionally relieved himself with the odd middle-aged foreign tourist, did still love his wife very much.

As was their custom, the Sarkissians kissed each other chastely on the cheek before retiring to their separate bedrooms. She still wore a gauze pad over the site of her latest surgical procedure, her chin, which he just looked under briefly for signs of infection before letting her go to her rest. Then, taking with him only a trashy detective novel from his considerable library, Arto too retired to his room, to think, as he always did, about the old days when they had been happy and young and sexy.

The novel, which was American and featured a detective with the unlikely name of Brick O'Hara, was entertaining in an undemanding sort of way. The challenge of the enterprise was to read the thing in the original English which demanded from the doctor some intellectual effort. But then it was still only eight o'clock and although his body had been tired, which was why he had come to bed, his mind was still fully alert and it was good to have something to distract him from the seemingly insoluble problem of the young boy in his mortuary. Besides, if an investigation into doctors who were known to be Christians were to take place, he would soon have very little time to think about anything else. As it was he was finding it difficult to tear his mind away from the notion that somebody he knew might be involved. Given the paucity of Armenian doctors in the city, unless the various informants and sex-sellers that the police had interviewed were wrong, there were only a finite number of people that it could be. It was difficult, if not impossible to imagine that if and when the offender was detected it would not impact upon him personally in some way.

And then, of course, there was that other thing currently

troubling his mind too. The thing that had happened when he had allowed these thoughts temporarily to overwhelm him. Had he told Avram Avedykian too much? OK, the man had promised to keep the information Arto had given him secret, but...He'd just wanted his younger friend to be prepared, that was all. The man was, he knew, homosexual and so would be doubly at risk of suspicion; he really did need to be prepared. Not that that in any way made up for what was basically a breach of security. Çetin Ikmen, he knew, would go berserk if he found out—not that he would. But...But then Çetin for all his kindness could not understand. Had he not told Avram there would, he knew, be those who would condemn his lack of community solidarity—not least amongst whom would be Avram's uncle, Father Tikon. And even though Arto himself almost never now attended sung liturgy on Sunday mornings, Maryam did and also lay great store by whatever the priest said even though that particular divine was not known to be fond of her husband. Once again Arto reflected that for one's family not to have noticeably suffered in the way that others were alleged to have done was a little like bearing the mark of the beast upon one's face—damning and ineradicable. May God rot your soul, Tikon, he said in his head just as the mobile telephone at his elbow began to ring.

With a sigh, Arto picked it up. 'Dr Arto Sarkissian.'

There was a short pause before the caller answered, but when he did his speech, unusually even in this household, was expressed in the Armenian language.

'Arto, it's Avram,' he said.

'Oh, hello,' Arto replied, a little taken aback by the identity of the caller, given his recent rather troubling thoughts.

'I need to speak to you about something. It's really very important.'

There was a distinct tension behind his tone and also a sort of breathlessness as if he had just recently been running.

'Oh,' Arto said, 'well, speak away, Avram, feel—'

'No!' It was said with such vehemence that Arto's hand just briefly moved the telephone away from his ear.

'No, not like this, not on the phone,' Avram continued, still apparently gasping for breath. 'I need to see you Arto.'

'What, now?'

'Yes!' Although he was shouting it was in the tone of one pleading, as if for his life. 'Yes, now!'

With a small struggle, Arto Sarkissian heaved his body upright in his bed and placed his book face down on the counterpane. 'Avram, what's wrong? Are you in trouble?'

'I've told you,' the other replied, now a little angrily, 'I can't say on the phone. Can we meet?'

'Well, you can come here, if—'

'No, no! Not at your house. No, I mean here at my apartment.'

'Well I can, if—'

'Then do so please! Now!'

'Avram, what—'

'Just come now, please, Arto. If you ever had any love for me please do this now!'

'Well, OK.'

He heard a sigh of relief from his younger friend. It was a very odd, almost occult moment—that one's presence could elicit such overwhelming relief was a heady tribute to one's powers of healing in the psychological sense and of friendship.

'Thank you, Arto,' Avram said, adding curtly, 'Come now.'

And then the line went dead.

Although bidden to do so, Arto Sarkissian did not immediately spring out of his bed and throw on his clothes.

For just a moment he sat quite still as if frozen. This, or something like this, had happened before. When Avedykian was a medical student precisely this kind of panic had been precipitated by something that had almost driven the younger man to suicide. Something, if he recalled correctly, that he had never really got to the bottom of, but which thereafter had been glossed over with quite forceful efficiency.

Just before they reached Ayşe's apartment in Taksim, the skies hurled down one of those huge and fierce autumnal rainstorms that can catch even the most seasoned citizen unawares. Although blessed with a car that his boss Ikmen felt was 'frighteningly efficient', Suleyman's windscreen wipers still found the sudden downpour a little much to deal with and he was relieved when his passenger told him that they had finally reached their destination.

Suleyman didn't pay a great deal of attention to precisely where they were as the two of them dashed from the car and into the stark but clean vestibule of the elderly apartment block. Even that short distance, a matter of just a few metres, had rendered them both absolutely soaked, if not to the skin, then very close.

'You'd better come up and get dry,' Ayşe said, mounting the narrow, twisting staircase that led to the upper storey.

'Oh, but I really should get back,' Suleyman replied, standing in what to his companion appeared to be his own private puddle, his hair slicked flat upon the top of his head like a close, black helmet.

Ayşe laughed. 'You can't go anywhere like that,' she said. 'Just let me give you a towel and then you can go on your way.'

'Well....' She did have a point and, nervous as he so obviously was around this lovely woman, he wasn't really happy about getting back into his nice pristine car in this state. 'All right.'

As he mounted the stairs, she smiled. Then, taking a large bunch of keys out of her jacket pocket, she stopped in front of one of the doors on the first floor landing and opened it.

'It's a bit of a mess, I'm afraid,' she said as she slipped her shoes off and placed them on a rack just inside the door. 'Ali left for Ankara early this morning and he tends just to drop things around when he's in a hurry.'

Ali was a mystery to Suleyman who, whilst removing his own shoes, simply responded with, 'Oh.'

Seeing the slight confusion on his face, Ayşe said with a smile, 'Ali is my older brother. When he got divorced last year we decided that, with both of us being single, we might as well share.' She put the hall light on, which revealed a large and comfortably furnished dwelling. 'It means that, being together, we can both afford somewhere nice to live and Ali can also keep watch over me for our mother—when he isn't working away, that is,' she added with a twinkle in her eyes.

'What does your brother do?' Suleyman asked as he stood, not really knowing how to progress from here, gently dripping on to the doormat.

'Ali is a computer programmer,' she said as she moved towards a door at the far end of the hall.

'Oh, that's very—clever,' her still stationary guest replied.

She looked back at him and then laughed once again. 'You know, you can come in,' she said. 'Rainwater is hardly going to do much damage to these old things.' She kicked one of the well-used rugs on the floor and then opened the door into what looked like a living area.

Suleyman, whose wet feet made unfortunate slapping noises against the threadbare floor-coverings, followed her.

As she had indicated earlier, the place was rather a mess. Discarded men's shirts and the odd shoe littered the floor and one of the two large red brocade sofas that dominated the room. Used tea glasses and plates bearing both food remnants and cigarette ends were also in evidence; it gave the whole place a somewhat 'student-ish' feel, or so Suleyman felt.

Ayşe disappeared briefly into a room that gave off from this mess and then returned bearing an armful of towels, three of which she gave to Suleyman.

'My brother, as you can see, expects the same sort of domestic service from me that he once got from his wife,' she said a little acidly. 'Sit down—if you can find somewhere.'

Draping one towel across one of the seats, Suleyman then sat on it and proceeded to dry both his hair and coat with the others. 'I take it,' he said, 'that you are not entirely happy with this arrangement.'

Rubbing her hair vigorously with another towel, she replied, 'Oh, I don't mind that much really. It's just that Ali sometimes behaves as if he is accustomed to servants, which he isn't. My father was a train driver and so there wasn't that much money about when we were growing up, and what there was our parents put into our education.'

'That's very commendable.'

'Yes.' She stopped rubbing for a moment and smiled. 'A very long way, I understand, from your own upbringing.'

He frowned slightly. 'What do you mean?'

'Well...' She reddened just a little around the cheeks. 'I've heard, or rather it is said that you were born in a mansion and that your parents are, well, you know, sort of...'

'I take it this all comes via a small, swarthy individual with whom I once patrolled the streets,' he said with a sigh.

'Well...'

Was it possible to have any kind of privacy if Cohen was your friend? And furthermore, what other little snippets of his life had the man revealed to this woman in whose apartment he should definitely not be sitting, protected by a thick layer of towels or not?

'Well, yes,' he said, 'I was born in what could be described as a mansion. It was a place where, I am told, we were attended by a small retinue of servants, but since we left that house when I was only four my actual memories of it are very scant.'

'Oh.' She looked down now as if either embarrassed or disappointed.

Suleyman smiled. 'I suppose Cohen told you that I was some sort of prince, didn't he?'

'Well...'

'I am, as you must have gathered, not. That was my grandfather, who is now sadly dead.' He laughed. 'The truth is always a little disappointing, isn't it?'

She looked up in what appeared to him to be a rather challenging fashion. 'No! If I like a person then I like them. I'm not so shallow as to only be interested in those I imagine have wealth or position.'

'I wasn't implying that you did,' he answered, 'I was just simply anxious, as you can appreciate, to put you right about Cohen's little fantasies. It's something I've had to do frequently over the years.'

They both sat in silence for a few moments after that—neither of them trying or even daring to guess at what might be the other's thoughts.

'Anyway,' he said at last, placing the towels neatly to one side. 'If I could just use your bathroom to sort out my hair, I had better...'

'Of course, you need to go, don't you?' she said, standing up and letting her own towels drop casually to the floor. 'It's just by the front door, the bathroom.'

'Thank you.' He stood up and left the room.

Ayşe moved over to the window to close the blinds on the teeming night outside. It was still raining really hard and so his attempts at grooming were all going to be for nought. Not that that was the only reason why she was still thinking about him. Having him here in her apartment had raised all sorts of feelings for Ayşe Farsakoğlu. Talking and laughing together had been, if difficult at moments, very nice. OK, when one actually got to know him, Mehmet Suleyman did prove to be a little more formal than the average person, but that did not detract from the way that she desired him, which was with a ferocity that had at times made her feel quite ashamed of herself. Was it just a sexual thing? Well, it had to be, because she didn't really know him. All they had in common was their involvement with that poor madman about whom they shared such guilt.

What could not be doubted, however, was that when Suleyman had waded in to save her from poor Lenin, he had done so with a rage that seemed, at least to the other men in the room, to indicate that he was desperately worried for her safety. He had said he would have done the same for any other fellow officer, but others said differently—well, Cohen, the weaver of stories, did, not that that, in the light of their recent conversation about Suleyman's origins, meant a great deal. Even though she wished so much that it did.

When he re-entered the room she was still standing by the window with her head bowed.

'Well, thank you for the towels and...'

When she did not react to his words he said, 'Are you all right?'

'No, not really,' she said leaving her panoramic view of the rain-soaked shops across the street.

'Still thinking about our poor crazy man, I suppose.'

'In part,' she said, feeling tears of either shame or disappointment or both rising up in her eyes.

'There isn't a lot that I can say that hasn't already been said,' he offered. 'Inspector Ikmen always says that you can't ever really get used to things like this but that in time you learn to live with them. I don't know...'

'Do you really have to go right now?'

She wasn't aware that she had been going to speak until the words had left her mouth. And as soon as she had done so, she wished that she hadn't and immediately covered her mouth up so that she couldn't utter such a thing again.

'Yes, I do,' he said quietly. 'We're in the middle of an investigation.'

'Right.' She turned and, despite the tears that were now stuck on to the tops of her cheeks, she smiled.

'Perhaps you would find it helpful to talk to a friend about this?' he said. But then he suddenly stopped and put his head down on his chest. 'This is impossible.'

'What is?'

He looked up as quickly as he had looked down. 'This,' he said, 'you and me here, like this, it's...'

'It's what?' She moved nearer to him but stopped as she saw him cringing away. 'It's what?' she repeated. 'You and me here, like...?'

'I don't think that we should discuss this further,' he said and turned back towards the door as if preparing to leave.

'Oh, I think that we should—Mehmet,' she said, daring once again to use his first name.

'I am married—to one of my own kind. An ersatz princess just as I am an ersatz prince. Quite right and appropriate.'

'But...'

'But nothing!' he shouted harshly. 'Nothing at all, Sergeant!'

'But...'

He held up one hand in order, it seemed to her, to ward her off. 'I'm going and that is—'

'No don't go!' she found herself screaming, adding the one thing she never intended to reveal. 'I want you...'

'And I want you too!' he said, the words coming tight and strangled from a throat that had not wanted to say them. 'But it...'

'But what is it?' she said as she moved around one of the settees that blocked him off from her. 'If I want and you want too...' She reached out and placed one tentative hand upon his shoulder. This time he did not flinch from her touch.

'Just because we might want...'

She gently and a little shakily placed one finger across his mouth in order to silence him. 'And just because we are not married to each other then why should that mean that we can't...'

'I...'

'I've wanted—no, I've lusted after giving myself to you since the very first time I saw you sitting next to Inspector Ikmen in that filthy old car of his.'

It was the most shameful and personal confession she had ever made, yet his face remained quite blank and impassive.

She was just beginning to wonder if he was going to respond at all when he leaned quickly down towards her and took her slightly parted lips between his own.

For the second time Ikmen looked across at his mobile telephone, which was lying on top of a dusty old metal filing cabinet. There was a smell of aged paper in his nostrils and, combined with the almost overwhelming silence of the basement, his sense of being disconnected from the world was beginning to spook him a little.

Should he or should he not call Suleyman? The man had said that he was coming back to the station after he had completed some errand that he had refused to be drawn upon. He had said that whatever it was he had to do wouldn't take long. That had been over two hours ago. Ikmen turned back to the flimsy piece of paper in his hands and read, for no particular reason, about the argument one Neşe Balaban had had with her father just prior to her disappearance in 1981. Predictably it had been about a boy. Gone but presumably still missed, young Neşe now, so Ikmen reckoned, had to be nearing thirty. He slipped the paper back into its cardboard file and then picked another from the stack at his elbow. He then looked up at the telephone again and sighed just as the instrument trilled loudly into life.

Ikmen stood up, walked across to the cabinet and picked the telephone up. 'Ikmen,' he said, fully expecting his deputy to reply.

'Dad,' a familiar female voice answered.

'Hello, Çiçek darling,' he said with a smile. 'This is a surprise. I thought that you were back at work tonight.'

'Oh, I am,' she said, 'just going in a minute.'

'Thought that you'd give your old dad a call before you left, did you? That's nice.'

'Yes, although...'

'Yes?'

'Well, I just wondered if you have any idea when you may be home.'

There was something in her voice that made Ikmen's heart beat just that little bit faster. 'Why? Is there a problem?'

'No,' she said, 'at least not at the moment. It's just that...Look, Dad, I'm not very happy about leaving Mummy alone with all the kids and Grandad.'

'She's always managed before,' he said, relieved that it was not a real emergency. 'She has Bulent and—'

'He says that he's going out drinking with some of his friends.'

'Oh, is he!' Ikmen clicked his tongue impatiently. 'Put him on, will you, Çiçek?'

He heard her put the telephone receiver down and was then aware of slightly raised voices in the background. Of course it was quite reasonable for his young son to want to go out with friends now that he was working, and besides, he'd be going away to the army soon enough, but, as Çiçek had rightly said, to leave Fatma alone with the five little ones plus the crazy old man wasn't really on. That it was he who should be there for her did briefly cross his mind but he dismissed it in a rapid flurry of inner self justification regarding his dead boy and the stagnant state of his case.

He heard the sound of footsteps growing in volume as someone approached the telephone.

'Bulent has already gone out, Dad,' Çiçek said.

Ikmen sighed and then rubbed his eyes with his fingers. 'That boy...'

'Are you coming home soon, Dad?' his daughter asked, her voice a little bit more pleading than usual.

'Not soon, no. I've got a whole stack of files to get through down here.'

'Can't it wait until the morning? Mummy—'

'No, it can't, Çiçek, I'm really under pressure for a result on this.'

'Yes, I accept that, but don't you think that Mummy's peace of mind is a little bit more important?'

'Oh, for the love of Allah, it's not like the old man's going to do anything that your mother can't handle!'

'Oh, yes, she just loves dealing with invisible Greeks and a frequently naked old man who has already made disgusting suggestions to me. She shouldn't have to deal with it. You should be able to sort him out!'

'Don't you dare speak to me like that!' Ikmen roared, enraged but also stabbed by guilt.

'I'll speak my mind in the way that my father always instructed me to if I witness an injustice!' she countered, successfully hurling back at him twenty-four years of his own ethical conditioning.

'Now...'

'And don't you dare even think about criticising me for this, Dad. You've been almost like a lodger in our apartment for I don't know how long. Coming in at all sorts of hours, only helping Mummy when you—'

'Now you look here—' he began, cut off only by the faint sound of another rather anxious-sounding voice in the background. 'Is that your mother there?'

'Yes. And?'

'Well, put her on.'

'No.'

'Pardon?'

'No, I will not put Mummy on because she'll just agree with whatever you say even if it means that she's unhappy herself.'

'Your mother is not—'

'Oh, yes she is!' Çiçek roared, now well and truly in her stride. 'She's quite miserable actually! She's very unwell herself and what with Grandad and all his activities she's totally worn out!'

'Your mother is quite capable of speaking—'

'Oh, no she isn't! At least, not to you!'

Shaking now with both anger and also misery at hearing the truth so violently, Ikmen said softly, 'Now is not the time...'

'Oh, now is never the time, is it!'

'I will sort it out in the morning.'

'I'll be in London by then!'

He heard somebody, presumably Fatma, shout something in the background which sounded rather like 'with who'.

'What's your mother saying?' he asked as Çiçek said something back to her mother which he also couldn't catch.

'Nothing of any importance,' his daughter replied when she came back to him. 'Now—'

'Look, Çiçek, you just go off to catch your flight and—'

'You'll come back right now and be with Mummy?'

'No—'

'Oh, well, there's not a lot more to be said then, is there?'

'Çiçek...'

'My taxi has just arrived. If Mummy has any trouble or—'

'Çiçek!'

'Oh, you're the most impossible man!' she spat and then, judging by the loud banging sound reverberating around the inside of his ear, she slammed the telephone receiver down.

Ikmen clicked his phone on to standby and walked back to his rickety wooden chair and the stack of files. Not that, despite the impassive look upon his face, he could concentrate on their contents, which concerned the disappearance of a middle-aged schizophrenic man from an institution back in 1982. So what? Was the man Armenian? No he wasn't. Did he have any children? Well, considering the fact that he had been institutionalised since the age of sixteen, that seemed highly unlikely. But he wasn't really concentrating on any of this. Damn that girl! And damn her great big honest mouth!

With a flick of the wrist he threw the file to one side and then picked up his telephone once again. Even before he had finished punching in the number he was muttering 'Come on! Come on!' impatiently.

'Hello?' said a slightly shaky female voice at the other end.

'Fatma?'

'Çetin, is—'

'Has that girl gone?'

'Çiçek just got into her taxi, I'm—'

'Fuck!'

'Çetin!'

He threw his forehead into his hands and sighed. 'I'm sorry, my love.'

'She shouldn't have bothered you like that, Çetin,' Fatma said. 'It was very wrong. But you know how headstrong she can be. She's just like...'

'Yes, I know she's just like me, she's my daughter,' he said, stating the obvious. 'Are you all right, Fatma? She seemed to think...'

'Oh, Çiçek just worries too much,' she said, a little laugh sitting at the back of her words. 'I'm fine. Bulent put Timür to bed for me over an hour ago.'

'I'll have words with that boy when I see him!'

'Yes, well...' She paused for just a second, as if gathering breath and then said, 'You know this captain Çiçek is going to London with?'

'Yes,' he sighed, really not that interested, 'says he's taking her shopping. So?'

'You do know that he's a, a Jew, don't you?'

'No, I didn't,' her husband answered, 'but I do now. I ask again, so?'

'Çetin!' She was always full of outrage when he was slack about issues touching on what was essentially her religion alone. 'Didn't you hear what I said?'

'I heard precisely what you said, Fatma,' he enunciated wearily, 'but quite what you want me to do about it I—'

'Well, she can't go around with him, can she? I mean what if she and he...What if they should become serious about each other?'

'Taking her shopping does not equal a proposal of marriage,' Ikmen said slowly, so that with any luck she might just take in what he was saying. And had he left it there she might have been mollified, at least for the moment. But he was tired and irritable and he just had to push the thing that little bit further. 'And besides, even if she were to marry him, why not? He's an airline pilot who earns good money, she could do a lot worse.'

'But he's a—'

'Yes he is, but if she loves him—which we don't know, remember—what can we do about it? You and I chose each other and, if you recall, you agreed to no arranged matches for the children. Apart from anything else it would be totally hypocritical.'

'Yes, but a...'

'Oh, so if I'd been an Armenian or something you wouldn't have married me?'

For just a second the other end of the line became totally silent before she answered, 'Well, no. I mean I would still have loved you but it would just have been...'

'Oh, thank you, Fatma,' he said acidly, 'that makes me feel just fine!'

'No, no...'

'And anyway,' he added spitefully, 'what you imagine you've gained by marrying somebody who doesn't believe in anything, I can't really imagine!'

'You went through sünnet, Çetin, and when you die you will be buried as a Muslim. You are really...'

'Oh, will you just stop deluding yourself for one minute, woman!' he shouted. 'Why, if my mother could hear you now she'd laugh herself sick!'

'Your mother?'

'My mother read cards, talked to the dead and—'

'Your mother was completely—'

'If you use the mad word I will stop this conversation right now!'

'Mad!'

'Right!'

He pressed the 'call end' button and then threw the hated instrument down on to the hard concrete floor. The little display panel shattered into an enormous number of pin-head-sized pieces at the same time as the back panel flew off. For several seconds he just looked at the thing, with no expression on his face. Then, as he turned away from this most recent scene of carnage and addressed himself once again to his stack of files, he muttered, 'Well, Mother, got me into trouble yet again, haven't you?'

He then heard, or perhaps imagined he heard, a laugh somewhere far above his head. That it sounded like his mother's crone-like cackle made Ikmen smile.

# 13

As ARTO SARKISSIAN pulled up in front of Avram Avedykian's apartment block, he could not help noticing that the people who lived on the floor directly above his friend were having a party. Loud music together with a selection of smart, if wet, young people skittering about on the rain-soaked balcony were obvious clues; certain youthful professionals were having a very good time indeed. Arto, however, thinking only of Avram and his apparently distressed state of mind, merely frowned as he got out of the car and then ran across the saturated hard-standing towards the entrance hall.

Although Dr Avedykian's apartment took up most of the ground floor of the block, his front door was actually towards the back of the building behind the stairs that led to the upper storeys. Shaking what was left of his hair whilst wringing out the collar of his coat on to the marble floor beneath his feet, Arto made his way quickly, if without great enthusiasm, towards the small vestibule hidden by the stairs. As he passed by them a very drunk young man in a Reebok T-shirt staggered down towards him mouthing a silent expletive to himself.

The door was slightly ajar and opened easily as Arto touched the handle. This was understandable given that his host had been expecting him, although quite why he should want to leave the door thus with a loud party going on, Arto couldn't really imagine.

As he closed the door behind him, the noise from above became more muffled as it was replaced by the far gentler strains of Gershwin's *Rhapsody in Blue*, which originated, he imagined, from his friend's stereo. Moving from the hall and into the lounge he called out, 'Avram? It's Arto.'

But there was no reply. Only the whiningly sensual strains of Gershwin came back in response to his cry. As he moved tentatively into the living room, Arto began to feel his hackles rise. Chiding himself for a suspicious old fool he tried to ignore this instinct, although over the years he had come to trust it. It was only when he heard, or thought that he heard, a sound coming from one of the bedrooms that he totally discounted his reaction. If he knew Avram, the latter had probably, in his misery, hidden away inside a bottle of something and would now be attempting to sleep it off. When drunk people did things like this: ring friends out of desperation and then inconveniently collapse upon them when they arrived.

It was probably as well just to check him out though. And as he opened the door to the bedroom the noise had come from he did indeed see Avram Avedykian laying face down on his tapestry-covered bed. Arto smiled. The man's posture suggested that he had fallen rather than placed himself on the bed. It was exactly as he had thought: completely drunk, his problems stowed for the moment inside the empty bottle of vodka on the night-stand.

There was nevertheless one thing about this scene that might be a problem for Avram when he woke up in the morning. His friend's head was lolling at a most uncomfortable angle over the side of the bed. Moving as quietly as he could, his ears clenched against the sound of his own footsteps, Arto moved quickly around to the other side of the bed. And then he stopped.

Initially, just a split second before he saw what was actually there, it was the feel of something slightly resisting against his feet that caused him to pause. Blood, he was stepping in blood! Running his eyes across the vast (or so it seemed to him) expanse of red that sullied the carpet beneath him, his gaze finally came to rest upon Avram's lolling head—or rather what was left of it. From where he was standing he could see that one cheek and a sizeable chunk of jaw had been quite literally blown away.

When he woke up he was, at first, quite alarmed to see that the light was still on. For just a moment he thought that he might have fallen asleep on the sofa in his living room, indeed he hoped that that was what had happened. The sight of his hastily discarded clothes beside the bed soon disabused him of that notion.

Oh.

He turned over and saw her lying beside him, apparently looking down at him, her face smiling as it rested against her arm.

'You fell asleep and so I let you rest,' she said. 'You seemed to need it.'

'Thank you.' On speaking he felt the muscles around his throat tighten as the memory of what he had done returned.

Guilt. He might have known that it would be like this. He should have had the presence of mind to stop himself.

'What's the time?' He needed to know what it was but was also anxious to say something—anything—to this woman he had so recently had sex with.

She glanced briefly at her watch. It was the only thing she was wearing.

'Ten-thirty,' she replied, still smiling.

'Oh, no!' He shot up into a sitting position and raked his hands through his tousled hair. 'The inspector will....'

It was at this point that his mobile telephone began to ring. Half falling and half hurling himself on to the floor, Suleyman strained to reach across to his jacket to retrieve the instrument. It was odd and even quite frightening to be naked in the presence of one who was effectively a stranger.

Having grabbed the thing, he pressed the 'receive' button and then held it up against his ear with his shoulder. 'Suleyman.'

'Are you on your way home or are you still working?' a rather taut woman's voice asked.

'Ah, Zuleika, ah...'

'I only ask because your brother is here to see you,' she said with what had become over the years a studied lack of interest.

'Well, I've still got a few things to do,' he said, both inwardly and outwardly cringing at the sound of his own deception. This kind of thing, this being in bed with another woman whilst speaking on the phone with his wife was something that other men did, men without either morals or honour. Men he didn't like.

'Well, when you've finished,' she continued, 'Murad has something he would like to discuss with you. Are you going to be long?'

'No...'

'Then I shall entertain him and Elena'—the name of his brother's unpopular Greek wife came out as if she were spitting something unpleasant from her mouth—'until you return.'

'Thank you.'

'I shall then go to bed,' she added, 'which I would quite like to do now.'

'I shall be home as quickly as I can.'

'Good.' The line went dead as she clicked the connection off: another of Zuleika's dismissive gestures.

Suleyman pressed the 'end' button and then threw the phone back on to his now crumpled jacket.

'I have to go,' he said, slipping his legs over the side of the bed and groping on the floor for his trousers.

'That was your wife, wasn't it?' she asked, already knowing the answer.

'Yes.' He kept his head well down when he replied, not wishing either to elaborate or catch her eye.

'And so, of course, you have to go.'

'Yes.' Zipping up his fly he reached across for his shirt and then turned to face her. The look on her face told him everything he needed to know about how she felt.

'I'm sorry,' he said, 'but...'

She smiled, a small, thin little thing. 'I know. I know. I always knew that you were married and so what could I expect?'

'I've really—'

'Oh, don't say that you've enjoyed yourself, please! And don't thank me.'

'I wasn't about to,' he said, and then, realising how she might construe this, he added, 'Not that I haven't had a good time because I have and—'

'Mehmet. Don't.' She turned away, hiding what he could only hope was not a tear-stained face from his eyes.

Buttoning his shirt, he sat down on the bed beside her. 'Ayşe...'

'What?'

'Look at me.'

She turned to gaze back at him; her eyes were indeed filled with tears.

'I took advantage and...I don't do this sort of thing every day.'

He stared down at the bed-sheet which he picked at nervously with his fingernails. 'I do like you. No, I both like and, and, well, I desire you too, you are very beautiful...' He looked up and smiled one of his dazzling grins that she loved so much.

'But?' she asked. 'There has to be a "but," doesn't there, Mehmet?'

He shrugged, seemingly in agreement.

'And it is, I suppose, your wife?'

'Indirectly.' He sighed. 'I don't love her, I never have.'

'Then?'

'My marriage was arranged. It was'—he searched for the right word, but when he had found a good enough approximation, he said—'expedient, in terms of my family. If I explain that my brother's wife is unwelcome not because she is Greek but because she is a grocer's daughter...'

'That mansion of yours hasn't really gone away, has it?' she said astutely.

He took one of her hands in his. 'No.'

'And nor, realistically, will it.'

He smiled. 'Perhaps one day.'

She leaned over and kissed him gently on the lips. 'Will you come here again?'

'I would like to...'

'But?'

In spite of the seriousness of the topic, he laughed. 'I want to. But I don't know whether it is a good idea—for either of us.'

'I can deal with it if you can.'

He touched her briefly, pulling his hand back quickly as if he had burnt himself. 'The truth is I don't know whether I can, Ayşe. I don't even know what I shall do when I see Zuleika tonight.'

'You don't think that you might tell her, do you?' Her eyes had widened now—this was not something that she had expected. Oh, she knew that he had the reputation for being honourable and everything, but to tell his wife about such an admittedly good but brief encounter seemed to her to be taking such qualities a little far.

He shrugged. 'I don't know.' Then, seeing the look of alarm upon her face, he added, 'Oh, I wouldn't tell her that it was you. But you must admit that unless I am to be like those awful men who creep around taking advantage of women and lying to their wives, then...'

'But what would she do, your wife, if she knew?'

He smiled. 'She would tell her mother,' he said, 'who would tell my mother, who would probably issue me with numerous threats and warnings.'

'And?' She moved over towards him again, folding one of her breasts beneath her.

He placed a small kiss on her cheek. 'She wouldn't and will not, I believe, divorce me.'

'But...'

'Apart Zuleika and I are nothing. Together?' He smiled again, sadly. 'She is the wealthiest of my cousins and I, thanks to my father, am the most aristocratic of hers. My mother's family are nothing if not ambitious. Even the fact that I have chosen to become a mere policeman has done little to devalue my worth as good breeding stock.'

'Oh.'

He stood up and then reached down for his jacket and mobile telephone. 'I really must go now.'

'Yes.'

'I can only say that I am sorry about—'

'Oh, don't be!' she said. 'Please. It was as much about me as it was about you. And, well, we were good—together.'

'Yes, we were,' he smiled. 'We were quite the best.'

'You really had better go,' she said, launching herself over on to her back and looking up intently at the ceiling.

'Now.'

'Yes.'

He looked back at her several times before he left her bedroom and then again at the blankness of her door when he reached the hall.

Out on the landing he took just a moment to collect himself before moving down the stairs towards his car. Like one running from some awful pursuer, he leaned against the wall panting with anxiety as he considered what he had just come from and what he was, possibly, now going to. Never, not even when he was a very young conscript in the army, had any woman, not even a professional, made him feel so good. Zuleika had admittedly tried in the early years of their marriage, but her basic disgust at the sexual act and everything that went with it got in the way of her good intentions. With Ayşe, however, everything, even things that he had never really considered doing before, had come so naturally that...OK, she was experienced, not a 'good' girl in the sense that she had waited for sex until her wedding night—she had quite obviously not done that. But...But whoever she was and whatever she had done or not done in the past was surely immaterial in the face of the fact that she had made him feel so good—so sexy and yet also so safe and comfortable too that...

Oh, he had to stop thinking like this! To keep on going over the thing would only make him feel like he wanted to go back to her and that, clearly, was not going to be possible. Perhaps later, at another time, some stolen afternoon while her brother was at work...

No! He turned his head as if physically removing himself from such ideas. No, that was not how he was, nor how he wanted or needed to conduct his life. Tiptoeing around like some tawdry little pot-bellied politician, slyly crawling into his mistress's bed behind his wife's back. Or at least that wasn't how he had been. But the last few hours had changed all that. Ayşe might not actually be his mistress (although she would probably not be averse to being so), but he had in effect crept behind Zuleika's back in order to satisfy his own lusts. He had even, to his shame, asked Ayşe to do such things as...But was it shameful? Given that all he had ever gone home to for the past five years was someone who occasionally deigned to give herself to him and then in a spirit of loathing for the flesh and all its works, could not his actions be seen as natural rather than shameful? Would not his friends and even his brother applaud his actions?

He put his hand up to his head and shakily wiped away the beads of sweat that had gathered on his brow. These thoughts were far too confusing not to mention totally unhelpful. What he had to do was get home, talk to Murad and then possibly sleep on the earlier events of the night. Yes. He thrust his hand into his pocket and drew out his car keys. As he did so his mobile telephone clanked against his fingers reminding him of something else that his brief liaison with Ayşe had prevented him from doing.

It was unlike Ikmen not to call him if he was late or failed to turn up for some appointment. Unless he knew that they were off duty, Ikmen was always too mindful of security not to want, in the main, to know where his officers were at all times.

As his conscience continued to plague his every thought, Suleyman dialled Ikmen's mobile number into his own machine and then waited. Quite what he was going to say when Ikmen did reply he didn't know. I'm sorry I didn't come back to you, sir, but I was having sex and now I've got to go and see my brother who has just arrived back from Bodrum wasn't going to be quite appropriate. But as it happened, the telephone just carried on ringing, indicating to Suleyman that either Ikmen had just dumped it somewhere and forgotten about it or he was still in the office. As he made his way slowly down the stairs and out into the street, he tried that number too, but to no avail. He thought about checking with the switchboard to see whether anyone had seen the 'old man', but then decided against it. Ikmen was probably at home by this time and if he wasn't he'd be propping up some bar somewhere. What was absolutely certain, however, was that he wasn't in the bed of some sexually athletic single woman. As he turned the key in the ignition of his car, Suleyman shuddered just a little at the thought and then, in spite of himself, he smiled.

When Ikmen next looked at his watch, he found that somehow, unaccountably, it had become ten-thirty. The small stack of files that he had read, compared to those he had yet to read, did not seem to tally with the amount of time that he had taken. But then, as he knew from past experience, a kind of bending or altering of time could take place in the basement. It had that sort of horror movie atmosphere...the kind of place that you enter in the twentieth century and exit into some nightmarish post-nuclear-holocaust environment.

'You've been watching too much television, Ikmen,' he said to himself as he surveyed the tiny pile of those files he deemed 'possibles' in relation to his investigation. These, two of them, consisted of one missing Greek eight-year-old and a thirty-year-old Syrian Christian, neither of whom had been seen since 1982. From his physical description the man could be a possible for Zekiyan, but the child was really quite wrong being both too old to match with the body and blond. But then even with the man there were problems. If he were indeed Zekiyan then why had no one reported sight of him over the years? The Syrian was a native of Sultan Ahmet and so surely someone would have spotted him in his new, Armenian guise? Zekiyan had, surely, to have come into the area from somewhere else, even if that were just another part of the city. To simply change one's name but remain in one's native area did not make any sense.

Ikmen sighed and then paused briefly to light a cigarette. It was very strange that Suleyman hadn't come back or even, seemingly, bothered to contact him. The man was usually so scrupulous about keeping appointments, however loose or voluntary they might be. But then with his mobile lying effectively dead at his feet how could he really know? Ikmen scowled. That had been a very stupid, petulant thing to do. How childish and also potentially expensive—if of course he decided to tell the truth about what had happened to the damn thing which he most decidedly did not want to do.

He picked up another file and briefly scanned some details about a Brazilian girl called Mira who had, apparently, last been sighted in the Bazaar in 1983. She had been eighteen at the time and was described in the notes as 'tall, black,' and 'of large build'. Not a common sight in the Bazaar; if someone like Mira could go missing Ikmen reckoned there was little hope for anybody who was more typically Levantine.

Throwing Mira carelessly on to what he had dubbed the 'done and useless' pile, Ikmen proceeded to the next file, which he left unopened in his lap for a moment as he considered once again the issue of where his victim and his captor/father/whatever might have originated from. They could not, he had already established, be local to the Sultan Ahmet district, although because the man apparently worked they or rather he had to be integrated into the city at some sort of level. In other words, somebody somewhere had to have knowledge of them or him, even if that were under another name. Knowing what that name, if indeed it existed at all, was could so easily provide the key to discovering who did what, why and how, but...But it was just the thing that he didn't have and so he had to rely, for the moment, upon all these old dusty files that would in all probability yield nothing more than painful memories for those these missing ones had left behind. And as time passed he and his officers were getting ever further from both the criminal events that surrounded the boy's death and the possibility of finding his killer.

He opened the file but, seeing a woman's face staring up from the top sheet, placed it down upon his useless pile and took another. It was then, probably prompted by the woman's photograph, that Fatma's plump little face popped into his mind. She had been totally unreasonable about Çiçek and her captain. As far as he knew the girl was just a friend to this man and even if she were more than that what did Fatma think she could do about it? Çiçek was, as far as he could tell, a well-brought-up young lady who was unlikely to throw herself into bed with the captain, but even if she did she would be no worse than her mother. Sınan, the Ikmens' eldest child, had actually been conceived several weeks before he and Fatma had married, up, as he so well recalled, in an old deserted house just below the Selimiye Barracks. And, as he also recalled, at the time Fatma would not really have cared very much whether he was Muslim, Jewish or some alien from a distant planet—that he was Çetin Ikmen, her love, was all she had cared about. How very much times had changed. Fatma had been young and smooth and passionate then, as had he—Çetin Ikmen, youngest son of the razor sharp and impeccably smart Dr Timür Ikmen, university lecturer, noted in academic circles as something of a wit.

Ikmen ground his cigarette butt out hard against the littered concrete floor and decided to curtail that particular train of thought in favour of what he should be considering. He picked up the next file and opened it.

One tiny beat of time later, he was clutching at his chest in shock.

Resisting the urge to touch anything either in, on or around the site of Avram's body, Arto Sarkissian merely looked in horrified fascination. That his whole body was shaking was only to be expected in view of the fact that the dead man had been his friend. Strangely, this irked him. He must have seen hundreds of bodies in better, worse or the same state as this one over the years and even though it was always different if you knew the person he couldn't help but be annoyed by what he saw as his lack of professionalism. Knowing that by being annoyed he was simply indulging in displacement activity in order to give himself time to absorb the shock was little comfort. Avram was dead and there was nothing he could do about that. He couldn't even, he knew, himself perform the all-important post-mortem to discover the 'how' of the matter. As a personal friend of the deceased he had to declare an interest and so preclude himself from the inquiry.

All that aside, however, his duty for the moment was clear. He must report Avram's death to the police and then try, as far he could to stop himself from disturbing the scene around the body. His shoes were covered in gore from Avram's appalling wound, but if that were the only disturbance of the scene that was not too bad. Just before he moved to take his telephone out of his pocket, however, he did cast a cursory glance around to see whether he could spot the firearm involved. The terrible damage to his friend's head could only, in his experience, have been inflicted by a gun and, given the agitation in Avram's voice earlier, Arto for a moment found himself thinking in terms of suicide. Obviously whatever the problem had been had proved too great for Avram to bear and he, Arto, had arrived too late. He felt his eyes fill with tears as he tried but failed to locate the offending article. It must have rolled under the bed or some other piece of furniture.

Arto took his telephone off standby and punched the first digit of the sequence into the machine. It was then that he located the weapon, or rather it located him. A split second after the barrel pressed itself into the side of his head, a hand came to rest on his shoulder and Arto, his telephone waiting for the rest of the number that would never be dialled, froze.

Zeki Ersoy had been five years old when he had gone missing. As Ikmen turned the pages of his file, which was considerable, back and forth in an effort to find out just exactly what had happened to this child he kept on returning to the first page whereon was written a short description of the boy. It was with one exception quite average and non-descript. But the exception was so very glaring that every time Ikmen read it he felt his skin crawl. 'Red circular mark of unknown origin below left jawbone', it said. Red circular mark—as in crescent.

As Ikmen attempted to place some sort of order on the chaotic file his mind turned endlessly on both this physical detail and upon the undisputed fact that he had been told this child had died. Without doubt this was Muhammed Ersoy's brother—son of Mr Hüseyn and Mrs Fikriye Ersoy of Yeniköy. A child born into great wealth and privilege who, unaccountably in the light of what he had previously been told, had ended up as an unsolved missing person case. What was particularly unhelpful was the fact that a large number of the documents in the file were written in what appeared to be Italian.

Piecing together what he could, which was not much, he surmised that the boy had in fact gone missing some-where in southern Italy. The police in what he recognised as Naples, Napoli, had become involved at some point, apparently liaising with an Inspector Hikmet, who he knew had now retired, in Istanbul. Quite what the boy had been doing in Naples was not clear, but that his mother, at least, had been present in Italy too was evident from what looked very much like a death certificate for a Mrs Fikriye Ersoy which had been written in Italian and signed by a Dr Craxi. How she had died he could not decipher but remembering what Arto had once told him about how both Mr and Mrs Ersoy had committed suicide he assumed that she had died by her own hand. Although in view of the apparent fact that young Zeki had not really died but simply gone miss-

ing he now had to accept that none of this could be quite
as it had originally seemed. Further, if the dead youth who
now lay in the morgue was this similarly scarred child, how
and when did he return from Italy to Istanbul—or was
Ikmen simply making wild connections where they did not
really exist?

In an attempt to make some sort of link between past
and present events, Ikmen held the one small photograph
of the boy up to the weak illumination of the basement's
single light bulb. Was it possible to project how this little
face would look fifteen years into the future—if indeed this
child were his victim? He had only ever seen the grown version as a corpse, his face distorted by the action of rigor.
That wasn't a good basis upon which to make a comparison,
which would be notoriously difficult to construct anyway.
The passage of time and life itself did things that could not
easily be predicted to people's faces as they aged, and considering that some of the most dramatic physical changes
took place within the first twenty years of life...

Ikmen put the photograph down and sat for a few
moments with his chin in his hands. This could all so easily
be a complete waste of time. After all, if this child had gone
missing, been abducted or whatever in Italy, why should
or would he turn up in Istanbul fifteen years later? But
then if, as they now thought, Mr Zekiyan—whose name,
Ikmen felt, had attained a spooky sound during the last
half hour—had had the child since 1982, that would mean
he would have to have been spirited somehow out of Italy
and brought home very rapidly after his disappearance.
And if that were so then surely it would have made far
more sense to keep him in Italy far away from those who
knew and loved him than to bring him home and to have
hidden him away for so long. And unless the Ersoy family

were being asked for money in lieu of the boy's safe return then even to have the child in the first place seemed like a totally pointless act. But whether or not this had originally been the intention was not clear from the file, what with all the Italian plus the confusingly sloppy state of Hikmet's paperwork. Nothing could really be seen clearly without, Ikmen imagined, speaking to the old inspector—providing of course that he was still alive.

If Ikmen recalled correctly, the rather religiously inspired Hikmet had retired to the holy city of Konya. Given the old man's frequently avowed love for the poet Mevlana and all things concerned with Sufism, the mysticism of Islam, that half-memory would make a lot of sense. He had never actually said that he was a member of any dervish order but his often bi-annual visits to the tomb of the holy Mevlana plus his quietly simple tastes in all things left those, like Ikmen, who had eyes to see in little doubt as to where his true ambitions lay.

What he needed to do now, of course, was to call the old man up. Hikmet had retired shortly after this Ersoy incident when he had been sixty, which meant that he had to be seventy-five now. That he had been neither a smoker nor a drinker had to bode well for his survival; not of course that such abstinence precluded heart attack, cancer or accident. But even if he were still around Ikmen had first to find his telephone number, and then persuade him to talk about something that he may well either not remember or prefer to forget. And it was already just past eleven o'clock. Ikmen, even if he could locate the old man thought it quite appalling to call at such an hour of the night, especially since he didn't really know whether any of this was actually germane to his current investigation.

In order to consider these issues in relative comfort,

Ikmen lit a cigarette and stretched himself out on the floor for a few moments, amid (he quickly discovered) the broken wreckage of his mobile telephone. What had prompted all this interest? Initially a familiar name and then a tiny sentence about a mark that either one or two little boys had under their chins. As far as he could see from the file there was no suggestion of kidnap for ransom; Armenians, be they doctors or otherwise, were conspicuous by their absence from the material. As he smoked Ikmen thought about all the other elements that had up until now both puzzled and obsessed him with regard to this case: the little models which seemed to be telling him a story about a boy caged and restricted according to some strange old Ottoman custom; the more contemporary use of drugs upon the child in order to keep him quiet or assault him or—what?

According to Muhammed Ersoy powerful families similar to his own had once employed the Kafes as a way of controlling and curtailing younger members of their powerful family and with an Armenian doctor as his lover Muhammed would have had access to the drugs that would ensure his little brother's silence without too much bother. But then surely Ersoy was far too well known to be able to engineer such a time-consuming project as hiding the boy away for so many years? And besides, to what end could he possibly have done this? With all his relatives—apart, presumably, from the boy—dead, there was no reason to keep him alive once he, Muhammed, had inherited all of his father's millions. And even assuming that the charming Mr Ersoy could be so wicked, why, knowing as he presumably did that this information on his brother did exist somewhere, would he then actively encourage a friendship between himself and the investigating officer? OK, he is an exhibitionist, Ikmen thought, but with all his money, power and advantage it hardly made sense to even so much as flirt with the possibility of being discovered.

So what else was there? Well, there was the fact that the boy was uncircumcised. As at least nominal Muslims, the Ersoys would have made sure that young Zeki went through sünnet in as honourable a way as possible. Even Ikmen, son of Timür the atheist and the witch from Albania, had been through sünnet. But then not all boys of five could be operated upon. Ikmen himself had been seven and, as was right and proper, all he could remember now about the event was the party afterwards. So it was possible that the Ersoy boy could be their victim. Had he been taken by a non-Muslim then sünnet would not have happened; even if his captor had been of the faith, given the circumstances of their lives would he have bothered with or even been able to consider such a thing? And what, if anything, did the little twins figure mean in all this? Did it, could it possibly point in the direction of the boy's brother Muhammed as his captor? Oh, but that had to be absurd!

What was clear from all this was that he had to speak to those who knew more about these events than himself: Hikmet of course, and then, depending on what the old man had to say, possibly to Krikor Sarkissian who appeared to know rather more about the Ersoy family than most. There appeared to be a sort of collective amnesia surrounding the disappearance of the Ersoy child—a group belief that the boy had died many years ago. It was an aspect that Ikmen was finding most interesting. Had the boy been found, either alive or dead, there would surely have been some record of it in this file which was essentially that of an outstanding and unsolved disappearance. So where this belief that the child was long dead had come from he didn't know, even though he, now, fully intended to find out.

Still, for the moment there was nothing for it but to contact Hikmet. Old men did not have the reputation for being easy to rouse from their sleep, much less being pleased about it, but once he told Hikmet how important it was, he imagined, or rather hoped that he wouldn't mind too much. Ikmen sat up and once again considered how stupid he had been to destroy his mobile telephone. All right, he hated the thing, but right now he could do with it. But the number —ah! All the directories were held up in the squad room, so he had to leave the basement anyway. Slowly he raised himself up from the ground and, grabbing hold of the file as he stood, wearily started to make his way towards the door.

A sharp tap upon her bedroom door roused Fatma from what had only been a doze rather than a full-blown sleep. Attempting to get comfortable with Kemal shuffling endlessly across her bed was not an easy task at the best of times and what with the constant pain in her abdomen real sleep had become largely a stranger to Fatma.

'What is it?' she called out, not even attempting to keep her voice down in the presence of her child. That one could sleep through an earthquake.

'Can I come in?' Bulent's voice was slightly slurred by the drink that he had consumed earlier that evening; Fatma frowned a little. So young and yet already so very like his father.

She pulled the covers modestly up to her chin before answering. 'Yes. Come in.'

As Bulent opened the door, Fatma noticed that he was still dressed for the street, which seemed to suggest that he had only recently returned.

'What do you want, Bulent?'

'It's Grandad.'

Fatma sighed. All she needed after a blazing row with her husband was for her husband's demented father to start acting up. 'If it's anything to do with his Greek, he can just get on with it alone,' she said, 'and if he's removing clothes then, drunk or not, Bulent, I think I might just leave that to you.'

'He's saying that he feels ill,' her son replied.

'He often says it.'

'His head is very hot, like he's got a fever. When he came into my room he said that he felt that his skin was on fire.' Either because he was tired or because he needed the support from somewhere, Bulent leaned against the doorframe. 'I think you do need to come and have a look at him, Mummy.'

Fatma sighed again, and yawned. Such midnight panics were not uncommon now that the old man lived almost completely inside an alternate reality. 'Oh, very well then,' she said, 'you go back to him and I'll be along in a moment.'

After the boy had left, Fatma slipped a long dressing gown over the old dress that now served her as night attire and then slipped her feet down on to the cold linoleum floor below. By the time she got to this age—she was now forty-six—she had hoped at least to have a small rug in her own bedroom. It wasn't much to ask in return for a lifetime of domestic servitude, but then rugs, not to mention comfortable beds plus a whole host of other household items were not things that Çetin deemed necessary for life. Provided they all had food, he had drink and cigarettes and the children could converse upon as wide a range of subjects as possible, Çetin was happy.

She made her way out of the bedroom and into the hall, coughing loudly as she encountered the smoke cloud from either her son's or her father-in-law's cigarette. The light, as usual, was on in the hall—Gul couldn't sleep without it, fearing the 'things' which lurked murderously in the darkness. As she pushed open the door of Bulent's bedroom Fatma briefly wondered whether the often unguarded talk that Gul's father indulged in about his work had anything to do with the child's anxieties.

The old man was sitting on her son's bed, his face the colour and texture of ashes.

'He's trying to burn me to the ground, that Nikos,' he said, waving a cigarette around in Fatma's general direction, 'sticking matches underneath my fucking skin.'

'Do you feel sick or in pain anywhere?' Fatma asked, alarmed by the old man's deathly pallor which was far too similar for comfort to that of her late father just before he succumbed to heart disease.

'He wants me dead and he's succeeding. I feel like shit.'

Gently but insistently, Fatma took the cigarette out of the old man's hand and then slowly stroked his bowed grey head.

'Yes, Timür, I know,' she said, 'but I'm just trying to find out how you feel ill. I mean, do you have any pains in your chest or arms or—'

'I've told you, I am on fire!' he shrieked, his eyes filling now with tears. 'He's burning me to the ground. Sticking matches...'

'I think we might need to get Grandad to the hospital,' Fatma said, looking up at the slightly flushed face of her son.

'Should I phone Dad?'

'No.' Fatma gently picked up a blanket that lay on the floor and placed it around the old man's shoulders. 'I don't think there's going to be time for that, Bulent.'

'Oh.' The boy suddenly, despite the strong smell of alcohol about him, looked very young and frightened.

'I want you to call for an ambulance,' Fatma said as calmly as she could, 'and then ring Uncle Halil.'

'But Dad—'

'I have no idea where your father might be right now,' she said. 'I tried to call him earlier on both his office extension and his mobile and I received no reply from either. Uncle Arto has been trying to reach him for most of the evening, and if he can't get him, well, I just do not know what to do.'

'Oh.'

'Now please go quickly and call the ambulance for me, Bulent,' she said. 'Right away.'

As the boy left the room Fatma leaned over and took one of the old man's papery hands in hers. 'We're going to go out for a little trip in a minute,' she said, 'to the hospital.'

He looked back at her blankly and then, his face a mask of confusion, he said, 'What we need is one of their priests, to stop him doing this to me. They always do what their priests tell them.'

'Yes,' Fatma smiled, 'but they do listen to doctors too, you know. And when we've seen the doctor I'm sure that he'll be only too happy to help you out with telling "him" that he mustn't ever do this to you again.'

'You know that he's...' He stopped, clutching his thin little chest, which alarmed Fatma yet more. 'That...'

'Ssh! Ssh! Don't try and talk now, Timür.'

'But there it is again, you silly woman,' he said, 'the burning, the matches under my skin, the—'

'Timür, you really mustn't—'

'I'm dying, you stupid whore! Can't you see that!'

For just a very short moment, his eyes, if not the rest of him, looked almost exactly as they had done before, when his brain had been fast and sure and sharp as a knife.

Perhaps, Fatma thought, in what could be the last phase

of his life, he was finally regaining some of the insight that had so tragically ebbed away from him over the years. Her father, just before he had entered his final coma, had been aware of his impending death too. Was she making too many connections between the living and the long since dead? Well, was she?

As she looked into the old man's pained, grey face she smiled—thinking all the time that no, she was sure her comparisons were justified.

# 14

MEHMET SULEYMAN HAD not slept since that all too brief doze he had snatched at Ayşe Farsakoğlu's apartment. As a consequence of this his drive in to the station that morning had been a somewhat surreal experience. When people who haven't slept are required to drive they tend to make a conscious effort to concentrate which looks, to the casual observer, rather like a form of wide-eyed mental disorder. His whirling thoughts had only added to his discomfort. As well as veering between rapture and despair at the memory of what had passed between himself and Ayşe, he was now also faced with the prospect of having to go with his brother to see their parents. Elena, Murad's wife, was pregnant and although in itself this was a wonderful thing and reason to be joyful, the old Suleymans would not see it that way. Mehmet had therefore volunteered to go along with Murad in order to lend him the support he knew he would need.

As he pulled into his parking space, Suleyman somehow developed the impression that someone was watching him. Guilt or just plain sleepless paranoia, he didn't know, but as he mounted the stairs to the office that he shared with Ikmen this feeling, rather than receding, just kept on growing. As he passed by a little group of constables on the landing they all turned and smiled at him before continuing with their earlier conversation. Did they know something, something that they shouldn't, something that perhaps in a fit of conquering bravado she had told them?

Continuing onwards and upwards, he then encountered Cohen who was looking particularly evil this morning.

'Did you have a good time last night, Mehmet?' the smaller man asked.

'What do you mean?' Suleyman snapped, only too painfully aware of the fact that he was almost shouting.

'Well, err...' Cohen was obviously quite taken aback by this reaction to what he had thought had been a perfectly innocent question. 'Um, your wife...'

'Yes?'

'She telephoned here last night, just before I went off duty. Said your brother had arrived from somewhere and—'

'What did you say to her?'

'I told her you were still out and about seeing people.' Rapidly and with wicked enjoyment his features broke out into a smile. He moved his head up closer towards his friend's and then said, 'You weren't doing anything that you shouldn't, were you, Mehmet?'

'No, I was not!' Then, regaining his composure just a little, he added, 'I was actually with an informant.'

'Oh, useful, was it?'

'What?'

Cohen laughed. 'Well, the information from your informant, of course! What is it with—'

'Oh, I haven't got time for this nonsense!' Suleyman

snapped once again and then pushed himself past Cohen and went on up the stairs.

Higher up however, things only got worse. She was standing looking out of the window at the car park below as he, foolishly, attempted to move behind her without being noticed.

'Everything all right, Sergeant Suleyman?' she said as he just lightly brushed past her back.

'Yes, thank you, Sergeant Farsakoğlu,' he said.

She didn't speak again: perhaps that was that, for now? He was wrong. As he put his hand up to push the door to the corridor open she added, 'May I have just a few moments of your time, do you think?'

'What, now?' He hadn't meant to sound that panicky, but it just came out.

'Yes. Is there a problem?'

'No, it's just that Inspector Ikmen—'

'Isn't in yet,' she replied with a smile, 'or at least he hasn't been seen yet. Can we talk in your office?'

'It is about work, I take it?' he said, instantly hating the haughty tone in which he expressed himself.

'Yes.'

'Oh, well, err...Just for a moment then,' he said and, pushing the door fully open, made his way down the corridor towards his office, her footsteps behind him echoing hollowly against the stark linoleum floor.

When he entered his office, he threw his car keys down on to his desk and then turned to face his visitor.

'Well?'

As soon as she had closed the door behind her back she ran lightly across the thin carpet towards him and then wound her arms extravagantly around his neck.

'I haven't slept for a second since you left,' she said.

'Every moment has been filled with the pictures I have in my mind of us and—'

'You can't behave like this here!' he cried, taking her wrists in his hands in an effort to remove her arms from his neck.

'What's the matter?' she said, her lips just brushing briefly against his face.

'Well, it just isn't appropriate!'

'What I feel I need now,' a disembodied voice interrupted the embracing officers, 'is a large glass of tea. In the absence of my toothbrush it may go some way towards alleviating the appalling taste of dead animal that I have in my mouth.'

Every bone and muscle in Suleyman's body screamed with both the embarrassment and the shame of his current situation.

'Sir?'

Only a cough, which originated from somewhere behind him, arrived by way of reply. Rapidly hurling Farsakoğlu's arms from his body, Suleyman spun round to find a very tousled and bleary-eyed Ikmen smiling up at him from his half-lying position across his desk.

'Good morning, sir,' Farsakoğlu said, for some reason smoothing the front of her blouse down as she spoke.

'Good morning, Farsakoğlu,' Ikmen replied as he plugged his dangling telephone extension lead back into the wall. 'Would you care to indulge me with regard to the tea while I attempt to haul myself back into the land of the living?'

'Oh, yes, sir, you—'

'Yes, plenty of sugar,' he anticipated correctly, 'and if you can lay your hands on some tobacco as well, all the better. I've only ten cigarettes left, which'—here he turned to look rather pointedly at Suleyman—'as you know, is a very dangerous place for a heavy smoker to be.'

'Yes, sir, of course,' she said and then, very quickly, she left.

A moment of pure silence passed between the two men before Suleyman, his face positively puce, said, 'Sir, I...'

An upraised hand from Ikmen silenced him immediately. 'Please don't make me do personal relations at this time in the morning, Suleyman,' he said, 'I've had a very bizarre night which I need to talk to you about right now.'

'Yes, but—'

'Look, Cohen is really your man for the sex thing, not me.'

'Ah...'

'Not another word!' Ikmen warned. 'We've far too much to do and I really need you to be fresh, awake and attentive. Do you understand?'

Suleyman looked down at the floor and then, with a sigh, said, 'Yes, sir.'

'Now,' Ikmen said, hauling himself painfully into a sitting position, 'I did a bit of research last night. Old missing persons. Which, by the way, you said you were coming back to help with.'

'Sorry.'

'You were, I take it...'

'I had to go home. A family matter,' Suleyman said, not daring to lift his eyes from the pattern on the carpet.

Ikmen sighed. 'Yes, of course.' Then, brightening, he continued. 'Well, I turned up some information regarding a Zeki Ersoy.'

Suleyman, raising his head a little now, frowned. 'Some relative of Muhammed Ersoy?'

'His brother actually,' Ikmen replied with a smile.

'But he's been dead for—'

'No. Not dead, missing. Now probably dead, but...'

'So why did I and, I believe, a lot of other people think he was dead?' Suleyman, his surprise overcoming his embarrassment, sat down. 'Apart from anything else the parents committed suicide—or were assumed to have done because of the loss of the boy. And if you are now saying that he was alive...'

'Mrs Ersoy did indeed die by her own hand,' Ikmen said, wiping his knuckles roughly across his tired features. 'In Italy.'

'Italy?'

'Yes. The family were cruising aboard their yacht in the Bay of Naples when it happened.' He looked up, his face grave and strained. 'Ingestion of cleaning fluid was the conclusion drawn by the Italian pathologist.'

Suleyman pulled a face. 'Nasty. However, forgive my ignorance, but what has this to do with our case?'

'Just read the description of the child, first page,' Ikmen said, flinging the thick cardboard file across at his deputy.

For a few moments Suleyman sat quietly with the material, his face impassive while Ikmen lit up one of his precious last ten cigarettes. Then Suleyman said, 'I see.'

'Do you?'

'Well, the boy in the mortuary and this child share a similar scar or marking on the face. Zeki Ersoy would also be about the right age to qualify as our corpse, and—'

'And because he is still, officially missing, we cannot and should not discount him from our investigation however unlikely that particular notion might be.'

'So did the child go missing here or in Italy?' Suleyman asked and then, leafing through the file for a few moments, noting that much of it was in Italian, he added, 'And how do you know all this anyway?'

'Before your time, until actually 1982 when all of this happened, there was an old inspector here called Hikmet. I never, I admit, knew him that well. He was of the pray-five-times-a-day variety whereas I was far more interested in cheap alcohol and bawdy jokes, as you well know. But anyway, he was the Turkish liaison point for the Italians with regard to this and last night I phoned him up.'

'And?'

'And he told me some very interesting things including the rather odd fact that young Zeki was not reported as missing in Italy until after Mr and Mrs Ersoy had died. Old Mr Ersoy was apparently very keen to have his wife buried in line with Islamic custom and so she was rapidly examined by a Dr Craxi, after which her body was interred in a small Muslim graveyard in Naples. He then, or so it would seem, returned to Istanbul where he died the next day.'

'And did he die by his own hand also?'

'His body was discovered in his boathouse, drowned apparently in the mooring bay.'

Suleyman frowned. 'So did Mr Ersoy report his son as missing before he left Italy?'

'That is unclear,' Ikmen replied, also frowning. 'According to the Italians as soon as he had buried his wife he left for home aboard an aeroplane, leaving his yacht in Naples harbour. Muhammed Ersoy later arranged for the vessel to be recovered after the Italians had released it from their custody—finding, so they said, no trace of the child.'

'OK,' Suleyman drawled slowly, 'so, assuming that he didn't report his son missing whilst he was still in Italy, how did the Neapolitan police get involved?'

'The missing person report was actually made here originally. On the seventeenth of April 1982, almost a week after his father's death, Muhammed Ersoy reported that the couple into whose care his father had put the child, some friends in Amalfi, had not yet made contact with him and in the absence of any essential details about them, he was beginning to feel out of touch and worried.'

'So did they find these people?'

'Oh yes, the Greko family were easily traced but were quite bemused when they heard that not only were their friends the Ersoys dead but that it was believed they had young Zeki in their care. The police apparently even dug up their lovely cliff-top garden just to make sure. Not the sort of thing they would have done for a Neapolitan street urchin but there you are.'

'So what about the yacht?' Suleyman asked. 'Wouldn't the crew know or—'

'Hüseyn Ersoy always piloted the vessel himself.'

'Yes, but—'

'There was a cook who also doubled as house- or rather boat-keeper for the duration.'

'And?'

Ikmen sighed. 'She always claimed, according to Hikmet, that the child had never accompanied his parents to Italy in the first place. Not that she was believed of course.'

'Why not?' Suleyman asked. 'I mean if this woman was actually there?'

'The child's nurse, who had remained behind in the Ersoy mansion, swore that the child had gone to Italy with its parents—as did the child's brother. And with no access to either of the parents it was assumed that these two people, who were so intimately connected with all concerned, not to mention in Muhammed's case, also very wealthy, had to be right. And indeed, later on in the proceedings, the cook did in fact tell the Italian police that she may very well have been wrong about the child not being on board.'

'Why would she do that?'

Ikmen shrugged. 'Perhaps in the face of such over-whelming evidence to the contrary from the rich and powerful she just felt that she had to fall into line. Or maybe she was mistaken, as she said to the Italian police, although personally I doubt it.'

'Why?'

'Well, although there is a record of both Mr and Mrs Ersoy entering Italy there is no mention of their son.'

'He could just have remained on the yacht?'

'In which case,' Ikmen said, 'somebody would have to have looked after him and the only candidate for that would have been the cook who claimed not to remember his presence. And besides, I may be wrong, but even when a foreign vessel just enters your waters, do you not have to make a record of who that vessel has on board?'

'I don't know, but...' Suleyman looked down at the file again and grimaced. 'So with all these inconsistencies, how on earth was it ever resolved?'

Ikmen sighed. 'It wasn't. According to Hikmet there was some frantic activity around this Greko family for a while who, apparently, have Mafia connections—but then what wealthy Italian does not? But there was no sign of the child ever having been anywhere in the vicinity of Amalfi.'

'And so?'

'And so after a few cursory inquiries back here the thing just died out. With no leads and, more importantly, no body, the police in both countries found themselves completely at a loss. Although officially unsolved the feeling seemed to be that the boy had either died or been drowned, whatever, somewhere between here and Italy. It could explain why Mrs Ersoy killed herself although it does little to illuminate her husband's death.'

'Which was, officially?'

'Death by misadventure. Muhammed Ersoy said that when his father went out to the boathouse on the night of his return he had been in a disturbed state due to the recent death of his wife and while in that state he must have slipped into the water.'

'It occurs to me that there is a lot here that depends almost solely upon the word of Muhammed Ersoy.'

Ikmen smiled. 'Yes, I thought so too.'

'I mean, I know that he is a powerful and respected man, but...'

'Yes. Which is why I am going to pay him a visit and, if I can, elicit from him, amongst other things, the whereabouts of the servants involved.'

'The cook and the nurse?'

'Yes.'

Suleyman paused to think a little before asking his next question. 'And so do you have a theory?'

'Not really,' Ikmen said, stubbing his cigarette out and then lighting another, 'beyond an idea that the boy never actually left Istanbul. I have a small notion about why this might have been, but it's a little mad for this time of day.'

'Is it?'

'Yes, at that dinner I went to at Ersoy's mansion he made a point of mentioning that the samovar he gave to Krikor came from the Kafes at a friend's house.'

Suleyman laughed. 'What?'

'Some friend of his father, one of you lot, I suppose, had a Kafes in his house. So, I presume in the past, he or his ancestors could lock away those who were a threat to them.'

'He told you that?'

'Yes.'

Suleyman sighed and then shook his head slightly from

side to side as if in a state of disbelief. 'Well, I can tell you for certain that that, if nothing else, is a lie,' he said. 'Only the Sultan had a Kafes. Nobody else, however rich, to my knowledge ever emulated that practice.'

'But Dr Sarkissian—'

'I think you'll find, sir, that Mr Ersoy is playing games with you—at least on this subject.'

'Is he, indeed. Well—' Ikmen was interrupted by the ringing of his only just reconnected telephone which he quickly moved to silence before the thing gave him the headache that he was fully expecting to get very soon. 'Ikmen,' he said, leaning heavily back in his chair.

'Çetin.'

The voice was instantly recognisable. 'Arto. Hello. You know I've had an absolute bastard of—'

'Be quiet, will you, Çetin, and listen to me.' There was a quality in his voice that made Ikmen sit up just a little straighter.

'Is everything all right, Arto?'

'I need you to come to Avram Avedykian's apartment, Çetin. Now.'

'Er, why?'

'Don't ask me that please, Çetin, because I can't answer you at this moment. Just come. Alone, if you will.'

'Yes, but...'

'Just do it.'

'All right. Can you give me his ad—'

The line clicked off into what Ikmen felt was an ominous silence. Slowly, he replaced the handset and sat for a moment staring gravely into space.

Suleyman, glancing up from the Ersoy file, said, 'Problems?'

'I think Dr Sarkissian may be in some sort of trouble.'

'What do you mean?'

'I don't know.' Ikmen suddenly and with almost furious resolve began shuffling amongst the huge heap of papers on his desk. 'Oh, it's got to be here somewhere!'

Standing up now and moving towards Ikmen, Suleyman asked, 'What? What are you looking for?'

'I'm looking for that list of committee members I showed you the other day,' he replied, knocking an ashtray containing a still burning cigarette on to the floor.

Suleyman turned, walked back to his desk and grabbed the corner of a piece of paper on top of one of his in trays. 'This,' he said, flinging it down in front of Ikmen's face.

'Ah,' the older man exclaimed. 'Thank you.' Then, frowning, he ran his finger down the page until he spotted the name he required. 'Ah!' he said again, triumphantly.

'May I know what's going on, sir?' Suleyman asked, still standing in front of his superior's desk.

'Yes and no,' Ikmen said, standing up and retrieving his jacket from the back of his chair. 'Dr Sarkissian has asked me to go to him at Dr Avedykian's home.' He looked up in order to emphasise his next point. 'Alone.'

'Do you think that's wise?'

'No,' Ikmen replied, bending to pick up the burning cigarette on the floor and then sticking it into his mouth. 'But he was very emphatic on the point and so I don't really see what choice I have. I know I'm probably being very foolish— Ardiç would kill me if he knew about this—but there was something in Arto's voice I just can't ignore. I can't!'

Suleyman frowned. 'I don't like it.'

'Neither do I. Which,' Ikmen said with a smile, 'is why you are going to take a squad over to Mr Ersoy's place and then follow me to Avedykian's.'

'But what if—'

'If I get into difficulty I can always call you, can't I? Keep your phone switched on and just be ready to come should the need arise. You won't need to go in mob-handed to Ersoy but if he sees we're out in force it might make him think.'

'So what, exactly, should I ask Mr Ersoy about?'

Forgetting his phone for a moment, Ikmen checked his pockets for keys and then put his cigarette out and lit another. 'You can tell him we think we might have some information regarding his brother and then ask him to tell you his version of events. If you can, get some information on those servants.'

'Right. And then?'

'Then get back to me either at Avedykian's or, if I'm finished there, here. We'll discuss what to do next then. I must go.'

As he opened the door to leave, he met Sergeant Farsakoğlu carrying a large glass of tea and a packet of Gauloises. Smiling, he deftly relieved her of the cigarettes and then said, 'Give the tea to Sergeant Suleyman, would you? I think he might need it.'

And then he was gone, leaving the two sergeants, for the first time, alone in the office.

Putting the tea glass down on Suleyman's desk, the young woman said, 'Now that he's gone, can I talk to you?'

'No.' He didn't even look at her as he made his way over to his telephone and dialled a number into the key-pad.

'You're going to have to talk to me some time, you know,' she remarked angrily, trying to position herself so that he had to look at her. 'I'm not some little whore that you can just use and then discard.'

And with that she left the room. Following her with his

eyes, Suleyman sighed and then said into the receiver, 'It's Suleyman, I need three men to come out to Yeniköy with me.'

Halil Ikmen looked down at the stylish gold watch on his wrist and then sighed. Sitting next to him, Krikor Sarkissian leaned over slightly and just gently touched his friend's hand. Several harassed-looking individuals in white coats hurried past, each one followed closely by the two men's searching eyes.

'Fatma is frantic with worry, you know,' Halil said as he picked uselessly at some invisible fluff on the sleeve of his coat.

'I'm sure that Çetin is fine,' his friend replied in what he hoped was a reassuring tone.

'Oh, yes,' Halil agreed, 'I'm sure that he is. My brother has nothing if not a talent for self-preservation, but that doesn't change the fact that he should be here, does it?'

'No.'

Over the tannoy system someone put out a call for a Dr Ali. Halil drummed a short tattoo on the side of his chair.

'How long might my father remain in this condition?' he asked, turning white-faced to his friend.

'It's difficult to say. He's had a massive heart attack. But,' Krikor smiled a little, adding, 'he is still breathing on his own and so—'

'And if he stops?'

Krikor sighed and then, looking down at the large pile of cigarette butts beneath his feet, said, 'The physicians will do everything they can to—'

'But if he stops breathing before my brother arrives, what will happen? I mean I'm not stupid, Krikor, I know that Father is gravely ill, but—'

'There may yet be—'

'Oh, please do not insult my intelligence with your bedside manner, Krikor!' Halil snapped. 'Just because we haven't, until now, said the word doesn't mean that it isn't true. Father is dying and not one of your calming words or assurances is going to make any difference to that.'

A moment of silence passed between the two men which was only finally ended by Krikor muttering, 'Sorry.'

Halil rummaged in one of his pockets for a few seconds and then took out a packet of cigarettes and some matches. 'I thought I'd done with these wretched things!' he said, lighting up and then wordlessly passing the smoking materials over to his companion.

Looking down at the cigarettes and matches before lighting up himself, Krikor said, 'You know that these have killed more Turks than even the most barbarous Christian adversary?'

Haul merely grunted by way of reply to that, then, turning, he said, 'You haven't answered my question.'

'No,' Krikor smiled. 'I haven't.'

'Why?'

'Because I think that we should only meet that contingency if it happens.'

'Well, I'd rather meet it now. Before it's too late.'

With a small gesture of helplessness, Krikor shrugged. 'If that's what you want.'

'And so?'

'Krikor drew long and hard upon his cigarette, preparing his mind, or so Halil thought, for what was to follow. 'If Uncle Timür stops breathing the doctors will try to revive him.'

'And if they can't?'

'Then he will die, Halil,' Krikor said gently.

'But isn't there some machine or something they can—'

'You mean life support? Well, yes, that is an option, but...'

'But what? I mean if it only keeps him alive until my brother arrives it...'

'Look, Halil,' Krikor said, taking his friend's one free hand in his and looking very intently into his eyes, 'if you want to do that then we can arrange for it to happen, but I would strongly advise you not to.'

'Why?' Halil's eyes were full of questions and a hurt that Krikor could only too easily recognise from a time long ago when his own father had died.

'Because, my friend,' he said, 'when you switch a machine on you must also at some time switch it off.'

'Yes, but...'

'And as his eldest son you and only you will have to take that decision.'

'Oh.' Halil looked down at the floor, close now to the tears he was only just controlling.

'The sort of questions you need to be asking yourself are things like: "Would my father want that?" and, more importantly, "Would Çetin want me to put myself through such a horrendous experience for him?" Think about it, Halil.'

Halil Ikmen looked up at the grey faces of all those others around him, people like him, waiting for news about loved ones. Some facing joy, others the kind of sorrow that he was anticipating. With some venom he threw what was left of his cigarette down on to the floor and ground it out with the heel of his shoe.

Çetin Ikmen was surprised when, leaning on the door to press the bell on Avram Avedykian's apartment, the thing gave and opened so easily under his hand. To leave a door open like this in a part of the city that famously housed so many moneyed people seemed to him like madness. Either that or, anticipating his arrival, the good doctor had decided to make his entry as simple as possible. Or, of course, something very sinister indeed was occurring which, given the tone of Arto's voice during their recent conversation, was probably the most likely explanation. He paused briefly to remove his gun from the holster underneath his armpit and then pushed the door gently with his foot.

The hall, a stark but stylish area, was, as far as Ikmen could tell, never having been to this place before, as it should be; it showed no signs of the chaos that usually accompanied a break-in. Looking down at the expensive carpet Ikmen felt a little guilty for dragging his mud-soaked shoes across its surface but then he didn't really have very much choice. There was something odd here, but it was a something he could smell rather than see that was alerting him to this strangeness. It wasn't a strong smell but it was vaguely familiar and not, he felt, in a pleasant way.

Tentatively he called out his friend's name. 'Arto?'

Nothing. Not a sound disturbed the peace that was beginning to engulf him.

'Arto?' He called louder this time and this time he was rewarded with a reply.

'We're in here, Inspector,' a voice that was not Arto's replied. 'The door just in front of you.'

It was, Ikmen assumed, Avedykian, although why he was not actually coming out to greet him he neither knew nor trusted. Walking forward, he held his weapon down to one side as he pushed the door open with his other hand.

The sight that met his eyes as he moved just inside the doorway was, on initial viewing, quite normal. The room, furnished in the same dark minimalist style as the hall, was very tidy and ordered looking, and what appeared to be the perfectly normal sight of his friend sitting in a large leather chair brought a brief smile to Ikmen's face. Had it not been for the expression on Arto's features, which was one of frozen terror, plus something that at first he did not understand about the angle of his friend's legs, he would have marched in without another thought.

Just for a second however, he paused. 'Arto?'

'Çetin.'

Something hard and metallic rammed itself into the side of his head, causing him almost to gag with shock.

'I'll take that gun, if I may, Inspector,' said a voice from beside the weapon at his ear. 'Just drop it on to the ground, if you please.'

Slowly, but not for a moment managing to lose contact with the weapon at his head, Ikmen bent down and laid the gun in his hand on the floor. It was as he did this that he saw what was odd about Arto's legs: they were tied at the ankles with tape. Why had he not seen that right away? Damn!

'Now move across the room towards your friend and sit in that chair next to him, please.'

Knowing of old that in the early stages of situations like this, one had no choice but to do as one was bid, Ikmen made his way slowly over to Arto and his seat. The carpet beneath his feet was, strangely, a little tacky underfoot, as if wet. As he passed his friend the doctor simply whispered, 'Sorry.'

'Well, you've certainly made us wait for your company, Çetin,' Muhammed Ersoy said with a smile. 'We tried many different telephone numbers during the course of the night, didn't we, doctor?'

Arto just cleared his throat in reply. Ikmen, however, remembering once again his childish altercation with his mobile telephone, plus his rather thoughtless unplugging of the office instrument so that he could sleep, put his head in his hands and groaned.

'But now that you are here I feel that the long boring watches of the night might just have been worth enduring for the benefit of having you with us.'

'I'm so glad you think that, Mr Ersoy,' Ikmen replied as he lowered himself into his chair, looking fixedly at the weapon in Ersoy's hand. 'Where is Dr Avedykian?'

'He's lying on his bed at present,' Ersoy said. 'Would you like to go and see him?'

Instinctively, Ikmen turned towards his friend before replying—a move which revealed to him a face that was tense and filled with a warning expression that he knew better than to ignore.

'Dr Sarkissian, I think, feels that this might be unwise,' Ikmen said.

'Very,' Arto said, finally rediscovering his voice. 'He's dead.'

'Oh.' Ikmen slowly crossed one leg over the other and then watched as Ersoy picked his service weapon up from the floor. So that was the smell. That would make sense. 'And how did that happen then, Mr Ersoy?'

'Avram's death?' He clicked the safety catch down on the gun and then put it in his pocket. 'I killed him.'

'But I thought that you, you and he were...'

'Lovers?' Ersoy smiled. 'Yes. But then his death was an act of love—my love for him.'

'I'm sorry?'

'Don't even start to try and make sense of it, Çetin,' Arto murmured.

'I have always thought,' Ikmen said slowly, 'that if you love a person the most usual urge that accompanies that is to keep the person alive.'

Ersoy laughed. 'In some instances, yes.'

'I am, I must admit,' Ikmen said with a shrug, 'struggling to imagine what instances might be outside of that general rule.'

Not taking his eyes or the barrel of his gun off the two men for a second, Ersoy slid down into a chair and then cleared his throat. 'You know Avram was really quite beautiful, wasn't he?'

'Dr Avedykian was an attractive man, yes.'

'Unlike myself he worked out continually. Did you know that?' Then, not waiting for either Ikmen or Sarkissian to reply, he continued, 'I have always abhorred exercise of any sort.'

Ikmen silently found that this, if nothing else, was a sentiment with which he could easily identify. Where this conversation might be leading in the long run was another matter.

'But,' Ersoy said with a sigh, 'time is such a heartless bitch and despite Avram's almost total dedication to his body he was beginning to exhibit distinct signs of ageing.'

Something that Ikmen could only describe as dread started to move slowly up the length of his body. 'And so you...'

'He would have hated to grow old and ugly—as would I.'

'And so,' Ikmen reiterated, 'you killed him.'

'Yes.'

'So that he wouldn't have to suffer the indignities of middle and old age?'

'Yes. Well'—Ersoy laughed again in that gentle, almost benign way—'in part. There were—'

'So like the Pharaohs and all those other great rulers and

whatever that you cited at that charming dinner you gave us all, you made sure that your friend would never grow old.'

'Yes.'

Ikmen struggled to find the right words to express what he wanted and needed to say. It was hardly surprising given both the outlandishness of his captor's opinions plus the danger inherent in the situation itself. 'You, who I believe are older than Dr Avedykian, must therefore now crumble into old age alone. I mean, given the direction of your logic...'

'Oh I do, I can assure you, intend to join Avram,' Ersoy said, and then, flicking the safety catch off his revolver, he added, 'Today as a matter of fact.'

Suleyman turned briefly towards the three young officers who stood behind him and then, with a sigh, resumed his conversation with the man at the door.

'You are certain that you have no idea where Mr Ersoy might be now?' he said.

'Yes.'

'He didn't give you any indication of how long he might be?'

'No.' The man, who was some sort of servant, briefly caught the eye of one of the young constables and swallowed nervously. 'Mr Ersoy is not in the habit of saying where he is going, at least not to me.'

'Would he outline his movements to anybody else then?' Suleyman's impatience with what he recognised only too well as the mindless loyalty of those who consider themselves inferior was beginning to show.

'No,' the man replied, 'at least not to staff.'

'And is there anyone in the house who does not qualify as staff?'

'No. Mr Ersoy lives alone.'

One of Suleyman's young companions smirked just slightly. Suleyman duly turned a vicious gaze upon him. The young man visibly shrank.

'So,' Suleyman said, summing up the conversation so far, 'what you are saying is that nobody knows where Mr Ersoy is at this moment.'

'No. Yes. None of us knows where he is, I mean.'

'Right.' Suleyman put his hands on his hips and sighed heavily. 'Does Mr Ersoy have a mobile telephone number that we might use to contact him?'

'Yes,' the man replied. Then he remained quite unmoving and speechless.

Eventually, Suleyman asked, 'Might we have that?'

'I don't know what it is!' the man said, obviously quite amazed that anyone could think he would have such information. 'That's for Mr Ersoy's friends!'

'Well, it looks as if we'll just have to come in and wait for him then, doesn't it?' Suleyman snapped.

'Oh no, you can't do that!' the man cried, holding one hand up to Suleyman's face as if somehow to ward him off. 'No one comes in while Mr Ersoy is out. It wouldn't be right!'

'In case it may have escaped your notice,' Suleyman said with increased venom, 'we are officers of the law.'

'Yes, but—'

'For all you know, I may wish to speak to Mr Ersoy on matters which relate to our national security.'

'Oh.' Then, bending forward a little so that only Suleyman could hear him, the man added, 'You do know that Mr Ersoy is a proper Turk, don't you? I mean he's not a—'

'It really is very cold out here,' Suleyman said, pushing the man back a little just lightly with his hand. 'I think that my officers could benefit from some of Mr Ersoy's tea, don't you?'

'Yes, but—'

'I will take upon myself any responsibility for Mr Ersoy's displeasure,' Suleyman continued, pushing forward at the head of his three young lads. And then, even though it galled him to do so, he added the arrogant but impressive lie. 'I was actually at school with your master and so I can't see that there would be a problem.'

'Oh.'

Suleyman entered what had to be the largest entrance hall outside of the royal palaces that he had ever seen. It was difficult, if not impossible not to be impressed. But Suleyman, who after all had some practice in this art, did a very good impression of aristocratic boredom with the whole thing.

As the last of the three young constables muscled his way through the door, the man whispered into his ear, 'He's very posh to be one of your lot! Who is he?'

'Sergeant Suleyman,' the young man replied, and then added with a shrug, 'He works for Inspector Ikmen.'

Whether that latter item of information was meant in some way to explain this Suleyman's behaviour the servant did not know. But the name Ikmen was, he felt, somehow familiar to him.

# 15

'MAY I HAVE a cigarette?' Ikmen asked.

'But of course!' Ersoy said with a smile, throwing one of his own packets and a lighter across at the policeman. 'Have one of mine.'

'You don't trust me to look in my own pockets then?' Ikmen asked as he caught Ersoy's smoking materials and then lit up.

'No, not really.'

'Right.' As he inhaled, Ikmen sat back a little further in his chair, his eyes fixed upon the face of the man before him. 'Would I be right in assuming, Mr Ersoy, that because you intend to die today, the doctor and myself are somehow involved in your plans?'

'Yes. You are both part of a rather clever plan of mine actually.' He laughed. 'I was with my dear Avram when he called the doctor here last night. He said he wanted to confess all to his old friend and I acceded, after a suitable show of shock and horror, to his demands. I must admit that I was amazed he trusted my acquiesence, but then he was not entirely himself by this time.' He smiled. 'It seemed like such a good opportunity. I must, I reckon, have shot Avram just as the doctor was leaving his house to help, or so he thought, my loved one with his problems.'

'His problems?' Ikmen asked. 'What problems?'

'Oh, don't play with me, Çetin!' Ersoy said, accompanying his mock surprise with a lascivious leer. 'You know exactly what Avram's problems were—you sent my old friend Murad Suleyman's brother to see Avram precisely because you knew.'

'If I may, sir,' Ikmen said, waving his cigarette rather nervously in Ersoy's direction, 'I think you may be ahead of me.'

'Well, the drugs, of course, you silly man!'

'Ah.' So Dr Avedykian hadn't simply been a good start with regard to 'getting in' with Christian doctors. Oh, Ikmen had played with the idea that he was 'the' doctor involved with the prostitutes but for such a kind, obviously concerned man to...

'The younger Suleyman, who, by the way, I was certainly shocked to discover works as a policeman, really frightened poor Avram, to the extent that by the time he returned home and telephoned me, he was quite hysterical.'

'I cannot believe,' Arto said with some anger, 'that Avram could possibly be involved in selling—'

'Oh, he didn't sell,' Ersoy said with a smile. 'No, he was much too moral to do that. He gave the little tarts their drugs and helped them out when they fumbled with their needles. He saw it very much as a social service.'

Ikmen frowned. 'How?'

'Avram, although latterly involved with the rather utopian ideas of your brother,' Ersoy said, addressing Arto with a bow, 'was in truth a realist. He knew that actually

getting these children off narcotics was virtually impossible—they take them in order to be able to cope with what
they have to do. Going down on really quite disgusting old
men requires either nerves of iron or a certain detachment
from reality that is easily obtained via the expedient use
of opiates.'

'But...'

'What he gave them was in effect a service. The clinical
drugs he obtained could be guaranteed free from harmful
additives, he could administer a measured and safe dosage
and his equipment, needles and whatever, was sterile.'

'His "service" wasn't free though, was it?' Ikmen said
gravely.

'Oh no.' Ersoy had a distinct twinkle in his eye. 'Why
step into the shop if you do not intend to buy?'

'But as his, as you say, lover, did you not...'

Ersoy laughed, this time loudly, almost braying. 'Oh,
yes, he was and is the love of my life, but what you must,
although I doubt if you can, understand is that devotion
does not necessarily preclude "incidents" with others. To
be fair, at the beginning Avram wanted to keep our relationship exclusive but I have, and always have had, other
interests apart from him. I even, contrary to popular myth,
sleep with women on a quite regular basis. They are so
much more submissive than men which, although I like
their bodies less, endears me to them.'

'So Dr Avedykian's pursuit of young prostitutes was...'

'An act of revenge?' Ersoy smiled. 'Initially, yes. Until
he discovered that I didn't mind and indeed found his
accounts of his adventures really quite exciting.'

Arto, his face now almost black with fury, nevertheless
controlled his temper enough to ask, 'He obtained these
drugs from the hospital then?'

'Yes. Although not originally for the little tarts. But that is another story'—teasingly Ersoy lowered his eyes just for a second—'which we will discuss later, I promise you.'

Unconsciously, Ikmen's mind moved to the dead boy in Sultan Ahmet, his system pumped full of pethidine.

Seeing or perhaps sensing something of this on Ikmen's face, Ersoy said, 'Yes, Çetin, you will get the chance to talk about your murder victim, don't worry. However,'—he lit a cigarette and then winced slightly as the smoke floated up into his eyes—'whatever the reason for which Avram was procuring drugs he always employed the same method.'

Arto sat a little further forward the better to hear.

'It could only be performed with patients who were in little or no danger.'

'What do you mean "performed"?'

Ersoy held one hand up to silence the plump little doctor, his face now a rather stern mask. 'I can only tell you what he told me,' he said. 'And as a non-doctor myself I could be wrong but...For those who came to him with minor or easily treated conditions, Avram simply added a little extra in terms of post-operative pain control to the prescriptions that he sent down to the pharmacy. These in turn were then entered on to the patients' records which Avram himself, as the consultant in charge of their care, was responsible for. He did, of course, sometimes make mistakes. Sometimes his theft would bite into the pain control that his patients needed; at times they became distressed, which did make him feel guilty. But that was usually when his need elsewhere, as it were, was at its greatest.'

'So what you are saying,' Arto said slowly, 'is that Avram was skimming small but significant amounts of opiates from off the top of patients' dosages—patients seen by him as not at risk and therefore not liable to be the subjects of clinical investigation or autopsy.' He turned briefly but significantly to Ikmen and then muttered, 'So my brother was right about Avram after all.'

Ersoy bowed his head slightly in recognition of Arto's words. 'Quite so. And because the increases were small and not constant, the pharmacist would think little of it. Sometimes, at various points after an operation, people do need either more or less pain control and with the pharmacy and the patient records always in agreement...' He looked across at Ikmen and smiled. 'Your colleague would have found little of interest in the vicinity of the pharmacy. Avram was always clever and rarely greedy—a point I tried to make to him last night when he was becoming hysterical.'

'Before you decided to kill him?'

Ersoy inhaled heavily before replying but when he did so it was, again, with a smile. 'Oh no. I had decided to kill him some time before—actually on my fortieth birthday.' He looked upwards as if appealing to some unseen power above his head and said, 'I made a lot of decisions on that day.'

'Did Dr Avedykian know that death was what you had in mind for him?' Ikmen asked.

Ersoy narrowed his eyes slyly before speaking. 'Now, I could at this point, I suppose, allude to suicide pacts and the like, but considering that a reduced or even a full prison sentence is not an option here I might as well tell you the truth. No, he didn't know, Inspector. Not until the very last moment, of course. I think I said something like, "I'll see you in paradise, my love," and although he went to say something, I had killed him before he had time to finish.'

'Considering,' Ikmen said sharply, 'that you both adhered to different religious codes the chances of your "meeting" in the afterlife are, do you not think, somewhat slim?'

Ersoy laughed. 'Oh, you know, I do really appreciate

your wit, Çetin! It is so very refreshing to meet somebody with whom one can easily converse on this level. I would not have had half the amusement I have elicited from this affair had it not been for you.'

'I'm so glad that I have been of service,' Ikmen said bitterly, looking across at Arto's shock-stained face.

'It would, however, be interesting, at this point,' Ersoy continued, 'to find out just how far you have progressed with the principal subject of, well, of my life, Çetin. In view of the little hints and pointers I have been giving you for the last however-many-it-is days.'

'Could we possibly be talking about the young murder victim in Sultan Ahmet?' Ikmen said, a now rapidly gathering realisation overcoming him.

'My brother, yes. Quite so,' Ersoy said, stubbing his cigarette out into his lover's favourite tortoiseshell ashtray.

Spitefully, or so it seemed to the two other young constables present, Suleyman slapped the third member of their party as soon as the servant girl had left the room.

'Don't leer!' he snapped. 'At least not at Turkish girls!'

'Sir...'

'Leer at foreign tourists if you must, but even then discreetly.'

'Oh, but sir, you...'

One of the others behind him smirked.

'Yes?' Suleyman asked, paranoia beginning to take hold of his mind. 'I what?'

'Well, you...'

Was this, could it possibly be an allusion to his recent liaison with the lovely Farsakoğlu? Surely, even amongst filthy-minded scum like these, so recently come from the army, such information couldn't possibly have reached the gossip stage yet, could it? Why, the thing, the—what had happened between them—had only occurred the previous evening. Unless she had told them herself! But she wouldn't do that, would she? However much she might feel for him, and in truth she must feel quite a lot to give herself to him with such enthusiasm, she would surely not put her own reputation at risk just to get even more of his attention? Such things can and did turn into disciplinary matters! Even so, perhaps it had been unwise to be as cutting as he had with her earlier that morning. But then, as a married man, even one who intended one day to tell his wife about what he had done, he had acted in the only way he felt open to him.

He turned back once again to the young boy at his elbow and said very clearly and slowly, 'I what, Öztürk? Come on, you were saying...'

Accompanied by a loud beeping sound, his mobile telephone started to vibrate against his chest. With a sigh he took it out of his jacket pocket and answered 'Suleyman.'

'Is the inspector with you?' Cohen's familiar voice inquired.

'No, he's...' Quickly remembering that Ikmen at that moment was not really supposed to be where only he knew him to be, Suleyman added, '...elsewhere. Why?'

'Because we keep on getting calls from his brother. I think it might be a family thing, but he sounds quite stressed.'

Suleyman sighed, briefly casting his eyes across a nearby painting of what looked like an Ottoman officer in a somewhat heroic pose atop his horse. If Ikmen's brother were calling then it had, he thought, to be a serious matter.

He knew Ikmen did not get on with his older sibling very well, so he doubted it was a social call.

'Have you tried the inspector's mobile number?' he asked.

'Yes. But it just keeps coming up dead,' Cohen replied.

'Oh.' Something vaguely unpleasant started moving from the back of his mind as he struggled to decide what to do next.

'What shall I say to this man if he calls again? I don't know what to do.'

If Ikmen was where Suleyman thought he was, at Dr Avedykian's apartment, it could be that something very serious was occurring. That Dr Sarkissian had asked him to go there alone had been unusual to say the least, and given that the doctor had been, according to Ikmen, very tense too...

'Look,' he said to Cohen, 'leave it with me. I'll get back to you.'

'Yes, but this man—'

'Just tell him that the inspector is out and at present uncontactable. Tell him he's with an informant—anything.'

'OK, but—'

'I'll phone you later, Cohen, when I know something.'

He then pressed the 'end' button and sat quite still and silent for a moment.

Two of his companions, including Öztürk, shuffled uneasily in their overstuffed chairs, but they remained silent. Good-looking and sophisticated he may be, but Sergeant Suleyman had, over the last few years, gained something of a reputation for being a bit tyrannical when his superior was not around to control him. Perhaps, Öztürk thought, it was his posh blood coming out?

When he did move Suleyman did so rapidly. Taking a sheet of paper from the pocket of his trousers he scanned down its length until he found what he was looking for and then dialled a number into his telephone. Raising the thing up to his ear, he clicked his tongue impatiently as he waited.

'So your brother Zeki and my victim are one and the same then, are they, sir?'

'Yes.'

Ikmen briefly paused to shake his head, as if in disbelief. 'I am interested, no, fascinated,' he said, 'to discover just how and why that should be so.'

Ersoy smiled a self-satisfied grin. 'Why, it is "so", as you say, Çetin, because I am, as I know you appreciate, a very clever fellow.'

'That's a fact,' Ikmen replied, 'of which I have always been aware. However, if I am right in my assumption that you somehow managed to detain your brother for what must now be fifteen years without detection, you must have had help. I mean, I am correct in my contention that young Zeki did not actually ever reach Italian soil?'

'You are right on both counts,' Ersoy said just as the telephone at his elbow began to ring.

As Ersoy picked up the receiver his eyes briefly left the faces of the two men who immediately turned and silently gesticulated wildly at one another. A millisecond later, however, his eyes were back on them again, smiling as was their custom, and all activity stopped.

Listening to what was being said at the other end, Muhammed Ersoy occasionally nodded. Finally he said, 'Your assumption that I am Dr Avedykian is erroneous, I'm afraid. The doctor is, sadly, dead.'

A few seconds then passed during which, so Ikmen assumed, the caller moved on to another subject.

'Ah yes,' Ersoy then said with a small laugh, 'they are both here, but...Yes, yes...Oh, yes, it is I. How very clever of you...' His eyes widened with something that looked very much like pleasure.

The reference to himself and Arto both being 'here' could, Ikmen thought, mean that the person on the other end of the line was Suleyman. In a way he hoped that it was, but in another that it wasn't...

'Ah, yes,' Ersoy went on magnanimously, 'of course you can, my dear fellow...Yes...Yes, but alone, Sergeant, you understand? I don't want to have to—'

Ikmen found himself shouting across the room. 'Suleyman, don't you dare come to this place without—'

'Çetin!' Ersoy yelled back, his hand over the receiver to conceal this altercation from the caller. Then, pointing his revolver most emphatically at Arto's head, he said in a milder tone, 'I do not want to have to do this before I am ready, so do not make me!'

Just briefly the charm slipped, revealing eyes that looked as if they could see through stone—cruel yet empty.

However, as he turned back to the caller, the smile returned and with it an almost tangible sensuousness. 'Oh, they are fine, for the moment...Oh, yes...But of course...' He laughed again, almost cooing into the receiver, 'Mmm... Very well...Very well...Until then.'

The call concluded, he placed the receiver back on to its cradle. Not once did his gun, pointing in the direction of Arto's head, waver.

'I do believe,' he said, 'that you and your sergeant are about to be reunited, Çetin. An unlooked-for but nevertheless interesting diversion.'

'Quite how you will keep all three of us under control will be the most fascinating part of the procedure from my point of view,' Ikmen said.

'Ah, but then perhaps I won't,' Ersoy replied.

'Won't what?'

'Keep you under control.'

Ikmen frowned.

'I think the doctor understands what I mean,' Ersoy said, looking across at Arto whose face was drained and alarmingly grey with terror.

A moment of silence then passed; a moment during which Ikmen quietly considered what had just been said. His stomach, unbidden, did a backflip. If Suleyman was indeed on his way all he could hope was that his sergeant didn't overreact. With one dead body in the bedroom and a carpet, he now knew, spattered with blood, this apartment could soon look like a slaughterhouse should his deputy decide to be brave.

'So,' Ersoy said, leaning forward and smiling at his two hostages once again, 'we were, I believe, talking about my brother, weren't we?'

'Zeki,' Ikmen said. The dead boy ought to be given a name.

'Yes, Zeki.' Ersoy sighed. 'As you know, he was actually my half-brother, the son of Fikriye, my father's little cousin from the country.'

'Your mother having died in childbirth.'

'Yes! You remembered.'

'Your father waited a long time to remarry,' Ikmen observed, 'given that your brother was twenty years your junior.'

'He had little need of marriage,' Ersoy replied. 'He had diversions, if you know what I mean. And, until it became apparent to him that I was not going to be the kind of son that he had always wanted, he had an heir too.'

'So what went wrong?'

Ersoy shrugged. 'The city, in two short words, Çetin. This naughty, vice-infested old whore that we all feast upon. As a lot of youths do, I started seeing boys, learning about boys and their bodies and what their bodies like. Naturally I gravitated towards Avram who, even at thirteen, was obviously a lover of men rather than women. Notes passed from my teachers to my father who first beat me and then presented me with a girl—which I must say that I took with relish. Not that I stopped seeing Avram and others too—the girl simply opened up another avenue for my pleasures. I had money, I could buy female whores if I wanted, which I did. Such an evil place, Istanbul.'

'Places cannot, of themselves be evil,' Ikmen said, grinding his cigarette out slowly in one of the ashtrays. 'Only the actions of men can make them appear so.'

Ersoy laughed. 'Oh, I accept that I am a most wicked boy, but...Anyway, when I failed the medical to gain entry into the armed forces Father felt that he had to act and so he took Fikriye for his wife and when Zeki was finally born he gave thanks to Allah for what amounted to his second chance. I, as you can imagine,' he said, his eyes slightly glazed at the memory of it, 'started to recede into the background.'

'Which, of course, you resented.'

'No. Not immediately. Father left me alone to pursue my own path which suited me until...' He took another cigarette from his packet which he played with rather than lit. 'Father called me into his office one day in order to tell me that he had amended his will. Rather magnanimously, according to him, he said that he had finally decided to let me share what was now essentially Zeki's inheritance. He said, I remember, that he hoped I would not use my share in order to bring shame upon my brother. After all, I loved the little boy just as much as he did, didn't I? I promised Father that I would certainly do my best. Then,' he said, his eyes now twinkling with what Ikmen imagined must have been a most bewitching light when he was a very young man, 'I went up to Zeki's nursery and fucked his little American nurse up against the wall while the child slept. I mention this only because that lady's part in later events is significant.'

'So what of Italy?'

'All in good time,' Ersoy said, holding up one hand in order to silence the policeman. 'Now, although my father really could not bear the sight of me, my new "mother", who was only the same age as myself, found me charming. To be fair, I did all those things that women, particularly ignorant ones, find charming. I kissed her hand, I opened doors for her, laughed at her boring little "adventures" in the great big wicked bazaar.'

'Seduced her?'

He laughed. 'Oh no! Fikriye, poor little pudding, was far too devoted and grateful to my father even to think of such a thing, and besides, she was most awfully religious. She was not, however, stupid. She knew that Father only married her in order to provide the family with a suitable heir. The occasional, I must say most violent beatings he inflicted upon her when her simplicity particularly irritated him, just served to underline this point. But when the issue of a family holiday was raised when little Zeki was five, she and I both agreed that perhaps she and Father should go alone in order to have some time together. She did, annoyingly, love him, you see. I, with the nurse, Jennifer, would gladly look after the child while Fikriye and Father relaxed on his yacht.'

Arto made a frustrated scoffing noise at the back of his throat. 'I cannot believe your father acceded to this!'

'Ah, but adore my brother as he did, Father also really adored money. Part of the trip was to involve meetings with representatives of an Italian company he wished to buy into and the boy would have been very much in the way—and bored. My father never took any significant crew on his voyages, people who could have cared for the child. Had he done so, word of his brutality to Fikriye might have got out. He also prided himself on his seamanship.'

'I can't understand,' Ikmen said, 'given the occasional but thorough brutality of your father, why Fikriye would have wanted to be alone with him?'

Ersoy smiled. 'She suffered from the delusion that she could tame him. I mean, with all his money and her son in his possession she could hardly leave him, could she? She had to try at least to make the best of the thing. And, as I have said before, the poor deluded creature loved him.'

Ikmen sighed. 'You know, I've never had any significant amount of money in my life, but I would not trade what I have for all your money, Mr Ersoy—or for the misery it seems to have caused you all.'

Ersoy didn't react to this; he simply lit his cigarette before continuing his story. 'So Father and Fikriye set off for Italy. I then gave all the servants a holiday and took Jennifer and Zeki over to my apartment in Beyoğlu.'

'Why did you do that?'

'From your point of view, Çetin, this is where my story is going to get interesting. Because this is when the plan that Jennifer and myself had formulated to teach my father a very valuable lesson came into being.'

'Which was?'

'As soon as I was certain that my father was in Italy, I contacted him to tell him that Zeki had been kidnapped and that a ransom was being demanded. I told him I had been forbidden by those who held him to contact the police but that I would deal with the situation as events demanded. The idea was of course for me to "rescue" Zeki in a heroic fashion and therefore secure my father's undying appreciation. He went berserk.'

'But surely,' Ikmen said, 'upon your father's return your brother would have said—'

'Oh, I hadn't thought that far ahead!' Ersoy cried with a chuckle. 'I was twenty-five and having a very good time. The boy was a dear little soul; my father was apoplectic, I was servicing both Jennifer and Avram and receiving rapturous praise for my performances. I was a young man having fun!'

'But?' There had to be a but, Ikmen knew. If there hadn't been a but they wouldn't all be where they were now—gripped by mortal fear in a fashionable apartment with a dead doctor in the bedroom.

'Things started to go wrong,' Ersoy said with a slight frown, 'when Fikriye killed herself. My father, apparently, blamed her for allowing Zeki to stay with me and registered his fury in his traditional fashion, with his fists. Not that that explains in full why my stepmother should take such a course of action. I can only speculate that Father made her feel so guilty that she reasoned that even if the child was found alive she would probably be denied all access to him from then on. Excessive, I know, but given my father's nature, probably correct.'

'She drank cleaning fluid, I understand,' Ikmen said.

Ersoy's eyes widened in what looked like appreciation.

'Why yes, how clever of you to have unearthed that little fact. You have obviously proceeded further along my clue-littered trail than even I had imagined. Inspector Hikmet, who you must know was the original investigating officer, was not,' he chuckled, 'nearly so astute as yourself.'

Ikmen, almost despite himself, made a little bow of recognition in Ersoy's direction.

'But when I discovered what Fikriye had done I must admit that I was sad,' Ersoy continued. 'I had never meant her any ill and that is the truth. However, the next thing I knew was that Father was coming home by plane.' He turned briefly to Arto. 'We are so hasty about the burial of our dead, are we not, Doctor? You must think, as I know Avram did, that Islam is very quick to despatch those who have departed. After all, you keep your dead for days, don't you?'

Arto, unable or unwilling to reply to this, simply turned his head to one side.

'So,' Ikmen said, becoming increasingly impatient with Ersoy's rather long and courtly expositions, 'what happened next?'

'What happened next, Inspector, was that I went home to meet my father with my head full of rather unformed ways in which to tell him that the whole thing had been a rather tasteless joke. But when he arrived I found that I just couldn't do that and so I pretended I was still in negotiation with the kidnappers, watching helplessly as he paced around the house like a maddened bear. He didn't even notice that none of the servants was home, that was how bad he was.'

'Your father, I understand,' Ikmen put in, 'died soon after he—'

'Which was, I assure you, an accident,' Ersoy said, his face now grave and, Ikmen thought, unattractively drawn too. 'In order to get away, just for a little while, from his anxieties, he decided to take his speedboat out on to the Bosporus. My father was an old man when he died, Çetin, almost eighty, and he was not in either the best of health or the most rational state of mind. Somehow he slipped whilst getting the boat ready in the boathouse, hit his head and just slipped beneath the water. I found him myself and, although not exactly devastated by his demise, I was nevertheless sorry that he had gone. After all, he was my father... The police found no signs of foul play, you know,' he added, 'and so I buried him the following day, having first prepared his body for the grave like the dutiful son I never was.'

'I take it,' Ikmen said, 'that your brother did not attend the funeral?'

'Oh, no.' Ersoy sighed a little at the memory and then said, 'It was just myself plus Father's lawyer and his accountant. I had, as you can imagine, a little thinking to do with regard to Zeki.'

Waiting in the car for the others to return from their various sorties was making Suleyman tense. Uncharacteristically he had even taken and smoked a cigarette that Öztürk had offered him, an action which recalled to him in horrible detail his brief romance with both cigarettes and alcohol while he was a conscript in the army.

Quietly, for they knew, in part at least, how very serious this situation could be, the three young men slid back into the car, trying to avoid the stares of various gawpers on the pavement.

'Well?' Suleyman asked, looking anxiously from one face to the next.

'All the shutters are drawn, sir,' Melik said, his one lazy eye looking, or so it seemed, across at a woman sweeping the doorstep of an apartment block opposite the car.

'But I could hear voices,' Öztürk added, ''round the back.'

'Could you make out what they were saying?' Suleyman asked.

'No, it was sort of muffled.'

Suleyman's telephone started to ring and he took it out and put it up to his ear. This was, he hoped, the call he had been expecting. 'Suleyman.'

'I've got Dr Halman for you, sir,' an unknown female voice said.

'Right. Put her on.'

A throaty feminine voice, just touched at the edges by the suggestion of a foreign accent, cleared its cigarette-scarred throat. 'Sergeant Suleyman?'

'Dr Halman. I'm in a bit of a situation here and I need some advice.'

'Go on,' the psychiatrist urged.

'Well,' Suleyman said, 'I think that I may be just about to become involved in a hostage situation.'

'Then call for back-up. Get yourself a professional negotiator. Do not—'

'I don't know that I have time to do that, Doctor.'

'Well, call them out anyway!'

'I think I may have to go in. I've spoken to the suspect and...Inspector Ikmen and Dr Sarkissian are in there with this man.'

'Well, what do you want me to do about it, Sergeant?' Dr Halman said, a little tetchily, or so he thought. 'Do you know anything about this man? His state of mind?'

'No.' He felt foolish now. Without details about a person even psychiatrists couldn't begin to guess at their motives. Just to say that Muhammed Ersoy was, in his experience, a spoilt rich boy and a bully seemed rather thin. But then perhaps what he wanted was more general than that. Perhaps he just needed some sort of ratification for what he understood should be done in such an eventuality. His hand shaking, he reached over towards Öztürk and indicated that he would like another cigarette. 'I think I should be both calm and unthreatening.'

'Whatever his state of mind,' the doctor said firmly, 'you must in no way antagonise this man. Do you know whether he is armed?'

'Yes.'

'And are you going in armed?'

'Yes.'

She sighed. 'I'm not sure that is a good idea. Are you wearing a vest?'

'No.'

'Then that is certainly not a good idea.' He heard what he thought was the sound of her puffing away on one of her trademark long black cigarettes. He then lit the one that Öztürk offered him and coughed.

'He's told me to come in to him alone,' Suleyman said when he had finished spluttering.

'But you have men you can deploy around the area?'

'Yes.'

'Look,' she said, sighing as she spoke, 'if you go in armed you could find yourself involved in a blood bath. He could easily take umbrage and lash out indiscriminately. If he's taken police hostages he's got very little to lose by adding murder to his list of crimes. And since we no longer execute these people what he's looking at is the rest of his life in prison, which, in my opinion, is actually worse.'

'But...'

'I don't know this man or anything about his background but what I do know is that if he's taken hostages then he is desperate. What you need to establish very early on is what he wants and then either give him that or rather the illusion of it until you or your men can get into a position that enables you to take him on.'

'So...'

'You must on no account either antagonise him or be taken hostage yourself. You must move gently, but you must also establish your absolute authority over the situation right away. You have something that he wants; make it clear to him that only you can give that to him.' Then, changing the subject rapidly, she said, 'You say you have spoken to him?'

'Yes.'

'Did he give you any sort of indication that he might be psychotic?'

Suleyman frowned. He'd heard this word many times before, most recently applied by the little blonde doctor herself in relation to the now sadly dead mad communist. 'Psychotic?'

'Has he or does he appear to have lost touch with reality?'

That was difficult to say. Ersoy's grandiose lifestyle had little to do with actual reality. On the telephone he had been calm and even humorous, emotions which, given the circumstances, displayed a certain lack of balance. But as for actually losing touch with reality...

'Did he articulate any sort of fantasy around the offence?' the doctor elaborated. 'Like a religious or political or even sexual justification for it?'

'No,' Suleyman said a little shakily, and then in a firmer tone, repeated, 'No. He just sounded sort of pleased.'

'Like he was having a good time? Having fun?'

'Well, yes, I suppose so.'

The doctor now sighed heavily and coughed into the receiver. 'You know that if you're really unlucky this man of yours could be personality disordered.'

'Pardon?'

'What we used to call a psychopath,' she said, articulating the last word in that strangely lilting foreign way that she had.

'Oh.'

'If he's clever, which he may well be, and he's having a good time, then that is a possibility. That or drugs, which can be equally lethal. I don't suppose you have a name?'

'Well...'

'You don't have to tell me,' she said quickly, 'I understand that until you have confirmed the assailant—'

'I'll do as you recommend,' Suleyman said. 'I'll call for back-up. But then I'm going to have to go in myself.'

'But a negotiator would—'

'Dr Halman,' he said, wiping one tired hand across his brow, 'this man has not only asked for me but he knows me also. He went to the same school as myself and was well known to my older brother.'

'It's not a personal thing between you and him, is it?' she asked, somewhat astutely, he thought.

'No!'

'Well, just be very sure that it isn't before you go in, Sergeant. Personalities are not things that we can afford to have in situations like this. Do I make myself clear?'

She did, although Suleyman was not sure whether or not he could obey this last instruction. Muhammed Ersoy, even putting aside the way he had treated Murad, was the sort of old Ottoman boy who gave those who now tried

to live normal, Turkish lives a bad name. He was, so Suleyman felt, like a bad smell from a previous, corruption-filled
age—something that he strongly felt should be left very
much in the past.

'Do you know whether he's hurt or killed anyone
before?' the doctor's voice broke through his musings like
an elderly, scarred record.

'I think he may have killed a doctor,' he said, wincing
as he heard her sharp intake of breath at his words.

'Then he really has got absolutely nothing to lose by
killing you, Sergeant,' she said firmly. 'I must admit that I'm
not happy about your going in there.'

'I don't have many options open to me, Doctor! And
the Inspector and Dr Sarkissian are—'

'All right! All right!' she said, throwing, or so he imagined, her short plump arms into the air. 'But if you have to
go, wear a vest, will you, for me?'

He smiled. Her concern, although couched in that rough
and almost mannish way of hers, was genuine. 'I will.'

'Ikmen and my old friend Arto Sarkissian have had
some life but you, I recall, are a young man,' she said.
'Don't throw it all away just for a moment of famous Turkish heroism.'

'No.'

'And call for back-up, now. If you've a psychopath in
there, you'll need it. Go straight to Ardiç, don't mess about.'

'No.'

'May God be with you,' she said finally, expressing the
form of the deity in the Christian fashion.

'Allah is merciful,' he said, feeling distinctly hypocritical, then he clicked the 'end' button.

Turning to the three constables who had been listening
in a rather bemused fashion to his conversation, he said,

'I'm going to call for back-up now. You two'—he indicated Öztürk and Melik—'get around the back of the property, but don't do anything unless you hear from me, do you understand?'

'Yes, sir.' They got out of the car and slowly began to make their way towards the apartment block.

'Once I've called in I'm going to go and knock on the front door. I can't, I daren't leave it any longer.' Then, looking at the remaining young constable at his side, Suleyman said, 'You stay here, Kemal, and liaise with the others when they arrive. Ardıç could well be with them so don't start spitting or blowing your nose into the street.'

'No, sir.'

Then with a sigh he picked up the telephone again and began to dial. His hands were shaking very violently now as if he were coming down with a fever.

'Aren't you going to wait for a vest, sir?' Kemal asked as he watched Suleyman tap the side of the telephone impatiently with his fingers.

'No, I'm not,' he said, taking his pistol out of the holster underneath his arm and placing it into his pocket. 'There isn't time for that.'

# 16

'I WAITED NEARLY a week before I took any action with regard to Zeki,' Ersoy said. 'The child appeared quite happy and I needed time to think.'

'What of the nurse, Jennifer?'

Ersoy laughed. 'I have a film to thank for her desertion, Çetin. So terrified was she of your officers as lovingly portrayed in *Midnight Express* that she just got up one morning and left the country. Glad, it would seem, to have escaped your interrogations with her life. Quite what she went on to do afterwards, I cannot say. However, during the course of that week Jennifer and I, to a certain extent, formulated a plan that came to dominate the rest of my life. Initially,' he said, shifting just slightly in his chair, 'I made up my mind to kill the boy. I suppose you now know I reported him as lost in Italy soon afterwards.'

'That was somewhat of a gamble, wasn't it?' Ikmen said. 'Given that the cook on your father's yacht you knew cannot have seen the child.'

Ersoy smiled. 'Even in democracies the word of a peasant doesn't hold anything like as much weight as that of a gentleman. And after the initial stages of Inspector Hikmet's investigation I did give Latife a small financial consideration to make certain changes to her story; I was also backed up by a most respectable foreign national.'

'Jennifer?'

'Yes. Which makes me think that it was a good thing that she left when she did. I don't know how she would have reacted had she had to endure interrogation at the hands of somebody besides Hikmet. He terrified her enough and he was, as I expect you recall, a most gentle man.'

'So you decided to kill Zeki. What changed your mind?'

With a sigh, Ersoy stubbed out his cigarette and then leaned back in his chair. 'It was Avram, of course,' he said wearily, 'or rather the reasons Avram presented me with.' Brightening suddenly he added, 'It is Avram you have to thank for the connection with the Kafes actually. It was he who pointed out to me the benefits our old rulers had obtained from the "putting away" of those they found threatening or inconvenient. It was also Avram who, on a more personal level, introduced me to the challenge inherent in this enterprise.' He smiled. 'Challenge was not a thing with which I had achieved intimacy before, you understand.'

'Avram was trying to curb your excesses just as he was due to take his examinations,' Arto put in sourly, 'I remember his state of mind well at that time—he was in torment, although not for the reasons he gave me then.'

'No.' Ersoy's reply was a little distracted, Ikmen thought. 'No, as I recall he fed you a lot of stuff about his doubts regarding whether or not he, as an Armenian, would even attain gainful employment.'

'Yes, he did.'

'Stuff that only partially reflected what was in his

mind. Not, of course, that your "Armenian experience", for want of a better term, didn't suit my purposes for a time, Doctor,' he said, smiling across at the now livid face of Arto Sarkissian.

'I can only imagine,' Ikmen said, 'that you are alluding to the non-existent Mr Zekiyan.'

'Yes.' Ersoy laughed, softly. 'The aptly named Mr Zekiyan, who, of course, was myself.' Then, leaning forward a little in his chair, he viewed both men gravely, 'Avram had this theory, you know, that Armenians are invisible. Live your life for a day in my skin, he used to say, and you will see what I mean. And so I did. Once I had taken the decision to rent a place in which to incarcerate my brother, a Kafes of my own, I went about my business as Mr Zekiyan, a very fetching crucifix ring upon my finger, and nobody so much as wanted to know whether I was even married. At a stroke and even in the face of pictures of myself that occasionally adorned the newspapers at that time, I had quite crushed natural Turkish curiosity and proved Avram right into the bargain.'

'I spoke to your landlord who described you as a model tenant,' Ikmen said, and then added with just a ghost of a smirk on his face, 'He wasn't even angry when I told him you had "altered" the top floor of his house.'

'Yes, it's amazing how far this paying rent routine can get one with the lower orders, isn't it? Mr Zekiyan always paid his rent on time, as you know, and when he went to buy cigarettes or drink from the grocer's shop opposite he was always most courteous, while never forgetting to let the peasants just glimpse his very valuable and very Armenian ring.' He paused briefly to take a breath and then continued, 'Of course all the business with the police had finished by that time. The boy had, or so it seemed, disappeared in Italy and despite the Greko family's pleas to the contrary there continued to be doubts about their part in the affair.'

'Did no officers ever come to your apartment?'

'Oh, they came. I invited them!' Here he laughed, loudly, some coarseness now just at the edge of his voice. 'Zeki and Avram hid in the bedroom when they came—I made it all one big game. That child had such fun!'

'Fifteen years later he's not having such a good time!' Arto Sarkissian spat.

Ikmen, rather alarmed now at his friend's growing anger, cast the doctor a warning glare. Ersoy, despite his charm, was, Ikmen knew, one of the most dangerous people he had ever had the misfortune to share a room with. 'But officially,' he said smoothly, 'the opinion was that your brother had drowned somewhere between here and Italy, is that right?'

'Fikriye's suicide had to have a cause and, to the Italian police at least, that seemed like reason enough. And besides, even when wealthy, we are only Turks, aren't we? Why should those who brought us Leonardo da Vinci, not to mention institutionalised crime, spare much thought for a group of dirty little non-Catholics? At least that was what I, with my limited but acute observation of Italian society, thought. And I was correct.'

'And the Turkish police, what of them?'

'As far as they were aware Zeki was a problem for the Italians. After all, that's what I had told them and I am, as you know, a man of some substance.'

'Just out of interest,' Ikmen said, leaning forward to take hold of another cigarette, 'did you bribe anyone?'

'Not as I recall, no.' Ersoy laughed. 'Quite amazing, no? But then confusion can do such a lot when used correctly, don't you think? That and the astute manipulation of the indigenous prejudices of disparate groups.'

'Ask him how he kept the child like that for fifteen years,' Arto said, his voice still showing signs of that rising anger Ikmen hoped that he'd halted earlier. 'It'll make you sick to your belly!'

Ersoy's only reaction to this was to laugh again.

'Well, sir,' Ikmen said, turning away from his friend towards Ersoy, 'How—'

'At first I told him that we were in great danger. When you are as wealthy as my family, you grow up understanding the realities of such things as assassination and kidnap. The poor little child was mortified when I told him that his parents had died but he did, nevertheless, understand why he and myself had now to be so quiet and careful. I spent, in those early days, a lot of time with him, and he knew that when I went out in order to obtain food and suchlike he was to be very quiet and stay in his room. When the workmen were building his new home I did get Avram to give him a little something. I don't know what it was.'

'The home, which having built, you eventually locked.'

'Yes. And as you now know as he grew older dear Avram augmented Zeki's generally passive nature with opiates. It was either that,' he said with a shrug, 'or have me kill the child. Challenge or no challenge, when things became more difficult I got bored. Going in to him every day, making sure that I was wearing the right jewellery and accessories that would identify myself as Mr Zekiyan...As you know, I adore every inch of this gaudy whore Istanbul, but sometimes not actually being able to travel was irksome. Although latterly when my brother was finally and completely dependent upon Avram's drugs I could get away for short times. As long as Zeki had his drugs he cared little, in the end, whether it was Avram or myself who gave them to him.' Then turning his head sharply to one side he said, 'Did you hear that?'

'What?'

'A noise outside.'

'No.' But he had and it had sounded like someone moving a little heavy-footed around the yard. It could be just another resident of the block but Suleyman was on his way, and even though Ersoy had asked him to come alone he would, surely, arrive with some sort of back-up. Unlike he, Ikmen himself, had done, but then that was another matter.

'Well, anyway,' Ersoy continued, his face slightly averted towards the shuttered window, 'that was how it was done.'

'So why did you eventually kill the boy then, Mr Ersoy? I assume that it was yourself?'

'Oh, yes,' he said quite matter of factly. 'Although his death was less connected with Zeki himself than with me and what was happening to me. You know, I found approaching the age of forty most awfully upsetting. For some time I had been noticing new and ever deeper networks of troughs crossing my face. Add to that a certain sagging in the skin around my arms and waist...You must, surely, have noticed similar things about yourself at my age?'

'No,' Ikmen answered shortly, 'can't say that I did. As far as I am aware I have always been the same ugly man you see before you today. And besides, Mr Ersoy, for a man in my position to give so much thought to such a trivial matter is, I believe, well nigh impossible.'

'You took a very long time to tell me that you consider me trite, Çetin.'

'But you got the message anyway.'

Ersoy smiled. 'Oh, yes.'

'But what of Zeki?'

'Drug addicts are supposed to be raddled, ugly things, don't you think?' he said, now staring glassily in front of him. 'But not my brother, for some reason. I injected him several times myself and made quite a mess, but Avram stopped that spiteful little game. Avram said his lack of ugliness—for want of a better term—was because Zeki always had drugs when he needed them, that he didn't have to go out like most do, into the cold streets, whoring for his fix...'

'Of pethidine,' Arto said, enunciating every syllable of the word with great care.

'Or heroin or morphine or any other opium derivatives that he happened to be using at the time. Medical men, as you know, Doctor, can and do choose the drugs that they prescribe and it was good for Zeki to have a change once in a while. Pethidine just happened to be the last incarnation of that process.'

'Which still doesn't explain why you finally killed your brother,' Ikmen said.

'Oh, have I omitted to tell you that?' Ersoy's face was first wreathed in its habitual smile, then fell quite dramatically downwards. 'Envy, to be brutally honest. Here he was—twenty, beautiful, clinging like the wooden embrace of the garrotte around my unwilling, forty-year-old neck. It wasn't fair and so, actually on my fortieth birthday, I went alone to see my brother and sent his innocent soul finally to paradise by way of a cord which, though not silken, could in all other ways be described as a bowstring.'

Having thought and read about this Kafes phenomenon, Ikmen knew that the bowstring had been the traditional method of execution reserved for those confined, but no longer wanted, within the walls of the Kafes. Drugged as he most certainly had been at the time, Ikmen nevertheless wondered what terrors and even pain the young boy might have experienced at the hands of this man who, seemingly, did not possess even one of the finer feelings of humanity.

'To overdose him would, I admit, have been simpler,' Ersoy continued. 'But this would have necessitated obtaining more drugs from Avram, which I did not want to do. I didn't want Avram to know what I'd done until I'd done it. As it was, he really went crazy when I told him later that day.'

'So you killed Zeki in order to free yourself from him.'

'In part.' Ersoy smiled again now, the cloud that was his brother's murder seemingly lifting from his shoulders. 'With all these hideous lines and bags crawling their way like a cancer over my body I had and have no desire to melt gracelessly into old age. I only killed the boy in advance of my own death. Remember it was I who gave you your ideas about Kafes in the first place, which I then underscored with those tasteless little figures that always so pleased my brother.'

'So it was you.'

'Oh, yes. Me, just wanting you to come along and catch me, Çetin.'

'Some of your references were a little too oblique.'

Ersoy laughed shrilly now, like a girl. It was unnerving just how many different types of laugh this man possessed. 'Oh, Çetin,' he said, fingering the barrel of his gun with almost loving intent, 'how very slow you are in comparison to myself. Ah, Allah, but what a sadness it will be when my fine mind has gone from the world!'

'I guess,' Ikmen said, at last managing to light the cigarette between his fingers, 'that you do, however, wish to die by the hand of another.'

'In the absence of an honourable suicide, which this could in no way be, to die in a hail of police bullets does have a certain mythical quality that appeals to me, yes.'

'I, however,' Ikmen said, smiling too now, as was his way when he wanted to be really hurtful or controversial, 'would far prefer to see you go to prison, Mr Ersoy. I—'

He was interrupted by the sharp, staccato sound of Dr Avedykian's doorbell.

'Ah, death himself!' Ersoy said with a smile. Moving over to where Arto Sarkissian sat, he said to Ikmen, 'Would you let your colleague in for me please?' He then jammed his gun hard up against the doctor's head and, grabbing him roughly by the throat added, 'And don't do anything stupid, Çetin. As you now know, I will not hesitate to kill if I have to.'

'Cohen!' she called out across the width of the squad room, the coarseness of her voice lending credence to the rumours that Sergeant Farsakoğlu was in a particularly bad mood today.

Cohen lifted his head from his paperwork and replied, 'Sergeant?'

'Come over here, will you, I need to speak to you.'

Cohen rose quickly from his desk and tripped lightly around various people and obstacles until he was next to her. 'Yes?'

'Have you heard anything about Inspector Ikmen and Dr Sarkissian being in some sort of difficulty?'

'No. I only know that the inspector's brother wanted to get hold of him urgently and that not even Meh— Sergeant Suleyman could say where he was.'

'I've just heard,' she said 'that the Commissioner is putting a squad together to go out and deal with whatever has happened.'

Cohen shrugged. 'Well, I don't—'

'You said that Suleyman couldn't say where he was or did he perhaps just not want to say?'

'I don't know. I suppose he...' Then, putting various thoughts both old and new together in his mind, he said, 'Why do you ask, Sergeant? Do you need to speak to Sergeant Suleyman?'

'No, no,' she said, raking her fingers through her hair in what seemed to Cohen a distracted fashion, 'I don't need the sergeant just now. It's just that...'

'What?'

She lowered her head to ensure that only he could hear. 'If the inspector were in trouble then surely it would be Mehmet, Sergeant Suleyman, who would initially go to him, wouldn't it?'

Cohen shrugged again. 'It might be,' he said and then added somewhat evilly, 'you're a bit worried about him, aren't you?'

'What? The inspector? Well...'

'No! Meh—Sergeant Suleyman! I mean he's such a nice man—I like him myself.'

'Oh, do you?' she said with the sort of expression on her face that could be used to sour milk. 'Well if that is the case I suggest that you—'

Suddenly the room went eerily quiet as all of those present realised that Ardiç had entered.

'All right,' he said as he waved a very obviously lit cigar into various people's faces, 'I want you all to listen very carefully to what I have to say.'

❀ ❀ ❀

As soon as Suleyman entered, Muhammed Ersoy's face broke into a smile, which, given that he was holding a gun to the doctor's head at the time, was creepily incongruous.

'Avram was right about you,' he said as the younger man came to a halt in front of him, 'you have grown both taller and slimmer than your brother.'

'Yes,' Suleyman said, stopping himself snapping back with some smart, acidic remark, trying hard to remember what Dr Halman had told him. 'Well, I'm here now, Mr Ersoy. Perhaps you could tell me what you want and then I can see what I can arrange.'

'Want? What do you mean?'

'In return for releasing the inspector and the doctor. What do you want. What are—'

Ikmen very gently tapped him on the elbow, bringing Suleyman's speech to a sudden halt. 'I think you'll find,' he said, 'that Mr Ersoy has no demands as such, Suleyman.'

'But...'

'Oh, Çetin is quite right,' Ersoy said, still retaining both his smile and his hold upon Arto Sarkissian's throat.

'So...'

'So, young Suleyman, if I may call you that?'

Suleyman bowed in reply. 'You may.'

'So, young Suleyman, it is now up to you to decide what happens next.'

Suleyman gave Ersoy and then Ikmen a quizzical look.

'What I mean,' Ersoy continued smoothly, 'is that I know what my aims are in this little venture. But do you know what yours are?'

'Eh?'

Ersoy laughed, the movement of his body against the doctor's causing the medic's large frame to vibrate incongruously under his grasp. 'I am correct, young Suleyman,' he said, 'in assuming that you are vainglorious enough to have come here armed?'

Instinctively, one of Ikmen's hands shot forward to restrain his colleague. 'Don't!'

Suleyman looked from Ikmen to Ersoy and then back to Ikmen again. 'I...'

'In order for you to do what I want you to, I think that you should take your weapon out now, young Suleyman,' Ersoy said, enjoying the fact that his use of the phrase 'young Suleyman' was obviously beginning to grate on the sergeant's nerves.

'I wouldn't do that if I were you,' Ikmen muttered at his sergeant's elbow.

'Çetin?' Ikmen looked up into a pair of eyes that bore into his with almost visible venom. Clicking the safety catch of his weapon off, Ersoy then added, 'Don't.'

With a sigh, Ikmen moved slightly backwards and then just shrugged helplessly at Suleyman. 'You'd better do as he says.' Slowly, lest his movements alarm his opponent, Suleyman reached into his pocket and withdrew the pistol, handle first, until he was holding it horizontally out in front of his body. 'There,' he said. 'Do you want me to place it down now?'

'No.'

Suleyman looked up into Muhammed Ersoy's mocking eyes, suddenly finding himself completely incapable of speech.

'I want you to turn the gun around and then point it at me please, my dear sweet little soul,' Ersoy said, pouting the words as if propositioning the officer as he spoke.

'But...' Looking first at Ikmen and then at the doctor, Suleyman cast around trying to find an explanation for this somewhere; finding none he reiterated, 'But...'

'My demands, if you like,' Ersoy said, jamming his gun

still harder into the side of Arto's head, 'are that we all play a game together.'

Suleyman slowly turned his gun around to face Muhammed Ersoy and then said, 'What do you mean, a game?'

'It is,' Ersoy said with a twinkle, 'a form of Russian roulette, except that all of the chambers of both of our weapons are full—well, my own is not quite, on account of Avram, but—Anyway, all of the chambers are as good as full and it is either the doctor here who is going to die, because I will shoot him, or it will be I who dies, because you can, if you wish, kill me.'

Suddenly Suleyman lost his composure. It came as almost as powerful a shock to him as it did to everyone else in the room. 'You're insane!'

Ersoy's face darkened for just a moment and then, inevitably, he smiled once more. 'The choice is yours, young Suleyman. You can kill me now and save the doctor or you can wait for me to blow his head off and then kill me. The only uncertain element in this equation is, as far as I can see, the life or death of the doctor. Do you understand?'

'Yes, but...'

'He's bluffing, Mehmet,' Ikmen said, now clutching at his rapidly pounding chest. 'He's got this crazy notion about wanting to die. He—'

'Can you be absolutely certain about that, Çetin?' Ersoy said, grinding the muzzle of his weapon ever further into Arto's temple. 'After all, I have absolutely nothing to lose if I kill the doctor.'

'But if you do that, how do you know that Suleyman and I won't just take you on without killing you? You must know that if a shot is heard coming from this apartment, our colleagues will come piling in here like a bunch of stormtroopers?'

'Who will,' Ersoy said lightly, 'in all probability kill me when they see what I have done.'

'Not if I can help it!' Ikmen said, barely controlling his anger. 'Whatever happens today, you are going to finish it alive and on your way to prison!'

'Then it would seem, if that is what you want, that you will have to trade the doctor's life for that particular pleasure.'

'No!' Instinctively, Suleyman took the safety catch off and pointed his weapon at what he could see of Ersoy's chest.

'Don't!' Ikmen said, only just restraining himself from grabbing at the younger man's hand. 'Don't get involved in his game, Suleyman! Don't play!'

Ersoy's eyes, which had until then been quite hard, suddenly softened as he looked across into Suleyman's face. 'Oh, come along now, Mehmet,' he said, 'we are both gentlemen, aren't we? And as gentlemen we keep our word, do we not?' Suddenly becoming steely once again he added, 'And so if I tell you that I'm going to kill the doctor I mean what I say. Don't listen to this peasant, believe the word of a gentleman and do what you and I both know you really want to do. I was, after all, quite unpleasant to your poor brother Murad for—'

'Don't for the love of life let him get inside your head!' Ikmen now almost screamed into Suleyman's ear. 'He's trying to mess with your mind!'

'You and I are, after all,' Ersoy continued smoothly, 'of a type. We both dress well, we are both well born, we are both, essentially, Ottoman gentlemen, are we not?'

Suleyman hesitated. his face dissolving into a morass of confusion, he averted his eyes briefly towards Ikmen. 'He's going to do it,' he said.

'No, he isn't!' Ikmen cried. 'If we talk to him, he—'

'You don't understand!' Suleyman replied and then, looking Ersoy deep in the eyes, he said, 'Please move away from Dr Sarkissian, Mr Ersoy. I will do as you wish, but—'

'Oh, please do not even attempt to insult my intelligence, dear boy!' Moving just fractionally back from the doctor's head, Ersoy took very careful aim and said, 'I will give you to a count of three. One.'

'If I shoot you, Ersoy, I will not aim to kill you.'

Ersoy laughed. 'Both you and I know that there can be no guarantees of that sort, especially when one is as nervous as you so obviously are.' Turning his face towards his proposed victim once more, he said, 'Two.'

Arto Sarkissian raised the fingers of one hand up to his head and crossed himself.

'Mr Ersoy!' Ikmen began.

'Time is up,' Ersoy said, screwing up one eye in order to see down the sight of his pistol. 'Three.'

❀ ❀ ❀

Sergeant Farsakoğlu handed Cohen back his box of matches and then breathed deeply on the smoke from her cigarette. Watching her shrewdly out of the corner of one eye, Cohen sighed a little before uttering what he knew had to be a most out-of-order, if not downright insulting question. But although surrounded by dozens of their fellow officers, they were quite alone crouched down behind the wing of the car, awaiting, as was everybody else, developments.

'You really care for Mehmet, don't you?' he said.

She gave him the kind of look that made him instinctively pull his cap hard down over his eyes. 'What do you mean?'

'Well...'

'If you're suggesting that anything of an improper nature has occurred, then—'

'No...' But he sounded just unsure enough to cause her to rise in anger.

'Well, it hasn't, Cohen!' Clearing her throat, she added a little more softly, 'Sergeant Suleyman and I enjoy only a professional association. I admire him but only in the way that lots of other people do, both women and men. And any rumours or talk you might have heard or even spread yourself is—'

'I don't spread rumours!' he said, genuinely hurt that she should think such a thing. 'Mehmet is my friend.'

'Then be a friend and keep all of your prurient speculations to yourself!'

'Well, I was only—'

'Shut up!' hissed Ardiç, who was positioned just behind the pair over by the scrub in the yard opposite.

Cohen lowered his head and then, pushing his cap up with the barrel of his pistol, wiped away some of the rain-soaked sweat that was gathering on his brow.

'I only mention this,' he said, whispering now into her ear, 'because—'

'Ssh!' she said, her eyes still riveted to the explosive face of Ardiç behind. 'Shut up!'

'But...'

The sound of the shot, when it came, was muffled because they were some distance from the apartment. But that it was a gunshot was indisputable; this group of people knew only too well what such things sound like.

With a sharp gasp, Sergeant Farsakoğlu threw one

hand across her mouth, her eyes staring in terror. And as all hell broke loose around them, Cohen pressed one small but consoling hand down upon her shoulder.

For a moment, which, in retrospect as indeed it did at the time, seemed like a small eternity, Suleyman just stood with the gun still outstretched before him, the barrel smoking gently in the chill silent air. Somewhere, someone started to weep with heart-stopping bitterness; for a moment he imagined that a woman had strayed unbidden into the room.

It was, finally, only the screaming that brought him to his senses—a sound that was both agonised and furious, like that of some hellish being, half human and half animal, squealing through a throat that was neither wholly with nor without a recognisable mortal soul.

'May I go blind!' Arto shrieked as he struggled to remove the tape from his shaking ankles. 'May God take my sight from my eyes!'

'Get an ambulance, now!' Ikmen yelled as the window behind his head, plus its shutter, exploded down on to the floor. 'You!' he said, indicating the shocked and gun-toting figure of the emerging Öztürk. 'Get out front and tell them that we have no men down. Do you understand, no men down!'

'Yes, sir.'

'And get an ambulance, right now!'

With just a brief glance at the spreading pool of blood on the floor, Öztürk sprang across the room towards the front door of the apartment.

Sinking to his knees beside the prone figure of Muhammed Ersoy, Ikmen took the man's wrist between his fingers, feeling for a pulse. As soon as he had located one, albeit faint, he looked across at Arto and yelled, 'Get over here and do some doctoring, Arto!'

'I...I'

'Now, man!'

As the doctor moved heavily across the floor, Suleyman placed his gun back into its holster and said, 'Sir, I...'

'Not now, Suleyman!' Ikmen said with a wave of one blood-stained hand. 'We've got to try and keep this bastard alive.'

'His shoulder is completely shattered,' the doctor muttered as he, with shaking hands, pressed down hard upon Ersoy's damaged carotid artery.

'Can I speak to Mehmet, please?' Ersoy's voice, thickened by trauma, still retained its smooth and slightly mocking quality.

Ikmen looked down into those narrowed but still amazingly bright eyes and then he said, 'Suleyman! Over here!'

As various heavily shod feet plunged into the room, their presence headed by the furious sound of Ardiç's voice, Suleyman moved quickly across to Ikmen's side, his feet slipping in the large amounts of blood that he had just shed. Then bending low across Ersoy's prone form he said, 'Mr Ersoy?'

'What a very bad shot you are, Mehmet,' Ersoy growled, gasping now in order to find the breath that he needed to speak.

'I told you that I would only wound you if I could.'

'You have dishonoured me!' And then, raising his head just slightly from the ground, Ersoy spat into Suleyman's face.

Arto Sarkissian pushed Suleyman roughly out of the way. 'I don't want him talking any more!' he said. 'Get away!'

Several officers that Suleyman knew, but at that moment could not even begin to name, pushed past him, making, at Ikmen's request, towards a room on the right of the apartment. 'There's another body in there,' he said, 'a Dr Avram Avedykian.'

'Don't touch anything in there!' the doctor added. 'We'll need forensic to secure the scene!'

'Right.'

Ikmen, his eyes now fixed once again on Ersoy's increasingly greying face, said to his friend, 'Will he live?'

'I don't know.'

'Are you all right, Arto?'

'Having been held hostage all night and then almost killed I would say no at this moment. But I will do.' There was an edge to the doctor's voice which, Ikmen felt, was directed solely at him.

'I don't believe that he would have killed you, you know, Arto. If I had—'

'What you thought, Çetin, was immaterial!' Arto said curtly. 'That gun at my head was, however, very real, and I will be grateful to Suleyman for the rest of my life for what he did here today.'

'Arto...'

'Look, I don't blame you for—'

'If,' Ersoy, his eyes now open and wide once again, rasped, 'three hadn't worked, I would have gone to five or...' Taking one final gasp of air, he lurched backwards. He did not appear to breathe again.

Without even hesitating, Arto Sarkissian launched his mouth down upon that of Ersoy's and breathed his air into his patient's lungs.

Realising that there was nothing he could do here now, Ikmen stood up and made his way across to Suleyman who was standing quite still and silent in the midst of the growing madness around him.

'You did a good job, Suleyman,' he said as he drew level with the younger man.

'How can you say that?' the other snapped.

Controlling his own rising anguish in the face of yet another outburst from a friend and colleague, Ikmen continued, 'You saved the doctor's life.'

'I thought *you*'—Suleyman said the last word with some venom— 'thought that Ersoy was bluffing.'

Ikmen sighed. In all probability Ersoy was going to die anyway and so what did it matter? 'He just said that he wasn't,' he lied. 'I was wrong. I got messed up in a psychology that I didn't understand and I...I made an error.'

'And I just killed a man, Ikmen,' Suleyman said, rudely using his superior's last name in a way his ancestors must have done to very powerful effect. And then, with one last withering glare at the inspector, he made his way out into the hall.

'But you...' Ikmen began but stopped as he realised that talking to Suleyman now was going to be impossible. OK, it had been Suleyman's decision to shoot Ersoy—he, Ikmen, had tried, for better or worse, to stop him. But none of that detracted from the fact that his sergeant was in a state of shock and...

'There was an urgent call for you, Inspector,' said Cohen, who had, as was his wont, simply materialised at Ikmen's elbow.

'What could possibly be more urgent than this?' Ikmen replied, looking around the room and then down at his own bloodstained body. 'What was it, Cohen? When was this call?'

'It was your brother, sir,' Cohen answered. 'Just before we left the station.'

'Halil?' Ikmen rolled his eyes dramatically just as two

members of an ambulance crew arrived and pushed roughly past him. 'What did he want?'

'I think that perhaps you should ask him yourself.' Cohen proffered a mobile telephone to Ikmen who took the instrument with a grunt.

# 17

HALIL IKMEN WAS standing outside the main entrance to the hospital staring into space when his brother arrived. He was, strangely, smoking a cigarette, which was something that Çetin hadn't seen him do since Halil had been in the army. But then, given the circumstances, perhaps it wasn't so odd.

His brother was also, Çetin noticed, completely oblivious to what the rain, which was now pouring heavily across the whole city again, was doing to his beautifully coiffed hair and expensive Italian coat. As Çetin approached him, Halil just nodded his head slightly at his brother and then looked back out at the nothing he had been observing earlier.

'When did it happen?' Çetin asked, gasping for breath as he made his way heavily up the short set of steps on which his brother was standing.

'Where were you?' Halil said, his voice cold and emotionless.

'I was...I was...' Çetin stopped. It seemed so difficult and somehow so trite to try and explain what had just occurred, and besides, tears were starting to form in

388

his eyes now. All that mayhem he had just left suddenly seemed totally alien and unimportant to him. 'When did it happen, Halil? And why did—'

'Father had a heart attack late last night. Fatma called me. She tried to call you too, Çetin, as we all did.'

'Yes, I know—now. I was—'

'You were working, yes.' Looking at his brother with eyes that were drenched in misery but also accusation Halil added, 'We know all about your work, your wife and myself.'

'Yes, but...'

'Well, Fatma got him to hospital,' Halil continued smoothly, stubbing out his cigarette with a scowl. 'I went to be with him and then at around about twelve this morning he had a stroke. A Dr Keskin, a very nice man, pronounced him dead twenty minutes later.'

'But...' Çetin could feel, inasmuch as the numbness that had taken hold of him ever since he had spoken to his brother on the telephone half an hour earlier allowed, that he was beginning to lose his hold on both his emotions and what was left of his cognitive faculties.

'There was just a moment when, had I wanted it, I could have requested that he be placed on life support until you arrived. But I took the decision not to do that, Çetin.'

'Oh...Yes.' Çetin sat down on one of the steps just below his brother's feet and put his head in his hands. 'Timür would have hated that.'

'Then you think that I did...'

'You did right, yes.' Looking up into his brother's now barely controlled face, Çetin said, 'You're a good son.'

'Thank you,' Halil Ikmen said and with one great gasp he dissolved into tears.

Rising rapidly from his step, Çetin Ikmen turned towards his brother and then, tentatively at first as he was so unused

to being like this with Halil, he put his arms around his sibling's shoulders and felt Halil's head fall forward to sob wetly
on to the back of his jacket.

'Oh, Allah! Oh, Allah!' Halil cried. 'We are alone!
Whatever shall we do?'

'I know. I know,' Çetin said, his own eyes now streaming with a misery that he could not even think about much
less articulate.

'It's just like Mother's death all over again—the pain!'
Halil wailed, his face now upturned and facing into the sharp,
rain-loaded wind that was blowing up from the Bosporus.

'Yes. I know.'

'And, you know, he was still going on and on and on
about that confounded Greek when he arrived at the hospital!' Halil said, moving slightly away now so that he was facing
his brother. 'About the man burning him down. The doctor
said that the burning analogy must have had to do with the
pain that he was experiencing, pain he'd had for some time,
in his chest and...that none of us had noticed...'

'That I had not noticed,' Çetin said, his eyes now turned
down and away from his brother's face. 'Because I avoided him
whenever I could. Because I could no longer deal with how he
was and the contrast between that and how he had been.'

'But the Greek!' Halil cried once again, his nose now running
with both cold and misery. 'The Greek always and forever.'

'You do know where all that came from, don't you?'
Çetin said, taking out a cigarette in lieu of weeping uncontrollably. 'That whole story?'

'No.' Halil suddenly seemed to wilt beneath a rather
quieter misery. 'No, he never told me anything much in
latter years. You and he were always closer.'

'The Greek was a Greek'—here Çetin smiled a little
at his clumsy use of language: Timür would have chastised

him for that—'who ran a brothel in Sivas. When Father was doing his military service he and his friends went there.'

Halil, somewhat embarrassed as Çetin knew he would be, cleared his throat.

'The story is that one of the girls fell in love with Timür. All she could think about was him and she became difficult. The Greek was quite naturally upset about this threat to his profit margin and so one day he threw Timür out, swearing that he'd kill him if he ever saw him again.'

'And it was that, that one little incident which so troubled him all these years later?' Halil shook his head in disbelief. 'I never understood what that was about until now. Why didn't he ever tell me?'

Çetin shrugged. 'Perhaps he didn't want to embarrass you.'

'But...' Halil sighed. What was the use of talking about it now? It, he, was over now and that was that. Now it was just himself and Çetin and things to do—many things. 'You'll have to get Sınan and Orhan back from Ankara,' he said. 'We'll have to inform the family. Everybody must come.'

'It's very quick, the way we deal with our dead, isn't it?' Çetin said, recalling an earlier, more malignant conversation.

Halil shrugged. 'It's the way,' he said. 'It must be done.'

'Seems wrong though, doesn't it, considering his beliefs—or rather the lack of them.'

The brothers shared a smile for just a moment and then Halil said, 'But he was born of the faith, Çetin...'

'When the Sultans were still Lords of the Golden Horn.'

'Yes. It's odd to think that he came from that time, isn't it?'

'It's frightening,' Çetin said, his eyes squeezing once more against the tears within them. 'Time is so...'

'I must go and prepare our father for his grave, Çetin,' Halil said, briefly squeezing his brother's arm.

Çetin looked down and nodded his head slightly. 'You are the first born, it is your right.'

'Will you contact the family and start to make arrangements?'

'Yes. Çiçek is in London; I don't know when she's due back. I...You know, I think that she had a feeling about this last night. She phoned me, very anxious and...'

'That girl is completely your own, isn't she?' his brother replied and then, smiling again into Çetin's face, he added, 'and Mother's of course.'

Çetin just shrugged by way of reply; it was such an obvious observation. 'You know, I thought I heard Mother laugh last night when I was alone. Do you think that she might have known, been happy that the old man's sufferings were over?'

'I don't know, Çetin,' Halil replied, placing one rain-soaked hand affectionately against the side of his brother's face. 'I don't know anything about anything I cannot experience myself.'

'We have a lot to do, don't we?' Çetin said, changing the subject to one he felt his brother could more readily relate to.

'So let us make a start then,' Halil said, offering his outstretched hand to his brother.

Then as the wind picked up yet again, the two brothers made their way hand in hand, for the first time since they were schoolboys, back into the hospital building.

Arto Sarkissian didn't rightly know why he was sitting outside the operating theatre except that to go anywhere else at this moment somehow seemed wrong. Even with him, a fellow doctor, the surgeon who had been charged with operating upon Ersoy had been very evasive. The patient had suffered massive loss of blood and his wounds, though not of themselves usually fatal if attended to quickly, could still carry his life away. As Arto looked up at the two young policemen who slouched beside the entrance to the theatre he could not help but be struck by the farcical nature of such a precaution. Ersoy was in no position even to breathe for himself at the moment, much less run. But then that was not really what the two policemen were about, not really. They were there because rules dictated that they had to be; unlike himself, they were probably quite happy. Outside the rain still continued to pour, bringing with it a wind that some said originated in Russia—cold and damp, whistling a hopeless lament.

Arto looked down at his watch and realised that he had been in this place for over an hour. Not that he'd thought about the man lying on the table beyond the doors for all of that time. Briefly it had occurred to him that there were still questions to ask him, like how he had managed to strip and clean that house of his so thoroughly of all forensic evidence and, further, if he had as he said wanted to be caught, then why had he done that? But what was really obsessing his mind now was Çetin Ikmen's father. Although he, as yet, knew no details about it, it would seem that old Timür Ikmen had died at some point after his own dreadful experiences had begun. It was the sort of news that made him feel guilty now that he had snapped at Ikmen so fiercely earlier on. But he had been angry that his friend, albeit with the best of intentions, had in a way gambled with his life in the face of Ersoy's unintelligible behaviour. That, from what Ersoy had said just before he fell out of consciousness, Ikmen's assessment of the situation seemed to have been correct did not really assuage his sense of having been used and let down.

But he was painfully sorry about Timür Ikmen anyway. His own father had died just a year after Timür's wife, Çetin and Halil's mother. And although always keeping a respectful distance from the grieving widow Sarkissian, Timür Ikmen had always ensured that the sons of his old friend Vahan, Arto's father, had free access to both his amusingly chaotic home and his own two boys with whom the Sarkissian children were good friends. It was not going to be easy telling his mother this unwelcome piece of news. Those to whom Mimi Sarkissian could talk about things that only the old could remember were getting few and far between now. Not, of course, that she had been able to converse with Timür Ikmen for the last few years. It still struck Arto as strange and wrong that a man with such a sharp and intelligent mind as his friends' father should succumb so cruelly and utterly to the ravages of dementia. Deep down inside he hoped that his brother Krikor might get over to Mimi's apartment before him and tell their mother the news. And because he assumed that the funeral would be both quick and Islamic it was not going to be possible for the old woman even to say a last goodbye. That was going to be very hard.

In the meantime, however, he alone would keep vigil for Ersoy. He knew he fostered the same hatred in his heart against this dreadful man that Çetin Ikmen also shared. Çetin wanted Ersoy to stand trial and then pay in prison for his terrible, disordered crimes and although Arto knew that in a way Çetin was right, he didn't just want the man to live because of that. Suleyman had shot Ersoy not entirely without anger and that was a very bad way for anyone to put an end to another—if indeed there could be said to be a good way. God alone, and presumably Suleyman himself of course, knew what terrible slights had been handed out by Ersoy to Suleyman's brother Murad, but whatever they were they would never, he knew, make right what the sergeant had done this day. If he died, Suleyman would not have Ersoy's blood only on his fine, tailored suit; it would be in his head too, where it would corrode something far more profound than mere cloth.

It wasn't often that Ayşe Farsakoğlu wished that her brother Ali were at home with her, but this evening he was just what she needed. Oh, she had spoken to him on the telephone about what had happened earlier that day, not of course that the injuries to Mr Ersoy were her real concern, and Ali had been as sympathetic as his rather practical nature would allow. But then in a way that was comfortingly familiar just by virtue of its very ordinariness. While Ali was speaking she could, for a time, blot out all thoughts of Mehmet Suleyman and how she felt about him, how she had almost died, right there beside that car, when she had heard the gunshot ring out from the Armenian doctor's apartment. Even just the thought of it now made her shudder. But then had Mehmet died, what would she, could she have done? She couldn't have keened her grief to the weeping skies like a widow in mourning, tearing her face and her clothes as a symbol of her utter desolation. However much she may have wanted to, she could not have done so. She would, she knew, have had to remain calm, detached, unaffected. Indeed Cohen who, as ever and despite her protestations, knew all, had grabbed hold of her very quickly after it happened and then kept her well out of the way until Suleyman's continued existence was confirmed. It was an act for which she knew she should thank him but acknowledged at the same time that she never could.

As she moved from the kitchen back into the living

room, she heard her doorbell ring. It was still quite early evening so it could be any number of friends or relatives, but with the force of the rain outside it was unlikely to be either of her parents who did not have a car and so travelled everywhere by, this time of year, rain-soaked foot.

When she did open the door she found someone who, by virtue of the strange dull light in his eye, looked rather more ghost than human being.

'What do you want, Mehmet?' she asked as her heart, even given his unnerving appearance, did a small sideways leap.

'May I come in?' he said, his head just a little bowed as if under some invisible weight.

'Why?' she asked in spite of her mounting desire just to pull him urgently inside her apartment.

'Because I don't know where else to go,' he said with a shrug.

A middle-aged man walked past on the stairs and tipped his head at Ayşe. When he had gone, she pulled Suleyman inside her apartment and closed the door.

'Can't just talk on the step like that, what will people think!' she said by way of explanation and then, pointing to the floor, she added, 'take your shoes off and put them there.'

'I'm...'

'I'm going to go into the living room now,' she said, viewing his grey countenance with what looked to him like disdain. 'When you are ready, come in and say what you have to.'

Once in the living room she found that she had to sit down because her legs were shaking so much. Why had he, who had ignored her so pointedly earlier that day, come here now? Surely he should be off to his wife after the kind of experience he had had? What did he want?

When he walked into the room she noticed that his feet were bare of both shoes and socks, which, together with the greyness of his face, gave him an uncharacteristically pathetic air.

'Why did you take your socks off?' she asked as casually as she could. 'I hope you're not planning...'

'They were covered in blood,' he said. 'I didn't want to soil your carpets.'

That was not all that was covered with blood. The front of his jacket was heavily stained too. It made him look like the victim of an accident—which in a sense he was.

'So,' she said, taking a cigarette from one of the boxes on the coffee table, 'what can I do for you, Mehmet?'

He shrugged his arms outwards and then let them drop limply to his sides. 'I don't know really.'

'Why aren't you going home to your wife? You could have died today and I'm sure that Mrs Suleyman would want to comfort you, sponge down that mess on your suit.'

'We don't love each other,' he replied in a matter-of-fact way.

'Well, yes, so you've said. But I hope,' she said, lighting her cigarette and then settling back in her chair to smoke it, her legs protectively crossed one over the other, 'that you are not now going to give me any little speeches about loving me.'

'No.'

That denial stung, although what she had been hoping for she didn't now know.

'Oh,' she said in spite of herself. 'Then all I can think you want, Mehmet, is perhaps to do what we did—'

'I want to kiss you again,' he said, now averting his eyes from her, pinning their gaze on the wall behind her head.

Outraged, Ayşe stood up and, flinging her cigarette

into one of the ashtrays, marched very determinedly across the floor towards him.

'You want to kiss me! You come here after treating me like some meaningless little tart you can just pick up and discard at will and you tell me that you want to kiss me!'

'Yes. I need—'

'I don't care what you need!' She was close up to him now, so close that she could see the muscles of his chest as they rose and fell beneath his heavily stained jacket. The smell had just reached her nostrils—musty and yet at the same time sweet.

In one swift movement, Ayşe clamped her arms behind her back lest she do something really stupid like reach out towards him.

'So,' she said, her nose now almost touching the tip of his. 'What news of Mr Ersoy?'

The sudden change of subject caught him temporarily off his guard and he just swallowed.

'Does he live?'

'Yes.'

'Although critically ill, I should imagine.'

'Yes. Ayşe...'

'Yes?' she said, still retaining a lot of her former arrogance despite the fear that seemed to be rising within her now.

'Do I look alive to you?'

On the face of it, it was a stupid question; logically, there could be only one answer. Yet as she paused to look, really look at him, she started to get a tiny intimation of what he was actually saying and what that meant.

'You shouldn't be here,' she said, a little more softly than she had spoken to him before. 'You should see a doctor. You haven't seen one, have you?'

'I just want,' he said slowly, articulating every word

very clearly so that there could be no misunderstanding, 'for someone to warm...I'm so cold, I feel like I've died.'

She couldn't help it. And as it later turned out, all they did that night was sit together, their arms wrapped around each other's shoulders, she occasionally talking about nothing much, just ordinary things, he getting near to but never quite achieving a smile.

She took his hands in hers and she kissed them.

'I thought you had died when I heard that shot ring out,' she said. 'I wanted to tear my face with my fingers.'

He rested one long finger lightly on her lips. 'Ssh,' he said, 'we must not talk of such things. We must never talk of such things.'

'No?' Still and completely illogically the hope broke through into her—a hope born of a night that she couldn't, wouldn't stop endlessly but compulsively replaying over and over in her mind.

'You are my friend,' he said as he bent down to kiss her softly on the lips. 'Just my friend.'

'Yes, of course I am,' she said, 'for tonight.'

'Thank you,' he said, 'I feel warmer now.'

As the moon rose up high above the buildings opposite it looked like a round face: in fact a dead face, so pale and almost translucent was it. Not, of course, that Muhammed Ersoy was actually seeing the moon or anything even remotely celestial, but the inner eye, especially when enhanced by heavy sedation, can throw up many bizarre pictures which may or may not be real. At times he seemed, just for a moment, to catch a glimpse of a room—a pale, stark room that couldn't possibly be his own. Whenever he caught sight of it a faint impression of fear would sweep across him before he descended once again into blackness or into some other scene that in real life would be utterly incongruous.

Perhaps this was death? It could be. Nobody had ever returned to tell what it was really like; maybe this was it after all. Perhaps one's life simply splintered as his appeared to be doing now—breaking up and scattering like dust into the depths of the universe. He hoped that it was so. There was no pain now, which felt so good after all the screaming agonies he had endured for some reason that he could no longer understand. If death were like this then it wasn't really bad. Just drifting was a sensation to which he knew he could become accustomed.

It was waking back up into life that made his heart jolt with fear. Quite what was waiting for him there he didn't know, but at the moment he felt that this drifting state, whatever it was, had to be preferable. If he could just stay here, then everything would be all right. If only that stark little room would stop coming into focus, if only he could get that to go away and fall back into the darkness...

# 18

F ATMA IKMEN SAT all hunched up over her large handbag, her face set into a kind of determined stare. She didn't want to look at any of the other women who sat in the waiting room with her, some of whom were opulently attired in tasteful French suits. Having said that, however, she couldn't help noticing that only the colourfully dressed Kurdish woman in the corner seemed to have the same large belly as herself. Two peasants in with a load of women who had probably come for sterilisations or in order to regulate their birth control or some other wicked, secular process that the state was always trying to encourage. With a small arrogant tilt of her nose she sniffed distastefully and then hugged her bag even more tightly to her chest.

Çetin, for all his 'reconstructed Turkish man' act, had left her at the door of the gynaecologist's office and then scooted back down that corridor like a kicked cat. Not nearly as 'reconstructed' as the smooth-faced young man who sat next to the heavily perfumed lady opposite. Obviously a lot younger than the woman, she thought that perhaps he was the lady's son until her mind, unbidden, drifted into far more salacious areas that shocked her. If the man were this lady's lover then perhaps they had come to see the doctor about getting an abortion. But that couldn't possibly be so, could it? Briefly she looked up at the couple; the woman gave her a rather sad and pitying smile in return. Perhaps, Fatma thought, the woman, looking at both her size and her headscarf, thought that she was one of those country women but lately come to the city with their hungry, work-seeking husbands. Being honest with herself, she had to admit that was an understandable assumption to make, given her appearance. She toyed, briefly, with the idea of informing the couple that she had actually been born and bred in Üsküdar, as had her parents, but she gave up on the idea as a waste of effort and energy. Besides, if the woman were there for an abortion she would have much more pressing things on her mind right now, like how she was ever going to live with herself afterwards.

A great deal of thought had gone into Fatma being where she was now. When all the family women had arrived for Timür's funeral some of them had been visibly shocked by her appearance. And when all the men had gone off to the cemetery in order to bury the old man two of her cousins had, after a little resistance on her part, managed to drag from her exactly what the problem was. Backed up, as usual, by Çiçek, she had made the decision that day to come back to the gynaecologist's office and really talk about what could or should be done in order to ease her pain. It would, she knew already, almost certainly involve her having her womb removed—a process that up until this time had filled her with so much dread and misery. Fatma, like most people, was instinctively afraid of the surgeon's knife, but that was not the most troubling aspect of this procedure for her. No. Not having a womb meant something much more profound than just having an operation to get rid of something that was hurting you. Not having a womb meant not having any more children—which was admittedly not very likely now anyway, but...But it also struck at something that made her the woman that she was. Traditionally men always put away, or rather these days divorced, those women who could not have children and although she had given Çetin more than enough children for any man's lifetime, she did wonder how he would feel about her when she was sterile.

Fatma looked briefly at her watch and then sighed. That old fool Çetin would be at his precious office now. He didn't need to be, he'd been given time off in order to mourn his father, but she knew him well enough to recognise the signs of boredom and frustration. Like Çiçek who could never wait to get back to her precious aeroplanes again, Çetin was not a lover of home and its comforts. Thinking of Çiçek again, she smiled. Of all of their children that girl was the one who had inherited most of the evil humour from her father. Like she had said when she had left just before Timür's death, she had indeed gone shopping in London with her Captain Lazar. What she had, however, initially omitted to tell her mother was that Captain Lazar's English fiancée had also met them there and the three of them had gone to lunch together. Rachel, the English fiancée, had even bought Çiçek a little present of cosmetics, so pleased had she been to meet her prospective husband's friend.

It was, Fatma felt, extremely modern behaviour and quite baffling.

But then the nature of life was to move on and change. Perhaps when the fibroids had gone she would get slim, which would be both interesting and satisfying. Her mother had been a woman of vast proportions when she died and Fatma had always feared such a fate for herself. Most Turkish men, especially those of a certain age like Çetin, didn't mind a woman with a little bit of fat, but there had to be a limit; she couldn't see that he would relish the prospect of a wife who had to be carried up the stairs as her mother had been for the last few years of her life. No, what she was doing had to be right. The posh women in their French suits could look down on her all they liked, but she was going to be brave and she was going to do this thing both for her man and for herself. It made sense, she would feel better and she would be so much more able to enjoy the younger children. Fatma sat back into her chair with a little sigh and closed her eyes.

'What are you doing here, sir?' Suleyman asked as Ikmen pushed his way into the office. 'I thought that you were still on leave.'

'I am, officially,' Ikmen said as he slotted himself back behind his unruly desk with a satisfied sigh, 'but I do, as you know, have a great deal to do.'

'But I thought that you submitted your report on the Ersoy affair?'

'Oh, all right then!' Ikmen snapped, but not without humor. 'I got bored. Satisfied?'

'Yes, but your father...'

'My father was, as you know, Suleyman, a very practical man who had little time for such things as mourning. Two days after my mother's funeral he was back at work and Halil and I were back at school. It's how he was. Nothing to do with not caring for my mother—he cared about her a great deal, he just felt that sitting about being miserable about someone who was dead anyway was a waste of time. He and Atatürk would have got on well. The Ghazi had no time for such sentimental waste either. Life was what he was about and that was what drove Timür forward too.'

Suleyman smiled. It was typical of Ikmen to use his avowed Republicanism as a vehicle for his own needs. 'So did the funeral' he said, spreading one hand out to catch a reply, 'Did it...'

Ikmen shrugged. 'It happened. My boys got here from Ankara in good time. Numerous awful relatives I had until then expunged from my consciousness arrived to behave in various insincere fashions and we put the old man into his grave. It's very odd not having parents, you know, Suleyman. My brother expressed it as our "being alone now," which we are in a sense.'

He dropped his head down just a little and then in order to distract himself from these thoughts he lit a cigarette. 'And what of you, Suleyman?' he said. 'I assume that my report into your part in the Ersoy shooting has gone some way towards making those above us happy about your actions?'

'Yes, although I think that the statement from Mr Ersoy himself has, with respect, done rather more to vindicate my actions than anything you or I could have said.'

'Oh?'

'Yes, like you said at the time, sir, Mr Ersoy said that he fully intended to kill Dr Sarkissian and that he had given me, in effect, no choice.'

This seemed to Ikmen to be a very strange turnaround after what Ersoy had whispered to him at the time. In fact it made him wonder whether somebody had actually 'got' to Ersoy before he made his statement. Arto Sarkissian had, he knew, been to see the patient at least once since the latter's admission to hospital. It was perhaps possible he'd spoken to Ersoy in an attempt to make him see sense about Suleyman?

But Ikmen kept his counsel on this subject and simply smiled. 'You know I feel very satisfied that Mr Ersoy is going to stand trial for his crimes, Suleyman,' he said. 'It is not often, thankfully, that one meets a truly wicked person, but if anyone is that thing then that person is Muhammed Ersoy.'

'Yes.'

They both looked away from each other for a few moments in silence until Suleyman, changing the subject, said, 'I have to go out for a few hours at midday today, if that is all right with you, sir.'

'Yes. Why?'

Taking a deep breath in, Suleyman then released it on a sigh. 'I have to go and visit my lawyer.'

'Oh?' Ikmen flicked ash down on to the floor and then leaned slightly forward. 'May I know...?'

'You might as well,' Suleyman said, his face if anything a little flushed, 'you'll have to in the end...I'm getting a divorce.'

'I'm very sorry to hear that, Suleyman,' Ikmen said, getting up from his chair and moving around to the front of his desk. 'I hope that you...'

'There is—no one'—he looked up briefly at Ikmen, his eyes containing what looked to his superior to be just the ghost of a challenge—'else—if you know what I mean, sir.'

'Ah.' This was obviously an allusion to the rather intimate embrace Ikmen had witnessed between Suleyman and the lovely Sergeant Farsakoğlu. But he kept his counsel on this subject too. A man, even Ikmen, did not speak about such things.

'So,' Ikmen said, 'you will I suppose be returning to your parents' home?'

Suleyman turned away and looked down at the papers on his desk. 'No, sir. As you know the apartment belongs to my wife so I will have to leave there but I am, in the short term at least, going to stay with the Cohens. Both their boys are in the army now and Mrs Cohen is happy for me to rent a room.'

'Well,' Ikmen said with a sigh, 'at least you'll be on the doorstep of all the action at Cohen's place.'

'Yes. He's told me that one of his neighbours is a pimp.'

'Just don't wear your watch when you come out in the morning is all I'll say,' Ikmen concluded. 'Either that or be prepared to fight somebody for it.'

'I know.'

'Ah, well.' Ikmen stubbed his cigarette out in an ashtray and then lit another.

A sharp knock upon the door followed by Cohen's face roused them both from their reverie.

'There's a lady to see you,' he said to Suleyman and then, looking towards Ikmen, added, 'oh, hello, Inspector, we weren't...'

'No, I've come back a little early, Cohen. Who is this lady?'

'Oh, it's Dr Halman,' Suleyman said, 'she promised to come and see me this morning to update me on Muhammed Ersoy.'

'Oh, well, that should be interesting,' Ikmen said. He waved Cohen about his business. 'Bring her in.'

Zelfa Halman, or 'Bridget' as she was known to her intimate associates, was a small blonde woman who, if she knew a person well, would occasionally own up to being the forty-five years old that she was. For much of that time she had worked as a consultant psychiatrist—first in Dublin, which was actually her home city, and then more recently in Istanbul. The result of a Turko-Irish marriage, Zelfa Halman's father had met her mother while practising as a paediatrician in the Irish capital where Bridget, which was her correct name, had been born. Coming to Turkey, which she had done with her father when she had been in her mid-thirties, she had adopted her second name Zelfa which, she reasoned, had to be a lot easier for the Turkish tongue to cope with. Although she had done well during her time in Istanbul she had not, as her father had hoped, found what he had described as 'a nice Turkish man to look after you.' But then having attended a school with the name 'The Convent of Our Lady of Mount Carmel' and having an uncle who was a Catholic priest did not, Zelfa thought, make her a tempting prospect vis-à-vis Turkish men. And this together with her age...

'Hello, Ikmen,' she said as she breezed into the office, tossing her blonde curls over the back of her shoulders. 'You look like you need a holiday.'

'I've just had one actually, Doctor,' Ikmen replied with a smile. She did not, he thought, know about the death of his father and it was not something that he wanted to get into again.

Suleyman walked across the room and retrieved a chair from the corner which he placed down in front of his desk.

'Please have a seat, Doctor,' he said. 'Would you like some tea?'

'Tea would be nice,' she said and then, turning to Ikmen as Suleyman called outside for drinks, she said, 'You know that little bastard just wouldn't start this morning. I had to come here on foot, for God's sake!'

Ikmen laughed. Both her direct manner and the fact that she was the only person he knew in the city who drove one of those weird little Austin Mini cars amused him immensely. It was, nevertheless, probably a contributory factor to why this wonderful but eccentric little woman was always on her own.

'Well, if you will insist upon driving something for which getting parts must be a nightmare...'

'Yes,' she said with a scowl, 'Father says much the same.'

Suleyman, who had now re-entered the room, sat down in front of his guest and smiled. 'Thank you for coming, Dr Halman.'

'I wanted to give you an update on my patient,' she said. 'I think you'll find it interesting and it might, I hope, provide you with some closure regarding the affair.'

'Closure?'

'It's psychiatric speak for finishing the case, Suleyman,' Ikmen put in.

She turned to him just briefly with a mock scowl on her face. 'Jesus, but you're a cynic, aren't you, Ikmen?'

'Yes.'

'Well,' she said, turning back to Suleyman, 'as you

know, Mr Ersoy is still under guard at the hospital recovering from his wounds, which I must say he is doing remarkably well with.'

'So how often do you see him, Doctor?'

'I've had five sessions with him so far. All very interesting, I can tell you.'

'So what do you make of him?' Ikmen asked. 'In your professional opinion.'

'I think he's very clever,' she said, taking out a packet of cigarettes and then lighting up. 'He is also personality disordered to a degree that I have rarely experienced before.'

'Meaning?'

'Mr Ersoy is what we used to call a psychopath. What this means is that he is anti-social in the sense that he can neither appreciate nor empathise with the experiences or views of other people. With regard to his wants and needs he is autistic, in that he sees them and only them—living as it were without reference to others.'

'So why—' Suleyman began.

'Why is he like this?' she sighed. 'Some people believe that psychopaths are born and others that they are made via their early experiences.'

'The Freudian view,' Ikmen put in a tad acidly.

'No, not as such,' she said. 'Of course I could, as could any practitioner, talk about the unresolved Oedipus complex he may have experienced as a result of the death of his mother but...'

'You would lose these two rather ignorant officers in the process,' Ikmen said.

'You said that, not me,' she said pointing an accusatory cigarette at his head.

'So are you saying that you believe that Ersoy was just born like this?' Suleyman said.

'No. Not exactly. From discussions I have had with him I do think that his father had much to answer for with regard to Muhammed's subsequent behaviour. However, Muhammed is a most accomplished liar and so we cannot be absolutely certain about anything he tells us.' She paused briefly to draw upon her cigarette and then continued. 'As far as old Mr Ersoy was concerned, young Muhammed could do no right. His mother, the woman the old man loved, died giving birth to the boy, which was the initial resentment. Then when Muhammed appeared to have an "alternative sexual orientation", the old man's fury became absolute. Muhammed was, he said, an insult to his noble Ottoman past and so he wounded the young man in the most profound ways that he could, firstly by marrying again and having another son and secondly by paying some dodgy doctor to certify Muhammed as unfit to perform national service.'

'Why did he do that?' Suleyman asked. 'Surely service could have, in old Mr Ersoy's view, made a man out of Muhammed?'

'Yes. But it could also have provided him with the sort of temptations which, if they became public, could have hurt the family.'

'I see.'

'So with no military service to perform,' Ikmen said thoughtfully, 'and, I presume, no employment...'

'He hardly needed to work, did he?' Dr Halman said.

'No. He had absolutely nothing to occupy his time.'

'Except pleasure,' she said with a smile. 'His pleasure.'

'Which was?' Suleyman asked.

'A lot of sex, a lot of drugs—and drink at times I believe—and a lot of thinking clever thoughts that he shouldn't.'

'He once said to me,' Ikmen said, his fingers laced like

thin strands of pasta underneath his chin, 'that it was the challenge of the enterprise with his brother that...'

'Oh, yes indeed,' she replied, 'and it is a tribute to Dr Avedykian that he put that idea to Muhammed in those terms. Muhammed just wanted to kill the boy as soon as all the business with his father's death and the 'setting up' of the Italian police was over. It must have taken some effort on Avedykian's part to come up with something that could both preserve the boy's life and appeal to the proud old Ottoman in Ersoy.'

'His very own Kafes.'

'Yes.' She laughed just a little and then continued. 'You know that when he brought out that samovar at the party you attended at his house and said it was from the Kafes, of an old Ottoman, Muhammed said that poor Avedykian nearly died of fright?'

'Luckily for him,' Ikmen said, 'we were all too ignorant to know that that institution only ever applied to the royal family. It was Suleyman who eventually enlightened me.'

'The poor doctor had not then quite caught on just how much Ersoy wanted to be found out—or indeed, what his somewhat unhinged plans were for the two of them, "old men" as he would have it.'

'But if he wanted to be caught,' Suleyman asked with a frown, 'why did he clean up the house so thoroughly after he had killed the boy?'

'Oh, he didn't want to make it easy for you! All the little crystals that he sent your boss here were very oblique and tantalising in nature. No, what he wanted you all to think as you shot his "old" life from his body was how clever he had been and how you all secretly admired him for it. He was still, and probably always will be now, looking for "Father's" approval for everything that he does. And, as this affair proceeded, you lot did in effect become father figures for Muhammed.'

'OK, I can see that,' Suleyman said, 'but what of Dr Avedykian's part in all this? I mean, he was an intelligent, successful, rational man—'

'Who was also hopelessly in love.' The doctor's face was a little sad now.

'With Ersoy.'

'Yes. Unlike Ersoy, Avedykian was totally homosexual and, despite his spiteful dalliances with prostitutes, he wanted nothing more than to be Muhammed's one and only love. Not that there was ever much chance of that.'

'So he persuaded Ersoy to keep the boy hidden—but for what purpose?'

'Because he knew that unless he came up with an amusing little alternative, Ersoy would kill the boy without a second thought. And as a basically good man, he could not countenance killing, but neither could he give his lover up to you lot either. Muhammed had the boy and if the child ever got out he could tell the world what his brother had done to him. Avedykian made the best of a bad job when he persuaded Ersoy to incarcerate Zeki.'

'And, of course, he then provided him with drugs,' Ikmen said.

'Yes. A very rational act.'

Suleyman frowned. 'How so?'

'Well, the drugs would keep the boy quiet and relatively happy. Locked up as he was, he could even be left for large parts of the day or night without supervision. As a doctor Avedykian knew that eventually the drugs would be all that the boy would care about, and also, given the doses he was administering, that they would, in the end kill him.'

'So the doctor was prepared to kill the child, then?'

'Yes, but one can convince oneself that a drug "casualty", as it were, is not one's fault. Like with the young prostitutes that Avedykian "fixed", the drug addiction was a fact that could neither be disputed nor cured and so he saw himself as simply making the best of a bad thing. Of course he fucked the young boys too, but then that is neither here nor there.'

Suleyman, who had felt his face blush as she, a woman, said 'that' word, cleared his throat.

'It occurs to me,' Ikmen said slowly, 'that the doctor must have loved Ersoy a very great deal in order to do all this for him.'

'Oh, indeed he did!' she answered. 'This is nothing if not a true love story, at least on Avedykian's level. He was, and I think always would have been, totally devoted.'

'Until Ersoy killed him.'

'Even then, according to Muhammed, he didn't protest. Just looked at Ersoy's outstretched gun and smiled.'

'So with the boy and Avedykian, are we at the end of Mr Ersoy's excesses?' Ikmen asked.

'I think so,' she said, 'although I believe Sergeant Suleyman here is doing something with regard to the boy's nurse, Jennifer Santiago, are you not?'

'I've made an initial request for information from the San Francisco Police Department, yes.'

Ikmen laughed. 'Perhaps if Ersoy hasn't chopped her up into small pieces you could find yourself over in the States for a bit.'

'Well...'

'There was also, well almost, what Muhammed calls the "madman" too,' Dr Halman said thoughtfully.

'The madman?'

'When the two of them, Ersoy and an apparently almost hysterical Avedykian, were cleaning the house, a beggar or some such saw them loading some things into the back of Ersoy's car. He ranted a bit so Avedykian chased him off. Ersoy would, he said, have liked him dead, but only for the sake of completion. My thoughts immediately leapt to our friend Lenin at this point, as you can imagine. In the light of this it is, I hope you'll agree, just possible that he was trying to tell us something.' She sighed. 'Something sadly clouded by the ravages of his psychosis.'

Ikmen and Suleyman exchanged a significant look—one which, in Suleyman's case, was also tinged with a little sadness.

The door then opened to admit a young constable with three glasses of tea.

'Ah, the cup that cheers, as we say back home,' Dr Halman said.

'Eh?'

'Nothing.'

She took one glass from the proffered tray and watched as the two men helped themselves. Then, dropping just one cube of sugar into the amber-coloured liquid, she said, 'You know what amazes me so much about all this?'

'No?'

'The fact that these two men could have survived the strain of doing all that for so long.'

'What amazes me,' Ikmen said, 'is that nobody was curious about what went on in that house.'

'But didn't Ersoy say something about how "being Armenian" helped him?' Suleyman said, stirring his own sugarless tea with his spoon. 'Made him invisible?'

'Oh yes, it did,' the doctor said with a smile. 'You Turks probably won't have it, but you are, just like the

Irish, just like everyone really, quite nervous of "the other" in society. We all tend to shun what we don't understand, we don't want to get involved in customs and practices we might find distasteful. My father, for instance, when he worked in Dublin, had friends who could only cope with him if they called him Sean or some such Irish name. Thinking about a Turk married to a good Irish girl was too much for them. It's also incidentally why I call myself Zelfa. My patients could not, I feel, handle Bridget, it would undermine their confidence in me as a Turkish practitioner.'

'And the house was in a tourist area with a shifting population,' Ikmen added.

'Oh, yes,' she agreed, 'and that did definitely help. The neighbours only became concerned about the place when the front door was left open after the murder which was, of course, a carefully planned strategy too. To have poor Zeki stinking away for possibly weeks on end would not have pleased Muhammed's finer sensibilities. As I've said before, Mr Ersoy is a very clever man.'

A short pause ensued during which a very thoughtful Suleyman formulated his next, rather delicate question. 'We, the police officers who were responsible for looking for Zeki Ersoy at the time, were very trusting of Muhammed's word. I mean, could he have bribed...?'

'He says not,' she answered with a shrug. 'He says he simply relied on his position in society, as a rich and powerful man, to pull him through. The cook on the boat who originally denied that the child was ever in Italy was an illiterate, easily bribable peasant and Ersoy was a rich old Ottoman. Need I say more?'

'Only that we are supposed to be above that sort of thing these days,' Ikmen observed.

'Nobody,' she said with a jaundiced grin, 'is above that sort of thing, Ikmen. Money and position are built into the bone, and that's not just in Turkey, that's everywhere. And anyway, whichever way you look at it, Ersoy was a master of confusion. He played his part to perfection, just like the classic psychopath that he undoubtedly is.'

'So what you're saying,' Suleyman said, slowly considering his own words, 'is that Ersoy is quite mad?'

Dr Halman laughed. 'Oh, now there is a contentious question if ever there was one!'

'Why?'

'Well, to go back,' she said, 'to our poor friend Lenin again...'

'Yes.'

'Well, if you remember, that gentleman's acts were informed by delusions of a political nature. He believed that he was being influenced by past political leaders to facilitate world revolution. Believed himself, on some level, to be Lenin.'

'Yes.'

'Quite obviously insane, you would say?'

Ikmen who had been listening most carefully, nodded his affirmation.

'Yes, he was I would say quite beyond the bounds of normal reason.'

'Good,' the doctor replied, 'and in that I think we are all agreed. With Mr Ersoy, however, I would take issue with the sergeant here.'

Suleyman frowned. 'Why?'

'Well, because he, unlike poor Lenin, did what he did because he wanted to do it, not because he was compelled by any disordered fantasy or belief.'

'Yes, but surely all that Kafes business...'

'I believe we've had a conversation along these lines before, Suleyman,' Ikmen said, 'about the pimp up in Sultan Ahmet.'

'Ah...'

'Muhammed Ersoy knew exactly what he was doing,' the doctor continued, 'no one like the devil or God told him to do it. Further he also knew that what he was doing was not in line with the normal dictates against killing. But he did it anyway because he wanted to.'

'But surely,' Suleyman said, his face now creased by effort as he attempted to understand what he was being told, 'that cannot be deemed normal behaviour?'

Dr Halman smiled again. 'No, it isn't. But as to whether it can be called insane is contentious. If a man kills in the full knowledge of what he is doing then he must surely be responsible for that act.'

'Yes, but if that man is ill...'

'Oh, now here we are on that dangerous ground again, Sergeant!' she said with a twinkle in her eye.

'Eh?'

In response to Suleyman's obvious confusion, Ikmen smiled across at his deputy and then said, 'I think that what Dr Halman is trying to say, Suleyman, is that academic opinion with regard to whether or not personality-disordered individuals may be deemed insane is divided. Is that not the case, Doctor?'

'That is certainly so and is most informed of your ignorant self, Ikmen,' she said with a small bow of her head. 'Psychopaths know exactly what they are doing and, in the absence of any treatment for their condition, they present both my profession and yours with a tremendous dilemma with regard to disposal. If I treated Mr Ersoy, for want of a better word, I would be surprised if I could actually do anything for him. But as to whether prison is appropriate...'

'I must say,' Ikmen said gravely, 'that I do feel that it is just, given the circumstances.'

She pulled a small, sour face. 'Well, I would disagree.'

'Anyone who takes the life of another, unless they performed that act without knowledge, in my opinion, forfeits his or her right to liberty,' Ikmen said and then added, 'unless of course the person is truly insane...'

'Which means what, exactly?' the doctor asked.

'Well, like that poor Lenin fellow, I suppose,' Ikmen said. 'Although I imagine that if we knew the precise answer to that question in all circumstances, we wouldn't be having this conversation, would we?'

'Precisely. The argument is, as you can see,' she said, turning to Suleyman, 'circular in nature. Madness as a generic term could be applied to all and any aberrant behaviours; the problem of course is to define what is aberrant. If you look at Muhammed's Kafes in the light of his ancestry his incarceration of the boy was really very merciful. Even his motivation, which was essentially first revenge and then greed, is quite logical, given who he is.'

'So...'

'What I am saying is that even given the label psychopath, Muhammed's actions according to his own values were quite correct. And given that all that any of us can do is operate within the compass of our own values...The fact that his values, unlike ours, do not correspond with the wider values of society is not his fault and does not indicate what could be defined as madness.'

'And the difference between him and that poor Lenin character?'

'Is that Lenin's personality had been entirely sub-

sumed by his delusion. Lenin as the ordinary Turkish man
he had once been had entirely disappeared. He possessed
neither malice nor real intent to harm. He was a man in
a different reality. Very unlike Muhammed who, though
aberrant, exists within exactly the same context as yourself.'

Suleyman felt a little shudder pass through his body
which was only curtailed by a knock at the door.

'Come,' Ikmen called out, hurling his latest cigarette
butt into an ashtray.

'Oh,' Arto Sarkissian said as he entered the room,
'Zelfa, I didn't expect to see you!'

'Well, I was just going actually, Arto,' she said.

'Çetin!'

'Arto.'

The two men smiled at each other while the woman
and the younger man looked on. These two hadn't seen
each other for some time and it was evident that there was
some catching up to be done.

'Well,' Dr Halman said, getting up from her seat and
stretching, 'I'd best get over to the bus stop.'

'Your car?'

'Yes, Arto,' she said with an acid expression, 'the little
bastard has done it again.'

'Oh, well, look,' Ikmen said, leaning across towards
Suleyman, 'why doesn't the sergeant here give you a lift?
You have to go out soon, don't you, Sergeant?'

'Yes.'

'Well, if that won't put you to any trouble,' Dr Halman
smiled at her prospective chauffeur.

'No, not at all, Doctor,' he said. 'You are, I take it,
going to visit the patient we've just been discussing.'

'The same.'

Taking his jacket from the back of his chair, Suleyman walked over to the door and held it open for the doctor. 'After you.'

'Thank you.' Over her shoulder Dr Halman said, 'Goodbye for now, Ikmen. I'll see you soon, Arto.'

'You will.'

When the doctor and the sergeant had gone, Arto and Ikmen embraced briefly before sitting back down.

'Are you sure it was wise to let him go like that with her?' the doctor asked as soon as he had made his considerable stomach comfortable.

'Yes. Why?'

'I've heard that she eats his type for entree and then spits out the bones.'

Ikmen laughed. 'Does she really! Well, well!' Then, lighting yet another cigarette, he changed both the mirthful expression on his face and the subject. 'I take it that Zeki Ersoy has now gone to join his ancestors?'

'His mother's father travelled from Iskender to be there for him.' Arto sighed. 'When the old man came to the mortuary to pick him up he was so grateful to me I almost cried myself.'

'Grateful?'

'Yes. To have an end to it all. For the family to know for sure where Zeki is. It was the not knowing all those years that, the old man said, placed the greatest strain upon them all. It must have been bad enough with Fikriye dying like that but...'

'Yes,' Ikmen said gravely, 'Ersoy's father must have been quite something to incur guilt in the poor woman. That, and of course, fear.'

'Yes.'

'And what of you, Arto? How are you managing with

having so recently almost died—as a result of a gamble I took on your life?'

'Oh, I think I can learn to forgive you in time,' Arto said, 'although you must admit that it is frightening to think that you would have let him fire on three had not Suleyman—'

'Ah, but didn't Ersoy say that he would have carried on counting?'

'Oh, no,' Arto said, a faint twinkle just touching the corner of his eye as he spoke. 'No, Ersoy said that he would have fired on three had he not been prevented from doing so by Suleyman. My report on Suleyman's actions is quite specific...'

'Ah, yes, but back in Avedykian's apartment before he passed out he—'

'Oh, no, Çetin,' Arto said, 'I think you'll find you must have dreamed that. I mean, after all, such an admission would not look good for our young friend, now would it?'

'No.' Ikmen started, very slowly, to smile again.

'I mean, poor Suleyman could be accused of all sorts of things by Ersoy's lawyer if that had been the case, but the facts as I have set them out are in Ersoy's own statement as dictated to one of his larger guards, if you get my meaning.'

'Thank you,' Ikmen said with a small bow. 'I appreciate that.'

'It's really the least I can do given my own rather unprofessional part in this affair,' the doctor said, looking down briefly at the floor.

Ikmen frowned. 'Unprofessional? I don't understand.'

'I went to see Avram just prior to Suleyman's visit. I told him what and where our thoughts were headed with regard to doctors and their involvement.'

'Ah. That.'

'Yes, that, Çetin,' Arto said with a small, sad smile. 'I allowed other loyalties, my affection for a younger protégé to...'

'Yes, you did, although that is over now.'

'Not for me it isn't.' Arto's face had taken on a slightly stiffer almost mask-like quality. 'I allowed outside and really irrelevant issues to cloud both my judgement and my actions. By wanting so much to believe that Avram had to be innocent I did something that was both dangerous and wholly unprofessional.'

'But you won't do it again.'

'Won't I?' The doctor turned his newly hardened eyes upon his friend and asked, 'Can you be certain? What if another Armenian friend of mine becomes involved in something?'

'Then we will meet that situation if and when it arises. I admit,' Ikmen continued, lighting yet another cigarette, 'that your actions did disturb me at the time, but—'

'I'm not so different to Krikor really,' the doctor interrupted. 'I criticise him for thinking too kindly of other Armenians but I do it myself.'

'We all think more charitably about our own, Arto,' Ikmen said. 'It's just human nature. And, OK, I was angry at first, but when I really got to thinking about what you did...Well, the difference between that and my, say, favouring Suleyman if I suspected he was in trouble, which we both know is pertinent...'

They exchanged a knowing look.

'Is not so far away from what you did. It's just that there are more of us than there are of you in this country. We must all be vigilant with regard to outside loyalties. We must all, furthermore, accept that even those we love may be capable of evil deeds. We have chosen to uphold the law with regard to criminal acts and so we must always put that first, irrespective of our personal feelings, because if we don't, who will?'

'I don't know.'

'People with rather more, shall we say, political motives? Like those who work in other areas of the field concerned with anti-terrorist activities?'

'Things we do not become involved with since we do not concern ourselves with either politics or religion?

'Exactly!' Ikmen smiled. 'Because while there are men like us the "others" cannot ever truly be in control, can they?'

Arto smiled back. 'No.'

'Every nation has both that other type of law-keeper and it has us, Arto, and'—Ikmen raised one finger to make his point clear—'those nations that don't have the likes of us are generally places where one is strongly advised not to go, aren't they?'

'Yes.'

'Which makes men like us, so I believe, extremely important.'

The doctor laughed. 'Well, if you look at it like that...'

'I do so value our friendship, you know, Arto,' Ikmen said, and then rising from his chair he moved across the room and kissed his old friend firmly on both cheeks.

Suleyman brought the car to a halt just in front of one of the side entrances to the main hospital building. 'I should imagine that Ersoy quite charms all the nurses,' he said as he put the car into neutral and pulled up the hand-brake.

'He tries,' the doctor replied, 'but they've all been chosen to be not easily susceptible to that sort of thing.'

'Rather, shall we say, plain women, are they?' he asked.

She laughed. 'That's very sexist of you but it's about right, yes.'

'He can get inside your head so easily,' he said. Looking down at the steering wheel he added, 'He got into mine.'

'Yes, but you coped,' she said.

'I nearly killed him, which is exactly what he wanted me to do.' He looked up at her. 'Not really coping as such, is it, Doctor?'

'Ah, but you didn't kill him, did you?' she said, placing one small but firm hand on to his shoulder. 'Ersoy lives and so, even more importantly, does Dr Sarkissian. That makes you what we call back home a fucking hero, Sergeant Suleyman.'

That word again! Once more the thought of such a thing coming from a woman's mouth made him blush. It also, secretly, made him want to laugh too. She was so very amusing, this strange, unkempt little medic with her funny Irish life and her Turkish father.

'You know that he resents you a lot, don't you?' she said, breaking his train of thought with her oddly accented voice again.

'Who?'

'Muhammed Ersoy. Because you didn't kill him. He's very bitter.'

'Oh.' There really was no sensible answer to that.

'Good thing he's not ever going to leave jail then, isn't it?' she said as she unbuckled her seat belt and swung her legs out of the car. 'He might come after you and I, for one, would not fancy your chances.'

'You wouldn't?' Suleyman looked suddenly very affronted.

Dr Halman laughed. 'Sorry to dent your machismo a

bit there, Sergeant, but given Mr Ersoy's record on clever crimes of cold violence as compared to your own I think he's just a little ahead at the moment, don't you?'

Suleyman smiled in recognition of her words and then looked up at her again, 'OK,' he said, 'I understand.'

'Good,' she replied and then, just as he was putting the car back into gear, she put her head through the window and said, 'Call me.'

Suleyman, a little taken aback, said, 'Why?'

She shrugged. 'To talk about Ersoy, to get some of that guilt out of your poor tortured soul.'

'You mean like therapy?'

'You're still, in my opinion, quite traumatised, yes.'

'But...'

'Oh, I won't charge you anything for my time,' she said with a smile, 'look upon it as a favour or, if you like, as closure for us both.'

He laughed. There was that psychological term again, the one Ikmen had almost sneered at. 'I will see,' he said, 'but thank you anyway, Doctor.'

'It's a pleasure,' she said as she pushed the door shut.

As he watched her hustling briskly towards the door of the hospital, Suleyman suddenly laughed out loud. The thought of what he and this small, dumpy, rude woman might look like walking together had entered his mind— and amused him quite considerably. It was the first time that he had really laughed in a long while.

Sitting at different tables, separated by what looked like an endless parade of sin in the form of chilled cakes and pastries, Zuleika Suleyman and Ayşe Farsakoğlu had both, independently, decided to subsume their woes within the confines of the Pera Palas Hotel patisserie.

Zuleika, whose husband had that morning placed his suitcases plus three boxes containing books and personal effects by the front door of the apartment ready for collection later that day, chewed almost without consciousness on a chocolate eclair. Very soon she was going to be a single woman again. Admittedly, she did not have the financial worries that caused many of her other divorced girlfriends so much grief. Mehmet's wages had only ever supplemented her considerable income and so his desertion would, from that point of view, make very little difference to her life. That he himself was removing to another place was, however, another matter. Once, long ago it now seemed, she had loved him with the kind of passion she could barely understand. Handsome, kind and clever, he had been, or so she had thought, everything that she desired in a man. Like her, he was 'old money', plus he was through his father's family a direct descendant of a sultan. It had all been so perfect. Except...She put another forkful of eclair into her mouth as she tried, in vain, to expunge the source of her failure.

Why and how could it be that none of the 'bedroom activity' had worked with her? She had both loved and desired him so...That first time had made her almost physically sick. Him grunting away on top of her, producing pain the like of which she had never experienced before; his hands, hands that she knew had fondled and caressed other women's bodies, roaming all over her torso. In spite of the fear and pain that he must have seen in her eyes, he had carried on pleasuring himself at her expense. Was it the knowledge that he had been with other women before that had made her feel like that? Or had it perhaps been the deadness in his eyes as he took her, the look of a man simply doing his duty which, as a good son of his family, he always did—until now.

He had, apparently, told his mother, Auntie Nur, that he had never loved Zuleika. Not that Zuleika herself had been unaware of this. Mehmet if nothing else had always been quite honest with her about that. Even before their actual marriage, he had spoken to her in terms of their both 'learning to love each other.' But it had never happened. He had, probably in part as a result of her horror of sex, remained indifferent, and she? Well, she had over the years slipped into the kind of carping bitterness that can only sour still further an already unsure relationship. And now he was going. Even in the face of his mother's wrath—she had even declared him dead to her—he was leaving, which had to mean that above everything else he actually wanted to go; he wanted rid of her. Although quite why it had happened at this moment in time as opposed to any other she didn't know and now probably never would. She bit back her tears as she chewed yet another lump of cake, contemplating the endless sea of loneliness that seemed to stretch out before her—a loneliness she knew that, at her age, would only be punctuated by men who were more interested in her money than her soul. But then perhaps, as she had said when she'd first been told about the separation, her mother could find some nice man for her daughter. Zuleika's tears dissolved into a short, bitter chuckle.

Ayşe Farsakoğlu's thoughts were punctuated by some bitterness too. As she looked across at the tall, immaculately coiffed woman sitting across from her slowly devouring a large eclair, she couldn't help thinking that perhaps someone like that was more suited to the attentions of her now ex-lover. Kind and courteous as he no doubt was, just by virtue of what he was, she had felt a little shabby by comparison. With her thick, unruly hair and slim but strong frame she could, she reasoned without too much effort, easily imagine herself in the role of the aristocrat's sexual plaything. In truth it was a role she had been very willing to play but now that he had told her that their affair was over, that he needed time to reassess his life in light of his recent separation, and in view of the admitted difficulties that being involved with someone in the office would bring, she was beginning to think differently about the matter.

OK, so she had thought for a while that she was in love with him—had even considered giving up her job after he dumped her—but in truth had her feelings for him ever been anything other than infatuation? He was handsome, charming, very sexy and he had been so gentle and loving to her when he'd arrived covered in blood from the carnage in Avedykian's apartment, but what they had in common outside of the bedroom was minimal. He enjoyed neither a drink nor a laugh in the way that she did. The earthy humour of the Anatolian peasant largely eluded him and although it was an odd thought, it occurred to Ayşe that when it came to a suitable life partner she really had far more in common with her lover's boss, Çetin Ikmen, than she did with Suleyman himself. It was such a bizarre, almost insane notion that, just for a second, she burst out in a small giggle.

Yet despite her laughter there was still, she felt, a very real message behind all this. Of course, Ikmen was totally out of the question, being too old, too unattractive to her and far, far too married. But...But somebody like him surely had to be more suitable for her than someone like Mehmet. Ikmen, although he frequently courted danger in low bars and cheap districts, was in a way safer than Mehmet. In times of real trouble, like when that poor madman attacked her, Ikmen was calm and rock solid in his resolve to attain a peaceful solution. There had been a wildness in Mehmet at that time—perhaps it was the craziness of what he imagined to be his love for her? The madman, Lenin, had seen it, dubbed him a killer even, and in truth there was something about him that was at root quite out of control. Perhaps she thought, sourly, it was his old aristocratic blood. They had all been, and if Muhammed Ersoy was anything to go by, still were quite unhinged. Perhaps in a way, given this evidence, she had had a rather lucky escape when he had dumped her—that or she was just deluding herself in order to feel better.

As she popped a small forkful of thick, sickly-sweet baklava into her mouth she looked over at the other lone woman, the elegant one, and smiled. It was a sad little smile and was greeted with an expression that was not dissimilar. It was hard to imagine, given the lady's polished elegance, but it seemed from her face that she was in the midst of some kind of woe also. Quite what that could be, given her wealth, beauty and the presence of a large wedding ring on her finger, Ayşe could not imagine. But then the rich did, had to, have worries as well as the poor. Cushioned by money, they could never really be assailed by concerns as great as those of the poor, but if the woman's face was anything to go by they felt just as keenly as other folk.

One thing that was different, however, was that Ayşe now had to get to work. The smart woman's numerous store bags attested to what was probably a day of shopping—something Ayşe on her meagre salary could rarely even contemplate. Nodding briefly to the proprietor of the establishment, Ayşe finished the last mouthful of her cake and rose to her feet. It would be interesting to know what exactly was making the elegant woman so sad, but she knew that one did not engage in conversation with such a person unless one was invited to do so. But as she left she did just briefly incline her head in the lady's direction and was once again rewarded with that slow, mournful smile.

Once the tired-looking young policewoman had left, Zuleika Suleyman put her head into her hands, taking care not to smudge her make-up as she lightly touched the skin around her eyes.

'You know,' Muhammed Ersoy said to the taller of the two large guards who spent such vast amounts of time in his room these days, 'if I were not as rich and powerful as I am and having done the things that I have done, I would probably be incarcerated in some dirty little cell right now— even with this very poor shoulder of mine.'

The guard didn't answer; he just kept looking straight and steadily ahead of him.

Ersoy was used to this kind of treatment now and he prattled on anyway. 'It must be so irksome for people like you,' he said, 'big boys just fresh'—he moved one hand suggestively up and down one of the bars on his headboard—'out of the rough Anatolian plains.' He laughed, amused by the complete lack of reaction he was getting from these men. He pushed it as far as he felt he could go. After all it, like life, was only a game and these men, unlike the dreadful beast who'd taken his statement did not, as yet, appear to be in the business of naked aggression. 'You know I've paid so many men like you to suck my cock it hardly—'

The door opened to admit that funny little psychiatrist woman, bringing Ersoy's obscene little speech to a halt, to the obvious relief of at least one of the guards.

'Oh, hello, Doctor,' he said, reverting to English which he knew made her feel much more comfortable. Then looking hard into her face, he said, 'Your pupils are dilated— have you seen someone you would like to fuck? Or is it myself you feel attracted to?'

'I don't know that that is any business of yours, Muhammed,' she said briskly and then, sitting down on the chair beside his bed, she asked, 'how are you today?'

'Oh, I'm still miserable to be alive, thank you,' he said brightly. 'Still hurt that one of my own kind should be so inept with a gun as to—'

'Your anger at Sergeant Suleyman seems to be achieving obsessive status.'

'Oh, no,' he said with a smile, 'I don't think that that is so, Doctor. After all, what would it profit me to pursue him when I am obviously so very unwell at the moment?'

'Unwell?'

'Yes,' he said, 'mentally. I mean, don't you—'

'You are not, as far as I am concerned, in any way psychotic, Muhammed,' she said, taking a notebook and pen out of her attache case. 'We've talked about voices which, if I recall correctly, you do not hear. Your obsessions although unbalanced could not be described as full-blown delusory...'

'Oh, but that was then,' he said, his voice honeyed to an almost tooth-rotting degree.

'That was when?' she said frowning. 'What do you mean?'

'That was before I became unwell yet again. I do get quite frequent bouts of it, you know. Yesterday afternoon...'

'Just after your lawyer left you,' she said with what both felt and tasted like a mouthful of bile.

'Why yes, it was just after he left, that's absolutely right,' he said smiling.

'Oh, give it up, will you, Muhammed, for the love of God!'

'Give...'

'If you're going to try and get out of all this on the grounds of being under the influence of Shaitan or some other crap, you can forget it. You're gonna live, you're gonna stand trial and you're gonna go to prison, old Ottoman money, hereditary madness or whatever!'

'Oh, I wouldn't be so sure,' he said, bending down to move his face just a little closer to hers.

One of the guards moved forward but she waved him away with her hand.

'Nothing is certain in this life, Doctor,' Ersoy whispered gently into her ear, 'and if it were that would be very boring, wouldn't it? That man, for instance, the one you would like to fuck so much, if you were sure of him there wouldn't be any fun...'

'If you don't stop talking about things that do not concern you, Muhammed, I will have to leave.'

'Oh.' It was a whine rather than a word; an expression more suited to a thwarted child than to a fully grown man.

'Now, look, we need to talk about you, that's why I'm here.'

'About me? What about me?'

'You know the form, Muhammed. You talk, I listen...'

'And write down things for the police to use against me. Yes?' He turned away from her, his face pouting in anger—again the thwarted child.

Dr Halman sighed heavily. He wasn't usually this difficult. She wondered what, if anything, was wrong or different about this day. 'Is there something you'd like to tell me, Muhammed?' she said. 'Something that is particularly troubling you today?'

He just grunted, still looking away from her.

'Well?' she said, as if to a child. 'Is there?'

'I went through sünnet,' he said, suddenly turning to face her again, 'this day 1964.'

'Oh, right.'

'I cried, you know.' His face was almost weasel-like in expression now. 'It hurt.'

'And did your father...?'

'Father beat me with his stick afterwards, said I was like a girl, said the surgeon should have cut my penis off and rammed it down my cowardly little neck!'

'That was a very cruel thing to say to such a young child,' she said, genuinely shocked at what he was beginning to tell her today.

'Yes it was,' he said, 'and it was something that I never put Zeki through. He died as he had been born, with his penis whole and unemasculated.'

'But, Muhammed, Islam demands and as a Muslim—'

'Oh yes, I know that,' he said, 'I know all about that! It's just that...'

'It's just that what?'

'It's just that I never got any credit for leaving Zeki alone in that sense. Not even Avram gave me praise for... All he said was that the having or not having or a foreskin was just a detail of religion.'

'Well, isn't it, Muhammed?'

'Oh, no, Doctor, no!' he said, his lips very slightly trembling. 'Not when it makes your father hate you, it isn't.'

'Ah, but,' she said, 'you've always said that your father hated you from birth.'

'Oh, yes, he did, he did! But it was only after siinnet that he could, as a good clean man of quality, start to take me sexually for himself.'

'But...'

Ersoy smiled, a slow, very calculating and disturbing expression.

'Well, somebody had to take the place of my mother, didn't they? And he at the time was far too busy to look for another wife.'

'But...'

'The sad thing though from your point of view, Doctor, is the fact that I really didn't mind. He hated me but while he was screwing me I had some sort of contact with him. Avram always said, for years, that my father just had to be the wickedest man in the world—quite a superlative, don't you think?'

'Well, yes, quite.'

Ersoy's smile turned into a laugh then, an unnerving sound in that tiny, sterile, unbalanced little room.

'And superlatives like that,' Ersoy said once he had stopped laughing, 'just cry out to be bettered, don't you think, Doctor?'

'Which is what...'

'I imprisoned, I killed, I drugged—I got no praise for failing to circumcise, but I think I'm winning ahead of some brutal old man who only ever managed—and then only just—to rape a small defenceless seven-year-old. What do you think doctor?'

He turned the kind of gaze upon her that one usually sees only in nightmares—that or films about creatures that are either not human or have lost their humanity. It was the face of someone who had completely lost all ability to feel.

'Well, Doctor?' he said.

'Well, I...er, I...'

'I think I am so far and away better than my father that to say any more now would be quite a waste of my breath and your time.'

And then, as she looked on, fascinated by what was really yet another virtuoso performance on his part, Ersoy turned his cold, dead eyes to the wall and started to hum to himself. Neither Zelfa Halman or the guards recognised the tune, mainly because it was entirely Ersoy's own: arrhythmic and totally, chillingly, unique.